NOBODY'S SAFE

ALSO BY RICHARD STEINBERG
The Gemini Man

RICHARD STEINBERG

NOBODY'S SAFE

DOUBLEDAY

New York   London   Toronto   Sydney   Auckland

PUBLISHED BY DOUBLEDAY
a division of Random House, Inc.
1540 Broadway, New York, New York 10036

DOUBLEDAY and the portrayal of an anchor with a dolphin are
trademarks of Doubleday, a division of Random House, Inc.

All of the characters in this book are fictitious, and any resemblance to
actual persons, living or dead, is purely coincidental.

Library of Congress Cataloging-in-Publication Data
Steinberg, Richard, 1958–
Nobody's safe / Richard Steinberg. — 1st ed.
p.   cm.
I. Title.
PS3569.T375492N63   1999
813'.54—dc21   98–19495
CIP

ISBN 0-385-49258-8
Copyright © 1999 by Richard Steinberg
All Rights Reserved
Printed in the United States of America
March 1999

3   5   7   9   10   8   6   4   2

For Robert Thixton: Agent, Counselor, Friend, Believer. "Mr. Science Affliction," who believed when damned few did!

NOBODY'S SAFE

PART ONE

BEHIND CLOSED DOORS

Locks, and the men who make them, are the reason that most thieves are in prison today.

Most thieves.

The most dramatic moment in lockmaking came in 1865 when an American, Linus Yale, Jr., invented the most secure key-operated lock known to man. The pin-tumbler-cylinder lock is still the state of the art; and will be, well into the next century.

Whether using a key, a digital code, a fingerprint, or retina scan, virtually all locks still require pins to be moved, drivers to be slid, and, most important, tumblers to be adjusted to a certain position before the bolt can be thrown.

Just as in Linus Yale, Jr.'s original design.

That's the name of the game.

Move the tumblers.

Just like people.

Cajole, force, or manipulate them into a particular place at a particular time.

Succeed and no door will ever remain closed to you.

Fail . . .

Well, that's why most thieves are in prison.

Most thieves.

ONE

GETTING ONTO THE ROOF was the easy part.
It was just past three that afternoon when Greg casually walked into the high-rise's lobby. An elevator to the forty-third floor, neither looking anyone in the eye nor looking away. Just another faceless visitor to the newly built high-rise on a crowded Friday afternoon.

As expected, he was the only one to get off on the still-unfinished floor; the last before the two private penthouse floors. And ten minutes after he'd entered the building, he stood in front of the secured fire door that led to the rooftop access stairway.

It was locked.

Of course.

He stood there, very still, carefully listening for any footsteps on the stairs below him. Finally satisfied (the closed-circuit cameras wouldn't be installed on this floor until next week), he set his briefcase on the ground and began to work.

The door was alarmed.

No problem.

Two small pieces of well-chewed bubble gum and four nine-inch-long, pale blue, pure silk threads and the alarm ceased to be a concern.

Attention on the lock.

"Oh, Linus, Linus," he barely whispered, "this is a most piddling little thing." He studied the lock as he reached into the case. "Quality control just isn't what it used to be." He sighed as he came up with what his fingers had been reaching for. "But then, what is?" A quick spray from a can of graphite, a slight push from an Allen wrench and . . .

On the roof, there was no hesitation.

A quick, casual-seeming look around to ensure that he was alone, then straight for the spot he'd been observing from a rented office across the street for the past week: an equipment shed for elevator servicing and light storage.

It was beige, as was most of the building's exterior. Three sides on the roof like some misplaced pigeon coop, the fourth wall just inches from the roof edge. With the bottom thirty inches of it in constant shadow from the roof's restraining wall.

He quickly reversed his jacket to expose its flat-black lining; pulled on a black hood and gloves from the case; took a last look around, a last listen, then slid into the narrow, deeply shadowed space.

And lay there, unmoving, for the next nine hours.

Normally he would've willed sleep to come. Forced rest and relaxation through his adrenalized body to prepare for the night's work ahead.

But ever since he'd decided on this job, sleep had become his enemy. A thing to be avoided at all costs.

Well, not sleep exactly, but the things that sleep brought with it. Phantom pains and fanged shadows that reached out for him from a place he'd thought no longer existed within him.

A place that had been mostly silent for so many years.

He never should've even considered this score. He knew that now. With the clarity of a man who has the time to think *Oh? I took that curve a little too fast,* moments before crashing over the side of a cliff.

But to walk away, even now, would be conceding a power over him to the dusty, moldy demons.

And this man conceded nothing to no one.

It was a little past midnight when he slowly, carefully crawled from his hiding place. His ears strained to hear everything, anything. Any noise that might give a second's warning of trouble or, worse still, that might give him away.

Once he was fully out of the crawl space, he rolled onto his back, staring up into the starry night, slowly counting to 300.

He felt the blood come racing back into previously cramped

limbs. Forced pinioned muscles to stretch, then relax. Rolled his neck to loosen his shoulders.

Felt himself come alive again.

Only then did he try to stand.

After testing his legs and arms, convinced that they'd fully recovered from the odd positions they'd been forced into all day, he moved silently across the gravel roof to the Gravesend Avenue side.

Avoiding any look down at the dark street, he spent more than a minute spotting the rented office across the street that he'd used for his reconnaissance. Then he checked his watch.

Nine minutes after twelve.

Counting down the seconds in his head, he kept his eyes locked on that distant office window. Where a steady light meant *Go. The target is dark and has remained dark for at least the last two hours.* Where a flashing light meant *Something is different. Beware! Take precautions!* And no light would mean . . .

Greg wiped his sweaty face beneath the nylon hood.

No light could mean *Abort! Something has been compromised! Return to hiding, then leave with the lunch crowd later in the day.*

Or it might mean that Foss just wasn't there.

Maybe he'd forgotten. Or was there and so stoned that he couldn't tell time or see across the room, let alone the street. Or maybe he'd been picked up on some bullshit buy-bust or reverse sting. Maybe he'd given Greg up to the cops already. Maybe they were waiting below, in the dark, to grab him.

All because he had a stone dope fiend for a partner.

For a friend.

"Be there," he whispered as he counted down the last seconds.

A light flicked on.

It shone brightly, steadily, for thirty seconds, then flicked out as suddenly as it had appeared.

The rest now depended on faith.

He glanced down at the street below. Gravesend Avenue. An empty, dirty street with only back doors, back walls, and no hope.

A street Greg used to know as intimately as any in the world.

But would rather die than return to.

It was a bad sign, Foss would say. A dark omen, Deo might laugh.

And Greg would agree.

But the building's address wasn't on Gravesend, but Beecher. A difference that Greg told them made all the difference in the world.

So long as he was awake.

After listening at the door to the stairway for long minutes, he put his hiding place behind him, silently descending toward the four luxury penthouses on 44 and 45.

Across the street, Bobby Fosselis sat shivering on the floor of the rented office.

He had no way of knowing if Greg had seen his signal. Or if Greg was even on the roof. But he gave it anyway. As he would three more times in the next hour.

He wiped the heavy sweat from his eyes and peeked out the window.

The targeted penthouses were still dark, had been since just before nine that evening. If everything was going according to plan, Greg should be walking around in the first one right now. It should all be over in the next forty-five minutes.

Should be.

But to an addict who hadn't fixed in six hours, forty-five minutes was a lifetime.

The late-fiftyish man (who looked twenty years older) glanced back at the desk where his works and a rock of black tar heroin sat waiting.

It would be easy, so easy for him to shoot up now. To feel the warmth course through his collapsing veins. It would steady him, he tried to convince himself, sharpen him for the vigil he must keep. It would make him more alert to any changes in the status of the penthouses. Changes that Greg must instantly be made aware of.

Hell!

Greg would understand, he continued in his silent argument. He always did. Right? He would sigh and say, "Hey, it happens." Then shake his head and walk away, a look of disappointment and pity on his face.

But Foss had given his word to the younger man. And, for the moment at least, that was a stronger, more visceral demand on him than the drugs.

For the moment.

He checked the penthouses again, then glanced down at the street below. Wondering if there'd be any dealers around when he left.

☐ ☐ ☐

A long black limousine slowly turned down Gravesend from a more heavily trafficked street, seemingly a mocking vision from another world.

Jack Kerry stared out from the luxurious, climate-controlled, fairy-tale world that was the passenger compartment, smiling as he took in the dismal sights.

"It never changes, does it?"

The young woman beside him looked up from her drink. "What?"

He never turned away from the window as he watched a woman with three small children walk slowly down the street. Clearly homeless, dirty, with that haunted/hunted look that he still remembered from his own childhood, so many years before.

"Life," he whispered softly as he leaned back into the plush leather of the seat.

The woman shrugged. "Whatever *that's* supposed to mean." She angrily lit a cigarette. "I wish we could've stayed. I really wanted to meet the mayor," she whined.

Kerry nodded without realizing it. He'd wanted to stay also, but the page alerting him to be home for "the Brugge courier" was more important. He would no sooner miss a visit from his Belgian money launderer's representative than he could stop breathing.

Sighing, he looked over at the woman beside him.

Under twenty-five, oozing sex and life, she was barely dressed in a $10,000 gown he'd bought her for the evening. More important, though, she was completely paid for. *His*—like his car, his penthouse, or his building.

So, after the courier came and went, if the meeting didn't last too long or sap his admittedly depleting energy, the evening wouldn't be a total loss.

Depending on the courier.

He smiled as he saw his building rise up ahead of them.

As the limo pulled into the high-rise's underground parking lot, Kerry glanced up at the dark upper floors, absently realizing that his servants, few neighbors, everybody would be gone. Either at the mayor's party or given the night off because of it.

The thought of being completely alone with his building, his money, his whore, *and* his superiority appealed to the older man. He just couldn't help smiling.

Four hundred and seventy feet above, Greg was also smiling.

The two apartments on 44 had yielded gems and jewelry worth at least $100,000. And the beauty was that he would have the pieces broken up and fenced days before anyone ever realized they were missing.

In the old days, the heyday of the top safe men, Greg would have been called a yegg, or a yeggman. His was the most specialized of the thieving professions. One that he thought he might well be the last practitioner of.

There was no safe, no lock, no security system that could keep him out. And his crimes were seldom discovered right away, because Greg was selective.

Three times selective.

First, there would be no obvious damage to the homes he burgled. No broken windows, kicked-in doors. No sign that anything was any different than when the owners had left or gone to bed. He left graffiti and vandalism to hypes and druggies who didn't know a Paul Revere silver tray from the carton of a TV dinner.

Second, there would be no sign that the safe had been touched (and Greg was primarily interested in the things that were kept in safes). He would never tear, chop, or punch a safe. Explosives were number one on his shit list; although in the dark old days, he *had* been made an expert in them. But all those techniques were too loud, too messy, too likely to alert the authorities or damage the contents.

He preferred to Jimmy Valentine each box. Combine touch with technology, insight with improvisation—and the world was just one, big, open door.

Third, and most important, he never, *ever* emptied a safe. True, he usually took the most expensive items of only the finest quality. But only very few of them at that.

When people open safes in their home, they almost never take an inventory. They glance in, see what looks like the right jumble of effects, take out or put in whatever they want, and close the door.

When, sometime after one of Greg's late night visits, they went to the safe for "Grandmother's earrings" or the "good diamonds," they would be mystified by their absence. Sometimes not calling the police right away until they checked with their spouses, jewelers, whatever.

And by that time . . .

The penthouses on 44 had been easy pickings. Routine dead bolts and amateur time alarm systems. The safes, they'd given up their treasures with the reluctance of a bored hooker on a Wednesday night.

Now, as he stood on the forty-fifth-floor landing, he flipped through Foss's hacked printouts of the insurance companies' inventories.

Units 45A and B were owned by one man. A media guy named Kerry. They shared one common wall, but their power was drawn from two separate circuits. No connecting doors, the balconies on different sides of the building, north and east. Each, however, blessedly insured by the same company.

There *were* things in 45B—listed as a corporate guest condo—that interested Greg. Knickknacks and doodads worth seventy or eighty thousand. A signed Melville first edition; a Mondrian oil; a relatively rare Brock table sculpture.

But it was penthouse A that really caught his attention.

Two safes, a floor job in the living room and one in the master suite; first-rate entry lockout system and an alarm that rated well above the value of any of the listed items; as well as something listed only as "special security measures—confidential."

Even though the listed insured items ranged from $10,000 to close to $100,000 each in appraisals, it seemed, to Greg's practiced mind, overkill.

And overkill meant only one thing.

There was something in the apartment so valuable that the owner couldn't (or more likely wouldn't) pay the exorbitant premiums to insure it. But he would damn well protect it.

He shoved the printout back into his case, checked a meter clipped to his belt that indicated the floor cameras were still off-line (playing the dummy tape he'd made before starting on 44); then he approached 45A.

Problem one, the door.

Slowly, carefully, he passed a handheld ion sensor over the perimeter of the fine mahogany, hand-carved door.

All things electrical, from the highest powered tool to a nine-volt transistor radio, "cooked" the ions that passed around the current, each singed ion giving off a telltale signal to the sophisticated machine in Greg's hand. It only remained to interpret the readings.

The sensor indicated three distinct power signatures.

Contacts—probably on a delayed system, near the door's threshold.

Something that looked very much like the signature of a series of pressure pads on the hinge side of the door frame itself, probably also delayed.

Finally a third, different kind of electronic signature. Seemingly phased, maybe timed, it came and went every twenty seconds.

"Special security measures—confidential," he mumbled as he fine-tuned in on the third power signature. Carefully studying its frequency, surges, and oscillations on his tiny glowing orange screen, picturing the charges and discharges of the ions in his mind, he began to frown.

"Mantrap," he whispered in an annoyed tone. "What kind of flaming paranoid puts a state-of-the-art microwave sweeper/motion detector in the middle of his goddamned living room?"

He put away the sensors, crouched by the foot of the door, rubbing his mouth with both hands.

"Gonna kill his plants," he said in a distracted tone.

He stared at the door, through the door, picturing the invisible microwaves covering an arc across the entire entryway every twenty seconds. Then waiting, like a tiger in the bushes, for a careless tap or touch to the door to pounce. Probably calling every cop in the western United States when it did.

Without taking his eyes off the door, Greg reached down and pulled a proximity voltmeter from his specially organized briefcase.

Carefully, with a rock-steady hand, he held the probe within a quarter of an inch of the door lock. He flipped the readout to wide frequency scan and waited.

Although his sensor hadn't shown it, he suspected there was an impedance alarm on the door handle and lock itself—at such a low power level as to go virtually unrecorded. But any touch by any conductive surface, such as a human hand, would probably trigger the microwave sweeper to go "full active"—flooding the living room and entry area with an impenetrable web of alarm triggers.

Then, oddly, he smiled.

Because it would probably also be hardwired into the microwave generator. And if that operated at the right frequency . . . It would be difficult but not impossible to convince the simple circuitry to *turn* on the more elaborate system, shutting down both systems completely.

He shook his head and the smile disappeared as the needles moved, barely.

There *was* an alarm on the lock, but its signature suggested it was hooked into some kind of a slave, probably infrared, preventing Greg from using one to beat the other.

"Someone does not want me going through that door, Linus, old pal," Greg said in a louder voice than he'd intended. "And who am I to argue?"

Shaking his head, he pulled out the floor plans for the apartment.

One minute later, he easily let himself into 45B.

The alarm, while expensive and well made, was easily and quickly bypassed. But the lesson of the high-tech motion sweeper was still on his mind. He stood very still while he scanned the inside of 45B. Finally satisfied, he moved quickly to the back bedroom.

Using a tape measure, a carpenter's level, a stud detector, and a hacked wiring diagram of the apartment's electrical systems, he found what he was looking for after five minutes of silent work in the dark.

He had to check inside three side-by-side cabinets until he found the one he was looking for, filled with sheets, pillows, blankets, and other bedroom stuff. He carefully piled them on the floor behind him, in the exact order that they'd been in the cabinet, then leaned inside.

He pressed his sensor against the back wall, meticulously sliding it along, not blinking as he waited for the digital readout to react.

Nothing.

"Oh, Linus," he whispered as he pulled a tiny electric saw from his case, "when will they ever learn?"

Then he stopped.

He stared at the wall, picturing the luxury apartment beyond, the riches it held, the unexplainably severe security it contained.

And he shivered.

Greg trusted his instincts, had lived by them since he was a child. Now they were screaming that something was very wrong. He crawled out of the cabinet, sat down in a luxurious swivel rocker, reviewing everything in his head.

Whatever was in 45A would more than make the trip worth it. Possibly more than he could get from the other three penthouses combined. But the risk was substantially greater as well.

The room beyond the wall was clear of mantraps, he was sure of that. But beyond there? Any man willing to put an industrial-level sweeper in his living room was capable of anything.

Special security measures, plural.

If there was a sweeper in the entry, what might the lunatic occupant of penthouse A have around his safes?

It all said *Walk away!* In capital letters.

But Greg wasn't in the business to play it safe. And, as he considered his options, he admitted that a simple, no-frills, no-problems score often left him feeling empty, unfulfilled.

Cheated.

Sure, he went after the expensive estates and penthouses for the riches they contained, but even more for the personal challenge. It was him against the best security systems, the most incorruptible security men, the finest locks and safes known to man.

A personal duel with the spirit of that beautiful, bloody genius Linus Yale.

So far in his career, the score stood at 122 for Greg, 5 for Linus, and 11 games called on account of instincts.

Now it should be 12.

Two minutes later, he pulled himself through an eighteen-inch hole in the small bedroom's wall of penthouse 45A.

Less than a minute later, his eyes more on the machine in his hand than where he was going, he slowly ventured out into the hall, heading for the master suite and safe number one.

"Okay, Linus," he said softly, "show me what else you've got."

The lights in the apartment suddenly flicked on.

"Jack," the beautiful young woman whined from the living room, "it's cold."

"So what?"

Out on the apartment's balcony, with the glass door wide open, Kerry never looked up from the telescope. As soon as they'd walked into the apartment, he'd rushed out to see if the homeless family they'd passed on the street had been attacked by the young gang-bangers he'd noticed as they pulled into the garage.

Disappointed that the young thugs were nowhere to be seen, he watched as the family huddled in a store's doorway forty-five stories below—the mother trying to wrap discarded newspaper around her shivering children.

"I love this shit."

"Jack?"

"What?"

The woman smiled what she hoped was a tempting smile. "I thought we were going to fly."

"When I say," he spat out as he walked into the living room, "and not one minute before!" He angrily reached out, slapping her across the top of her head.

The woman toppled off the couch onto the thick, plush, white rug. But she looked up with a playful smile.

"So, Daddy wants to play." She slowly pulled her clinging dress over her head. "Wants a little bit of the rough?" She reached up, grabbing him by the necktie.

"I've got a meet . . . I have to . . ." he mumbled gutturally as he allowed the woman to pull him down to her.

"Later," she rasped out, pressing her naked body against him. Her mouth seemed to be everywhere—kissing, licking, biting. "Now, where has Daddy hidden it tonight?" She tore open his $200 shirt, roughly massaging his steel-gray-haired chest. "Not there?" She sounded like the pouty little girl she knew he would like. She quickly undid his trousers, savagely thrusting her hand between his legs.

"Ah! I think I've found baby girl's little toy. Oooh!" she purred. "Two little toys. This—" She squeezed his balls, enjoying the expression that was equal parts pain and passion. "And these!" She pulled out a small plastic envelope of white powder.

She dumped the contents on top of the glass coffee table. "First baby girl has hers," she whispered as she prepared the cocaine with a custom gold grinder, "then Daddy gets what he deserves."

"I couldn't have put that better myself, young lady," a cold voice from somewhere behind them said in a sad tone.

They whirled around, staring at the entryway to the penthouse.

A man, as old as or older than Kerry, stood there, flanked by two younger men. All three wore dark, conservative suits that seemed to blend with their completely expressionless faces.

"It's been a long time, Jack," the older of the three said flatly.

Kerry didn't move, seemed not to breathe. Seemed completely paralyzed—except for a small vein in his forehead that suddenly distended, beating furiously.

"Tom?"

The girl looked from one to the other, then seemed to realize she was lying there naked. She grabbed for her dress as she wiped the powdery residue from her upper lip. "Hey! I *don't* do parties!"

The man Kerry'd called Tom nodded slightly. "Pity."

Instantly one of the young men came up to the girl, wrapped his arm around her neck while pressing her head to the side. There was a thin snapping sound, then he let her dead, limp body drop to the floor.

Kerry ignored it. "Am I next?"

Tom raised his eyebrows, smiled, then wandered out to the balcony. "That remains to be seen." He looked through the telescope. "Interesting view." He adjusted the focus slightly. "Have you been talking out of school lately?" he asked without looking up.

"What?"

"Telling old war stories, perhaps. Reminiscing about the good old days, past conquests . . . Joe and Max?" His voice seemed calm, but also flat of affect. As if he already knew the answer, was only seeking confirmation of it.

"No," Kerry said as he slowly, deliberately stood up. "Why should I?" His tone was a measured calm that barely covered the growing panic he felt at the sight of the man who had *died* twenty years before.

"No reason. I just wondered." Tom turned back toward the living room.

"Have you?"

Tom smiled, an expression that oddly stopped at the bridge of his nose, as if the upper half of his face was paralyzed with an expression of cold disregard.

"As a matter of fact, I hope to be seeing them quite soon."

He calmly walked back into the room, stopping inches from the clearly shaken man. He looked down at the body of the dead girl.

"She's a bit young for you, don't you think?"

No answer.

Tom shrugged. "A question of taste, I guess." He paused, looking directly into Kerry's eyes.

Frightened eyes.

"I understand that you've acquired some interesting tastes in the last few years, old friend. Expensive tastes."

Kerry never took his eyes off the man he'd thought he'd never see again.

Prayed never to see again.

"Is that what this is about? The coke? It was for her! A little game we played. I wouldn't ever—"

"Now, me," the man interrupted, "I never developed any taste. Just . . . appetite."

The two young men came up alongside Kerry, beginning to search him as Tom wandered around the living room.

"And it's a voracious bugger, my appetite is. Requires a great deal to satisfy it. But then, we've been well provided for, old friend. Right?"

He didn't wait for an answer from the man whose eyes remained locked with his. Even though he was being meticulously stripped and his clothes searched by the two young men.

"Now I'm sitting at home, bouncing my first great-grandchild on my knee when I get a telephone call. There's this voice on the other end. A young voice. An unfamiliar voice." He paused. "An *official* voice. You remember the kind, Jack?"

Kerry nodded weakly, standing there naked, as the young men turned away from him, beginning to ransack the elegant living room.

Tom stepped out of the way of one of the men as he began tearing apart each book in an antique, mahogany bookcase.

"This official voice says to me, '*Mr. Kilbourne,*'" he smiled. "That's my name these days. Kilbourne. I chose it myself. What do you think?"

"Go on." Kerry ignored the men as they moved to other rooms in the penthouse.

"Well, this voice says, '*Mr. Kilbourne, we understand that someone has been leaking information about Joe and Max. We don't like that very much, Mr. Kilbourne,*' they said."

He walked over to the now-shivering man. "Actually, neither do I, Jack."

"It's not me." Kerry's voice came out in a hoarse whisper. "I wouldn't." His skin had lost its color, he was sweating heavily, and a nerve began to twitch uncontrollably in his neck.

"I'd really like to believe that, Jack," Kilbourne said with what appeared to be deep emotion. "I really would."

One of the young men returned from the back of the penthouse. He spoke softly to Kilbourne for a moment.

"And what would be the combination to the safe in your bedroom?" Kilbourne said with purpose.

The second of the expressionless young men was just finishing tearing apart the contents of the bureau when his partner returned.

"Here's the combo."

"Great." The second man threw down the shirts in his hand as he walked over to the safe, now exposed from behind a newly torn Chagall original.

"You get to the closet yet?" the first asked casually.

"Just to look in really. Hardly got started."

The first man nodded, reopening the closet's double doors.

Rows of fine suits, custom-tailored casual clothes, and accessories lined the dark inside. It seemed that everything was in its assigned place on its assigned hanger or shelf.

The man tried the light switch, but nothing happened.

"Guess the bulb's out," the man by the safe said as he worked the combination.

The first man nodded, pulled a Mag-Lite from his jacket pocket, shining it in the closet. "Geez! This guy's wardrobe is worth more than both our salaries."

"Tell me about it," the other said as he swung open the safe door. "But great taste."

"Oh yeah," the first man said casually as he started working his way through the racks and hangers. He carefully checked the clothes, inside the shoes, steadily working his way back to an old, antique cabinet.

"There's nothing but money, jewelry, and stuff in here," the man by the safe called out. "Take a look."

The first man started to turn, paused, then turned back to the six-foot-high cabinet.

Topped by an elaborately carved panel, the double-doored antique seemed to be locked. The man pulled on one of the doors, feeling the resistance of some unseen force. Then pulled again, harder.

Still, it refused to open.

"You got a key to this cabinet in here?"

"Screw it. He wouldn't keep it in there."

"Right," the first man said as he turned to leave.

Suddenly he stopped, whirled around, kicking at the cabinet's door. His foot partially went through the old wood, requiring him to use his hand to free it.

His partner rushed over at the sound.

"What the hell?"

"You never know, right?" the first man said as he reached inside with both hands, roughly pulling the doors open.

"Hats? Who the hell locks up his hats?"

"Gentlemen," they heard Kilbourne call from the living room.

Shaking their heads, they left the bedroom.

Never seeing the eyes of a hooded figure peek out from behind the top panel of the cabinet.

"Nothing yet, sir," the first man said to Kilbourne.

"But to give this place a real thorough going-over would take a couple of hours," the other quickly added to cover himself.

Kilbourne nodded at the young men, then looked deeply into the eyes of the terrified man in front of him. "Save us a lot of trouble, Jack. Tell us where it is."

The naked man looked as if he was about to collapse. "What?" he whimpered. "I don't know what you want!"

"We all have them, don't we, Jack? Souvenirs, mementos, keep-sakes." Again the half-faced smile. "Insurance?"

"Nothing! I—I don't have . . ."

His words were cut off by a nod from Kilbourne and the rough gloved hand of one of the others covering his mouth.

Kilbourne studied the man for long seconds. Finally he exhaled long and loud.

"And you haven't been trying to . . . *expose* Joe and Max? Haven't been helping others look into things better left forgotten?"

Kilbourne seemed to be convinced, and Kerry visibly relaxed as the hand was removed.

"Never. You know I wouldn't."

"I think I probably believe you, old friend," Kilbourne said as he turned toward the front door. "Still, I have to be certain, don't I?"

A knife was suddenly produced from the sleeve of one of the young men, who expertly thrust it up, under the nude man's rib cage. As Kerry stiffened, the young man gripped the handle of the knife with both hands, pulling it first to the left, then to the right. A crimson arc appeared in the path of the blade.

As Kerry fell to the floor, the young man allowed the body to slip from the knife.

"He didn't suffer," the young man said as he wiped the blade on Kerry's discarded shirt.

"Pity," Kilbourne said without turning around. "Walk me downstairs, boys." The three of them quietly, calmly walked out of the apartment.

His clothes plastered to his body from the sudden, heavy sweat, a deeply shaken Greg climbed down from the closet cabinet soon after the men left the room. Tossing the closet's lightbulb onto some folded sweaters.

Quietly, he tried to understand the voices he heard coming from the living room. Suddenly the voices stopped.

Barely breathing for fear of the noise bringing the men back, Greg strained to listen. To be sure he was alone.

Before he got the hell out!

It wasn't the unexpected arrival of the old man and the girl. These things happened in Greg's line of work.

He'd ducked behind the three-quarter-opened master suite's door, to wait them out.

If they started to come in, he would have time to retreat to the closet, then wait for them to fall asleep before he would leave quietly, invisibly.

If they began to screw in the living room, as he expected, he would use their distraction to hit the bedroom safe, then leave.

But it was the others turning up that had shaken him.

That, and the too-recognizable sound of a body dropping to the floor.

He instantly recognized the tone of the older man, if not the words. He'd heard it many times before.

From the men who'd refined his talents, who had nurtured and supported him, given him a sense of purpose—before using him for their own.

It was the voice of the faceless demons of his nightmares.

The older guy was a stone killer; a man who'd decided to kill before he ever set foot in the apartment, but needed something first.

Some *thing*, Greg realized, that despite his relaxed manner the man was deeply worried about.

Greg had known enough of those guys in the past to realize that whatever was happening would, inevitably, become terminal.

Quick.

So he had retreated behind the heaven-sent panel on top of the old Sheraton tallboy.

The tone of the men as they searched, sometimes within inches of him, sent another chill through him.

They were professional, trained, searching through the room rapidly but methodically. Missing very little, caring nothing about the money or jewelry lying in plain sight in the half-open safe. Caring only about the object of their search.

Whatever *that* was.

Finally, satisfied that he was alone in the apartment, Greg moved to the open safe.

He grabbed two large rings, maybe thirty carats combined weight of decent-quality diamonds, and two of the several bundles of hundred-dollar bills. Probably ten-thousand-dollar packs. Then he padded to the doorway, listened, and stepped out.

Halfway to the small bedroom and a quick, clean escape, he stopped.

Something in the apartment so valuable, a little voice seemed to whisper, *that the owner would use a heavy industrial security system to protect it.*

A microwave mantrap . . . which was now clearly turned off.

Holding his breath, he slowly turned, moving silently toward the living room.

And safe number two.

TWO

FOSS CROUCHED in the dark office, as frozen in time as any photograph ever taken.

He'd seen the lights come on in 45A, seen Kerry come out on the balcony, stare through his telescope, then return to the living room. He'd seen another man come out on that balcony fifteen minutes later.

But he had no idea where Greg was.

He could be in another of the apartments. Could even be back in his rooftop hiding place or on his way out of the building.

Should be.

Must be.

Please God, let him be!

But deep down, Foss knew he wasn't.

The panic of the moment had dropped the burning pull of his addiction. At least for the moment.

Reacting out of fear for Greg, and for himself if anything should ever happen to Greg, he turned on the small strobe light by the desk.

For a full minute, he allowed it to steadily flash, filling the office with a bright blue light, then returning it to near-total darkness. In five more minutes, he'd do it again. Desperately trying to warn Greg of what was happening.

Get out, the flashing light silently screamed across the void separating the two buildings. *Run away! Go no further!*

The problem, it occurred to Foss as he reached for his cell phone, was that Greg had to look out a window to see it. And if he didn't . . .

He dialed a number that was answered on the first ring.

"Grey at point one," a voice said tensely.

"Blue at alpha," Foss responded. "Possible alternate." He spoke carefully; quickly but clearly.

"Shit," the other voice whispered. "Point two or three?"

Foss thought about Deo Hartounian sitting in a used, temporarily stolen sedan.

Temporarily . . . because it had been taken off a used-car lot shortly after closing and would, ideally, be returned (odometer rolled back) before it was missed.

Deo was the third part of the team. Older than Greg, but younger than Foss, it was his job to get the burglar out of anything he couldn't get out of himself. Or to just casually pick him up at a designated spot if all went as planned.

He would willingly drive through a storefront window, crash a police roadblock, drive through attacks from automatic weapons (by police or others), so long as the risks had been explained and paid for (well paid for) before the job began.

Tonight, if everything went as planned, he might not have to do a thing; other than wait for an all-clear from Foss, then return the car to the sales lot. It all depended on Foss's instructions.

And he would do nothing without those instructions.

Deo wasn't the best driver in the business; not the fastest or the most reckless; and he never, ever carried. Anything. Neither gun nor swag.

He was known in the business as a "vanilla." A man who did what he said he was going to do, be where he was supposed to be. But seldom, if ever, volunteered, suggested, or improvised. It was his way of remaining blameless if anything "wrong" happened on the job.

It was an accepted, if somewhat disparaged, way of doing business.

But it was how he'd become that rarest of things in his business . . . a middle-aged wheelman.

Tonight, in twenty-one minutes, Greg would be relying on Deo to be at point two.

Unless he was instructed otherwise.

"Talk to me, Blue," the voice on the phone said nervously.

"Go to point three," Foss whispered without breathing.

"Copy, Blue. Point three," Deo said flatly as he disconnected.

Foss shut his phone, then looked out the window at the brightly lit penthouse.

Willing his friend to glance out a window.

Any window.

Standing at the edge of the living room, Greg was only looking in one direction . . . down.

Two bodies. Not one. Both nude, both showing the obvious violence that had been used against them.

He stood there for the longest seconds in his life. Unwilling to move, to blink, until he was sure of what he was going to do next.

The bodies lay near each other, the man having fallen across the girl's legs. Blood was pooling on the thick carpet, coming from a hideous wound in the man's stomach. It matted the thick shag, staining the white—pink on the edges, growing thicker, almost black in the center of the grotesque puddle.

The girl's head lay loosely on her shoulder, at an impossible angle. A look of surprise on her once beautiful face.

Greg looked up from them, glanced at the closed front door, then firmly stepped forward.

"Five minutes. Just five minutes," he repeated slowly as he moved toward the bar. "Then I'm outta here."

It wasn't the fact of the bodies. He'd seen that before.

Enough to drive a sadist mad.

No, it had more to do with the tone of the old man; the Cold Man, as he'd begun to think of him. Combined with the casual professionalism of the two younger killers.

People like that didn't just leave bodies lying around.

He walked behind the bar, forcing himself to concentrate on the job ahead.

Despite the indications on the floor plans, there was no sign of the floor safe. He studied the carpet, pulled at it, tested to see how secure it really was.

The back of the bar contained what the back of a bar should. No hidden switches, control panels, or disguised latches. It was as innocuous a place as such places could be.

Crouching on the floor, he opened his case and pulled out a disc-shaped object, about the size of a dinner plate. Snapping in a nine-volt battery, then plugging in a single earphone, he lay down on his side.

He began to slide the disc along the floor, listening to the return of the low-frequency radio wave "thumps" as they bounced off the subflooring, barely whispering as he moved.

"Wood . . . wood . . . conduit . . . wood . . . rebar . . . wood . . . ah."

His mind counting down the seconds left in the five minutes he'd given himself, he carefully examined the spot where his device had indicated a steel construct. It was just inches from the end of the bar, at a place where the floor jutted up against the wall molding.

Putting the disc on the floor behind him, he ran his hand along the carpet, up onto the wall. He suddenly stopped, smiled, then knocked on the wall.

It sounded hollow.

"You were a devious son of a bitch, Mr. Kerry. I'll give you that," he said with genuine respect.

He easily slid open the hidden panel that revealed the round, glistening, stainless-steel safe embedded in the floor within the wall.

Greg quickly pulled his case over to him and pulled out his ion sensor.

Then he hesitated.

People liked safes where they could get at them. Even floor safes, which were designed for maximum concealment. Why would an old man put a safe, which he presumably used regularly, in such an awkward, hard-to-reach spot?

Special security measures—confidential.

Every instinct in Greg's body told him to pack up and leave.

Now.

Shaking off the feeling, driven to know what was worth so much effort, from so many people, he continued working.

"Now, Linus," he said in a halfhearted humor, "let's see what you have in store for me next."

Almost in answer, he heard the front door open.

"Like I said," he heard one of the young killers say, "routine."

"Yeah, yeah," the other one said in a clearly annoyed tone. "But it would've been a heckuva lot easier just to work on the geezer."

"Man said no. You want to argue with him?"

Greg, frozen on the floor behind the bar, heard two somethings of plastic drop on the floor of the living room.

"No," the second voice said after a moment. "I don't think I would. Move him off her."

As he heard one of the men move Kerry's body, Greg silently, carefully moved his sensor over the safe's door. His rock-steady hands, equaled by a steely gaze, concentrating on possible alarms in front of him. His ears listening to every movement from the other side of the bar.

As his mind raced.

If he was discovered by the men, he was dead. No question. On the other hand, if they were going to move the bodies, and if he was completely silent . . .

A single drop of sweat fell off his soaked hood, while the beating of his heart filled his ears with a dull roar.

As he continued to watch the sensor's readouts.

"Nice-looking."

"For a whore, I guess. But I don't like to pay for it."

Greg could hear something, presumably the girl, being rolled in plastic.

"You want to take her, then wrap him? Or what?"

"Uh, let's do him, then make one trip." A pause. "If you think you can carry him by yourself."

"Why can't I carry the girl? She's gotta weigh half what he does."

The unmistakable sound of Kerry being rolled in plastic.

" 'Cause she weighs half, and I'm senior man."

"Oh."

There was the unmistakable power signature of a CPU coming from within the safe. Probably the main central processor for the entire apartment's alarm systems. As Greg withdrew the sensor, he had to blink the sweat from his eyes.

But his hand remained steady, his body motionless, his moves deliberate. Painfully splitting his concentration between the men and the safe.

Thinking.

Planning.

Praying.

"Get some neckties for the ends."

"Okay. Make me a drink, will ya?"

Greg froze, his hand half in his case as he watched a shadow come across the wall.

"What am I, your bartender? We'll get something later."

Greg heard the man sit down on one of the barstools. Looking up, he could just see the man's hand as he drummed his fingers on the glass bartop.

For what seemed like forever, Greg stayed there, bent over, almost on all fours, breathing shallowly. Watching those fingers, hoping the man wouldn't change his mind about the drink.

"How are these?"

The fingers stopped their drumming as the hand was pulled away.

"Great. Let's do it."

"Geez! They're never gonna get this carpet clean."

"Damn shame, too. Probably cost a fortune."

"Yeah. Looks it. But you got to pay for real quality."

"Believe it. Lift him up for me."

"Over the shoulder?"

"No. Uh, maybe a fireman's carry'd be best."

"You got it."

The sound of a heavy plastic-wrapped package being lifted, then, a moment later, another.

"Let's go. We still gotta finish going over this place before the next security shift comes on. We only got an arrangement till five."

"Right."

The sound of the front door opening and closing.

This time Greg didn't wait, didn't check to see if he was alone.

Grabbing a towel from behind the bar, he pulled off his hood, wiped his face and hands dry, then plunged his hands into his case.

He grabbed something—it looked like a flashlight without a lens—in one hand. It had a bulbous end with an almost thread-thin, light blue cable coming from where the lens should be. In his other hand he held a digital keypad and an apparent carton of Camels unfiltered. Almost in the same movement as he returned to the safe, he plugged wires from the keypad into the carton.

"Don't think, act. Don't think, act," he kept repeating to himself as he laid the carton and keypad to the side of the safe's door.

Carefully he threaded the blue fiber-optic cable under the combination dial.

"Be a C, baby. Be a C."

The safe was either a Banham Locks Model 263 C or D. From the outside, it was impossible to tell. If it was a C . . . no problem. The fiber-optic cable would easily reach past the drivers to where it could light up the CPU.

If it was a D, however . . .

The thought of being caught between the cops (when the cable triggered the alarm) and the young killers was equally unappetizing.

It slid in a half inch.

An inch.

An inch and a quarter . . .

"Ah."

The safe was a Model C.

Another quick reach into his case for some green duct tape, which he wrapped around the dial and the cable. Then, to be sure all external light was blocked out from the dial, he folded the towel over the dial several times.

He flipped the switch on the ultraviolet generator.

Biting his lower lip, he silently counted to 20, then shut the switch.

Quickly ripping the tape and towel from the dial, he ran the sensor over the safe door once again.

The needles never even tremored.

"Never met a microchip that could hold a decent shot of UV light," he muttered as he pulled out the cable.

Three quick dimensions measured out and the cigarette carton was meticulously placed above and to the right of the dial, at an odd angle. He entered a three-digit code on the keypad, then the carton seemed to suddenly hug the safe's door as if being pressed down by a giant hand.

"Ninety seconds," he mumbled as he keyed in another code. "Just ninety seconds more and . . ." He watched as a red light began to flash rhythmically on the keypad.

Never taking his eyes off the flashing light, Greg began loading his other tools back into the case. He started to reach back behind him for his disc-shaped "safe finder" just as the light flashed green.

Grabbing the cigarette carton that contained the high-intensity, tunable magnets, he pulled the safe door up and open.

There was no time to be selective now. He grabbed a small jeweler's envelope, a thick manila folder with rubber bands around it, and a long, thin leather case.

Maybe nineteen inches by five by two, the case had double lock latches, was expensively made, seemed very old. But Greg wasn't about to take the time to open it now.

"Okay," one of the men's voices said as the door opened. "But I'm thirsty. I'm starting at the bar."

"Whatever. We've got to search the whole place anyway. Just stay off the booze."

One of them stepped behind the bar.

Greg silently closed and locked his briefcase. His fingers tightened around the handle, he took then exhaled a long, deep breath.

"I'll just get a seltzer," the man said as he looked back over his shoulder. "You want . . ."

He never finished the sentence, as he was suddenly bent in half from the impact of the thief's case as it violently impacted deep into his groin.

The man let out a high-pitched scream, his face turning a deep purple as Greg exploded to his feet. Greg's shoulder collided with the man's chin, knocking the man over and back as he rushed past.

The man's partner, standing by the balcony, took two seconds before he understood what was going on. He immediately reached into his jacket.

"No guns," the purple-faced man wheezed from the floor. "No guns!"

Two more seconds passed as Greg almost flew across the living room, into the hallway. The second man in deadly pursuit.

As the door to the small bedroom slammed shut, almost in his face, the second man stopped, pulled his gun, then took a breath.

"There's nowhere to go, asshole! You're forty-five stories up with no freakin' fire escape. Right?" He listened, but only heard a rapid moving sound from the other side of the door. "Give it up right now and we can work this out." He glanced behind him as his out-of-breath, heavily wheezing partner caught up.

"No goddamned shooting," the purple-faced man slurred out as he pulled down his partner's gun. "Only as a last resort, damn it. You"—he bent over and puked on the floor—"you heard the man," he said in a weak voice.

Reluctantly the second man put his gun away.

The purple-faced man grabbed at his groin, then held up three fingers.

The first man nodded.

Three seconds later, they burst through the door into the room. It was empty.

Both men produced knives, then spread out through the room.

"Come on, pal. Let's do this the easy way, right?"

No answer.

"Check the closet."

"Closet my ass!" the purple-faced man screamed as he almost threw a slightly askew oak night table across the room. "We got us a rabbit!"

The second man rushed over, dropping to his knees, leaning into the hole.

"He's gone next door," he screamed, his voice muffled by the linen closet on the other side. "Go around." He barely pulled himself through as the purple-faced man limped hurriedly out of the room.

Ten seconds later, the chair by a writing desk seemed to move itself backward, and Greg crawled out from under the desk.

He grimaced, shook his head, then walked quickly out of the room.

The sedan sat quietly in a convenience store's parking lot, half a block from the building. At a major intersection, the driver could see halfway down Gravesend Avenue, and well down Third. He sat there, parked, trunk in, at the space—Walkman earphones on, seeming to sway to the unheard music.

"Six Adam fifty-six. Six Adam fifty-nine. Six El forty. Possible four five nine there now. Silent ringer, one one niner four Beecher. One one niner four Beecher. Penthouse four five Baker. Six Adam fifty-six handle code three."

Deo started the car as he pulled the right earphone back. He picked up his cell phone, speed-dialing the number.

"Blue at alpha." Foss's voice was clear but tense.

"Grey at point three. We just had a shake at patsy three."

"You sure it's three?" Foss sounded confused. Not disoriented, not stoned. Well, hopefully not. "We have a problem with patsy four but . . ."

"Confirming," Deo said as he checked the traffic in the intersection. "I have three unfriendlies responding to patsy three. Please advise."

He hated working with junkies. Didn't know why Greg, who was so careful in every other way, kept him around. After all, as they said, you can always count on a junkie . . . to let you down.

"Uh, wait a minute. I have lights in patsy three," Foss said in a thin, fragile voice.

Deo took a deep breath. "Blue, please advise."

There was a long silence on the line.

"Grey, hold at point three. Will advise."

Deo tossed down his phone, sliding down in his seat as two police cars came speeding by, red and blue lights flashing.

Greg hesitated at the door to the apartment. But making decisions was never much of a problem for him and he didn't wait long. As soon as he was sure that the hallway was empty, he was out the door, speeding for the stairs.

He was sure that the men after him would've set off the bypassed silent alarm in 45B. That meant that even if he got away from them, there would still be a thorough search of the building by the police. So his rooftop hiding place was out.

He started down the stairs, reviewing his options as he went.

He hadn't considered that he might be on the run from professional killers, but he *had* considered fallbacks. If an alarm should inadvertently be triggered (unlikely at best), or if something unforeseen should disturb him.

He shook his head as he carefully opened the already-bypassed stairwell door to 43.

"He's on the stairs," an angry voice screamed from above him.

Almost immediately there was a shot and plaster flew off the wall, slicing into Greg's face.

Now it was a footrace.

The building was basically a box. One long corridor going the length of the building, with a shorter one meeting it at a "T" leading to the elevators. He ran down the long way, cutting sharply to his right down the elevator corridor.

And he heard the stairwell door crash open behind him.

The two men, guns drawn, slowly moved down the long corridor, checking doors as they went. They didn't say a word, but their intentions were clearly written on their faces. The second one continued down the long way, while the purple-faced one limped down the elevator way.

He stopped, looked down at the yellowish carpet, then nodded.

"Over here," he called.

When his partner came running up, he pointed down at two still-wet blood drops; followed a distance later by two more.

They moved slowly now, guns pointed at each of the doors they checked. Halfway to the end, with more blood drops in sight, a cell phone rang in the purple-faced man's pocket.

"Yeah?" He listened for a long minute. "No, sir. That's not a problem. We took care of them first."

He paused, and even the second man could hear the angry tone coming over the small phone.

"Not our fault, sir. Uh, we were . . ."

"Interrupted," the second man offered in a bare whisper.

". . . interrupted . . . No, sir. No . . . We were just . . ."

He held the phone away from his ear as the voice on the other end screamed at him.

"Yes, sir. Right away, sir." He shut the phone, glanced down at the remaining doors, then over at his partner. "Cops are downstairs."

"Shit."

"We're to make a quick pass through the target, then split through the secondary route."

The second man looked skeptical.

"What about the cops?"

"Man says the target and the route will remain clear for ten more minutes. After that, no guarantees."

"Let's book."

"Wait a minute." The purple-faced man walked over to the last visible blood drops, then stared alternately at the doors to either side of it. "Son of a bitch is here," he growled.

"We don't have time for this shit," his partner almost yelled. "We're on the clock, damn it!"

The purple-faced man reluctantly nodded, took a step back up the corridor, then spun around—firing two silenced rounds through each door.

"This ain't over, asshole," he called out as he followed his partner back to the stairway.

"Old man ain't gonna like that," his partner said as they half jogged back to the stairs.

"Fuck him."

Across the street, Foss was chugging down his sixth soda pop of the last half hour. Its sugar and caffeine would help to hold off his need for a few minutes more. But it would do nothing about the fear and adrenaline that were pulsating through his body.

Deo had called twice more, anxious to move up to a better position.

Lights were coming on all around the building. So far, above the third floor, only the penthouses were lit; but the search seemed to be moving upward steadily.

And a police helicopter was shining its searchlight on the building's roof.

All while marked police cars were continually racing down Gravesend, then turning up toward Beecher and the front of the building.

But none had taken a position behind the building on Gravesend itself. At least that was a small comfort.

One thing going right on a night of disasters.

Foss had been with Greg for years, maybe thirty, forty scores, and none had ever gone so wrong. For the first time, torn by the call of the drugs, his fear, his confusion, Foss began to consider a life without Greg.

A short life, almost certainly.

Greg had found him in a run-down, downtown mission. He'd said he was looking to hire a homeless man, ideally with a college education. Had said he was interested in "trying to give back a little something to the community," or some other meaningless crap.

Hell, there'd been ten or twelve men more qualified, Foss always believed. Men with better educations, without substance problems; without yellow sheets. There was no good reason for Greg to hire a stoner with a penny-ante record for slipshod cons.

But he had.

First, as a personal assistant, helping the younger man to learn about computers, programming, hard- and software. This had been Foss's specialty before his addictions had gotten him tossed out by a Silicon Valley software design firm, tired of unaccounted-for expenses and missing days.

As his trust in Foss had inexplicably grown, Greg gradually introduced the old man into his real line of work.

Which Foss had taken to with grateful enthusiasm.

Nobody trusted junkies, and with good reason too. But Greg had trusted Foss, and although he'd let the burglar down on more occasions than he could remember (always on the little things), he'd never completely betrayed that trust.

Would rather die first.

But why, that was never completely clear to the older man.

Why he'd let down just about everyone else he knew. Had done nothing in his life to deserve a—what was it? A fiftieth chance?

Or why Greg was willing to trust a man, not a man—a long-poisoned corpse, walking around waiting to find a place to drop—instead of getting himself a young, clean partner. Someone he could trust no matter what.

Foss wiped his face on his shirt, continued to twist a tissue into nonexistence and to blame himself for everything.

Greg had put the old man in several detox programs over the years. They all worked, for a little while. But invariably he found a syringe, an eyedropper with a needle, or whatever, shoved in his arm or up his nose.

But Greg was always there.

And, although Foss never quite knew the reason, always would be.

Paying off the dealers he'd ripped off. Bailing him out of jail.

Keeping him alive.

But now, with all the commotion across the street, Foss felt more impotent, more useless, than ever before in his life.

And for a junkie, that was saying something.

He flipped on his cell phone at the first ring. "Blue at alpha."

"Still straight, old man?"

"Greg!"

"Yeah." He sounded exhausted. "You straight or not?"

Foss wiped his nose on his arm. "Straight, but I'm bad." He paused. "Patsy three and four are lit up, man. And I got people movin' around in four."

A long silence filled the air.

"Cops?"

"Three units. Also a chopper."

Foss could hear Greg's heavy breathing in the background.

"You straight enough to do some things?"

Foss knew Greg expected an honest answer. "Some."

Again, a silence.

"Write this down, old man. And do it to the letter. Right?"

Foss flipped on a desk lamp and looked around for a pad. "G'head."

"Call Grey. Tell him to go to Flash Alternate. Flash Alternate. Repeat that."

"Flash Alternate."

"Then go to a pay phone and call Carlisle. Don't use your cell and *do not* call him from the office. Right?"

"What do I tell him?" Foss's hand was shaking, the sweat from his hand staining the paper, but he managed to make the notes as Greg talked.

"Don't use any names, but tell him what happened." He paused. "At least as much as you know."

"What does that mea—"

"Never mind," Greg said, suddenly lowering his voice. "Just do it. Then go home. Straight home. No stopping, no dealing, no buying. Right? And don't fix till you get there."

Foss took a deep breath, then slowly pocketed his tar rock. "I promise."

The line went dead.

He hadn't the time to pick and choose when he needed a place to hide. Instead, he just hit the first office door that didn't *look* alarmed. Pulling a locksmith's "shooter" from his pocket, he was in and had relocked the door before his pursuers ever saw him.

He'd been close enough to hear their end of the phone call; barely avoided the two shots that thudded through the door—into the wall behind him. Had heard them leave; but still waited ten minutes before he dared move around. Even then, he stayed as quiet as possible.

After calling Foss from the office receptionist's desk—a risk, but a necessary one—Greg finally took stock of his surroundings.

It was apparently some sort of accountant's suite. There were two connected offices, a third, larger office; reception area and a supply room. There were no indications of alarms or the need for them. He estimated all of the office contents at less than ten, maybe fifteen grand.

Feeling secure, if not safe, he stretched out on a couch in the large office, allowing the debilitating effects of an adrenaline rush to wear off, as he reviewed his options.

If the killers' call hadn't been a ruse, and he wasn't at all sure it was genuine, the killers would be leaving the building about now. Then, there was the matter of the police downstairs, maybe upstairs by now. He had to allow for any possibility. Which begged the question.

"What next?"

He said it out loud, surprising himself. He looked around, suddenly worried he might've been overheard, then shook his head as he got up, walking to the window.

He couldn't see Beecher or Gravesend. Just a bit of Third, and the edge of the intersection where Deo should be waiting.

Would be waiting, he told himself.

He reached up to mop his forehead with a tissue taken from a desk. As he brought it back down, he noticed the blood.

He stared down at the stained tissue, not thinking about his wound. Instead, his mind returned to the Cold Man, the bodies, and the contents of the second safe, now safely locked away in his ever-present case.

But he wouldn't look for answers now. That could wait till the more immediate problems were solved.

With a mirror and first-aid kit found in the supply room, he bandaged the deep but superficial scratch. But even while doing that, his mind remained on the business at hand.

Getting out.

Later, when he was safe and rested, he would think about what had happened. About the young killers.

About Cold Man.

But right now he had some stairs to deal with.

After listening at the door for five minutes, he stepped out into the corridor. Walking quickly, not running, he headed for the stairwell. Opening it a crack, he listened again.

Voices. Calm, collected, professional. But not the voices of the killers. And above, not below him.

With the calm that only a lifetime of burgling can bring, he slowly started down the stairs.

After a brief stop on the twenty-fifth-floor landing to catch his breath, he continued down, increasing his pace as he went.

The bodies might be gone, the killers escaped, but the ugly flood on the pristine carpet would be all the police would need to call for more units. Lab techs, detectives, patrol units to guard the scene and secure the building.

Maybe he had five minutes left, maybe not even that. Only one thing was sure.

The way out was down.

Fifteenth floor.

Tenth floor.

Second floor.

Ground floor.

Basement.

He stopped at the door to the upper level of the subterranean garage. It was thick, designed to keep the noise and fumes of the garage out of the stairwell, so there was no hope of hearing anything on the other side.

Wishing he still had his hood to conceal his face, taking a deep breath, and praying to his gods, he opened the door, then stepped out.

Greg kept to the north wall of the garage, staying between the parking stones and the wall. It was the only place that wouldn't be seen by the building's closed-circuit cameras. Cameras, he was sure, that were searching wherever the police weren't.

As he carefully climbed over the hood of a car parked in his way, he got his first good look at the gate.

It was an aluminum-mesh overhead type. Gear-driven, activated either by security, an internal pressure hose on the floor of the garage (inactive when the door was locked), or a key switch on the outside. Although lightweight, designed more for aesthetics than security, it would keep people out.

But not in.

Edging his way around to the gearbox on the top left of the ten-foot door, he looked through the mesh, freezing as he saw the two police cars blocking the intersection of Gravesend and Third. He slowly pulled back from the door, set down his case, and opened it.

Now was not the time for high-tech gadgets or stealthy, touchy-feely gimmicks. He pulled out a small hatchet from the bottom of the case.

Taking a last look at the gearbox above him, then out to the street, he looked down at his wristwatch.

Less than two minutes later, a used sedan came slowly swerving down the street.

Music turned up loud enough to rattle nearby windows, the driver waved happily at the police as he drove over the center line. The seemingly drunk driver brought the car onto, then off, the sidewalk, then scraped one of the patrol cars as he waved and smiled at the angry officers.

As they screamed at him, Deo dropped the car into gear and sped away.

Followed an instant later by the police, their sirens covering the sound of a blade slicing into and through a garage door's gearbox.

Nobody noticed the darkly dressed man who rolled under the partially opened door, stood, seemed to listen, then walked away quietly.

A fanged (hopefully invisible) shadow melting into the dark.

The long black limousine cruised silently, seemingly randomly along the inner-city streets. In the back, Kilbourne fingered the black nylon hood and the disc-shaped object that his men had brought him.

"And this was all? Everything?"

"Yes, sir," one of the men said firmly.

"The floor safe was empty, sir." This in a reluctant voice from the man whose groin still throbbed from earlier.

"Yes," Kilbourne said as he held the disc very close to his eyes. "The floor safe. The one you didn't find." He didn't sound angry, just disappointed.

"We would've, Mr. Kilbourne. You can believe that."

"Hell," the other said quickly, "it's because we were starting behind the bar that we found the guy."

Kilbourne nodded. "After *he* found the safe."

"We talked about that," one of the men said with emphasis. "We figure the guy must've worked with Kerry, must've known right where to go."

"Probably had the combination," the other quickly added. "He shouldn't be hard to find. We'll just track Kerry's inside circle, right?"

"Right," Kilbourne agreed in a distracted voice. "Of course, if he *were* an intimate, he'd hardly have made the hole in the wall you described." A brief but malignant pause. "Or necessitated the shots you were not supposed to take."

The two men looked out the window rather than into those unsmiling eyes.

The car pulled to a stop in a warehouse district as Kilbourne gestured at a nearby Cadillac.

"Your ride, gentlemen." He opened the door.

They quickly climbed out.

"We'll have the little bastard by noon, sir."

"Count on it."

Kilbourne smiled. "Of course." He closed the door as the limo started to pull away. "When they're in the car, Paul."

"Yes, Mr. Kilbourne," the driver said as he concentrated on the rearview mirror.

Less than a minute later, an explosion pounded the neighborhood. Two pounds of Centex, expertly placed beneath the cushions of the front seat of the Cadillac, vaporized the young killers. As well as a fifteen-foot-wide, three-foot-deep chunk of the highway behind the limo.

Kilbourne never flinched.

"Find out what this is, Paul," he said as he passed the disc-shaped object over the seat back. "And who it belongs to."

THREE

"THERE ARE always possibilities."

His father's favorite phrase.

He surprised himself by mouthing the once familiar saying.

But the real problem, as the man who had called himself Kilbourne for the last twenty-plus years thought, was that there were usually too many possibilities. So many, in fact, that their consideration inevitably led to a near-total paralysis.

A condition Kilbourne despised.

Also, he was quite sure his father had never considered the kind of possibilities he faced now, in the absolute twilight of his life.

Had Kerry been the one trying to expose Joe and Max?

Was it someone else? Someone not connected to the old days? Was it someone who was merely guessing; or not even guessing, just capriciously examining a historical riddle?

And of most immediate concern, who was the man in the penthouse? Did he work for Kerry or someone, like himself, who needed to know what Kerry knew?

Or was there actually nothing behind all this after all? Was it merely all a pretext to clean up some long-festering office politics? An elaborate exercise in cover-your-ass.

If not, what would happen if Joe and Max *were* exposed?

Those possibilities, he refused to even consider.

In all, it made him feel old.

Not just the constant internal pressures of being an eighty-two-year-old man in a society that worshiped twenty-two-year-old boys.

Not because of the occasional, in the last hours near-constant, chest pains that reminded him that soon he would have to account for . . . Too much to think about and still sleep.

Certainly not as a result of the stark reality that he was almost the only one left from the days he thought of as his prime.

No.

It was this job.

For almost forty years, he'd lived a life built around moral certainties. Certainties growing out of a time when morality, right and wrong, were finite things. Clear. Easily recognized.

For almost twenty years, he'd been able to put even those memories behind him. Secure in the knowledge that whatever he'd done, or caused to be done, it was for a higher purpose. The greater good.

But then *they* called. Those others; the new ones to whom morality and higher purpose were abstract concepts to be used like weapons. When and *if* needed.

He'd been surprised at first. But now, sipping coffee at an all-night burger stand, he realized how naive that had been. Of course, they called. It made perfect sense, what he would've done.

They knew all about him, of course. They had to. That's what *they* did.

Where he was. What he'd been doing. What he'd believed in.

Still believed.

Oh, they themselves might not know the reasons for the occasional surveillance, wiretapping, letter opening, or computer checks. Hell, they probably didn't even know the real meaning of the message they'd relayed to him.

And he was certain they'd never met Joe and Max.

But others knew and others had.

Others who still sat in their corner offices. Who gazed pacifically across the Washington Ellipse, or the Pentagon's Core Park, or the thickly forested woods outside Langley, Virginia, that covered, well, he wasn't sure exactly what they covered.

But the others knew, and they were not about to account to people who weren't born when the decisions were made. The lies told. The secrets simply and completely vanished away for the national security and the greater good. Or so they'd all said to each other at the time.

Whether they believed it or not.

But Kilbourne *had* believed; took it as an article of faith. He'd been there, tasted the fear, and saw. Whether the others in their cool, political analysis set the thing in motion with noble intentions or not, he was *certain* that it was the right thing to do.

As the others well knew.

So they'd given him the men, almost unlimited funds, and support. All with one simple objective: Joe and Max were not to be disturbed.

At any cost.

Now, as he revisited the places and people (those few still alive) of his youth, it all poured in on him. An avalanche of experience, feeling, life.

He would chase down every lead.

Question former comrades.

Kill old friends.

Yet he would do it all with the detachment that had served him so well in the past. A thing he thought he'd framed and hung on some long-forgotten wall. A disconnected part of the former Kilbourne.

Before he was Kilbourne.

And it was that, in the final analysis, that accounted for the feeling of age.

Like a lonely old lady in a nursing home, blankly staring into a photo album, trying to remember the young girl she saw in the pictures. Feeling older from the effort.

This temporary resurrection of his former self was aging him beyond measure.

Making him seem, at least until this abortion had been properly and antiseptically performed, older than any other living thing on the planet.

Faced with almost endless possibilities.

"Mr. Kilbourne?"

He looked up as his driver walked over from the nearby limo. "Yes, Paul?"

"It's four A.M., sir."

"Thank you, Paul."

The driver nodded, then took a seat at a nearby table. Out of earshot, but close enough if needed.

Kilbourne pulled a cell phone from his jacket pocket, dialed a number, then impatiently waited for the connection to be made.

"Randle."

Kilbourne smiled without realizing it. "Hello, sweetie."

The bright, female voice seemed puzzled. "Gramps? That you?"

"I'm not disturbing you, am I?"

"No. I just got in five minutes ago. Still on my first cup of . . ." She paused. "What are you doing up at six? What's wrong?"

He laughed. "I'm in New York, remember?" he lied easily. "It's seven here."

"Oh. Some archivist I'm going to be if I can't remember that. What's going on?"

He paused, always shaken by how closely her voice on the phone resembled his late wife's.

"Bad news, honey. I'm not going to be able to get back in time for Kim's birthday."

"Oh." Her voice was genuinely sad. "You're not working too hard, are you? Remember your blood pressure."

Kilbourne smiled weakly. "I'm fine. Just disappointed that I'll miss her big day."

"Grandpa Tom, she's only two. The party's more for all of us than her. She'll be fine."

"Still . . ." He paused, fighting off yet another sharp pain from somewhere deep inside him. "Listen, I'm FedExing something for her. Make sure she knows it's from me, okay?"

Laughter.

"Sure. Sure. You just come back real soon, that's all she really wants." Light laughter. "She misses Grandpa Teddy Bear."

"As soon as I can, Julie."

"Listen, my boss just came in. Was there anything else?"

"Just my love to everyone."

"Back at you."

He disconnected, looking away from his driver as he wiped a tear from his eye.

"Mr. Kilbourne?"

He quickly pulled himself together. "Yes?"

"I have a lead on the device."

Kilbourne nodded as he faced the man. "Go ahead."

"It's a sophisticated echo locator. Very sensitive. Very complex. Very unique. If it was manufactured locally, I've been led to believe there are fewer than five possible sources for it. I'll have a list in ten minutes."

Kilbourne nodded. "And the second team?"

The driver gestured toward two men standing just behind the limousine. "They arrived while you were on the phone, sir."

"Let's hope they're more durable than the last set," Kilbourne said as he laboriously stood up.

The driver helped him. "Yes, sir."

Kilbourne walked over to the new men.

"Two rules," he began without preliminaries. "First, no guns unless absolutely necessary."

The men nodded.

"Second," Kilbourne continued, turning to the limo as he talked. "Leave no witnesses."

Being a witness was about the furthest thing from Greg's mind as he walked away from the high-rise. He had much more immediate concerns.

Cops were everywhere, starting to set up on Gravesend, throwing a 360-degree perimeter around the building.

He was without immediate means of transportation. Deo would need time to lose the cops on his tail; and cabs never came to calls on or near Gravesend after dark.

Then there was the fact that he was forced to walk almost the length of the dismal street by himself. He knew from personal experience the type and numbers of young punks hidden in doorways. Young predators just waiting to jump some poor, unsuspecting schlub who opted for a shortcut down the aptly named avenue.

So he walked briskly, but didn't hurry. Changed sides of the street often, ignored the few poor souls he encountered, but didn't look away either. Did everything he could not to paint himself as a victim.

Trying to ignore a long-buried memory—that demanded substance—of other walks on this same diseased street from a time that he denied.

He wasn't surprised when he heard the two sets of footsteps fall in behind him.

"Hey!"

Taking a deep breath, Greg stopped, then turned to face the voice behind him.

There were three, not two, young men standing there. Torn, dirty jeans, loose-fitting long-sleeved shirts worn untucked, baseball caps pulled low over their angry, hating eyes.

And the one closest to him held a nine-millimeter Glock semiautomatic pistol in his hand.

As he looked into the mirror of his childhood, Greg's face remained impassive.

"Yeah?" His voice was completely without emotion.

"Wha'chu got in da case?"

Greg thought of the several hundred thousand dollars' worth of things in the soft-sided case.

"I've had a bad night, guys, okay? Why don't we just let it go this time?"

Something about the flatness of his tone, the lack of fear in his eyes, something, made the two boys with the gunman fidget nervously.

"Come on, Ty," one of them half yelled. "Let's just do it!" The other one looked around while biting his lip.

"I said," the gunman repeated, "wha's in da case, motherfucker?"

Greg looked down, sighed, then barely shook his head before looking up. "Fine," was all he said as he dropped the case to the sidewalk.

As the gunman looked down, smiling, he suddenly felt his arm being forced up, as his head exploded from the impact of the heel of Greg's right hand.

The next thing he, or any of his friends, knew, Greg's right arm was wrapped painfully around the boy's throat. The gun in Greg's left hand; the barrel screwed into the boy's ear.

The three young thugs froze.

"Like I said, I've had a bad night." Greg's voice was relaxed, frighteningly calm. "Why don't we just let it go this time?" He pointed the gun at each of the terrified punks before returning it to the gunman's ear. "Okay?"

The two boys in front of him eagerly nodded. Greg gestured with the gun and they ran off. He waited, feeling long-suppressed instincts begin to rise up in him, then released the young gunman, who took off on a dead run.

Greg watched them go, shook his head, turned, then continued down the street. When he was sure he was no longer being followed or watched, he tossed the gun down a nearby storm drain.

An hour later, grateful to put the night and the street behind him, he arrived at the Flash Alternate fallback.

Union Station, although open twenty-four hours a day, was usually more than three-quarters empty in the early morning hours. But tonight, due to the once-a-week arrival of the Sunset Limited from Chicago and the pending departure of the biweekly Southern Plains Express, it was almost half full. A place where one man could easily spend several hours unnoticed.

Which is why it had been chosen for the Flash fallback.

If Deo could shake the police pursuit, he would ditch the car, steal another, then pick up Greg. If he hadn't arrived by the time the Express pulled out, at 4:45 A.M., Greg would simply board the train, ride up the line a bit, then get off, get a hotel room, and make phone calls to determine how safe it was to return.

After what had happened earlier in the evening, he almost hoped Deo would be late.

He bought a newspaper, a pint of milk, then wandered into the departure lounge.

There was a low buzz of conversation drifting through the air as the fifty or so travelers waited for their train. Greg found a seat in a row half hidden behind the snack bar. To his left, a young couple excitedly chattered about his meeting her parents. To his right, obviously a traveling rep for something or other, his sample case securely stowed between his legs as he pored through a pocket organizer.

And, over the top of his newspaper, Greg had a clear view of anyone who walked into the terminal.

"Ladies and gentlemen," an almost indecipherable voice said over the loudspeaker. "Update on outbound trains. The Southern Plains Express, Amtrak 1189, will be delayed. Boarding is now expected at 4:50 with departure at 5:02. Amtrak apologizes for this delay."

As the announcer repeated the message, Greg ignored the groans of frustration around him and opened his paper. Ambivalent about the extra fifteen minutes Deo now had to pick him up.

For the next hour and a half, he read, peeked out at the crowd, generally trying to clear his mind of everything except the newspaper. But it was useless.

Without realizing at the time, he'd bought the newspaper that Kerry published; actually seeing the man's face smiling back at him from the top of the Op Ed page. He studied that face, like a plastic surgeon an aging movie star. Looked into the eyes, the laugh lines, the wrinkles, the firm, conservative expression. Trying to equate that man with the naked corpse he'd seen scant hours earlier.

And although Greg's face never reflected it, staring into those eyes began generating a turmoil in the burglar. Some form of deep, visceral rage directed at Cold Man and his killers.

It wasn't that they'd killed Kerry and the girl. That was between Kerry and Cold Man. It wasn't for the killers' pursuit of him. That was an unfortunate part of the game.

No. There was something more to it. Something about the carefully controlled, even more carefully hidden, fear in Cold Man's voice.

Cold Man ordered the killings despite the fact that Kerry had, or was at least suspected of having, something that Cold Man needed. And he was killed before Cold Man had gotten it, because he couldn't be allowed to live knowing that, whatever it was, it was no longer in Cold Man's control.

As Cold Man would kill or have killed anyone who knew he, or his masters, had lost control of whatever it was.

As Greg now knew.

He fingered the top of his briefcase, thinking about the small leather case and the two envelopes. He considered going into the bathroom to check the contents. But no. That was too risky, and Greg felt he'd run his luck right to the edge this night.

But the possibilities ran through his brain, refusing to allow him to concentrate on his reading.

After ten minutes, he got up, looked around, then walked over to a pay phone. He dialed a number, deposited a dollar ten in change, then waited for the connection to be made.

"Carlisle," a deep, gravelly voice answered.

"Glad you're up and about," Greg said in a casual tone, aware of others around him.

There was a pause, then the three clicks that told him a tap alert was being activated. The tiny device, when plugged into the phone, would beep five times if anyone else came on the line. Either on another extension or covertly.

"Greg?"

"Yeah."

"What the hell happened over there?"

"Why don't you tell me?" the thief said in an annoyed tone.

"They've got almost a full task force gearing up. So far, they're

not saying much, but I've heard enough to guess that they're treating it as a high-priority murder investigation."

"Go on."

"They've got an all-points out on that media guy, Jack Kerry.
Although, privately, I've been told they think he's dead. Something
about too much blood at the crime scene." A pause. "And they've
got a short goddamned list of who they like for it."

This time the pause came from Greg.

"Like who?"

"Your name came up."

"You know better than that," Greg said in a too-loud, angry
whisper.

"I know. Hell, even *they* know," the lawyer said patiently. "But
they also know that four high-security penthouses got hit, without
force, in a state-of-the-art-security building." He was silent for a
brief, frightening moment. "They aren't stupid."

"Any warrants out?"

"Not yet. But I wouldn't answer the door or the phone for a few
days."

Five beeps could be clearly heard on both ends of the conversation.

"You in the house alone?" Greg asked.

"Yes," came the terse reply.

Greg quickly hung up. As he turned away, he forced a blank
expression over his angry emotions.

He walked slowly around the terminal, his mind racing.

He'd expected a major effort from the cops, but not until they
were sure that the blood on the carpet was Kerry's. Then, only after
maybe half a day of checking with the man's staff to be sure that he
was missing. Even then, they'd had no reason to check any other
apartments in the building than on the Forty-fifth floor. So there
was no way they should have him on a short list now.

Someone was making this a major priority.

Making *him* a major priority.

"Ladies and gentlemen," the announcer's crackling voice in-
truded on his thoughts. "Announcing the first boarding call for
Amtrak 1189, the Southern Plains Express. Now boarding on Track
G as in golf. All aboard for Amtrak 1189, the Southern Plains Express. Track G for golf."

Greg started to wander over to the boarding area.

Just as he was about to step into the tunnel that led down to his train, he glanced back at the departure lounge to notice Deo come hurrying in.

For a full minute, the two men locked eyes across the crowded terminal. Deo's face blank, waiting patiently for Greg to make the decision.

Greg's mind screamed at him to get on the train. To ride the length of the line; to figure all this out when he was safe on the other side of the country. Maybe on a plane from New Orleans to South America. He even turned, taking a step toward the train.

Five minutes later, sitting next to the driver in an old, stolen Dodge Dart, he turned to Deo.

"Any problems?"

Deo shrugged. "I handled them."

Greg nodded. "You clean through the weekend?"

This wasn't all that unusual. On any job that went bad, no matter how bad, he would often end up with extra assignments.

"An hour or a day, it's all the same to me," Deo said lightly as he pulled onto the deserted freeway. "Five hundred." He saw the way Greg studied his side-view mirror. "If the risk's the same," he quickly added.

"One large per," Greg said softly, his eyes locked on the mirror. "Three-day minimum." He pulled his emergency "out money" from his jacket pocket, counting out $3,000.

Deo was silent for ten minutes as he randomly changed directions, lanes, destinations. Making sure he wasn't being followed. For five hundred a day, he was expected to deal with almost anything that might come up during a score.

But for a thousand . . .

"Where to?" he finally said as he took the money.

"My car's by the pier. Then pick up something cold, something real safe. Then meet me at the place."

"The place" was a 7,500-square-foot ranch house on twenty-two acres just outside the city. It had two guesthouses, stables, a performance ring and grazing field for the twelve American Saddle Horses that Greg owned. It was rustic, quiet, and most important, isolated. The house was at the end of a long driveway with multiple curves peppered with sensors and early warning detectors.

While he might not apply it to others, Greg highly prized his own security.

He parked his car around the side, then walked to the back of the house, to a backyard with a sheer cliff drop to the Pacific Ocean seventy-five feet below. He closed his eyes, breathed in the sour, salty air that meant a red tide, and began to undress.

There'll be dead fish on the beach, he thought distractedly as he stripped, throwing the clothes into a large brick barbecue. Everything went, reversible coat, shirt, pants, even underwear, shoes and socks.

He frowned as he remembered the missing hood.

After dousing the pile with a can and a half of starter fluid, he lit a match, then tossed it in.

Never underestimate the police, he thought as he stood there naked, watching to make sure that everything was being consumed. The same modern technology that he used to break into places would be equally effective in tracing him back to those places. Wherever we go, we leave traces of ourselves, as well as take traces of that place back with us.

And Greg was not going to prison because of fiber evidence.

Finally satisfied, if somewhat annoyed, that his favorite jacket (and other clothes) would soon be reduced to ashes, he entered the house through a side door after deactivating the alarm.

He immediately reactivated the system.

He was overwhelmed by exhaustion and hunger. Maybe it was the natural result of nearly twelve hours of high-adrenaline actions. Maybe it was just that he hadn't eaten since the day before.

Or maybe it was the sense of relief and security he felt standing in the one place in the universe where he felt truly safe.

Regardless, after dressing in jeans and a T-shirt taken from the laundry pile, he headed for the large kitchen before going to his study to go over the night's haul.

"Unbelievable," he muttered as he looked in the refrigerator. "Unbeliev—"

He stopped, a confused expression coming over him.

"I know I had some," he mumbled. "Just bought it yesterday, for God's sake."

He began rooting through it, pushing things aside, looking in every drawer and compartment with a growing sense of frenzy or visceral anger.

"Son of a . . . Where the hell is the bast—"

Then something on the counter caught his attention. An empty pink baker's box with the crumbs of the chocolate cake he'd been searching for.

"Foss," he said beneath his breath in dark tones. "Goddamned Foss. Selfish, unthinking, doesn't care about anyone but his own junkie self . . . Son of a bitch!" He slapped the carton off the counter.

Angrily returning to the fridge, he grabbed at a carton of milk (knocking over several bottles in the process), then slammed the door hard enough to knock the cupboard doors open.

As he slammed each of the cupboard doors shut, the anger intensified, becoming a living thing that the exhausted thief seemed to be doing battle with.

"All I ask is that I have a little cake or something when I get home, but no! Nobody gives a shit about that!"

He slammed the final cupboard closed, but it obstinately swung open again. Greg looked up at it, took a deep breath, seemed to calm, then reached up, grabbing it with both hands and ripping it from its hinges.

He threw it across the room hard enough for it to shatter against the far wall.

He walked over, looking down at the splinters, then sighed.

"Shit," he said softly.

And the genuine rage (what Foss called "the nothing storms") was gone even before he'd carried the milk and his briefcase into his study.

The room was small, comfortably furnished with a love seat on the opposite wall from a large desk set. A stereo/bookcase lined the third wall, with dark paneling and a door on the fourth.

He settled behind the desk, drank a long hit of the milk directly from the carton, then lifted his case onto the desk. But he didn't open it.

Instead, he turned to a large monitor that was mounted on the wall to the side of the desk. He punched a code into the computer beneath it, then studied the display.

Greg knew only too well how easily alarms and sensors could be defeated, so this was his backup. His fail-safe, just in case the worst happened. A system that only went active when someone actually entered the house, thereby undetectable.

Anytime any of the access doors to the house opened, this un-passable sensor system recorded the entry and rolled video on that particular door.

The system had recorded three hits.

The first and the last he knew were only his leaving for the score that morning, then his arrival five minutes before. He called up the second hit on the monitor.

He watched as the machine played back Foss's entering the house at 0246:17. The cameras followed the man, turning themselves on and off, as he went straight upstairs to his bedroom, lit a candle, then pulled out his works. Greg shut the playback and reset the sensors before he saw Foss shoot up.

He was upset enough already.

He flipped the monitor to active mode, calling up a display of the old man's bedroom. Foss lay on his bed, his eyes half open, the drug-induced stupor clouding his otherwise strong features. The remnants of the cake staining the sheet by his head.

Sighing, Greg shut the monitor.

Now he turned his attention fully to his case, emptying it of the loot from all four apartments. This he ignored as he took the case over to a storeroom just off the den. It was only while unloading and inspecting the equipment, putting each item back in its own place, that he noticed his echo locator was missing.

Another frown as he remembered the rush to get away from behind the bar.

Sloppy.

Expensive.

Maybe terribly so if the police could trace the components. But he would be long gone before that ever happened, he reminded himself as he returned to the den.

Now he concentrated on the things he'd stolen earlier in the evening. Intentionally ignoring the three items from Kerry's floor safe.

The haul was better than he'd thought originally. Just over $30,000 in cash; $45,000 in negotiable securities; jewelry worth in excess of $250,000 (maybe $75,000 from the right fence, more if he broke it up—sold the stones and mountings separately); as well as other things worth around, oh, $50,000 easy.

Two hundred thousand.

Before the floor safe.

He put the jewelry and expensive knickknacks in *his* floor safe, hidden beneath the carpet under the heavy love seat. He withheld the cash and securities. These, without really knowing why, he put in a windbreaker on a nearby coatrack.

Then, as if looking for something to do before getting to the things from Kerry's floor safe, he took another drink of milk, then listened to early, vague reports on the morning news about "the mysterious police activity surrounding media mogul Jack Kerry's glamorous penthouse home."

After ten minutes of seeing nothing helpful, he turned to the contents of Kerry's floor safe.

First, the jeweler's repair envelope.

Wearing rubber surgical gloves, he carefully opened the small flap, allowing the contents to slide out onto his desk.

A something, encased in Lucite on a thick gold chain.

Greg frowned as he pulled his swing-arm, lighted magnifying glass over.

The Lucite block was thin, maybe a quarter of an inch thick, three inches long, one inch wide. In the center, a tiny silver object, just over an inch long.

At first glance it appeared to be a piece of ballpoint pen shaft. Maybe silver aluminum, definitely tubular. But under magnification Greg could barely make out some kind of writing near the chain end of the thing, on one side, as well as what appeared to be ridges near the other end of the thing.

"What the hell are you?" Greg said as he reached into the desk for a more powerful jeweler's loupe.

The loupe revealed the writing to be hieroglyphic in style, or at least geometric shapes that seemed to be placed in more than a random pattern. The ridges ran completely around the thing and, although Greg knew it wasn't likely (or really possible for that matter), seemed to have some kind of printed circuitry markings between them.

But he would need a microscope to see anything more.

Looping the chain around his neck, dropping the token, or whatever it was, beneath his shirt, he turned to the fat manila envelope.

He snipped off the tightly wrapped rubber bands, slit it open, pulling out a sheaf of papers.

A quick glance through them revealed fifteen or twenty Xeroxes of old newspaper articles, some almost fifty years old. Along with what appeared to be several lists of names, places, dates, and an organizational outline for something called the Umbra Project.

Certainly not the kind of thing you keep in a floor safe.

Ignoring the Xeroxes, lists, and outline, Greg read a brief note that Kerry had apparently written on a Post-it that had fallen loose.

It read simply, "Life Insurance—Kerry Eyes Only."

Sighing deeply, feeling the exhaustion of almost twenty-four hours without sleep under great tension bear in on him, he put the papers back in the envelope. Later, when he was more rested, mentally sharper, he would try to wade through them.

Finally he turned to the leather case.

It was locked, but only a paper clip was required to deal with that.

"Probably his prized toothpick collection," Greg said bitterly, expressing the disappointment he felt over the lack of any prize from the safe.

"Mantrap, maybe twenty grand in living room alarms alone, hidden panels, and the bastard used the damned safe as a junk drawer."

Then he thought of Cold Man.

Greg carefully opened the case.

The case had a red velvet interior, with a brass plaque just inside the top which read:

Giant Rock Collection
Numbers 61 through 80

But it was the bottom of the case that riveted Greg's eyes.

There were two rows of dimples in the red velvet. Ten dimples in a row. And in fifteen of the dimples, a large, round, glass ball.

But the way they seemed to catch the light, the rainbow greens, reds, blues, that seemed to erupt from each one, was astounding!

His exhaustion was instantly swept away.

Slowly, carefully, he picked one up, holding it under the magnifying glass.

It seemed heavier than it should have, clearly not hollow. Was perfectly round, about an inch and a half in diameter, showing no marks of tooling, sculpting, or molten casting. It appeared to be completely clear, without any internal clouding, distortions, or facets, yet the light seemed to explode within it. A prismlike effect that just wasn't possible in a simple, unfaceted glass ball.

He seemed to focus deep within the unusual thing.

Just then his computer monitor flipped on.

Looking up from the perplexing object, he opened the front gate, allowing Deo to drive through in a late-model Volvo. As he buzzed the driver through the front door, instructing him through an intercom to make himself comfortable, Greg returned to the business at hand.

Studying the ball, frowning, he stood up, walking into his storeroom and a small table that had been set up as a jeweler's bench.

Years ago, he'd realized it would be a massive help on the job if he could easily identify the good jewelry, stones, etc., from the garbage. So he'd taken the GIA (Gemological Institute of America) course to become a certified gemologist. A skill that had served him well over the years.

Forty minutes and a half-carton of milk later, he looked down at the small form on which he'd been making his notes.

Diameter—22 millimeters
Weight—15.714 carats
Color—transparent
Refractive index—2.418
Specific gravity—3.53
Hardness—10+
Dispersion—0.46

He checked three more of the "marbles" just to be sure.

They were identical.

When he was done, he put all but one back in the case and locked the case in his floor safe. After he pushed the love seat back into place, he sat down on it, his mind racing.

The marbles seemed organic, not manufactured. And even under the closest inspection he could give them, they showed no sign of having been artificially shaped or altered in any way.

Which left him with a fundamental problem.

Gemstones, minerals, even silica nodules, are not spherical. Never. Not out of the ground, seldom after cutting, almost never. Besides, the technology didn't exist to create perfectly round stones out of what his tests showed the marbles were made of.

But every test he could run shouted back the same results.

Diamond!

Which meant . . . But even his last possible answer didn't work.

Assuming for the moment, and it would be a massively insupportable assumption, that nature did produce one perfect, round, with-out-angles-or-flaws diamond, that through some freak of volcanic and tectonic activity this mutant diamond was formed, how could you explain fourteen—maybe nineteen if you counted the empty dimples—other absolutely identical stones?

Greg tried not to think about it as he set up three portable alarms to augment the systems he already had on the storeroom and den.

He grabbed the manila envelope and his windbreaker as he pushed the remote that activated all the systems.

Trying, but failing, to ignore the never-before-felt tremble in his hand.

It was almost noon as the long limousine pulled onto the potholed, asphalt parking lot in a low-rent suburb of the city. The driver paused, confused for the moment by the lack of anything that looked like it might be the right place. Then he saw the second team's car parked in front of the fourth of five stores.

Deutchmeur's Car Stereos

Glancing in the back of the limo, he saw that the old man was still asleep, so he parked the car lengthwise through four spaces in front of the store and got out quietly.

One of the second-team men came out of the small shop through a door with a Closed sign hanging on it.

"This is the guy," he said flatly.

The driver's expression never changed. "Which guy?"

The man seemed confused for a moment, then suddenly understood. "No, this guy's way too old to be our guy. But he *did* build the thing."

"And?"

The man hesitated. "Hey, we were told to locate, detain, and notify. Anything else has to come from the man."

The driver sighed. "Get the guy ready."

The man nodded, returning inside the store.

The driver thought about the old man in the back.

He was exhausted, been going almost nonstop for at least the last twenty hours he'd been in the driver's care. Probably hours before that as well.

And the driver's orders had been unusually clear. The care of the old man had priority over everything. To that end, the driver had a full cardiac-care kit in the trunk of the limo, always stayed conscious of where the nearest hospital was, anything to help care for the impressive Mr. Kilbourne.

And one other thing. He liked Kilbourne, a rarity in his job. There was no nonsense in the man. Like a guided missile, he seemed to unemotionally home in on his targets with skill, precision, devoid of interfering, bullshit morality.

He was the kind of operative, the old kind, that the driver had read about in history files. The kind he hoped to be one day.

As he climbed back in the car, he regretted that he had to wake Kilbourne. His complexion was pale, his breathing getting a little labored. But he'd come to know the man, he thought, and the man would want to question this Deutchmeur himself.

As he lowered the center divider, his Car-FAX chirped to life. He decided to wait on waking Kilbourne until he saw the message.

He hoped it wouldn't be the one that *must* come at some point, the one ordering him to kill the old man.

He smiled as he read the unspooling message.

"Sir," the driver called out softly. "Mr. Kilbourne?"

Kilbourne blinked himself awake, seeming to be confused by his surroundings.

"Oh," he finally said, "Paul."

"Yes, sir."

"Where are we?"

"Second team has found the man who built the echo locator. We're there now." A pause. "Shall I have them begin the questioning?"

Kilbourne shook his head, wiped the sleep from his eyes, then sat up straight. "I'll talk to him."

"Very good, sir."

Paul got out, hurried around the car, opening Kilbourne's door, helping him out. Then he handed him the fax. "The list you requested. It just came in."

Kilbourne nodded, reading while they walked.

In the back of the closed-up stereo shop, Deutchmeur sat on a stool, with the two men from the second team standing behind him. He was fat, fiftyish, and clearly scared. His eyes locked on Kilbourne as he slowly walked up.

"I want to assure you, Mr. Deutchmeur," Kilbourne began without preamble, "that we know who you are, what you do, and who

you do it for. Any lies in those areas will be most unappreciated."
He paused as he walked within a foot of the man. "As well as punished."

"I don't know what you're talking about," Deutchmeur stammered out. "I just . . ."

His words were choked off by a large hand clasped over his mouth
from behind.

Kilbourne sat down in a chair that Paul brought over.

"That lie, I'll allow. We'll chalk it up to your inexperience." He
pulled out the fax from his jacket pocket. "I assume you're a brave
man, Mr. Deutchmeur. Witness the profession you've chosen. Providing sophisticated electronics to high-rent burglars." A pause.
"Yes?"

Deutchmeur, the hand still firmly over his mouth, sat still.

Kilbourne sighed. "I'm on a schedule, Mr. Deutchmeur. Nod for
yes, suffer for no."

Slowly the terrified man nodded.

Kilbourne held out his hand, and one of the men handed the
echo locator past Deutchmeur to Kilbourne.

"You built this?"

A slow nod.

"For a burglar." It was a statement.

Another nod.

Kilbourne looked down at the thin paper in his hand, the fax that
listed the top, most talented burglars in that area.

"Was it Cesar Luis Rodriguez?"

No reaction.

"Robert Brawley?"

No reaction.

"Gregory Picaro?"

Again, no reaction, except for the slightest twinge of a muscle in
the man's cheek. It was probably nothing, just the understandable
tension of the frightened man physicalizing itself. The other three
men in the room hadn't even noticed it.

But Kilbourne had, as long-rusted-over instincts seemed to
emerge from hibernation. Instantly translating that one slight
twitch.

"Let's talk about Mr. Picaro," he said as he waved the killer's
hand away. "Who he is, what he does, and where he might be
found."

FOUR

T HERE WAS surprisingly little fire, but the thick choking smoke was everywhere.

He shouldn't be there, it was a completely unacceptable risk. And he hadn't planned to be anywhere near the Fifth Arrondissement—but a disturbing feeling, left over from the night's work, beckoned him.

And this man lived by his instincts and feelings.

He wandered through the debris, stunned (as was everyone else) at the complete obliteration of the place.

"Who would do such a thing?" he heard someone cry out.

"What kind of monsters are they?" from another.

"They say the target was the Islamic Center on the third floor," a woman whispered to a friend.

The second woman, standing inches away, shook her head. "They must've known about the day-care center."

The man wandered away head-down—to avoid identification as well as to hide his look of shock and pain—as members of the local gendarmerie began to cordon off the debris field.

He *hadn't* known.

But the others must have.

Suddenly he tripped, almost falling over into the still-burning ashes. Steadying himself, he froze, staring down at a small, thin, child's arm; lying by itself in front of him.

It was a pale, dismembered reminder of the power of the blast.

And it still gripped a smiling doll in its dead, innocent fingers.

□ □ □

Greg blinked open his eyes.

In that instant between the last of sleep and the first conscious thought, the smell of charred flesh and wasted humanity morphed into bacon and eggs.

But the faded sense of the nightmare remained.

He hadn't experienced the full nightmare—more accurately, memory—in years. Thought he'd neatly stored it away in an unopenable box, buried deep within some forgotten spot. A thing he'd long ago decided to deny any life to.

But it was with him this morning nonetheless. As suggestions of its full horror had been with him for days.

He sat up in the king-size bed, dangling his legs, clenching the thick carpet in his toes as he tried to empty his mind of everything but the problem at hand.

The cops.

The strange stones.

Cold Man.

He stood, pulled on jeans and a sweatshirt, then stretched. He walked over to a mirror, running his fingers through his hair, rubbing his eyes; silently deep in thought.

Of course, the stress of the night before had accounted for the nightmare/memory's return. Of course, he should have expected it after the pains and tension of his near escape from the killers.

He never should've put down a score anywhere near Gravesend Avenue.

A nightmare memory generated by a nightmare job on that nightmare street of his childhood.

He nodded as it all fell into perfect place for him. He started for the door, then stopped, turned, walking with purpose back to the bed. He reached beneath the mattress.

A moment later, he checked that the clip in the .45 automatic was loaded before shoving it into the special pocket inside his windbreaker. He carried it and the envelope from Kerry's floor safe out with him.

He found Deo sitting in the dining room, watching the two TVs.

On one set an insufferably cheerful, well-past-her-prime beauty queen chirped her contempt at a world that recognized her for the no-talent that she was. All while her seventyish, trying to look thirty, former game show host companion nodded his eager support.

Deo barely nodded as Greg sat on the other side of the table, concentrating on the other set.

There, alternating views from the nine security cameras around the ranch flashed for seven seconds each. A groom was combing one of the big horses in the barn. A gardener rode his mower across the island of grass that the driveway circled. Deo's Volvo sat, parked nose toward the gate, near the front door.

And just outside the gate, a cable TV truck with two workers leaning against it sat by a power pole.

"How long?" Greg asked as he used the remote to freeze that camera's picture on the screen.

Deo glanced over at it. "About an hour." His voice was flat, quiet, unconcerned. "Definitely heat."

"I hope so."

Deo glanced over at him, then returned to the talk show. "Not bad legs for the miles on her," he said as the camera pushed in on the talk show host. He knew he would be told what he needed, when he needed to know it.

Foss walked into the room with a breakfast plate.

"Figured you'd be down a few more hours at least," he said casually as he sat down and began to eat.

He was a different man from the night before. His face, stretched so tightly during the score, had relaxed. A comfortable smile replaced the nervous tic; and he seemed younger, more alive. But all that would change in a few hours . . . after his "wake-up" had run its course.

"There's more inside."

"No cake, though." Greg's voice was still angry as he kept his eyes on the cable truck.

Foss knew that his boss/partner/friend/savior was the coolest man in the world in any crisis. Always calm, detached, icily efficient no matter what overpowering odds they faced.

He also had learned that it was the little things that would set him off; sometimes into a fiery fury that shocked those few closest to him.

He decided not to say anything about it, offer no excuses, and hope the mess he'd cleaned up in the kitchen when he'd gotten up would be the extent of the man's anger.

"I'll fix you a plate of something," he said quietly.

Greg shook his head as he continued to study the cable truck. He tossed the envelope over to Foss.

"Run it down for me." He adjusted the camera to push in on closer detail of the men by the truck. "Start with the typed sheets."

Foss shrugged as he pulled out the papers. Between forkfuls of bacon, or toast dipped in the runny eggs, he began to read.

"Organizational breakdown and funding channels—the Umbra Project," the old man mumbled as he found the papers. "Majic— Eyes Only." He paused "Governmentspeak. Can't just come out and say what they're talking about like regular people," he grumbled. He continued to read as he ate.

"Tell me about the wheels," Greg said as he poured himself a cup of coffee from a pot on the table.

Never taking his eyes off the cable truck.

Deo flipped from the talk show to cartoons. "Volvo 350-S. Can't get them in this country. Sturdiest high-impact chassis in the world."

"And?"

"Passenger compartment has one-inch wraparound titanium on all sides. Glass is half-inch, impact-resistant polymers. Kevlar over the fuel bladder, which is tucked under the rear seat and enlarged. Go upwards of five hundred miles on one tank at speed. Not bad for the overall weight and engine size." He paused, laughing at an outrageous moment in the cartoon. "I love this shit. Think it clears out all the bad karma in the air. Engine's a 410 V-8 with turbos."

"Anything else?"

The driver shrugged. "Few custom tweaks. Nothing special."

Greg nodded as he returned the set to its alternating display and tried to empty his mind with the cartoons. The ringing of his phone disturbed the already-failing attempt.

"Three-five-one-three," he answered in a consciously changed voice.

"I thought I told you not to answer the phone."

The click of the tap alert was obvious on the line.

"What's going on, Carlisle?"

The lawyer's voice sounded tense over the electronically swept line. "Nothing good."

"Hang on." Greg put the call on hold, then walked into the kitchen. Taking a deep breath, he picked up the phone there. "Go ahead."

"All of a sudden, the cops are treating the Kerry thing like a routine disappearance. No task force, no priority. No nothing."

"And that's bad?" Greg asked without a smile, already suspecting the rest.

Carlisle's deep breath could clearly be heard above the occasional electronic chirps and white noise that kept the line clear of eavesdroppers.

"Specifically," the $750-an-hour criminal defense lawyer said slowly, "the chief called the head of Homicide Special and ordered them off the case. Also, my man in Residences and Lofts says your package got pulled."

"We knew that, right?"

"But now we know who pulled it. As my man put it, 'a drab man in a drab suit with no particular expression and a little plastic card that says he can do like he likes.' Get it?"

Greg considered the impact of this newest piece to the puzzle. Somehow he didn't feel quite comforted by the possibility that the cops might no longer be looking for him.

Because someone else was.

"How old's the information?" he asked after a time.

"I just got off the phone."

Greg quickly reviewed his options. Something he was doing too much of lately.

"I have a current will on file?"

This time the hesitation was on Carlisle's end. "Yeah," he said in a stunted voice. "Less than a year old."

Greg nodded. "Just remember that I'm not feeling suicidal, right?"

"I'll make sure one of my guys does an autopsy," Carlisle said after an even longer pause. "Do you really think it'll come to . . ."

His words were cut off as Greg hung up the phone, hesitated, then returned to the dining room.

"Cable guy's got high-priced assistants," Deo said coolly as he pointed at the security monitor.

A stretch limousine was parked just behind the truck.

Greg pulled on his windbreaker as he watched the driver get out, walk over to the cable repairmen, conversing as they looked toward the house.

"Give me something, Foss." His voice was flat, emotionless, but somehow . . . taut.

Foss looked up from the paper. "Doesn't make much sense yet. Give me a couple of hours and some Internet time."

Greg watched the driver return to the limo, then lean in a back window. "I'll take what you got."

For the first time, Foss noticed the tension in his friend.

"Uh, the Umbra Project—probably a code name or call sign—is run by something called MJ-12, which is also referred to as Majic 12 or something or other. Specifically, by someone designated as MJ-7."

"And?"

As the driver got back into the limo, Deo pulled off his boots and pulled on canvas Velcro-tie tennis shoes. He pulled the straps tight.

"Umbra is set up like some sort of weird pension fund," Foss continued. "Accounts for fifteen or twenty people, paid out annually through a series of dummy corporations."

"That it?"

"So far," the old junkie said softly. "Except that all these papers are, or more likely were, classified 'Eyes Only' to the attention of this Majic organization. *M-a-j-i-c.* Might be an acronym or abbreviation for some covert ops or something."

He paused, looking at the monitor that seemed to rivet his companions' attention, then back into Greg's worried eyes. "We leaving?"

Greg didn't move as the limo pulled up to his gate. He watched as the driver pushed the intercom button and the phone on the table rang.

Greg picked it up on the third ring. "Yeah."

"Mr. Smith for Mr. Picaro."

Greg pressed the code to open the gate. "Come ahead." He turned to Foss as he watched the big car drive through. "Get the crash bags." Then he turned and walked to the front door, followed silently by Deo.

The long car slowed as it approached the front of the main house.

"Be friendly, Paul," Kilbourne said from the backseat. "Friendly, pacific, just a driver who's being paid for his time."

The driver nodded. "Yes, sir." But his voice was decidedly less than enthusiastic.

"What is it, Paul?"

"Sir, no disrespect intended, but shouldn't we take this guy like the others? You said that time was of the essence. And he *is* just a burglar. No different than the other lowlifes that led us here."

Kilbourne nodded as the car pulled to a stop opposite the front door. He thought about the technician, Deutchmeur; of the fence, then the man who laundered stocks and bonds that they'd been led to, as they steadily tracked down the only witness to the night before.

"Just a burglar," he repeated softly. "Perhaps. But this burglar, Paul, this one might not be like the others." He gestured at the surrounding lush ranchland. "Not quite what I would expect for the home of just a burglar."

"Me either," the driver admitted reluctantly as he put the car in park but kept the engine running.

"So," Kilbourne said as he arranged himself in the backseat, "we make a small investment in time." He paused. "Then, if all is as it should be, if he is what we believe him to be . . . we proceed."

The front door of the house opened. Greg stepped out, followed by Deo. The limo driver took a deep breath, forced a natural, open smile on his face, then got out of the car.

"Mr. Picaro?" he asked in a casual voice.

Neither man reacted.

"I've got a Mr. Smith here to see a Mr. Picaro."

"And?" Greg stood stock-still, studying the tinted passenger compartment window in front of him.

The driver started to step around the car. "Mr. Picaro? If you'd just step inside, I think . . ."

"I'm not really interested in what you think, Smiley," Greg said in an annoyed voice. "Smith wants to talk, he steps outside."

The driver paused, surprised by the confidence he heard in the burglar's voice. He hesitated, then got back in the car.

A full minute later, the rear door opened and Kilbourne stepped out.

He blinked against the bright morning light, then reached into his pocket . . . for sunglasses.

This simple action had been carefully thought out. Something the old man had done hundreds of times in the past when faced with similar situations. It never failed to provoke a flinch in the opposite side as the thought would flash through their minds that he was going for a gun.

And the man behind Picaro *had* flinched.

But the burglar had only smiled.

"You have the advantage of me, gentlemen," Kilbourne began brightly. "Which of you would be Mr. Picaro?" he asked, although he knew the answer.

"Smith, huh," Greg said in a disappointed tone. "You couldn't come up with something better than that?" Again, he smiled. Calmly, loosely, as if he didn't have a care in the world.

But inside, he was chilled to the bone as he finally put a face to the voice of the Cold Man.

Kilbourne shrugged. "Any name will do. So long as our conversation is productive."

He cut himself off as Deo stepped past Greg, seemed to come toward him, then walked over to the nearby Volvo. He perched on the hood, his eyes locked on the limo driver's.

Kilbourne looked back at Greg. "Shall we leave our . . . associates here, and step inside?"

"Take a look around, Smith."

"What?"

"Look around." As the old man turned, Greg stepped forward. "I got gardeners, I got stable hands; I even have a vet on the grounds looking at one of my horses."

Kilbourne turned back, surprised to see how close Greg had come to him.

"Your point?"

"No point," Greg said in a relaxed tone. "Just an audience."

"Point taken."

"So?"

Nothing was as the old man had expected, not this place. Certainly not this man. So Kilbourne retreated to a decades-old, carefully honed routine.

"So I believe you, shall we say . . . came in contact with two associates of mine last evening."

"Let's skip the word games, Smith." Greg's voice had dropped to a low, almost threatening tone. "What do you want?"

Kilbourne paused, impressed by the display from the man in front of him.

"Very well." He took a few steps away. "What were you doing in the Kerry penthouse last night?"

"I'm a burglar. It's what I do."

"A burglar, yes." He nodded in appreciation of the breathtaking view of the Pacific Ocean to the side of the house. "A burglar with no recorded past, prior to ten years ago."

Greg lifted his eyebrows. "How far back does your past go, Smith?"

Not the expected answer.

"Who do you burglarize for, Mr. Picaro?" Kilbourne kept his feeling of being slightly off balance completely out of his voice.

"I'm usually self-employed."

"Usually." Kilbourne smiled. "Would you consider last night's work usual?"

Now Greg shrugged. "You learn to adjust in my line of work."

Kilbourne laughed, a cheerless laugh. "Two bodies, a rather grotesque-looking scene as I recall; chased by two, I assure you, quite ruthless men through a building in the dead of night . . ." His voice trailed off. "As you say, let's not play word games."

"It's your meeting."

Despite the rock steadiness of his voice, Greg's stomach was turning over. The dark images that had stayed with him since he'd first stepped into Kerry's living room had suddenly become crystal-clear. His worst case playing itself out before his eyes.

Shadowed flashes of men who'd possessed Kilbourne's voice, without his face, laughing at him in his mind.

Kilbourne was openly displaying an arrogance of power. His admission to complicity in the killings, to the phony name; the ostentatious limo, the obvious surveillance beyond the gates, all spoke to Greg in bright red-lettered words. It said: *You are insignificant to me. Of interest only for as long as is necessary. Live or die, all of little consequence to me.*

"I'll make this simple. Tell me why you were there," Kilbourne said as he stared unblinkingly into the burglar's equally intense stare. "Who sent you? What did you find in the floor safe?" He paused. "Convince me that our interests lie in separate areas and we will never set eyes on each other again."

Now Greg was certain that the rock-hard old man was going to kill him. The only question left was when.

"I've got a question."

Kilbourne sighed deeply. "I hope it's to the point," he said as he turned away, fussing with his fingernails. It was a move of calculated unconcern.

"Do you believe in magic?"

Kilbourne spun around. "What?"

"Do you work for the Umbra Project, or directly for MJ-12?" The burglar's voice was casual, as if he was only mildly interested in the answer.

Kilbourne stiffened.

"Not that I care, really," Greg hastily continued as he noted the reaction. "I'm just curious."

It was the only thing he had; his only means to slow the Cold Man down. To make him think, question, hesitate.

"I believe you just answered my questions, Mr. Picaro."

Greg forced a relaxed smile to his lips. "Did I? Really?" He paused. "Yes," he finally said as he seemed to consider some deeply complicated issue. "I see your point. But then, I don't think you've quite thought it through, have you? I mean, the fact that I know about Umbra and MJ-12 *may* mean that I've gotten it from the safe."

A vein in the old man's temple began to pulse slightly at the mention of *it*.

Most wouldn't have noticed.

Greg did.

"Then again," he continued casually, "it may only mean that I work for the same people you do. Just trying to find out whether we have the same boss, or if it's our boss's boss that we have in common."

He paused, smiling sympathetically at Kilbourne.

"How embarrassing that would be for you: destroying someone from the same team. I mean, what would MJ-7 say?"

Kilbourne took several steps toward the younger man. "Who *are* you?" he said in a hoarse whisper.

Greg seemed about to answer, then he suddenly reached inside his windbreaker. He chuckled as Kilbourne flinched. "Go away, Smith," he said in an imperious tone. "Leave now, and I'll say no more about it." He turned, starting for the house.

"Picaro!" Kilbourne's voice wasn't quite a shout, but it was choked with threats.

Greg stopped, then turned to face the old man. "Yeah?"

Kilbourne walked over to him. "You had better pray that your story checks," the man said in a menacing whisper.

"Which story is that?" Greg said in an amused tone. He gestured for Deo to join him, waiting until the wheelman was inside the house before turning back to Kilbourne. "Go away, Smith. Before I call the cops on you for trespassing." He turned and walked into the house, slamming the door behind him.

Kilbourne stood there, staring at the closed door for two full minutes. In his mind, he flashed over the conversation, every word, every nuance, every suggestion. Finally he returned to the back of the limo.

"Sir?" the driver said as Kilbourne slammed his door.

"I want three more surveillance/entry teams here within the hour."

"Right away, sir." The driver started the car. "So he *is* the one, then."

Kilbourne didn't answer, just stared at the floor as the limo headed for the gate. He pressed the button to raise the black privacy divider; wondering, as it cut him off from the rest of the world, whether he or Picaro would be dead in the next few hours.

In the dining room, Picaro watched the limo pull off his property, parking halfway down the street.

"That," Deo said with emphasis, "is a very serious individual."

Greg nodded, then turned to Foss, who had eavesdropped on the conversation from the entryway. "We're leaving."

"Thank Christ!" Foss, with two suitcases, a duffel bag, and a toolbox by his feet, looked grim. "When?"

"The sooner, the better." Greg turned, heading for his office. " 'Cause I'm flat out of bullshit."

While Foss loaded the bags in the car; while Deo called the local Highway Patrol to check on road conditions for various possible routes; while three nondescript sedans (with equally nondescript men) pulled up near the entrances to the ranch, Greg worked in his office and around the house.

The men didn't talk, just silently went about their jobs. Foss going over a checklist; Deo looking at maps; Greg carrying a large box filled with strange-looking machines around the house with him, before disappearing into his office one last time.

Forty-five minutes after his meeting with Kilbourne, Greg joined the other men in the kitchen.

"Way I figure it, they'll come around seven, maybe seven-thirty. After most of the staff's gone for the day."

Deo nodded toward the security monitor.

"Looks like there's maybe eight, ten guys, and they're settled in. In no damned hurry right now."

Foss finished filling a thermos. "Car's loaded."

"What about you?" Greg asked in a serious tone. "You up for this?"

Foss looked hurt. "Why'd you have to say a thing like that?"

But Greg never looked away. "I mean it, old man. Things could get kind of . . . *difficult* out there. I need you to be . . ." He paused as he looked deeply in the man's eyes. "Maybe you'd better sit this one out."

An uneasy silence settled over the room.

"We going or what?" Foss finally mumbled.

Greg continued to stare at him. "You're up front with Deo," he said firmly.

"Wonderful," the driver said as he shook his head. "We'll get pulled over for speeding, then all go to jail for possession."

Foss turned to him, a smile slowly growing. "Probably preferable to what that old fart has in mind for us." He paused, a serious expression crossing his eyes. "Besides, I'm not carrying."

"And Smith is selling Girl Scout cookies," Deo said as he got himself a bottled water from the refrigerator. "When do we do this thing?"

Greg picked up a canvas gym bag, the only remaining item in his box. He reached inside, pulled out a remote control, then pressed a three-number combination, waited, and pressed a fourth number.

Clicks of devices turning on, hums of hidden machinery, and the slightest acrid electrical taste of microwaves filled the air around them.

"Now."

From the power pole by the front gate, one of the phony cable men spoke softly into his voice-activated radio.

"Three white males, getting into the car."

The limo driver turned to make sure Kilbourne had heard the message.

"Unit five to remain, watching the house, Paul. The rest in casual pursuit."

The limo driver nodded and relayed the orders.

Less than a minute later, the Volvo pulled out onto the street. Quickly followed at a discreet distance by the limo and three sedans.

"Your show, man," Greg said as he looked out the thick rear window.

Deo nodded. "Not much they can do down here. Too many homes, too many pedestrians, too much traffic. They'll wait for us to hit the access road to I-24. It's four lanes, usually empty this time of day, perfect place to take us."

"You sure?"

Deo smiled, a genuinely relaxed, open expression. "It's where I'd do it."

"Swell," Foss mumbled as he checked his seat belt.

"No refunds once the car's in motion," Deo said in a serious tone. He slowly accelerated to forty-five miles an hour. "Don't want them to feel too comfortable."

One of the sedans drove past them, taking a position about five car lengths ahead. The two others stayed behind the escape car, about the same distance, but in the lanes to the left and right. The black limousine forming the bottom tip of a diamond formation around the fleeing car.

"Access road in a mile and a half. Go, no go?"

"Do it," Greg said firmly.

The Volvo slowed, just a hair but enough for the car ahead to reach the beginning of the curving access road critical seconds before they did.

Suddenly the little silver car jumped forward as Deo jammed the gas pedal deep into the floorboards. The reinforced metal grillwork on the front seemed to almost reach out to the left rear corner of the sedan in front, sending it into an uncontrolled wild spin across the highway.

With his foot pressing still harder on the pedal, Deo flashed the car past the spinning, soon-to-be wreck, onto the access road at close to seventy miles an hour.

The driver of the sedan to the left rear never had a chance to avoid his out-of-control partners. The two cars collided, the one stopping the spin of the other as they slid in a shower of sparks, screeching metal, and screaming men, over the side of the fifty-foot embankment.

The last sedan and the limousine careened wildly, barely avoiding them. As they slowly recovered, the two cars hurried in pursuit of the Volvo.

"Jesus!" The limo driver's knuckles turned white as he fought to keep control of the big, swerving car.

Kilbourne pulled himself up from the floor of the backseat, ignoring the bleeding from his nose as he leaned across the divider, straining to see where the Volvo had gone.

But the long, curving access road ahead was empty.

"Catch them, damn it." Kilbourne's voice was filled with an almost animal rage. "Faster!"

As the sedan and the limo came around the bend of the curve, they were stunned to see the Volvo stopped at the far end of the access road.

Facing them.

Almost before they could react, before any curses were uttered or acts of final contrition made, the little car shot forward, aiming directly for the limousine.

There was no time to think, no time to reason, as the limo driver, a mountain at his left, pulled his wheel hard to the right, just catching the left rear corner of his companion sedan.

The sedan, its passengers screaming, fishtailed to the right, then, as the panicked driver tried to recover by pulling his wheel to the left, it was slammed into by the Volvo.

The little reinforced silver car seemed to shudder a moment, then dragged the sedan backward twenty meters before it continued on unabated. Leaving the sedan a crushed wreck, pinned against the side of the hill.

The limo driver fought the wheel, ignored the sparks that flew off the thin guardrail (all that prevented the big car from going over the side), and fought to regain control of the car. As the right front tire blew out, followed almost immediately by the right rear, the limo coasted to a stop.

Neither Kilbourne nor the driver said a word. They just sat there for almost five minutes, the only sound their heavy breathing. Finally the driver forced open his jammed door. A minute later, he helped the bruised, bleeding old man out of the car.

"Are you all right, Mr. Kilbourne?" His voice was shaky, as if what had happened still hadn't fully registered on him.

"Fine," Kilbourne said in a quiet voice as he stared down the road where the Volvo had disappeared. He daubed at some blood on his upper lip. "Just fine." He seemed to notice the smoke com-

ing from behind and below them for the first time. The flaming
wrecks of the first two cars.

"Poor bastards," the limo driver said as he walked around the car,
standing by the guardrail, looking down. "They never had a
chance."

"Check the others," was all the old man said.

The driver hurried down the road to the twisted wreckage of the
third sedan. A quick look inside, then he turned back to Kilbourne,
slowly shaking his head.

The old man took a deep breath, straightened his jacket, then
leaned into the driver's door, pulling out a small microphone.
"Unit five?"

"Five by."

"Five, this is leader. Terminate surveillance and pick me up at"—
he paused, looking for a sign—"access road, Interstate 24 West."

"Five, roger. En route."

He tossed the mike back into the car, then sat in the door frame.
Waiting. Staring down the road where the Volvo had vanished.

Trying to anticipate the burglar's next move, while already certain
of his own.

He patted his pockets, then stood up with a grunt of pain and an
even more pained expression. It took him more than three minutes
of searching through the shambles of the backseat to find his cellular phone.

While his driver tried to open the crushed and jammed trunk to
get to the first-aid kit, Kilbourne dialed a number. It was answered
during the first ring.

"One-one-seven-two. Duty Officer Lieutenant Mendez."

"Routing Office, please."

"Authorization."

Kilbourne hesitated before saying the words that he hadn't uttered in almost thirty years.

"Authorization," the voice on the other end demanded.

"San Augustin four-seven."

"One moment, please."

Two quick rings, then another voice.

"Routing Office, Major Rogers."

"Request priority routing to Habitat," Kilbourne said in a near
whisper, although the line was scrambled and there were no live
ears close enough to hear.

A long pause on the other end of the line.

"Sign?" the voice finally said.

Kilbourne took a deep breath. "Robert. Alpha. Alpha. Foxtrot. Four-seven."

"Authority?"

This time, Kilbourne actually looked around before speaking in an even more quiet voice. "Joe Gray. Max Gray."

"Stand by, routing you now."

The old man ignored the pain exploding through his left side, radiating up the left side of his neck.

And prayed for a quick death once this was all over.

Seven hours and three hundred miles later, Deo pulled the beaten-up car into an alley behind a just-closed strip mall in Northern California. Almost before the car stopped, Greg was out of the front passenger side, hurrying over to a steel door marked "Cyber Barn."

"Warning," he read from a red, white, and blue shield-shaped sticker pasted in the middle of the door. "These premises are protected by a silent alarm and armed patrol response."

He shook his head as he pulled a can of spray cooking oil from his gym bag, attached a thin straw to the nozzle, then sprayed inside the lock for ten seconds. Then he drove three heavily rusted nails into the door frame at the appropriate spots.

"I'll make you a deal, Linus," he mumbled as he attached bare copper wire to the nails, sliding the other ends between the door frame and the top of the door. "No surprises," he said as he carefully opened the door, "and I'll pay for the merch."

He disappeared inside, after jamming a wedge under the opened door.

Ten minutes later, he was back. A large box cradled in his arms. Deo hopped out, helping to load it into the trunk.

"That's the Packard Bell 300 megahertz," Greg said as Deo secured the box. "What next?"

The driver checked a list. "HP 5L LaserJet printer. Two Packard Bell peripheral drives. A Hewlett-Packard . . ."

"Give me the list," Greg said in an annoyed whisper as he grabbed the paper from Deo's hand. "Can't he just use what I can buy at this hour?"

Deo shrugged. "You're the one who wanted him to start tonight."

He smiled. "Don't forget the mouse pad. He wanted a blue one." He immediately suppressed a chuckle.

Greg gave him a dirty look, then returned to the computer store.

An hour later, the two men were working under Foss's direction, setting up the equipment.

"Make sure none of the cables are touching the others."

Greg looked up, his eyes flashing angrily.

"You going to be able to do anything once this thing's up and running?"

Foss knew that look. It was Greg's "don't give me any shit" look. He was angry, legitimately angry. A rare state for the always steady burglar.

It wasn't really directed at Foss, although that's how he would express it. No. The anger was aimed at that old man, Smith. At being forced to run like a common thief.

Greg hated being thought of as a *common* thief.

On the drive here, he'd told his companions the details of what'd happened in Kerry's penthouse. Everything he'd heard, seen, and thought. Including the fact that he was certain that Smith would be coming after them.

"Who the hell is this guy?" Deo had asked. "If he's crook, then he knows you're not about to cop to the jobs just to rat him out. And if he's straight, why didn't he just call the cops?"

Greg had been silent for a long time after that. "I think he's government. Ex-government anyway," he finally said.

"Our government?"

Greg had shrugged. "Somebody's."

"Shit. Whose?"

Then Greg had turned to Foss, who had taken over the backseat.

Sitting there with a lap desk and battery-powered lantern they'd picked up in a sporting goods store, he was reading through the papers from Kerry's "Life Insurance" envelope.

"Any answers for the man?" Greg had asked in an urgent voice.

"I don't know," he'd said. "All this stuff's almost fifty years old. Postwar things. References to appendixes that aren't included. Lots of militaryspeak."

He'd paused then, letting the titles, designations, and acronyms swim before his eyes. Letting them sort themselves into some kind of order. It'd been his strength when he was a star in Silicon Valley.

When he'd routinely solve incredibly complex, highly abstract problems just by letting his mind wander over the data.

But that had been lost years and countless syringes ago. A mind not polluted by his thrice-daily poisonings or his mostly lost life. Whether it could still function on that kind of level, he wasn't sure. Was afraid to find out. So he'd asked for high-powered computer equipment to check the answers that were already forming in his besotted mind.

Which left them in this small hotel bungalow, with a telephone line "stolen" from a nearby pole and the W-3 search engine menu flashing before him.

"Give me a couple of hours," he said as he began punching in access codes and routing instructions.

Greg nodded reluctantly, then walked to the door. He looked out at the deserted street in the run-down neighborhood.

"You got to do anything to the car?"

Deo shook his head. "I checked her last time we stopped. She's good to go." He stretched out on one of the two beds. "You're taking the first watch?"

In answer, Greg opened the door and stepped out into the night.

Deo exhaled deeply, closed his eyes, trying to ignore the constant clicking of the keys on the computer console.

Far to the south, Kilbourne sat in a lawn chair, looking up at the early evening stars over the blue Pacific.

For the last five hours, he'd had marine military police search teams going over every inch of the ranch. The barns, stables, outbuildings, had all been made short work of. Flooring torn up, holes punched in walls, every drawer, case, cabinet; every piece of paper carefully examined, with every item of possible interest brought before Kilbourne. Who sat in his lawn chair like a king surveying his army in battle from a high ridge.

But nothing that mattered had been found.

So, for the last few hours, they'd been concentrating on the house. And *that* search was going painfully slow.

"Mr. Kilbourne?"

"Yes, Captain."

The young marine captain shook his head as he walked up to the bandaged old man who held priority orders. "We're still hitting those damned booby traps in every room." He wiped his soot-stained face. "Whoever owns this place *does not* want us poking around in there."

Kilbourne ignored the man's tone. "How far have you gotten?"

"We're in the front third of the place. Kitchen, a bedroom, dining room. And we've got the door to what looks like an office open. We've also finally made it up the stairs."

Kilbourne suppressed a smile of sympathy for the man's problems.

Ever since they'd entered the house, they'd been forced to go at a snail's pace. Open this door, you get teargassed. Cross that threshold, the lights go out and smoke bombs fire off. Along with the occasional deafening explosion and the odd blinding flash.

He was beginning to understand this burglar's mind. And he was now convinced that Greg *was* a burglar. But he was a burglar who knew things he shouldn't know. Showed up places he shouldn't be. Had an almost uncanny resilience.

It could all be coincidence, and once they caught up with him they would definitely find that out. But either way, he knew too much, or might know too much, and that alone sealed his fate.

"Keep at it, Captain."

The captain nodded, then turned to leave, just as a lance corporal came running up. He took the offered envelope from the young man, shook his head, then turned back to Kilbourne.

"They found this on the floor, just inside the office door." He handed the envelope to Kilbourne.

For a moment, the briefest flicker, the old killer wondered if the envelope labeled "Smith" might contain a letter bomb. He smiled at the thought.

It was what *he* would do. Not this intelligent, almost practical-joking burglar with the steel balls; the man who set off nonlethal obstructions in the path of the searchers.

Things to annoy, to slow down, but not to hurt or kill.

He tore open the end of the envelope, pulling out the single sheet of paper within. He quickly scanned the two paragraphs, then looked up at the marine in front of him.

"I suggest you get your men out of the house immediately, Captain."

"What?"

Kilbourne struggled to his feet, starting for a nearby unmarked helicopter, helped by his assistant. "At least a hundred meters away should be safe," he said casually as he went.

The captain watched him for a moment, then picked up the microphone to his handie-talkie.

"Recall! Recall! Everybody out and to the other side of the lawn! Now!"

As the helicopter lifted off, to take him to the private jet that would eventually leave him at Habitat, Kilbourne looked down at the men pouring from the building like ants from a burning anthill.

He smiled as he checked his watch. "Ask the pilot to hold here for a moment, Paul."

His assistant nodded, then spoke to the pilot on the intercom. A moment later, the chopper seemed to be pushed straight up in the air as it was caught in the shock wave from a huge explosion below.

The large house seemed to collapse into itself, as thick dark smoke poured from the growing wreckage. Occasional deep orange flames could be seen slipping between the fallen roof tiles and collapsed walls.

"All right, Paul. We can go now," Kilbourne said distractedly as he reopened the note.

Mr. Smith:

Seven minutes after this note is taken from the floor of my office, a series of explosions will begin. These will effectively destroy my house, but should also end your unwarranted and ill-mannered invasion of my privacy. In addition to alerting everyone within a mile of your presence. I advise you to leave now.

Whoever you are, whoever you represent, understand this: any further attempts on my life or attempts to locate me or retaliate against my friends will result in significant repercussions. For you, for Umbra, for MJ-12. I may not have your resources, but then you have no true understanding of mine.

Or of my will to use them.

Nobody's safe!

Gregory Picaro

As the helicopter banked, heading for the air base to the east, Kilbourne closed his eyes and smiled.

He was beginning to like this man he must destroy.

And, somehow, that made it all right.

PART TWO

STRANGER THAN FICTION

It was in the years before. A time when fully grown precision, definiteness, exactitude, and steeled nerves were prayed-for—not realized—qualities. A time for fear, for dread, for soul-deep suspicion of anyone and anything.

A time dedicated to forgetting cadaveric mothers that may have only existed in the heart, and not the life.

The little boy was warm, protected, looked after, and loved . . . after a fashion. But still, something wasn't right.

As he grew in his newly found middle-class existence, as he tried to embrace the suburban values of his foster family (a locksmith, his wife, and three "real" children), he never forgot Gravesend and the lessons it had taught him.

Even in his brief time in a group home, he'd worked to stay ahead of the system he was now submerged in. The smiley-faced counselors were not the enemy, but close. The doctors, benevolent fools. The other children . . . the competition.

There were late night escapes from the comfortable dorm. What were Masterlock Standards and file cabinet minikeys to a child who could disassemble any padlock he came in contact with; then reassemble it blindfolded, his act in the dorm talent show. They served as little or no impediment to this "gifted" child.

So these carefully planned, near flawlessly executed forays into the locked administrative offices became a regular event.

To manipulate possible adoptive parents' application files, according to his own requirements.

To read his case reports, in order to come up with the responses the authorities wanted.

To review his options.

Sure, he'd be caught, rarely. Punished, forced to spend hours at a time in the isolation room. Not a prison cell by any means, and certainly nothing daunting to a little boy who'd grown up where and how he had.

But other things, things he couldn't con, cheat, or steal away, *did* punish him nonetheless.

The looks from the doctors who called him "a classic case of betrayal response." From the prospective families who, as one possible father had said, saw him as "damaged goods." From the little face in the mirror that tried but failed to inject a believable look of joy, happiness, or innocence.

The look he knew the families wanted to see.

For he had learned his first lessons about this system. You must, no matter what, give them what they expect.

He would be judged by his appearance. By his demeanor, looks, congeniality.

Where he'd come from (still a closely held secret from the beneficently stupid adults) your value lay in your survivability. Your strength. Your connections.

Things of little import to a couple or family that wanted "a little angel."

Or cheap labor subsidized by the government.

It all confused him. He'd lash out over the lack of a second helping of ice cream, or an early bedtime, and be called "unstable."

He would be analyzed and reanalyzed by a staff he was terrified of confiding in. That believed he had been "irreparably traumatized by his parents' desertion." That saw him as "a brave little soldier with only a fantasy view of the real world."

He longed for, cried for, just one chance, one opportunity to scream out the truth to them. To, just once, let them see the frightened little boy who had survived so much.

But he didn't dare.

Because for all their seeming concern, for all their attempts at comfort and solace, they were still a part of a system that he was desperate to escape from.

He would be rescued, in time, by a locksmith from the suburbs (he'd acted duly surprised, of course); a man who'd seen him playing with his combination lock in one of the early news stories.

He wasn't a bad man. Not a perv or a user or a schemer. And he would teach the instinctively talented boy the niceties of what would become his life's trade.

But if the check from the county was late, if the boy were to get in trouble at school; if he stayed out too late or just acted up (far less than the man's other children), the look would come into the man's eyes.

The look that was always followed by "you know we don't have to keep you."

So the little boy learned, as he had learned in the group home, as he'd learned with the cops who'd found him, and as he'd learned the night he walked away from Gravesend Avenue. The only one he could trust, truly depend on no matter what . . . was himself.

And he was nine years old.

FIVE

"LADIES AND GENTLEMEN, the majority leader of the United States Senate and Mrs. Van Ness."

Scattered applause, almost drowned out by the clicking of shutters, whirring of film and video cameras, and the hushed but excited conversation among the media present.

Jesse James Van Ness, the senior senator from Nevada, thirty-five-year Washington insider, and presumptive Democratic nominee for president, was holding his first press conference in a month.

An extraordinary month.

Since he'd wrapped up the nomination in the New York primary twenty-nine days before, the majority leader had been in a weird semiseclusion. He'd appear on the floor of the Senate, at the most important meetings, some party functions, but nothing involving press or anyone outside his most intimate circle of friends and staff.

The rumors had flown fast and furious, of course.

"Senator's Mistress Threatens Exposure," one tabloid had ventured.

"Jesse James Past Drug History Implied," another suggested.

"Nevadan Van Ness in Casino Scandal?" the *Post* wondered.

But today, as Van Ness's press flunky had suggested in a brief fax to the nation's leading news organizations, "the senator will have a statement" for the media, addressing the rumors.

Three networks were covering it live.

The senator smiled as he walked into the room, his arm around his wife. Deeply tanned, wearing a beige jacket over his usual jeans and turtleneck, he shook hands as he moved.

His wife smiled beautifully, peacefully, with just a hint of aged sexuality. Just like she had in all of the senator's campaigns.

Known as Molly the Trooper, she routinely traveled twice the schedule of her husband. Always with a kind word while visiting a hospital; a caring hand to children at day-care centers; awestruck grin in high-tech factories.

But this was also a woman who sat in on all his important staff meetings. Often (some said usually) understanding the issues presented better than her husband.

But that was a side of both that the public was never allowed to see.

"Wow," Van Ness began without preamble, the trademark smile bearing down on the press corps. "There must be free booze and food hidden 'round here or somethin'."

The assembled media laughed. They liked the senator.

True, he was old enough to be the grandfather of most of them. He did seem driven by an out-of-date view of morality and the world. But in these days of overhandled talking heads, wimpy nothings who mouthed platitudes to cover their own lack of any moral foundation, the man (like his name) was refreshing.

Like everybody's favorite uncle who said whatever he thought, whenever he thought of it.

When the laughter died down, he continued easily, never seeming to refer to the notes his aide had covertly laid on the lectern before the senator's entrance.

"Well, as y'all can see, I'm still in one piece. An' I'm sorry to disappoint you, but there's no mistress, skeletons, or financial irregularities 'bout to jump out of any closet of mine."

He paused, glancing down in a self-effacing way. "Hell, if the ladies present will excuse my language, at my age, irregularity is not a word I even like *thinking* about!"

More laughter.

The senator's face suddenly became solemn. The grin transformed to a look of deep regret. His shoulders slumped, seemingly under the weight of a thousand worlds.

The shutters clicked, the cameras pushed in tighter, as Molly put her arm supportively around his waist.

"Just under a month ago, right after the New York primary, it

suddenly became clear to me the awesome responsibility I was facing. The people of the party and cause that I have so long worked
for had confided in me their hopes, dreams, and trust. The enormity of it would overwhelm any normal man." He paused, looking
more vulnerable than seemed possible for a hardened politician.
"And I assure you that I am a most extraordinarily normal man."

A squeeze from his wife, along with a supportive nod.

He took a deep breath. "Then, just four days after that incredible
victory in Manhattan, a tragedy befell me that, frankly, I'm only now
just beginning to overcome. A dear friend, a man I've known since
the dark days of the Second World War, was murdered in his home.

"Jack"—another pause, as if speaking the name seemed to
wound his soul—"Jack was more than a friend. Since 1944, he has
been an intimate adviser; a trusted comrade and ally. Hell! He was
like a brother to me."

His voice drifted off as his wife embraced him, whispering apparent comfort in his ear.

"Now," she said in an almost silent voice. "You've got them, play
them."

He nodded, as if pulling himself together required the most maximum effort he'd ever given.

"In the cauldron of emotions that boiled around me then—my
exultation, which Jack was doomed not to share, and the grieving
for his senseless slaughter, which seemed about to consume me—I
discovered something."

He pulled himself straighter, seemed almost to youthen and grow
stronger before the cameras' piercing gaze.

"Jack and I grew up in another time. A time where good and evil
were clear, easily recognizable opposites. Where men said exactly
what they meant, and a handshake was good enough to seal any
deal. A world where people never locked their doors, neighbors
helped neighbors; where women and children could walk the street
in safety no matter the neighborhood or time of day.

"Jack Kerry and I fought in a world war to preserve that way of
life; the image of which kept us going in our lowest moments." He
began to gesture with his fist; short punching motions in the air,
flawlessly tied to the increasing rhythms of his speech.

"Somewhere between then and now, between the idylls of the
fifties and the despair of the nineties, we lost all of that. That faith.
That belief. That trust. And when that despair invaded the very

hearth and home of my friend, my brother, when it crushed the breath of life from his body and that of his secretary, I . . . I . . ."

His voice seemed to lock up, becoming a choked sob. But this time he remained facing the crowd. Letting them stare in amazement at a deeply private public man who was willing to reveal so much of his inner self on camera.

"I gave way to that despair. Wallowed in the feeling of utter hopelessness that this senseless killing stirred up in me. 'How,' I asked myself, 'how can I possibly go on?' "

A last pause to stare painfully out across the room.

No one moved, no one spoke. Sixty-five statues frozen into rapt attention by this emotional display from a man many of them secretly hoped would be elected the next president.

"But I must go on," he said after almost thirty seconds. "Jack Kerry's death, the deaths of all those other Jack Kerrys who have been callously victimized by the drug addicts, the thieves, the parasites of our communities, must have a meaning! There must be purpose to this random act of inhumanity and all the others like it. We must give them purpose!

"This campaign, this crusade, must and will be carried on in my friend's name. In the names of my friend and all the others like him, I do hereby rededicate myself, this campaign. We *will* return hope to America! We *will* return sanity to our communities! We will triumph over the doom and gloom, emerging newly ennobled in the golden light of peace, prosperity, security, that is the right of each and every American!"

This time the applause was full-blooded. Strong and enthusiastic.

Almost completely from the sixty or so Van Ness supporters that had been infiltrated among the press corps during the last moments of the speech.

A long, passionately supportive hug from Molly, followed by the appearance of whispered soothings.

"How was I?"

"You left out the bit about ghosts demanding justice," she said as she embarrassedly wiped lipstick from his cheek.

"We've got another one of these things at four. I'll do it then." He kissed her on the cheek.

"I'll take a few questions," he said into the microphones, in a voice choked with emotion and commitment.

Forty-five minutes later, it was over.

He shook a few hands, made small talk with some old friends, harmlessly flirted with some of the ladies. Then, arm and arm with his lady, the "love of his life," he retreated to an elevator with two aides and his Secret Service contingent.

"Great speech, Senator," his appointments secretary said without looking up from his always open notebook. "We're clear till three-fifteen."

Van Ness shrugged. "Timing's off. Let's get a video of that sucker an' see what we kin do with her."

"Right away, Senator."

They exited on the twenty-first floor, picking up still more body-guards.

Van Ness shook the hands of some staffers, slapped some shoul-ders, much as his wife did on the other side of the corridor as they walked. Near the door to their suite, they were met by the senator's chief of staff.

"Great job, Senator. Not a dry eye in the house."

An indifferent shrug from the man who would be president as he walked into the Presidential Suite. He walked straight to the bar where he quickly poured a bourbon and branch for himself, then a white wine for his wife.

"The man here yet?"

"In the next room, Senator."

Van Ness waved with his glass. "Well, bring the old boy in." He noticed the hesitation in his most senior assistant, then followed his gaze. "Uh, Agent Grover?"

The Secret Service agent seated at a small desk across the room looked up. "Yes, Senator?"

"Could y'all excuse us for a time?"

"Of course, Senator." He gestured for the other two inside agents to follow him as he opened the door. "We'll be right outside, Sena-tor."

Then he paused, as would any other older agent who had served White Houses past, as a man (at least in his nineties) was wheeled in from the bedroom.

"I thought he was dead," one of the other agents whispered to Grover after they closed the door from the corridor side.

"Don't think so much," Grover admonished his younger col-league as he began to busy himself with routine matters. Unable to shake the oddly unsettled feeling that swept over him.

The old man was helped to a place by the couch, given a bottle of chilled mineral water, before Van Ness's aides left the senator and his wife alone with the man.

As he came out from behind the bar, Van Ness exchanged drinks with his wife, cradling the delicate wineglass by the base as he sat across from the man. His wife took a slug of the bourbon before joining them.

"Interesting speech, Senator." The old man's voice was surprisingly strong. Exceeded only by the fire in his eyes. "I never realized that you and Kerry were that close," he said with a hint of a reproachful smile.

Van Ness sipped his wine. "Press would've made the connection eventually."

"Would they?" The old man paused. "I suppose," he finally said in an offhanded way. "Beautiful as ever, Molly."

She leaned over, kissing him delicately on the cheek. "It's been too long, Mr. Secretary."

"The Secretary," a man long out of the office that he'd once been indistinguishable from, seemed to think about that for a moment as he studied the woman. Then, as if casting off some unexpressed doubt, he turned back to Van Ness.

"I must admit, I do like the image of the late Mr. Kerry as a martyr to the cause of truth, justice, and the American way."

"We'd already received some vague questions," Van Ness said defensively.

"Vague but pointed," Molly quickly added. "We had to act before things got out of hand. Call it a preventive strike, if you like."

"I don't like," the Secretary said between sips of his water. "I don't like at all."

Van Ness put down his wine. "We're working with our people in Kerry's organization. The only story that'll go out is ours. Hell, even his own people believe it." He seemed satisfied.

"When was the last time you actually saw Kerry, Senator?"

Van Ness shrugged. "Everybody knows he was a private man. Almost fanatic about it."

"We'll say he didn't like to flaunt his relationship with Jesse," Molly said easily. "It'll play even better that way."

"Let's hope so." Another sip of the water, then the Secretary pulled a folder out of the pocket of his chair. "The briefing you requested."

Both Van Nesses tried to read the papers upside down.

"Of the original Umbra team, excepting the obvious," the Secretary began slowly, not really referring to the papers, "six are left. Including the formidable Mr. Kilbourne."

"What about the other five?" Van Ness's voice had dropped to a respectful whisper.

"Two have been located abroad. Other . . . *organs* will deal with them. Mr. Kilbourne has been instructed to concentrate on the remaining three individuals."

"Who are they?" Molly asked.

The Secretary smiled spasmodically while taking in their equally concerned, almost identical expressions. Then he paused ever so briefly on the person who might have been his lover once. In a time and place where it had been impossible.

In a time so long ago that he wasn't quite sure if the sweet-scented recollection was memory or fantasy.

"There is also the other problem," he continued, ignoring Molly's question. "One I should think you would be more concerned with than the name of imminently deceased former friends."

Molly looked into the man's dead eyes. He was hiding something. She was almost sure of it.

"We assumed you'd taken care of the situation," she said seriously. "When we'd heard nothing for the last three weeks . . . ."

"Besides," Van Ness interrupted, "if this guy had anything . . . ."

"He might well wait until closer to the election before using it. Or even after the election." He seemed to consider the prospect.

"Have you heard something?" The senator suddenly seemed spring-coil tense.

The Secretary continued to stare into Van Ness's eyes, then barely shook his head.

"Do you need anything?" he asked in a quiet voice.

An unspoken understanding passed between them.

"Not till after the convention. Whatever you can get us on our opponent's strategy or scheduling would be the priorities."

"Of course." The Secretary replaced the file in his chair's pocket. "In the interim, we'll keep you fully informed of all developments. We expect the situation should be wholly resolved long before then."

"He's lying, Jess." Molly's voice was flat, stating a rock-solid fact.

The Secretary glanced at her, then back to Van Ness. "Am I lying, Senator?"

Molly stood up, refilling her bourbon at the bar. "Look at him," she said, "you can smell it on him."

The man in the wheelchair continued to stare at the senator across from him. "Senator?"

Van Ness rubbed his chin. He knew he wasn't the smartest man in the world. Not the best educated or the most intuitive. But he knew two other things besides.

First, he was married to the smartest, best educated, most intuitive person he'd ever known.

Second, the man in front of him was one of the most crafty, amoral people, he felt safe in saying, in the universe.

He sipped his wine and waited.

The man in the wheelchair remained impassive.

"Kilbourne's no closer to finding out who's been breaching security than he was when this all started, is he?" Molly walked over, standing over the crippled man. "Is he?"

"It doesn't really matter, does it?" the man in the wheelchair finally said.

"Doesn't matter!" Molly looked as though she was about to slap the man. "Doesn't matter? All we have to do is keep clean between now and November and we're in the White House; and he says it doesn't matter if Joe and Max appear on *Oprah!*"

"I hardly think they'd do that." The Secretary smiled strangely.

"Calm down, Moll," Van Ness said without taking his eyes off the Secretary. "What he means is that anybody that could get through, who might even remotely be able to connect us to"—the briefest of pauses—"anything will be . . . handled?" He tried to stare into the black heart of the man before him. "Or am I mistaken?"

The Secretary sighed. "We should've done it years ago, really." A long drink from the bottle of water clutched in a liver-spotted hand. "Removed the old, rusted, useless links from the chain." He paused, turning to face the angry woman beside him. "We had visionary hopes that tide and time would do the deed for us. But now events have forced our hand."

"What about this burglar? This Picaro?" Molly, her legendary temper vented, was quickly calming down.

"He's ours whenever we want him, dear, sweet Molly," the old man said. "You'll be able to serve him up to your media contacts as the quintessential symbol of the decay of morality in America." He smiled. "Before the convention, of course."

"Served up dead, I hope."

"However you like, bright angel." The old man, old even in this company, coughed lightly. "Would you mind getting my pills from my aide. He's just down the hall in 2108."

Molly hesitated, until her husband nodded at her. She smiled her practiced smile as she patted the old man's back. "Of course, Mr. Secretary. I'll be right back."

Almost as soon as the door closed, Van Ness moved to a place on the couch beside the suddenly healthy old man. "Liar."

The Secretary raised his eyebrows.

Van Ness chuckled. "You really think Kilbourne can put the genie back in the bottle?" His voice was mockingly light.

"Umbra's the only lead we have," the Secretary said with genuine regret. "There's no one else on the outside, besides the retirees, who could possibly be leaking the information. Certainly no one in . . ." He smiled weakly. "So we're left with one of your old . . . ?"

"Associates," Van Ness said too quickly.

The Secretary seemed puzzled by the choice of words. "It has to be one of your old 'associates.' No one else can do us, you, any harm." The Secretary's voice was suddenly, well, human.

Van Ness nodded. "There's always someone else. You taught me that." A pause. "What about this TV producer you mentioned last time? Then there's the burglar."

"The producer's questions *have* been closer to the mark than I think she realizes," the Secretary admitted with a sigh. "But so far she only has random pieces of the puzzle. Nowhere near enough to see the overall form or design. MJ-6 seems to think her source is holding back as much as he can. Hoping she'll figure it all out before he has to reveal himself through more detailed information."

"I assume she's being watched."

The Secretary laughed. "Don't be insulting."

"What about the burglar?"

For the first time, the old veteran of countless black wars seemed unsure of himself. "He seems to have burst whole from nowhere ten years ago. No files, no records, a carefully orchestrated file drawer filled with volumes of nothing."

"You think he's community?"

"Reeks of it, as your blushing flower would say." He took the senator's hand in his, patting it consolingly. "We'll find him, Jess. I promise you."

Van Ness looked into the old man's eyes, trying to find the reassurance that wasn't in his voice.

"What's he have? How badly can he hurt us?"

"I wish to God I knew." The voice was choked with fear and despair.

Van Ness took a deep breath. "I really do want to be president, Michael. Think I'd make a good one, too."

"We want you to be, Jess." A pause. *"I* want you to be." He pulled the younger old man's hands to his lips, briefly kissing them. The barest touch of cracked, dry lips.

Dead man's lips, Van Ness thought or, perhaps, remembered. Their past and present seemed so intertwined, so tangled in the morass of service to the public and personal insulation from that service, that they might have played this moment out at any time in the last forty years. *Had* played it out.

And the brush of those lips had always seemed to be a last caress from a desiccating corpse. Whether in the idealism and innocence of his youth, or the cynicism and stark reality of his presidential ambitions.

"You'll keep me informed?" Van Ness said in a voice that was part cajolement, part seduction.

"Always." The Secretary paused, considering for the hundredth time whether or not Van Ness *was* the best choice. But he forced the feeling down.

Whatever his real feelings toward the man might be, either now or in a past that may or may not have existed, Van Ness was the *only* choice. The only one who understood, who had seen and acted. The only one who could carry on plans begun so long ago and so cryptically that their shape and purpose now grew hazy and indistinct. But Van Ness, for all his other flaws, still saw things with a crystalline clarity that the Secretary despaired of finding anywhere but his mirror.

So the act must seem to be one of love, not expediency; or that crystal might shatter and the work of a half century lost.

"Always, Mr. President." The Secretary smiled as he squeezed the senator's hand. "Always, Jess."

□ □ □

Halfway across the country, in the midst of the Kansas prairie, thoughts of power, ambition, and conspiracy would have seemed completely out of place. This was the heartland of America; a place where people said what they meant and did what they said.

At least that's what was written on the two-foot-by-three-foot poster boards that served as cue cards for the out-of-place reporter.

Standing in front of a red, wood plank, one-room schoolhouse, the camera crew waited for that reporter to signal that he was ready. The man wet his lips, carefully arranged a single lock of hair so that it would barely blow in the light wind, took some deep breaths, then nodded.

"All right," the segment producer said with a groan born of impatience as she replaced the old cards with the new ones. "Let's try and get it in one."

"You want me tight on the door or the window, Megan?" the cameraman said without looking up from his viewfinder.

Megan Turner, segment producer, researcher, writer, director, and sometimes minicam van driver, pointed at the school.

"Tight on the window; pull back to the door, then pan left as Steve Stunning makes his entrance."

"Got it." A pause. "Rolling."

"I heard that," the reporter said acidly. "Talk like that will not get me to work for you on the new mag."

"Promise?"

Megan smiled as she walked in front of the camera with the digital clapboard. "Segment 245A, Stranger Than Fiction. Stand up. Take one." She hit the clapper, then quickly stepped off camera as the reporter began.

"Maybe we'll never know exactly what has been happening in this isolated schoolhouse. Is it a portal to another world? A place for the restless spirits of the plains to gather to tell their pioneer stories? Or is it actually a psychic battery, having stored the energy of the hundreds of children it has served so faithfully in the last hundred years?"

He paused as the camera pushed past him, the cameraman steadily walking toward the door, which seemed to open by itself.

"Or is it only a piece of our history, of all our histories, fighting to survive against an ever-increasing urban sprawl? Who knows? But one thing is certain."

He paused dramatically.

"Truth is stranger than fiction. Luke Kellog, outside Grand Junction, Kansas."

Megan waited a moment before stepping forward. "And . . . cut. That's a wrap, people. Thank you very much. Let's set up for the tour."

A small woman in jeans and a "Save the Schoolhouse" sweatshirt peeked out from behind the door. "Was I all right, Ms. Turner?"

Megan smiled at her. "You were perfect, darling. Right on cue."

The woman beamed. "I just wish I could've gotten one of the spirits to show up. They're usually much more social than this."

"Uh, yes." Megan looked around for someone to rescue her from the pleasantly demented old woman. "Luke!" She reached out, grabbing the reporter away from a mirror he'd set up in the van. "Mrs. Johnson, this is Luke Kellog."

The woman, easily in her eighties, blushed and giggled. "Oh, Mr. Kellog! I watch you every weekend. I'm your biggest fan!"

The vain man beamed. "Always nice to meet a real fan."

"Oh sure. I've watched all your shows. No matter how bad they've been. I'm your loyal audience."

"I thought Mrs. Johnson might take you on a walk-through before we start shooting inside," Megan said as she stepped out from between them, stifling a laugh.

"Of course," the reporter said as he started to walk into the schoolhouse with the woman.

"I can't wait to introduce you to the spirit of Old Man Hammond," the woman bubbled. "He's even a bigger fan than I am."

"You've got a nasty streak in you, little girl," the older cameraman laughed.

Megan laughed along with him, checked her clipboard, then looked around. "Where do you want to do the sunset coverage?"

The cameraman shrugged as he cleaned the lens. "Wherever. This ain't *60 Minutes,* right?"

Sighing deeply, Megan nodded. "This ain't even *twenty* minutes."

She wandered off a bit, ostensibly to check out the vista from a hillside to the east.

Stranger Than Fiction not only wasn't *60 Minutes,* but it even felt embarrassing to mention the godfather of all magazine shows while wearing a *Stranger* windbreaker.

The one-hour reality show specialized in stories that made the tabloids nervous. Haunted schoolhouses being the most normal of the shoots she'd produced in the last six months.

From demon possessions of teenage boys who pled innocent to the gang rape of a prom queen, to the eyewitness account of Bigfoot stealing pro football cheerleaders to make his sex slaves. From aliens abducting rednecks to repopulate their planets, to accounts of covert government programs to recapture the demons that had escaped from Hell when Mt. Saint Helens erupted.

She'd shot them all, however, with a serious eye, a snappy pro style, and a bottle of Mylanta in her purse.

All the while sending out her résumé (which left off the specifics of this particular job) to every news organization in the country.

As she checked various views of the western landscape with the schoolhouse in the foreground, she let her mind wander.

With a master's in journalism, three years as the police reporter for a major midwestern daily, then five more on the city beat in Chicago, she'd expected her move into television to be a smooth, rapid ascent. Ending, of course, as the Washington Bureau director for CBS or CNN, or maybe a coanchor position on *60 Minutes*.

But it hadn't happened that way.

Instead, while more photogenic, more cosmetically talented (or enhanced) talking heads became the feature reporters, the weekend anchors, the rising stars of every network's news division, she'd been left behind. Establishing an impressive record for segment producing.

Even if it was for the lowest rung of the TV news food chain.

She'd taken the job with *Stranger* because she'd seen it as an entree to the newly formed network's inner circles. When they eventually formed their news division, she'd be there, already inside, homegrown talent for them to recognize and reward.

Megan had worked hard to make it happen too.

On her own time, she met, wined, dined all the important government officials she could. Established a reputation with them for being able to keep a secret, protect a source.

Heck, it'd been easy. She'd had damned few outlets to run the stories even if she'd wanted to. Just the occasional spot on an affiliate's "Around the Nation" news segments.

After the news division had been formed, she made a point of doing favors for the division's executives, often warning them of a major story that the other networks had missed. Ghost-producing

segments for all of the network's reality shows. All the while producing the highest quality segments for this dung heap show that were
possible.

Then, after all the work—the exorcisms, UFO sightings, cattle
mutilation stories—she'd been called to the network president's office.

"Megan," the woman had said to her, "we think this network
needs a prime-time magazine show to compete with *48 Hours* and
Dateline NBC. You think you can make that happen?"

She'd almost cried when she heard the words.

Then did cry when she heard the rest.

"We want it to be a high-class, think piece kind of thing. Call it a
thinking man's *Stranger Than Fiction.* We could call it *Beyond Bizarre.*
What do you think?"

What could she think?

Finally settling on the spot for the spooky sunset shot, she started
back toward the schoolhouse.

Well, she'd convinced herself, if that's all they were going to give
her, then she'd better make the best of it. Working with her minimal
budget and three-person staff, using *Stranger* crew and correspondents, she was slowly bringing the show to life. When this shoot was
over, she had a swamp creature story in Louisiana to do, then she
was full-time on the new show.

Questions, as she insisted the show be called, was her last opportunity. An opportunity she was determined to make the most of.

The network might want a tits-and-ass, depraved-sex-scandals, and
crazed-people-in-pain show, but that's not what they were going to
get.

When *Questions* debuted, it would be a hard-hitting, unflinching
examination of some of the great mysteries of our time. Carefully
researched, each claim well documented; it would probe into the
black hearts of corruption, deceit, and the unexplained that (as she
would say in the show's intro) "exist in our own backyards."

For weeks, she'd taken every moment of free time she'd had to go
through old newspaper accounts. To interview anyone that seemed
to be involved in any of the types of covert, possibly illegal things
that she hoped to focus on.

It took a while, but she'd finally decided on the right mystery to
open the show with.

The first episode of *Questions* would focus on a mysterious military convoy that had traveled through the Southwest in the late forties.

As well as the series of unexplained deaths that seemed to follow its path.

It might not be what the network wanted, they might well fire her after it aired. In fact, it had none of the grotesqueries that the network seemed to thrive on.

But she didn't care.

It would be sixty minutes of film that would show her talents to the people who really counted. Those few remaining devotees of Cronkite, Murrow, Edwards, and Sevareid who recognized that a dog possessed by the spirit of Ted Bundy wasn't news.

If it failed, well, at least she'd have taken her best shot, honestly, her way.

Her way!

She wasn't a *trophy anchor*—a man or woman whose on-camera beauty concealed a basic dumbness or inner ugliness that the masses would never see.

She wouldn't sleep her way to the top, although she often honestly wondered what she would've done if the opportunity had ever presented itself. But it never did, so she comforted herself that she wouldn't have gone the way of so many men and women whose sexual acrobatics—not their ability to find, analyze, produce (or even read the word) news—had propelled them to the prestige positions.

And she wouldn't sell out!

Well, not completely, anyway.

Because *the demon* must be fed.

Megan pictured her demon sitting comfortably on her shoulder. Contenting itself with the occasional rabid whisper or perfectly timed ambition.

It's all yours for the taking, the demon would say in the sleepless nights born of frustration and glass ceilings. *You're smarter than they are. Sharper. Reach out, feeeel it. Caress it. The sound you hear, the fragrance you smell, the touch you feel. It's there. It's your moment. And all you have to do is . . . take it!*

A long-gone mother and distant father had created a woman who was mentally tough, physically courageous, and—most especially—longing with all her heart's desire for the demon's promise to come true. She believed in the basic truth of the message, so set aside all else—personal happiness, friends, lovers, a semblance of a life—in a headlong pursuit of the brass ring.

Of defining her life by the attaining of that most glorious—if most indefinable—triumph.

And until she had it, well, everything else would just have to wait. Except *Questions*.

For that first episode, she and her small but dedicated staff had interviewed long-retired sheriffs and police chiefs who'd dealt with the mysterious convoy. Who'd been ordered by mysterious men not to investigate the strange deaths in their towns. Several of whom pointed her to others who told of "strange happenings" or late night visits from government agents.

Much was still unclear. But enough evidence had been uncovered to show that the government (which agency was still a mystery) had made thousands in payoffs. Bought farmers or ranchers new equipment. Sold government land to them well below market rates. All in exchange for their silence. Many still refused to discuss it.

And no one would talk directly about the deaths; how many there'd been, what had happened to the bodies, and so forth.

She had her story, but she needed to fill in the blanks.

More than sixty-five Freedom of Information Act requests for classified documents later, she'd been on the verge of giving up. The National Archives, CIA, the Pentagon, all had either refused her requests outright or had given her documents so heavily redacted, so completely blacked out with their black markers, as to be virtually useless.

She'd clearly stumbled onto something. But exactly what it was, wasn't at all clear. Until she was able to answer that question, she knew the story would never air.

Then she'd gotten the phone call.

A man's voice, of indeterminate race or age, told her to check beneath a roadside trash can near her Los Angeles home. Curious, thinking that this was some elaborate practical joke, she'd gone.

There were five photocopied, reduced sheets. They purported to be a briefing paper from one administration to another. The chain that would link a conspiracy across the decades in the government's most inner sanctums. They detailed the deaths (seven in all) and gave cryptic references to "the need to protect Joe Gray and Max Gray from any exposure" resulting from the deaths.

Other sources had authenticated the style, if not the substance, of the documents that had been stamped "Majic Eyes Only." More research (through local papers and sources, retired military who'd been ordered to "clear certain intersections at certain times" for a classified convoy) allowed Megan to begin to see, if not clearly, then at least generally.

Further calls from the source had led her to more documents, had answered more questions, provoked new ones.

As well as reactions.

The source told her, which she confirmed, that her phone was tapped. Her mail was also being delayed, probably opened. But a close friend in the FBI, a man that she trusted more than she loved, confirmed that whatever it was, whoever was doing it, it wasn't the Bureau. He'd promised to get back to her after more investigation.

Then had refused to take her calls or see her.

But the source's calls kept coming, along with the precious documents.

Until just over three weeks ago.

Suddenly, without warning, they'd stopped. No more advice, no more documents. Just a strange, somehow foreboding silence.

She'd continued on, she had enough to do the story now. But all it would do was ask questions. Not much different from what they did here on *Stranger*.

Hardly what she'd set out to do.

Her cameraman waved her over to the van. "You got a call."

She nodded, reaching out for the unit's cell phone.

The cameraman shook his head, pointing at the schoolhouse. "Who'd you give that number to?"

Megan shrugged as she walked inside. She found the phone on the teacher's desk in the front. "Turner."

There was a pause on the other end.

"Miss me?"

She froze as she recognized the always muffled sound of her source's voice. "Are you all right? I thought that maybe—"

The voice cut her off. "You're running out of time," the source said urgently. "You must move faster or you'll find the cupboard bare."

Self-consciously Megan looked around the empty room.

"I need more. I'm being stonewalled everywhere."

"Try harder."

She paused, thinking of the list of questions she needed answered.

"We've documented most of the convoy's route, except for its start and destination. I know about the seven deaths mentioned in the documents; also three others farther north. But I need to wrap it all together. I need the whys."

She held her breath during the long silence from the other end of the phone.

"What about the ODM traffic? Did you check it?"

Megan breathed again. "I've found eight references, in declassified Office of Defense Mobilization telex traffic, to Joe or Max Gray. But nothing since 1954. Never going into any detail about who they are, what they've done, or why almost every other reference to them is highly classified." She paused again. "You're sure they were part of the convoy?"

"They *were* the convoy, in effect."

She thought about that. "Are they still alive?"

No answer.

"Were they in command of the convoy?"

This time a light chuckle. "An interesting perspective."

The source was in one of his playful moods, she thought. Best to play along.

"Why?" she said in a forced light tone. "Were they visiting dignitaries? Was the convoy just a road tour of the American desert?"

"Let's just say," the voice said after a too-long pause, "that they were the driving force behind the convoy. After all, what's a convoy without drivers."

"Drivers," she repeated softly.

Megan had come to understand that although this source was incredibly well informed, he preferred to drop hints, rather than come out and say things. Just before the disappearing act, he'd been providing documents only when she'd become completely stymied.

"Were the drivers attached to the military?" She held her breath. The invisible voice often severed the connection if pressed too directly.

"Hurry, Ms. Turner. You have so little time."

The line went dead.

Megan hung up, pulled out a pocket pad, making notes of everything she could remember from the conversation. Then she hurried out to the van.

"Megan, can we get this done?" The reporter looked upset. "This Johnson woman is seriously strange."

Megan waved him away as she retrieved her cell phone and speed-dialed a number. "Tell James to set up by the teacher's desk. I'll be right there." She looked down at the cell phone as if willing it to connect.

"*Questions*. This is Tracy."

"It's me. Write this down."

She heard a shuffling of desk debris before the young woman came back on the line.

"Go."

"Check with that guy from the National Archives. Fred what's-his-name."

"Burkhardt? Modern Military Branch?"

Megan thanked her personal gods that there was at least one other person who took the job seriously. "That's the guy. Find out what transport units were stationed in Arizona, New Mexico, and western Texas in 1946, '47, and '48. Get the names of the command-ing officers, then track them down."

"Going to be a helluvalot of names."

"Like you've got something better to do?"

The woman laughed. "When you getting back to help out with this latest snipe hunt?"

"Day after tomorrow, swamp devils notwithstanding." Megan paused, remembering the warning about lack of time from the source. "Call that journalism professor over at LACC."

"The one that keeps giving us hell for 'shitting on the profes-sion'?"

"That's the guy. Tell him if he really wants to change what he sees on the air, he should loan us about five or ten of his students to help with the calls. Offer them per diem and screen credit."

"Geez, you *are* getting serious about this."

"Why are you still on the phone, Tracy?" Megan disconnected, tossing the phone back into the van.

As she returned to the haunted schoolhouse, in the midst of the gathering gloom, she could hear the source's voice call to her in the growing, cold prairie breeze.

"Hurry . . . You have so little time."

SIX

IT WAS AFTER MIDNIGHT when the Northern Illinois People Movers' taxi slowly cruised down the residential, no-sidewalk, bedroom community of Chemung, Illinois. Near the Wisconsin border, it was a quiet, two-main-street, middle-class town. Clean. Suburban. Safe.

As the cab turned down treelined Concord Avenue, it shut its lights. Two streetlights located on either end of the long street made the cab specterlike as it inched its way through the shadows between.

"Remind you of anything?" the driver said quietly.

"Yeah. *Leave It to Beaver,*" the passenger said as he studied the houses they passed.

"I don't think we're in Chi-town anymore, Toto."

"On the right. The one with the green trim."

The driver nodded, then cut the engine, allowing the car to glide to a stop at the curb opposite the house that had been pointed out.

The house was an old two-story Midwestern Victorian with an attached garage. An oval lawn to the side of a small curving walkway was lined with immaculately trimmed ivy. In all, it seemed the perfect cover for *Suburban Home Beautiful.*

But the passenger ignored the aesthetics, concentrating instead on the front door, the windows, the path that led around the garage side of the house to the rear.

"What's around the back?"

The driver checked a Xerox-reduced map. "Subdivision plot shows another house sharing a rear wall separating the backyards."

"Let's take a look."

Two minutes later, they were around the corner heading the opposite way down the street behind the house on Concord.

The second house was almost identical to the one with green trim. Except here the trim was peeling, the lawn was overgrown with weeds, and an obviously aging "For Sale by Owner" sign lazily swung in the light breeze.

"Looks good," the driver said. "You want to set up here?"

The passenger nodded, then got out of the car. "Easy access to the score. Quiet. Neighbors' windows dark by twelve. Yeah." He stopped as, off in the distance, a dog began to bark. "Pick me up in ten minutes." He walked casually toward the front door as the cab pulled away.

Glancing down at the dimly lit sensor in his hand, the man studied the walkway. It was clear where raindrops had left their muddy impression. Dirt and dust coated the small porch, showing that no one had been in that way in a long time.

The man slid his feet as he stepped on the porch, leaving no clear impressions among the dirt. He could tell, even in the minimal light, that the doorknob was dirt-encrusted as he looked back down at the sensor.

All readouts registered a big, fat nothing.

"Oh, Linus," the man said in a whisper as he smiled for the first time in almost a month. "Sometimes you make it too easy."

The smile was instantly replaced by his look of the last few, hard weeks . . . pained exhaustion.

"Thank you," he said softly in a heartfelt voice as he let himself in ten seconds later.

The woman was out of breath as she answered the phone on its seventh ring, putting down the grocery sacks at the same time.

"Yeah? Hello?"

"Lewis McCutcheon, please," a young voice said through the bad connection.

The woman slipped her shoulder bag off and turned to look around the living room. "One, two, or three?"

"Uh"—the voice sounded unsure of itself—"I'm looking for the

Lewis McCutcheon that served in the army in the late forties and
early fifties.''

"That'd be Lewis One, my father-in-law." She looked toward the
open kitchen door. Although no one could be seen, a cloud of blue
smoke hung low in the air. She cupped a hand over the receiver.
"Dad?''

"What?'' was the ill-tempered raspy reply from the unseen man.

"Telephone.''

"Who is it? What the hell do they want?''

Shaking her head at the man's increasing irritability, she turned
back to the phone. "He's a little busy right now. Can I ask what this is
about?''

"Uh-huh. I'm an intern with WIN News,'' the young voice said as if
reading. "We're doing a special on the American postwar experience
in the southwestern states. We'd like to talk to Mr. McCutcheon
about his military service. Maybe do an interview for the special.''

"Really?''

The woman smiled, thinking that this was exactly what the old
curmudgeon needed. A new audience to tell his fanciful, deadly dull
stories to. Maybe even be a little money in it. And God knew they
could use it.

"Just a second. I'll see if I can get him to come to the phone.''

She put down the receiver, picked up her packages, then carried
them into the kitchen.

Her father-in-law stood by the kitchen sink, looking through the
window into the backyard.

"There's leaves on the deck again,'' he mumbled as she came up
to him. "That kid never gets all the leaves.''

"We'll take care of it, Dad.'' She touched his shoulder. "Didn't
you hear the phone? There's TV people who want to talk to you.
They—''

"Nothing decent on the damned box since they took *Gunsmoke*
off,'' he interrupted.

The woman ignored him. "They want to talk to you about your
time in the army. Maybe even do an interview. Wouldn't that be
nice?''

His expression remained gruff, but she saw him straighten, just a
little, as he turned to go into the living room.

"Better be a network. Man like me's got no time for the local
fools.''

The woman smiled. "It's the network, Dad," she called after him, then quietly lifted the kitchen extension as he picked up the receiver in the living room.

"What is it?" he barked into the phone.

The voice on the other end seemed nervous. "Mr. McCutcheon?"

"You want to talk to me or what?"

A pause.

"Uh, Mr. McCutcheon, I'm an intern with WIN News."

"So?"

"Um, sir, we're trying to locate the commanding officers of military transport units in the Southwest right after the war. Say 1946 through 1950. And—"

The man interrupted. "Why?"

"Uh, well, we're doing this special on the American postwar experience in the—"

"How'd you get my name?" he insisted.

"Well, uh, like I said, we're trying to talk to people who served and, uh . . ." There was a sudden pause. "Could you hold on for a minute, sir?"

"Barely."

Less than a minute later, another voice came on the line.

He smiled at the confirmed kill. His last remaining hobby was trying to irritate telephone salespeople into hanging up on him. So far, he'd gotten rid of seven this month alone.

Make it eight with the young network intern.

"Mr. McCutcheon," the new voice began, "this is Megan Turner. I'm the producer of a new show on WIN called *Questions*. May I have a few words with you? If it isn't too inconvenient."

McCutcheon smiled at the confidence in Turner's voice. As he had instantly assessed the first voice as an underling, a nobody, somebody he could make short work of, he immediately had Turner down as a somebody. A more fitting challenge.

The most fun to irritate.

"Of course it's inconvenient," he growled. "But I can spare a few minutes."

Megan seemed undeterred by the words or the tone.

"I really appreciate it, sir," she said easily. "Just a couple of brief things first. Just to make sure I'm speaking to the right man, you understand?"

"Go ahead."

"You *were* First Lieutenant Lewis McCutcheon in command of the 2nd Truck Squadron of the 23rd Transport Company, 183rd Battalion, 9th Infantry Division, Mechanized?"

"Yeah," he said brusquely. "For a few months, anyway."

His eyes seemed to unfocus as a distant memory of purpose, youth, vitality, started coming back. He quickly pulled himself back from that place he'd been going to far too often lately. Afraid that on one of these trips, he might not find his way back.

"Course," he rushed out, "I retired a major."

"Were you in command of the 2nd Squadron in the summer of 1947, Major McCutcheon?"

He paused, nodding. Then, with a start, realized the ridiculousness of the act.

"From May until just after Halloween. First or second week of November, I was transferred." He stopped himself from going into more detail. "Somewhere else."

This time the pause came from Megan.

"Major, do you remember a convoy in that period that went from somewhere in the Southwest through . . ."

McCutcheon laughed. "Lady, you sound a little young to know better, so allow me to continue your education. We run convoys all the time back then. Ask anyone who lived along them desert highways. Back then, there was more military traffic on the roads than there was civilian."

He sat down, putting up his feet as he began to enjoy himself, forgetting his little game as he once again relived the times he thought of as the living years.

"I understand, Major. But I'm interested in one particular convoy. It went through Moriarty, New Mexico; Holbrook and Quartzsite, Arizona; and Landers, California. It started sometime before July ninth and ended sometime after July seventeenth."

"That don't sound right," McCutcheon said in a low voice as he thought about it. "Never took more 'n a day, day and a half, to go from New Mexico up to California." He paused. "You sure of them dates?"

"Yes, Major." She sounded disappointed. "So you don't remember that convoy?"

"We must've run about three convoys a week back then. Movin' everything from men to toilets. East and west." His voice trailed off as a distant memory demanded his attention.

As a distant voice demanded he reject it.

"Well, thanks anyway, Major. Like you say, there were a lot of convoys."

McCutcheon wasn't listening as he got up, walked over to some nearby bookshelves, then pulled out an old, dog-eared atlas.

"Before I let you go," Megan was saying, "do you remember the names of any of the other truck squadron comm—"

"Give me those cities again."

"What?"

The old veteran sat down with the atlas opened to a detailed map of the Southwest. "The cities? What were they?"

"Okay. Uh, Moriarty, New Mexico."

"Right," he said after taking a moment to find it on the map.

"Holbrook, Arizona."

He ran his finger along the map until he found it. "I wonder," he muttered.

"Excuse me?"

He ignored the obvious interest in her tone. "Quartzsite next, right?"

"Right. Then Landers."

"Gotcha."

He traced the route on the map, making marks at several points that Megan hadn't mentioned. Then he leaned back, smiling as if he'd just discovered the fountain of youth.

Which, in a way, he had.

"Took them over a week to run the old Muroc Express, you say?" His voice was quiet, strong, somehow . . . triumphant.

"Muroc? What's Muroc?" Through the bad connection, from halfway across the country, Megan's excitement was plain. "Major McCutcheon?"

No answer as the old man closed his eyes, smiling as the half-century-old memories mixed and mingled with his unrealities.

"Major McCutcheon?"

Despite the warning bells that were clanging in his head; in complete rejection of decades of personal discipline, he answered.

"You're talking about Operation Gray, aren't you?"

In the cramped office that WIN had given *Questions* (a space filled with seven college students, three regular staffers, two Xerox machines, and Megan); in a place where the noise level was never much below a dull roar, Megan froze.

Hearing only the disembodied voice of the old veteran who'd been call number 34 by the volunteer student from a list of fifty names.

"You still there, Miss Turner?"

Megan quickly recovered. "It's one of the things we might be interested in," she said, trying to force every ounce of calm and unconcern into her voice possible.

She heard the old man laugh over the other end of the connection.

"Damn, that's going back a few years," he said lightly. "I always knew there'd be a helluva story in it. That's why I kept mimeos of all the paperwork." He actually chuckled. "Really I kept them to cover my aspidistra, if you'll pardon my French. But I always thought it'd make a good book. Got all the elements. Intrigue. Mysterious happenings. Dead bodies. No sex, but I always figured . . ." His voice trailed off. "Course, they'd never let me write it."

As she listened, Megan looked frantically around the room for her assistant. She saw Tracy talking to one of the volunteers. For a full minute, she tried to get her attention. All the while listening to McCutcheon talk about how "it's one of my best damned stories and no one would ever believe the damned thing." Finally she threw a pad, hitting Tracy in the back.

"Hey!"

Megan waved her over while talking into the phone.

"Uh, Major McCutcheon, would it be okay if I put you on hold for a minute? I'll be right back, I promise."

"Hell," the man on the other end said in a far-off voice, "I wonder if I still got all that stuff out in the garage."

"Hello? Hello? Major?" There was no response from the other end, but she could hear movement and nonspecific sound. "Major McCutcheon? Shit!" She handed the receiver to a volunteer. "Keep listening. If anyone gets back on, keep them talking." Then she turned to her assistant.

"What's our closest affiliate to"—she checked the call sheet— "Chemung, Illinois?"

"I don't have a clue," Tracy said in confusion. "What's going on?"

Before she could answer, the volunteer thrust the phone receiver up to Megan. "The woman's back."

Megan grabbed the phone. "Hello?"

"I'm really sorry," the woman said simply, "but he does that sometimes. Is, you know, *off* sometimes. His mind wanders. One minute, he remembers things from decades ago, the next, he can't remember his grandson's name; and it's the same as his." A weak, embarrassed laugh.

"Can I speak with him again?"

"He's sort of wandered out to the garage. It's his special place. We don't like to bother him when he gets like this. Just keep an eye on him until he, well, comes back, you might say." A brief pause. "I could have him call you later."

Megan scribbled a note to her assistant on top of the call sheet with the information on McCutcheon on it. The words were chillingly cryptic.

Get me there with a crew! Claims he has proofs!

The assistant took off on a dead run.

"Um, I'm sorry, I never got your name," Megan said in as friendly a voice as she could muster.

"Betty McCutcheon. I'm his daughter-in-law."

"Hi, Betty. I'm Meg Turner, a producer at WIN News. The major was saying that he might have some old papers that we might be able to use. He wasn't, uh, *off* then, was he?"

"Oh, those," the woman laughed. "God, no. The man's an honest-to-God pack rat. We even had to get a bunch of those cardboard file boxes when he came to live with us. He had papers everywhere—in cases; stuffed in boxes; even in pillowcases, if you can believe that. My son, Lewis Three, helped him organize the stuff a few years back."

The woman paused and, for a terrifying second, Megan thought she'd lost the connection.

Then she was back.

"I always said Dad should write a book or something; you know, from twenty years of army paperwork, there's got to be something. Right?"

Megan was nodding as the woman talked. "I'm sure there is. The thing is . . ."

"It's just," the woman continued almost without pause, "that since he refused to take any more of that special pension money he was getting, things have been tough for him. For us too, actually."

"I can imagine," Megan said, realizing what the woman was leading up to.

"If these papers of his, if you can use them, would there be something, I mean . . . Would it be worth anything? I'm just thinking of him."

Megan knew that WIN never paid a source for information. Not as a matter of journalistic integrity, the network of *Stranger Than Fiction* had no illusions about that. No. It was simply that they were cheap. An underfunded news division run on a shoestring that was constantly fraying.

But Megan also understood what the woman on the other end of the line was saying.

"It's possible," Megan said after a long pause while she tried to figure how much she had left in her bank accounts. She needed the daughter-in-law on her side. "It's possible, depending on what the documents are, of course."

"Oh, of course."

"I'm going to put you on with one of my assistants, Betty, to get some information from you. To help us with the story."

She handed the phone to the volunteer with instructions to find out exactly where the McCutcheon house was, then transfer the call to her office.

Tracy came rushing up to Megan as she handed the phone to the excited college student. "Affiliates in Madison, Wisconsin, or Rockford, Illinois, are about equidistant."

Megan thought for a moment. "Go with Rockford. We used a crew of theirs for a haunted farm story about a year ago. Get me the next flight out of LAX and have someone from the station meet me." She was already hurrying toward her office. "Call the news director over there." She paused. "What's the station?"

Tracy grimaced.

"Would you believe W-I-N-K?"

Megan raised her eyebrows, then continued on. "Call the news director over at WINK-TV and get him to find out everything he can about our Major McCutcheon. Anything and everything, without him or his family finding out."

Tracy was taking notes. "You know they're going to ask about a supplemental budget for this," she said without looking up.

Megan shrugged as she checked the fully prepared Val-Pack she kept in the back of her office. "Promise them whatever you have to. I'll deal with it later." She sat down at her desk as her phone began to ring. "Now get out of here and get me a flight!"

She picked up the receiver. "Betty? Hi. Let me tell you exactly what we're looking for."

The luxury sedan drove steadily through the late afternoon. As a light rain fell, the car slowed down slightly, the driver conscious of oil rising up in the roadbed ahead. As he adjusted the cruise control down to sixty miles per hour, the cell phone on the seat next to him began to ring.

"Klein." A pause. "Right away." He handed the phone into the backseat. "For you, Mr. Kilbourne."

Kilbourne sighed, put aside the crossword puzzle he'd been working on, and took the phone.

"Kilbourne . . . Yes . . . I'm fully aware of . . . Of course . . . When did that . . ."

A long pause.

"I understand."

He disconnected, then handed the phone back to his driver. "Paul?"

"Yes, sir?"

"When do you expect us to arrive in Chemung?"

The driver checked his watch. "An hour and a half. More or less."

"Make it less, please."

The driver nodded, slowly accelerating to seventy-five miles an hour.

An all-night flight to Chicago, then a short commuter flight in a turboprop that was more antique than airliner, left Megan exhausted on the ground in the Rockford airport. Her disposition wasn't improved any by the absence of anyone from WINK. Two angry calls and ten minutes later, the evening anchor from the station was loading her Val-Pak into the trunk of his car.

"God, I'm sorry about this," the man with the plastic-perfect hair said in a carefully toned voice. "But we've been working on this all night."

"We?"

"News director, me, two of our reporters, and a couple of stringers."

Megan was impressed with the effort the small affiliate was making. "I appreciate it."

The man shrugged. "With a supplemental budget for a new satellite downlink, we'll all gladly work through the night." He smiled at her as they pulled away from the commuter airport.

Megan smiled back . . . nervously.

Making a mental note to congratulate Tracy on her creativity, just before killing her.

"What've you got?"

At a red light, the man handed her a file of photocopied newspaper clippings.

Megan gasped when she saw the thickness of the file. "What about the highlights?"

The anchor nodded at her reaction. "We had two stringers in the library all afternoon and three hours after closing to put that together. Luckily for us, the head librarian does a show on the WINK, Sunday afternoons." He paused, noting the lack of reaction from the woman who had been described to him as "a would-be network honcho who might be able to do us all some good."

If they could make her happy.

And while the news director lustfully eyed the new satellite system, the anchor had something else on his mind . . . Newsmagazines, *network* newsmagazines, needed correspondents.

"That goes back to 1945," he said with genuine enthusiasm in a perfectly modulated voice. "McCutcheon was born and raised here. Joined the army in '44 through the local ROTC. As a second lieutenant, he was posted to an immigrant relief corps in Germany at the end of the war in Europe. Transporting displaced persons from one camp to another, is how I read it."

He paused at an intersection. "You want to go right to the station or stop at a hotel first?"

"The station," Megan said as she flipped through the well-ordered, chronologically arranged clippings.

The anchor nodded as he turned the car. "After the war, McCutcheon came home twice. First time, for a parade honoring Chemung's veterans. The second, when his father died.

"Far as we can tell, he had three postings after the war was over. First at Fort Stewart in Georgia with a supply command. Then a promotion to first lieutenant and command of a transport unit in New Mexico."

Suddenly the professional tone vanished, replaced by a genuinely confused tone. "It's kind of weird after that. He's transferred out of the transports almost as soon as he gets there."

"I heard. So?"

"Well, the next reference we can find is seven years later. The clip highlighted in pink," he said, nodding at the folder.

Megan pulled it out and began to read.

Monday February 22, 1954
CHEMUNG MAN DINES
WITH PRESIDENT
Captain L. F. McCutcheon
Honored at Ike Barbecue

Dateline: Palm Springs, Calif.

At a gala barbecue last night, President Eisenhower took time out to personally compliment Chemung Favorite Son Captain Lewis F. McCutcheon on "his dedication, intrepidity, and devotion to a cause higher than self" for his work in "preserving the national security of our precious country."

The President, who is fully recovered from a minor dental procedure, made the remarks at a star-studded barbecue at Smoke Tree Ranch in Palm Springs, where he is enjoying a well-deserved, brief vacation.

The remarks came during impromptu comments by the President during which he singled out Captain McCutcheon, as well as 18 other members of a local Joint Services Unit, as examples of the "strength America will need to face the tests ahead."

Megan skimmed the rest of the article. It only listed some of the movie stars, golf pros, and celebrities that had been in attendance that night. "What was this Joint Services Unit?"

The anchor pulled into a parking lot, behind the cinder block building that was the TV station.

"That's the weird part," he said as he parked. "We've got an old bio on the major. His daughter-in-law apparently sent it to us with the idea that the old gentleman could be an on-air expert for us during the Gulf War. According to that, McCutcheon served in Greenland from late 1947 until his retirement in 1974."

"Ever check out the discrepancy?"

The man shook his head.

"Why bother?" he said as they got out. "The guy was almost twenty years retired by the time the Gulf War started. We never even considered him for the gig. Besides, we heard the guy wasn't all there. You know?" He nodded at the remainder of the file. "The rest is about members of his family."

After a brief tour of the even briefer newsroom, and feigned appreciative introductions to "the team" that had assembled to do the research, Megan sat down in a conference room with the news director and the anchor.

She was surprised at how quickly they worked out their plans.

She would travel with a camera crew and the anchor to Chemung in the early afternoon, after going over all the local research; additional background developed by the L.A. staff; and making a call to Betty McCutcheon to assure that the major was home.

As well as *there*.

While the anchor and the crew did local research and shot "B" roll color on Chemung, she would do an evaluation interview with the old veteran. Then, if the man or his documents looked promising, she would call for the anchor to conduct the on-air interview from her notes.

A task, a promotion really, that the plastic man was nakedly ambitious to embrace.

Just after noon, they left in a WINK-TV News van for the hour-and-a-half drive to the northern edge of the state.

"Grey at point three."

"Blue at alpha."

"We've got a shake at patsy one. TV truck."

"Stand by, Grey."

"All units from one. Does anyone recognize the woman who just got out?"

"Two, negative."

"Three, negative."

"Four, negative. But the guy getting back in does the six and eleven news in Rockford."

Tension filled the suddenly silenced radio air.

"All units from leader. Be advised, female suspect may be target designated 'Stranger One.' Stand by for orders."

□ □ □¹

"Grey?"

"Grey at point three."

"Blue at alpha. Black en route to alpha. ETA, one zero minutes. Recommends you check for unfriendlies in interim."

"Hate to break it to you, Blue, but the street's full of 'em."

It was a ten-minute drive from the roadside motel to the empty house. But to Greg, it felt like hours.

For the last month, he had consistently come up a day late and a dollar short in his search for answers. He accepted as fact the old saying that nothing good comes easy, but the last month, well, it had more than proved the point.

The first week after his confrontation with Cold Man had been spent playing hide-and-seek from the police, along with the *other* authorities along the West Coast. His picture had been run in every one of Kerry's newspapers, flashed on reality crime TV shows, been given out to seemingly every patrol cop in the country.

Then there had been the attacks.

Whoever it was that Cold Man worked for, they'd been brutally efficient, finding the fleeing felons three times in the first ten days. It had only been by the slightest chance that Greg, Foss, and Deo (who'd been hired full-time for ten thousand a month) had escaped from burning motel rooms, car chases, and shots fired from the dark.

But they *had* escaped.

Ten days after it'd begun, the three found themselves on the ferry to Vancouver, British Columbia; then, three days later, safely tucked away in a remote cabin in the Canadian wilderness.

For the first time, they had a chance to breathe, to rest . . . to try to figure out what had happened.

Calls, through third parties, to his lawyer had let Greg know about the explosion at his house; along with the tapped lines and active surveillance of most of his friends. They also revealed that, although he and Foss had been listed in the Most Wanted circulars, Deo had remained unidentified.

Three weeks after it had all begun, the driver was released with a full month's salary. Deo was safe, Greg assured himself. Not the kind of man that would shop them to the cops or break under pressure from the others. He felt comfortable relying on the driver's obsession with professionalism and their long, shared history.

But Greg and Foss moved two more times anyway.

The next few days had been quiet, comfortable, depressurizing. Foss continued to work through the Majic Eyes Only papers on the Internet, through hacked databases, or whatever other ways he could. Greg easily arranged for financial transfers to be made from offshore accounts.

With occasional trips to Red Deer for supplies, or Calgary for Foss's more discreet needs, they could live safely and quietly for a long time.

But the nightmares had continued.

Greg would see himself wandering the streets of some unidentified European city. Find himself surrounded by faceless men who all sounded like Cold Man. Would watch himself open the doors, bypass the alarms, make the faceless men's killing easier, more efficient. Would watch as they, he, would commit their brutalities. Would stand by helplessly (or worse, helpfully) as the bodies piled up. High enough to block out the sun.

To hide him from the accusing eyes of God.

Then he'd wake in a sweat. Drenched from the only slightly exaggerated nightmare/memory.

Then he'd run.

For hours at a time, while Foss worked the computer looking for answers that were carefully and professionally hidden, he'd run; forcing himself to remember that he'd gotten out from his past. Had simply decided that he could no longer, *would* no longer, play their hideous games that were cloaked in convenient excuses of patriotism, loyalty, and duty.

He'd volunteered (sort of) to become part of their system. Believing, through his rather unique naiveté, that by joining the system, he could beat the system. Finally and completely. Fade into the woodwork of a bureaucracy that had been his longtime foe. Find safety in the camp of his enemy.

How wrong he'd been.

So, he reasoned, if he'd volunteered in (however reluctantly), he would volunteer himself out.

The decision made, the rest had been relatively simple.

He used the skills they'd taught him, along with that native talent for which he'd been recruited from a Paris jail at twenty-three. Over an eighteen-month period, he'd lied . . . as they'd taught him; co-opted . . . in the approved fashion; and stole . . . a highly developed skill he'd always had. Turned it all against them until finally, one quiet winter's day, he committed the ultimate burglary.

He removed his identity, every trace, photo, file, and whisper. Stepped easily into the new one he'd prepared, and literally *stole* away into oblivion.

Into freedom.

At least as free as he could be, as he now hid in a three-room cabin in the border woods of Canada.

Almost as though he'd sensed his friend's inner turmoil, Foss had suddenly announced that his computer search was over.

Greg slowed as he approached the residential neighborhood. He wanted to take a look at the front of the McCutcheon house. With a Chicago Bears cap pulled low over dark glasses and a recently grown scraggly beard, he turned down Concord.

He saw the stakeout at once.

Four vehicles, each with two or three people in them. One apparently broken down with the hood up and a second car with occupants allegedly helping. A cable TV truck with three men lounging against it. A pickup with what looked like gardeners sitting in the back munching on hamburgers.

All within direct line of sight of Deo, sitting in the taxi across the intersection, studying the scene through a monocular. He nodded as Greg stopped at the light, waiting to turn the corner.

Foss's research had revealed that each of the men who had received laundered pensions through the Umbra Project had also retired from the military on the dates that their pensions kicked in. For the most part, their military records had been normal, routine, undistinguished. With one exception.

Each of the men had served more than twenty years of their thirty-plus-year careers in units that existed only on paper. Organizations that were duly noted in government tables of organizations and military manpower reports, but that had never received so much as a single communication, cable, written order, or supply allocation from the Pentagon in all its years.

And one other thing.

Foss had discovered, through the Military Personnel Records Repository's database in St. Louis, ID photographs of all nineteen men. It had been mistakenly filed under a unit heading one digit off from the odd unit's telex identification number. With a start, Foss had recognized a young Jack Kerry's face among them.

But under the name of Captain Lane P. Kilgallan.

Every instinct in Greg's body screamed at him to let it go, to make a life for himself either there in Canada or perhaps in Gypsy Europe. To stay as far away as possible from whatever all this was.

But some hidden thing was driving the thief. A festering, infected place deep within him that was demanding instant attention.

He might steal from anyone and everyone (and had). He had no compunctions, drew little or no distinction between wealthy and not-wealthy victims. They had what he wanted, and if they weren't good enough, tough enough, smart enough to keep it, well . . .

Morality was not the issue.

No. It was far simpler.

And more complex.

His entire life, sometimes he thought lives, had been spent in a careful, well-ordered denial. Of his childhood; of his life in suburbia; of the black days in Europe working for the Cold Men.

But in recent years that had begun to change.

Maybe it was age. Looking down the road, there were few sixty-year-old thieves. Whatever, he'd begun to feel a need, a subtle desire, to find something out about himself. Who he really was, perhaps.

Or, more likely, who he might've been if not for the accidents (or incidents) of birth, death, and life that had so determined his course.

Somehow, he knew (thought or prayed, he wasn't sure which) that this latest accident, this maelstrom that he'd been thrown into (literally on the doorstep of that pitch-black street that had been his cradle), had a purpose. A meaning or a path that somehow he must follow.

So, if only to silence the voices that came in the dark, he would journey a little farther down that path that Cold Man had set him on.

And there was one other reason besides; a thing that was so much instinct to the thief that he was, at best, only slightly conscious of it.

Whether as a small boy cast adrift into a nightmare existence of cover stories, lies, and manipulations in order to cheat Destiny's choices for his life; or as a yeggman in Europe—a thief of such skill, tenacity, intelligence, and personal force that no one would dare cross or betray him—Greg had *never* been a victim.

And he wasn't about to start acting like one now.

Even if it was absolutely the wrong thing to do.

Two days later, Deo met them at the Des Moines airport and their search had begun.

McCutcheon was the fifth stop on the trip.

Melvin Rogers had been killed in his sleep when his home's gas heater had malfunctioned.

Thomas Webster had a fatal heart attack.

James Kenyon had disappeared from work one day, found shot to death in his car three days later. A presumed carjacking gone bad.

Leonard Blythe was missing, presumed dead, on a flight in his private plane.

Each of these deaths or disappearances having taken place either just before or in the weeks since the murder of Jack Kerry.

Frankly Greg had almost given up hope of finding anyone on the list alive.

Until they'd arrived in Chemung, Illinois.

His plan was simple, actually would've been the same whether he'd found McCutcheon alive or dead.

He would set up the man's house just like he set up every score. Foss, Deo, and he would scout the neighborhood, record the movements of the occupants of the house. Find out what they could about local police responses, 911 capabilities, private security patrols, then he would strike. Breaking into the man's home to search for the answers he so desperately needed.

Four times now, Greg had broken into dead men's homes only to find professionally emptied safes and file cabinets. Blanked computer disks or torn-apart metal storage lockers.

Finding McCutcheon alive was a godsend. Finding the virtually abandoned house was just frosting on the cake.

Foss had been set up inside to man communications and to keep a continual watch on the back of the McCutcheon house over the fence. If he'd been discovered, he would be just another homeless junkie that had found a safe warm place to crash. But even that possibility was blessedly remote. A quick computer search of the records showed that the owner lived in Florida and that the house hadn't been shown by anyone other than the owner in almost a year.

Deo and Greg rotated in the taxi at various points in front of the McCutcheon house, keeping a careful log of everyone who came and went. They'd been there for three days and nights now.

If everything went as planned, Greg would make entry either in the coming night or the next.

But then the call from Foss had come.

The arrival of someone from a TV station, whether or not part of a larger conspiracy, clearly indicated that something was up. Something darkly confirmed by the sudden presence of the "unfriend-lies," as Deo called them.

The men without faces from Greg's nightmares and waking reality.

He tried to put his growing fears aside as he turned the car to go around the block to the abandoned house.

Then he froze.

As he saw, clearly profiled against the slightly tinted glass of the top-of-the-line Cadillac, Cold Man talking rapidly into a cellular phone.

"It was unforeseen," Kilbourne repeated into the cell phone. "That seems a most tame way of putting it." He studied the Car-FAX photo of Megan that had just come through to him.

"We informed you that she had made contact with Umbra 14."

"And neglected to include the information that she was en route." Kilbourne quietly popped a small pill into his mouth.

"An oversight," the voice on the other end said after a brief pause. "But a singularly fortunate one. At least, now we know where she's been getting her information."

Kilbourne laughed bitterly. "Do we? That remains to be seen."

"How will you handle this"—a long pause—"latest development?"

"The reason I called." Kilbourne glanced out the window toward his support units. "It's just after three here. Broad daylight on a relatively well traveled street. Not exactly conducive to what we have in mind."

"Then wait until tonight," the voice said in an annoyed tone.

Kilbourne shrugged. "An action that might well find us terminally compromised if Umbra 14 *is* the source. The producer could leave with enough information to make our prophylactic actions quite meaningless."

Another pause from the other end. "Then do it now," it finally said.

"The other problem," Kilbourne said flatly. "The producer was dropped off by a three-person news crew. One that will undoubtedly return to pick her up. In any event, moving directly against a media person who has been engaged in, shall we say, *researching* us would, in all probability, cause the very exposure you've asked me to prevent. You see my problem?"

"What do you propose?"

Kilbourne took the offered bottle of water from his assistant/driver. "I thought, this once, you might like to make the decision yourself."

A pause. "I'll call you back."

The call was terminated from the other end.

Kilbourne put down the phone as he took a drink of the cool water.

He was tired. Soul-tired.

He smiled spasmodically at the thought.

His soul, he was sure, if it hadn't withered completely away in the face of his actions in the last five weeks, was certainly well beyond exhaustion. The killing of friends tended to do that.

After three days spent in the company of Joe and Max, spent renewing his commitment and purpose, he'd continued on his grisly quest.

Of the nineteen original members of Umbra, sixteen were now dead. Twelve men and four women, any of whom might have been the one trying to compromise security.

Any or all of whom might have been completely innocent, but who'd been sacrificed for prudence' sake.

Leaving Kilbourne, crazy old Mac McCutcheon, and one other.

The untouchable one. The one that Kilbourne was now certain the entire exercise was dedicated to.

So now it was McCutcheon's turn. A nice guy, as Kilbourne recalled. That rarest of all the Umbra retirees—a man of conscience and dedication. The dichotomy of which had finally torn his always too-sensitive psyche apart. Leaving him a helpless, doddering old man; a senile cipher struggling to remember a past that didn't exist in order to avoid the pain of the one that did.

Waiting to be put down like an old war horse that had responded to the war klaxon once too often.

To be put down, as Kilbourne was now certain he would be too. But not before the suits and the bosses were certain that the dirty work was completed. The manure bagged and secured just as neatly as the piles he'd seen in the burglar's barn.

The burglar.

Was he alive or dead? Had the suits and the bosses reached out to him, crushing the cocky brass-balled man beneath their unassailable weight? Or had he somehow eluded them, as he'd eluded every effort Kilbourne had made to catch up to him?

He liked to think the last was true. It was the last remaining vestige of a formerly full-blown romantic.

No.

That was a lie.

He wanted to see the young burglar save himself because, in the end, after order had been restored and the legacy of Joe and Max secured for some later generation to judge, it would be nice to meet his own black implacability, knowing that someone still existed outside of the suits' and the bosses' control.

The last egotistical wish of a man who had once deluded himself that he had been independent, with free will and clear eyes.

He picked up the phone on its first shrill ring. "Kilbourne."

"Please proceed at once. We'll manage any collateral damage from this end." The line clicked off.

Kilbourne took a deep breath, tossed the phone down on the seat as if throwing away the perverted intelligence on the other end, then turned to his assistant/driver. "Paul?"

"Yes, sir?"

The old man wiped his face with a red silk handkerchief. "Inform the team we go in ten minutes."

"Yes, sir."

As the driver turned to his radio, Kilbourne glanced out the window at the clean little community in the heart of the America that he had dedicated his life to preserving.

Praying that Hell didn't really exist.

SEVEN

"I JUST CAN'T UNDERSTAND IT," Betty McCutcheon worried as she poured the coffee in the kitchen. "Just yesterday, he was all excited about it. He even stayed out in the garage most of the night rummaging through his papers."

Megan sipped her coffee. "He seemed eager enough on the phone."

"That's just it. He even had my son and me help him look for things."

Megan stared down into her cup, trying to decide what to do next.

She'd arrived a half hour ago, met by an eager daughter-in-law. For ten minutes, they'd discussed the terms of the interview, something Betty had clearly prepared for.

McCutcheon would retain all publication rights to his papers; would receive screen credit as "Major Lewis McCutcheon—Noted Military Archivist"; would have his on-camera appearance edited to eliminate anything that "might make him look, you know, doddering." Also, there was the fee.

Betty would receive $2,500, as a research assistant, regardless of the results of the interview. An additional $2,500 would be paid if the material was actually used in the special. In exchange, Megan or her researchers were to have full access to the major's papers, as well as to the major himself.

That's when the problem cropped up.

After a hastily drawn-up agreement had been signed, combined with a personal check from Megan, they went into the garage to talk with the old man.

The two-car garage had been converted into an office of sorts. File boxes were stacked against one wall, the year of the documents they contained carefully written on each. A card table with a typewriter had been set up in one corner, and a well-worn couch, chaise, and lawn chairs were in another.

McCutcheon sat at the card table, two boxes marked "1947" open on the floor beside him. He was bent over, reading each paper, then sorting it into one of three piles. He never looked up as they walked in.

"Dad," Betty had begun, "that woman from the television is here to see you."

"Not now," the old man barked as he checked a paper from the smallest pile before going to the next from a box.

"But, Dad, Lew, it's the woman you wanted to show the papers to."

"Make an appointment with the company clerk through the proper channels," he said gruffly without looking up.

"What?"

But the man had ignored them, muttering beneath his breath. "But it didn't happen. How can I remember something that didn't . . ."

Megan and Betty had retreated to the kitchen for coffee.

"He was so excited. I mean, when I went to bed last night, he was still reading. Mumbling happily, the way he does."

Megan worked to keep her voice calm and relaxed. "Does he get like this often?"

Betty shrugged. "More and more. But he was always like that a little bit, I guess. I remember when I married Lew, he used to refer to his father as 'the secrets man.' He was always like that. You spend your life keeping secrets for the government up in the Arctic Circle, it just becomes a way of life, I guess."

She sounded embarrassed.

"Even after he retired, he'd get mixed up, kind of talking code, like. Say sand when he meant snow. Heat exhaustion and the like when he meant freezing. Say he'd been places or met people he just couldn't have possibly."

Like barbecues with Eisenhower in Palm Springs, Megan thought.

"When he gets . . . confused," she said with as much sensitivity as she could muster, "does it last long?"

Betty glanced at her watch.

"No." She paused. "Not usually. It's hard to—"

Megan cut her off. "Did you see the documents he was talking about yesterday?"

As if the act would somehow reassure the producer, Betty nodded energetically.

"Oh, yes! They're there, all right. Dispatch orders; telexes; something called a briefing packet; and a bunch of other things. All from July and August of 1947." She sounded as if she was describing baby pictures. "In pretty good condition too."

"Did you read any of them?"

"Well, no actually," the woman said in a reluctant admission. "Dad just let us read for the date, you know, and the heading. Then he took it."

"What heading?" Megan tried to say casually.

"Uh, anything marked Majic, that's with a *j* not a *g* for some reason. Also some stuff marked 'MJ-12,' I think."

Megan nodded casually as she covertly looked at her watch. Anything to cover her growing excitement. As well as unease.

She wasn't sure when the news crew would be back, how much time she would need for the preinterview, which she hadn't even started yet. If the worst happened, if the old man was just some attention-starved media star wannabe, if all of her instincts were wrong, she wanted to find it out on her own. Not in front of a local crew.

"Maybe I should try talking to him by myself," Megan ventured as she stood.

"I'm not sure," Betty said suspiciously. "Dad doesn't really like strangers."

Megan smiled what she hoped was her most charming smile.

"I'm sure you want to get ready for your part of the interview. I think we'll get along fine."

"My interview? Oh. I didn't realize . . ."

"Of course. You're part of the story. A woman opening her home to one of our country's heroes."

Betty grinned.

"I suppose . . . yes, well . . ." She stood, glancing at the stairs that led to the second floor, then at the door to the garage. "I guess

I might put on some makeup, at least. Wouldn't want Dad to think I wasn't proud of him.''

"Of course." Megan took a step toward the garage door. "We'll be fine." She turned, walking through the door into the garage before the woman could say another word.

McCutcheon lay on the chaise, eyes closed, a pile of papers clutched to his chest. For a long, terrifying moment, she thought he might be dead. Grotesquely another, perhaps final, victim of the strange convoy that had already claimed at least seven victims that she could prove.

Then she saw the steady, if wane, rise of his chest as he took a breath. Quietly she approached him.

"Mr., er, Major McCutcheon? Sir?" She stood next to the chaise. "Major McCutcheon, it's Megan Turner from WIN, sir."

He slowly opened his eyes, taking almost a full minute to focus in on her.

"Major McCutcheon, are you all right?" Megan leaned over the pale, barely breathing man. "Should I get your daughter-in-law?"

"True."

Megan could barely hear the weakly muttered word. She bent low over him. "What?"

He smiled, a weak but seemingly satisfying act.

"True," he repeated through lips that barely parted.

"I—I'm going to get . . ."

As she turned, McCutcheon reached up to her, grabbing the sleeve of her jacket. His grip was shockingly strong.

"Always true," he stammered out. Patting the pile of papers on his chest, he added, "I was, I guess, doubting some."

From somewhere in the house, Megan heard the doorbell. Assuming that Betty would be bringing the camera crew in shortly, she turned back to the seemingly exhausted old man.

"What were you doubting?"

McCutcheon's eyes became teary. "When you spend so long, so long, denying what was, and you train yourself to only remember what wasn't, you . . . I started to doubt."

Megan reached for the top paper from the pile.

"What?" she said quietly as she tried to pry his fingers off the pages. "What were you denying?"

He smiled again. This time fully, with his entire face, especially his tearing eyes. "Joe. Max. The truth."

"What truth? Who are Joe and Max?" she said as she heard the kitchen door open behind her. "Joe Gray? Max Gray? Was it the convoy? What *is* the truth?"

McCutcheon, gripping the pile of papers tightly with one hand, pointed behind Megan with the other. "What you see here," he mumbled.

"What you *hear* here," a man's voice said from behind Megan.

She whirled around to see Kilbourne framed in the kitchen door, flanked by two men, one of whom was holding a struggling Betty McCutcheon.

Stunned, Megan instinctively turned back to McCutcheon as he began to speak again.

"When you leave here," he said in a faraway voice.

"Let it stay here," Kilbourne said sadly.

Deo nervously fidgeted behind the wheel of the stolen taxi. Since Cold Man and three of his men had entered the house, there had been a marked increase in the activity on the street.

No longer were the surveillance teams trying to remain unnoticed. Now they were in their cars, engines running, some with sidewalk-side rear doors open. The cable truck had moved out into the intersection, less than ten meters from Deo's position, setting up a temporary detour. It effectively closed off any access from that side of the street.

And, although he couldn't see it, he was confident that there was another one down the block, fully isolating the house with the green trim from any possibility of help from the outside.

Frankly the professional driver was shocked into a near daze by the recklessness of these men. Up until now, their every move had been coolly calculated, carefully planned. This seemingly improvised home invasion smacked of panic.

And panicked men, even hardened professionals, were the most dangerous on the planet.

He picked up his radio, checked the time for the right frequency, set it, then pressed the call button.

"Grey at point three," he said quietly, his eyes constantly scanning the street in front of him.

"Blue at alpha."

"We've got a serious shake at patsy one, Blue. Multiple unfriendlies inside, repeat, *inside* patsy one. Looks like their friends outside are getting ready to book too." He paused. "Request Black advisory ASAP."

Foss's voice came back with more than a hint of fear in it. "Black has committed, Grey. He went over the top, one zero ago."

"Grey, copy." Deo tossed down the radio.

With Greg somewhere in the backyard or, worse, inside the house, at the same time as Cold Man and the others, the situation had turned from dangerous to critical.

Slowly, making sure that none of his movements would draw any attention, Deo fastened his seat belt, then started the taxi. He glanced down at the local street map that he'd already committed to memory. Just to be sure.

Then he slid down in his seat, never taking his eyes off the front of the McCutcheon house.

Ten minutes of pure terror followed by fifteen minutes of the most savage silence Megan'd ever experienced.

Before she'd been able to react, to move, scream, or even breathe, two men rushed past Kilbourne. One clamped his hand over Megan's mouth as the other pushed her backward, against the garage wall.

Both men violently searched her. Lifting, grabbing, tearing. Only after the second man had finished was she allowed to pull her torn blouse closed as she was forced into a nearby chair.

She was quickly handcuffed, her arms pulled painfully back, then gagged with a strip of duct tape.

For ten minutes, she'd sat there, watching while Betty McCutcheon was handcuffed and gagged across the room. Watching as Kilbourne stood by the kitchen door, whispering orders to men who would disappear into the house, could be heard moving around inside. Watching as McCutcheon was allowed to get up to check on his daughter-in-law.

Apparently satisfied, he was helped to a chair by the table. Then one of the men who'd gone into the house returned.

"Place is locked up tight," he said in a loud whisper. "No one's getting in without we know and we got total surveillance on the front. One man in the back also. Just in case."

Kilbourne had nodded, then taken a seat next to McCutcheon.

For fifteen minutes, he read the papers that McCutcheon had been holding. He would carefully read a page, two, sometimes as many as five, then glance up at McCutcheon, before returning to his reading.

When he was finished, his expression was an odd mixture of surprise and admiration.

"I always thought that you were unappreciated by the higher-ups, Lewis," Kilbourne said in a voice that was at once compliment and threat, "but I think even I underestimated you."

McCutcheon maintained steady eye contact with Kilbourne.

"They told me you died." His voice seemed to be stronger than before. "So I believed it . . . like I was supposed to."

"You were always good at that," Kilbourne said as he put the six-inch pile of papers on the table between them. "Too good for your own good, I understand."

For a brief moment he looked genuinely concerned about the man across from him.

"I'd heard you had . . . lapses near the end. That it'd been getting worse in the last few years." He paused. "I'm sorry."

McCutcheon slowly shook his head. "Compassion?" he stammered out. "It doesn't suit you, Barry."

"It's Tom now."

"Tom." He rolled the name around his mouth as if tasting it. "Tom. Whatever." McCutcheon looked over at his daughter-in-law, then at Megan. "You don't have to involve them."

"You know better than that."

McCutcheon seemed to be concentrating very hard as he looked down at the floor.

"I know." He paused. "I'm never sure anymore what I know." He looked back up at Kilbourne. "I know you always tried to keep innocents out of the line of fire." He paused again, suddenly looking uncomfortable. "Didn't you used to say . . ." He looked confused. "Uh, say . . ." His voice trailed off.

"Barry," he said after another long pause, "they said you were dead."

Kilbourne looked physically uncomfortable. As if he had his past on his stomach. "Lewis?"

McCutcheon looked around the room, the confusion evident in his eyes.

"This isn't Habitat," he finally said in a strong voice.

Kilbourne shook his head. "Lewis?" He gently turned the man's face toward him. "Concentrate on me, Lewis. It's Barry, remember?"

McCutcheon's eyes seemed to come into focus.

"Good," Kilbourne said softly. "Now stay with me, Lewis."

"They said you were dead."

Kilbourne sighed, then turned away. "What happened to you?" he said under his breath in a pained voice.

"It was easier than remembering."

Kilbourne looked back at him. "What?"

McCutcheon took a deep breath. "Remembering the wasn't."

Kilbourne chuckled lightly. "That's right," he said with growing understanding. "How did you used to put it? Forgetting the was . . ."

". . . is harder than remembering the wasn't," McCutcheon finished.

Kilbourne nodded as he looked at his former comrade-in-arms. "But at how high a price?"

McCutcheon just shrugged. "I'm okay when I've got things to cling to. Stuff I can prove, can see. Sometimes lets me focus. Remember some things."

Kilbourne nodded again, then looked over at Megan. "And have you been remembering what *was* to her? Have you been telling her things, Lewis?"

McCutcheon shrugged. "I sorta drift sometimes. Hard to find things to hold on to. Things I know are real. But she knows about the convoy. She told me, so it must be real, right? She told me, and I remembered them old mimeos."

Kilbourne nodded at the papers. "But now you've found something she doesn't know, haven't you?"

"I was thinking . . . ," McCutcheon stammered out in a frightened voice.

"Always your problem, Lewis. You always thought too much." Kilbourne stood up, beginning to wander through the garage. "You've put me in a rather difficult position, Lewis. I hope you appreciate that."

McCutcheon looked exhausted. Twenty years older than his eighty-plus years. "You used to," he mumbled.

"Used to what?" Kilbourne asked as he looked through one of the 1947 boxes.

"Think."

Kilbourne froze, eyes staring into the box, but his focus deep inside of himself.

"You remember," McCutcheon stammered out. "We did what we did because we thought it was the right thing to do. And there were some things, after we'd think about them, that we wouldn't do. And things we shouldn't have done. Afterward, when we *thought* about it, there *were* things we knew were wrong. Were, were so . . ." McCutcheon seemed to be trying to look through Kilbourne. "You remember."

It was a statement, not a question.

After two long minutes, Kilbourne straightened, turning to the retired major.

"I'm sorry," he said with genuine regret in his voice. "But I only remember the wasn't."

He turned his back on McCutcheon, walking over to Megan.

"Ms. Turner." He seemed to study her for a moment. "You would tell me who your source is, in time." He shook his head sadly. "But I'm afraid I don't have that luxury." He paused. "At least, not at the present."

Megan stared at the hard eyes, heard the resoluteness in his voice, and for the first time in her life thought she was going to die.

Kilbourne stood there, staring down at her, then suddenly turned away, facing his driver/assistant. "Let's get this over with, Paul."

"Yes, sir," the young man replied softly.

"Take the boxes marked 1947," Kilbourne said crisply. "Burn the rest."

"Yes, sir. And the, uh . . ." He looked over at McCutcheon.

Kilbourne started toward the door. "No pain," he said softly as he scooped up the papers from the table. He indicated that two of the men should bring Megan along, then strode purposefully from the room.

Never once looking back.

After whispering detailed instructions to the remaining two men, the driver/assistant walked over to the two 1947 boxes. He easily picked them up, then turned to the door.

"Hey?" one of the men called after him.

"What?"

"Where do we go after?"

The driver/assistant paused. "I'm not sure. Better check with me at Fox Lake in twelve hours."

He left the garage, never reacting to the two heavily muffled shots or the telltale sounds of bodies falling to the floor.

"Grey at point three."
"Blue at alpha."
"Three unfriendlies, including Cold Man, just pulled out from patsy one. Woman from the TV van was with them. And she didn't look happy about it."
"Copy, Grey. How many unfriendlies left inside?"
Deo paused, watching the Cadillac with Kilbourne and Megan pull away, turning left, scant meters away from him.
"At least two in the score and two more on the street, Blue. Maybe more. Any word from Black?"
"Negative."

The two remaining gunmen stood in the kitchen, looking around.
"How we gonna do this?"
The tall one opened the refrigerator, glancing in. "All that paper back there," he said casually. "A cigarette butt misses an ashtray." He closed the door. "What worries me is how do we get it to spread to the upstairs. We got a linoleum floor and a fiberglass door in between."
The short gunman wandered out toward the living room. "This place natural gas?"
The tall one followed him out.
Magically, as if pulled by an invisible hand, the cabinet door under the sink slowly opened.
First an inch, then two, then a long pause. Finally, after a full thirty seconds, Greg noiselessly uncoiled from the cramped space.
After checking to be sure the two gunmen had gone upstairs, he turned to peek through the garage door. Seeing no one, he moved through.
He could smell the burned powder from the shots in the air as he stood just inside the door. Then he saw Betty McCutcheon lying on the floor at an awkward angle. He started over to her, then stopped ten feet in.
The shot had entered her right temple, but had blown off the left front side of her head, which lay in a growing blackish puddle of gore.
Then he saw the major.

He lay half under the card table, a deep red stain spreading across his white shirt. Greg listened to try and hear the men upstairs, then hurried over to the old man.

He'd been shot once, in the middle of his barrel chest. But that chest was still rising and falling beneath the crimson-stained shirt.

He bent down to the old man, whose eyes blinked as Greg's face came into view.

"McCutcheon?"

"Who . . ."

"What's it all about?" Greg begged in a rushed whisper. "Who did this?"

"Is . . . Betty . . ."

Greg measured the old man's life in seconds, and his own possibly in minutes. There was no time for soothing lies.

"She's dead," he said flatly. "Who did it, McCutcheon? Who are they, how do I get to them?"

The old man barely shook his head, as though it took all the strength he had left.

"I . . . never . . . should have come . . . home. My fault. My . . . sins." He closed his eyes as a single tear worked its way down a blood-spattered cheek.

"Damn it! Who are they?"

McCutcheon's eyes blinked, as if he was trying to force them open.

"Come on, McCutcheon." Greg slapped the old man, hard on both cheeks. "Report! Major McCutcheon, report!" He could hear the men talking on the stairs.

McCutcheon opened his eyes, focusing on the young man over him.

"They can't be . . . You can't . . . stop them. Only Joe. Only Max."

"Joe and Max," Greg repeated as he bent low to hear the old hero's last, fading words. "Can Joe and Max stop them?" He could hear the men in the living room.

McCutcheon suddenly smiled. "They . . . Majic 12 . . . do anything to . . ."

He closed his eyes for a long moment, as if gathering his strength for one final push.

"Get Joe and Max. Get them. Use . . . them to stop the . . .

Majic." He winced as a body-shuddering wave of pain swept over him.

"How do I find them? Joe and Max! How do I find . . ." Greg straightened as he heard the men enter the kitchen.

"Find . . . the girl. She knows . . . some of . . ."

And McCutcheon was gone.

"I'm telling you," the short gunman said as he entered the garage, "it'll be fine."

"Furniture polish?" The tall one seemed skeptical as he followed his partner in. "That's a new one on me."

"It's the perfect accelerant. Flame burns quickly, real hot too. And the best part is that the arson guys'll miss its residue, 'cause it looks almost like floor wax. We just spray a line from the garage door to the living room carpet, then up the stairs. Place'll be fully engulfed inside five minutes, we do it right."

The tall one shrugged. "Better than anything I can come up with. Where'd you see it?"

The short one stepped around the card table toward a half-open broom closet. "I saw some in . . . *ahhhhh!*"

His hands flew up to his face while he screamed in pain from the steady spray of furniture polish in his eyes.

"What the hell?" The tall one rushed forward, realizing what was happening just a fraction of a second too late.

Greg grabbed the .380 automatic from the short one's waistband and fired; all in one motion.

From ten feet away, even Greg couldn't miss.

The tall one doubled over as the bullet tore through his stomach, lodging in his lower spine. After he was down, Greg spun on the short one, firing once into his shoulder.

As the man's screaming intensified, Greg shoved him out of the way, stepped two paces forward, took careful aim at the stricken tall one, then fired point-blank.

Greg could feel pieces of brain, skull, skin, and gore fly into his face. He blinked the man's stinging blood from his eyes, immediately returning to the short one.

"Shut the hell up!" Greg said in an angry growl as he shoved the man down into a chair. "Now, I don't have you boys' training and all, so I'm going to ask just once. Lie to me, make me even think you're lying"—he moved his blood-spattered face within inches of the man—"and you're dead."

He shoved the hot barrel of the still-smoking gun hard against the semiblinded man's left eye.

"Where's the girl from the TV van?"

Wincing in pain, confused, unsure of what was happening or who he was dealing with, the wounded man took a deep breath. Faced with the pain in his shoulder (the almost psychic pain of the gun in his eye, wielded by the cold-eyed, blood-covered man in front of him), the short one answered.

"Fox Lake facility."

"Good decision," Greg said as he released the breath he'd been holding since he'd first hidden in the closet. "Now, tell me about Fox Lake."

"Blue at alpha."

"Black."

Foss pulled the microphone closer to him, as if the act somehow brought him closer to his friend. "Go, Black."

"Have Grey go to point one. We go as soon as I get back. I'm leaving now."

"Thank Christ."

"Pack it up, we won't be coming . . ."

Greg's voice cut off, then, a few seconds later, the sound of a single muffled shot came over the radio.

"Black at patsy one?"

No answer.

"Black? Come in, Black."

Still no answer.

Foss tried twice more, then relayed the message to Deo. Sweating heavily, he grabbed the two gym bags of equipment, left the back glass door open, then hurried out front. As soon as Deo pulled up, Foss threw the bags in the back, then climbed in behind them.

Deo opened the front passenger door. "What's going on?"

"Trouble."

The two men sat there, barely breathing for what seemed like an eternity.

Foss moved toward his door. "I'm going back to . . ."

"Here he comes."

Greg walked slowly to the taxi from around the side of the house. Deo accelerated away before he got the door closed behind him.

"What happened back there?" Deo glanced at the heavily breathing burglar. He saw but didn't say anything about the blood on the man.

"Foss?"

"Yeah? You okay? We gotta get you to a . . ."

Greg barely breathed as he pulled off his blood-soaked shirt.

"It's not mine," he said with a deathly casualness.

Foss leaned over the front seat, handing a rag to his friend. Greg slowly wiped his face.

"Stupid," was all he said until they pulled off the interstate twenty minutes later, stopping behind a large billboard on a deserted rural road.

After stripping and burning all of his clothes, using bottled water to clean himself off, he matter-of-factly told the others where they were going.

"Give me some numb," he said to Foss as they got back in the car. He sounded about ninety.

Foss looked shocked, then reached into his pocket, pulling out a plastic pill bottle. He took two dark blue capsules out and handed them across to Greg.

"Careful with those, man. Take enough, you won't feel a thing till the end of the century." His humor was forced but unnoticed.

"Fine," Greg said quietly as he swallowed the pills.

Deo had known Greg for almost ten years, and he'd never seen him take drugs before.

"What the hell hap—" A look from the burglar silenced the rest of the question. "What's in Fox Lake, Wisconsin?"

But Greg just closed his eyes, feigning sleep for most of the rest of the trip.

The building sat off by itself in the middle of the calm natural beauty of southeastern Wisconsin. With the impressive Fox Lake Dam in the distance, the deep blue lake just to its rear, it might well have been taken for a luxury office building. Or maybe the corporate headquarters for some computer company or other environmentally friendly entity.

It might have been, if it wasn't for the double chain-link fence circling it, the heavily armed guards at the only entrance . . . and the sign.

There was no mistaking the meaning of the bold white letters set against the navy-blue field, or the lightning bolts on either side of the octagonal sign.

WARNING!
This Is a Secured Area.
The Inner Perimeter Fence IS ELECTRIFIED!
Passage Beyond This Point Is Strictly Forbidden!
Any Unauthorized Entry May Be Met by
Deadly Force!
As Authorized by
Section 21 Internal Security Act of 1950
WARNING!

At just past nine that night, a stolen utility company van pulled to the side of the road, its three passengers studying the sign.

"Not a lot of places to set up surveillance," Deo commented as he looked around what was mostly grassland.

Foss, who had shot up two and a half hours before, seemed alert as he looked around the unlit road.

"Have to go back, then around. Maybe try coming up on it from the other side. We go 'round that bend up there"—he gestured ahead—"they gonna make us for sure, man."

Greg continued studying the countryside with night-vision binoculars. "Yeah," he said casually.

"Gonna take a week at least to case the place properly," Foss added as he joined Deo in studying a local map. "Maybe a couple weeks."

"We go tonight," Greg said flatly.

Both men violently snapped their heads up as if they'd been hit from below.

"What?!"

Greg turned slightly as he focused on the fence, about half a mile away. "No time to case it. We'll just have to play it on the fly."

Deo looked at him as if his friend had gone insane.

"That," he said in the voice a parent uses to scold a stubbornly insolent child, "is a sure-as-shit *federal* something. You make one mistake, and trying to bust in there without proper intelligence is your first mistake, they'll throw you in some hole for a thousand years or so."

Greg nodded as he walked over to study the map. "Probably," he agreed simply.

"You did see the sign?" Foss said, his voice filled with disbelief. "You'll be lucky if *all* they do is lock you up for a thousand years!"

"Agreed," the burglar said calmly. "Now, either of you want to know how we're going to do this?"

Twenty minutes later, Greg and Foss lay on their stomachs, just inside the first fence.

"I can't believe I'm doing this," Foss whispered in a near panic.

Greg ignored him as he studied one of his sensors. "No motion detectors or proximity alarms this side of the fence. And I think those cameras on the building have the wrong angle to see this part of the fence."

"You *think?*" Foss groaned. "I never go in," he almost whined. "You always said it was better that way."

"No choice," Greg said as he laid out what looked like jumper cables from a duffel bag at his side. "The fence's a two-man job."

"I'll get Deo."

"He's got other things to do." He raised to his knees, passing a sensor over the fence. "Three main circuits. Top row. Row five. Row nine." He ran wires from the cables to a small box with an analog meter. Then he handed the left end of the cables to Foss. "We've got to make contact almost simultaneously or we'll trigger the impedance alarms."

Foss finished pulling on heavy rubber gloves.

"I hate this shit," he mumbled as he followed Greg to the fence, moving five feet to his left.

"Start with row nine. We'll go one, two, three, clip. Got it?"

Foss nodded as he wiped his face on his sleeve.

"Okay," Greg said, smiling. "One. Two. Three. Clip!" Tiny blue sparks flew out at them as the alligator clips locked into place.

Greg checked the needle: it had moved a quarter inch to the left. He used a large knob to bring it slowly back to the center of the display. Satisfied, he and Foss repeated the process twice more. Each time, the needle was adjusted back to the zero mark in the center.

"Okay," Greg said as he stood and stretched, "here's where you earn your keep."

"Swell," Foss grunted.

"When I hit that fence, the impedance is going to jump like hell. Use the regulator knob to keep it at zero." He looked at the clearly frightened man. "Think of it as a video game." He turned to the fence.

"What happens if I lose?"

One last smile from the burglar. "Then I'm fried and you have half the cops in the world rain down on you." He paused. "I go in three, two . . ."

Foss grabbed the knob, staring at the barely lit needle with all the intensity he could muster.

". . . one!"

Greg leaped at the fence, froze for a moment, then climbed to the top. He pulled himself over like a seesaw, allowing the weight of his upper body to catapult his lower body over.

He hit the ground with a thud, freezing for two full minutes. Finally he looked through the fence at Foss, who was still staring at the display.

"Stay on it. I may have to come back this way."

Foss only nodded, refusing to take his eyes off the needle.

Greg turned, slithering through the grass, more reptile than human, eventually vanishing in the dark.

When he reached the edge of the fence's ionic shadow, the closest spot to the fence where other alarms or detectors could be put without being triggered by the fence's current, he stopped to check his sensor.

"Oh, Linus, these are *seriously* unfriendly individuals," he said quietly as he read the display that indicated motion detectors fanned out irregularly in front of him. "Let's try and stay more than three feet from each, shall we?"

It took forty minutes to cover the 150 meters from the fence to the end of the electronically monitored part of the lawn. Forty minutes of sliding on his stomach, sometimes his side; of contorting his body into odd shapes to avoid the field of detectors. Finally his sensor showed the lawn was clear ahead.

He lay there, willing himself to be just another shadowy little lump of nothingness on the lawn. Nothing for the cameras to focus on, to push in on.

Moving as slowly as he could, as quickly as he dared, he pulled a red LED digital stopwatch from his backpack. He held it at arm's length in front of him. When he was satisfied with his view of the two cameras on the wall of the building in front of him and the watch's display, he began to time the cameras' rotations.

For fifteen minutes he lay there, trying to find a gap in their automated coverage of intersecting arcs of ground.

A seven-second gap in a narrow path maybe four feet wide, maybe three feet to his left, existed on every third pass.

"Thirty meters in seven seconds," he muttered. "Seven seconds."

He put the watch away, watched the cameras turn, then raised himself to the balls of his feet and his fingertips. Like a runner in the blocks, he concentrated on the cameras, waiting for his one, brief, bare chance. Praying that his guesses of angles and distances were right, that the grass wouldn't be too slick for him to get the traction he needed.

And he was off!

Mind a blank, muscles pulling, tearing from the sudden change of position, he sprinted forward. Eyes glued to a spot on the side of the gray building.

Fifty feet.

Twenty-five feet.

Ten feet.

He flattened himself against the building as the cameras swept back toward him. He stayed there, panting, hurting, waiting. Trying to regain his breath, soothe torn muscles, all the while watching for the errant guard or previously unseen security device.

Ten minutes later, after checking that he was too close to the building to be seen by the cameras, he began sliding along the side toward the door that was his eventual target.

Painfully aware of the contrast of his stark black coveralls and hood against the soft gray of the building.

His sensors showed a sophisticated but not unpassable alarm on the door, but before he addressed it, he pulled out his palm-sized radio, pulling the antenna to its full six-inch length.

"Grey from Black," he said quietly as he checked the grounds around him for signs of a patrol.

Deo's hushed voice came back instantly. "Grey by."

"Black by. Do you have"—he paused, looking for a word—"acquisition?"

"Grey by. Affirm."

"Black by. Move to point two and stand by. Out."

"Grey copy and out."

Greg looked over in the direction where he knew Foss was hunched over the impedance modulator. "Blue from Black."

There was a frightening pause of fifteen seconds before Foss's voice came through. "Blue by."

"Black by. How's it holding up?"

"Blue by. Better than I am."

"Black by. Stand by point one for one hour, then move to point three and execute primary."

"Blue by. Copy. Are you okay?"

This time Greg paused.

"Let you know in an hour ten. Out." He shut the radio, quickly storing it back in the pack.

As he passed his sensors over the outside of the door one last time, he thought about the part to come.

There might be cameras in the corridors. Possibly roving patrols or checkpoints. Hell, there might even be a guard station just inside the door.

Then there was the problem of finding one unidentified woman in a building that was three stories aboveground, who knew how many below?

Hiding in the Canadian wilderness was looking better and better.

He used a handheld microwave transmitter and some small magnets as he began to work on the door's alarm.

This was all stupid, he was thinking as he worked. A waste of time. If this, whatever it was, was government-sanctioned, then there was nothing he could do. With the girl's help or without it, the government had the money, the resources, the *time* to make sure it always came out on top.

His own young adulthood had been living proof of that truth.

The sensors showed that the alarm had been disabled without incident. He put the equipment away, pulling out his locksmith's shooter.

He knew he wasn't motivated by revenge. He didn't know the McCutcheons, or Kerry and the girl before them. As for the men back at the McCutcheon house, well, they'd been responsible for their own deaths. Their faces, at least, wouldn't stare back at him from any nightmares in the future.

He hoped.

And Greg certainly had no clear idea who the woman from the TV van was, or what she could do to help him get out from under all of this. Beyond McCutcheon's cryptic dying exhortation: *"She knows . . ."*

Even *if,* and that was a big word at this point, he could find and free her.

But one other thing drove him on. Beyond that which had compelled him from the Canadian backwoods. This wasn't about the woman's knowledge or information—although that certainly had contributed to his decision to go in—it was about power.

Cold Man wanted, and now had, the woman. Somehow she was essential to whatever his plans or goals were. And that alone was reason enough to break in and take her away from him. Pure vindictive, blissful revenge. If only in small measure. And if she *did* have the information Greg so desperately needed to get out from under, well . . .

But, he admitted with a bitter smile as he felt the shooter take hold, one small other thing besides.

He'd established a nice, comfortable, well-cushioned existence since he'd left people like Cold Man behind. Four or five scores a year, maybe fifteen weeks of work (including job prep) to earn him the four or five hundred thousand tax-free dollars he lived on.

Until Cold Man and company had taken all that away in one brutal night. Stolen all that he'd worked for and achieved.

He opened the door a crack, then waited. No shots, no screams; no one coming to check or indications of hidden alarms.

Taking a deep breath, he slid around the door, into the building.

No one, he thought as he moved through the door, *no one steals from Gregory Picaro.*

EIGHT

SHE LAY IN A DAZE, not sure of where she was, what she was doing. Not certain if what was happening was real or a bizarre dream/nightmare.

Men and women in surgical greens stood around her, completely expressionless as they worked. Speaking in a flat nonintonation that screamed professional disregard. They occasionally glanced down at her, but for all intents and purposes, it was as if she wasn't in the room.

She giggled. Why, she wasn't sure.

A familiar voice, an older voice, seemed to be talking in low tones somewhere near the foot of the . . . whatever it was that she was lying on. She tried to lift her head to see him, but it felt heavy, clouded. She instantly decided it wasn't worth the effort and lay back.

"What did you give her?" the older voice was saying.

"Rohypnol. Fifty milligrams, dissolved in orange juice," one of the men in green said.

"It's the so-called date-rape drug," one of the women in green added. "Causes instant, extreme intoxication, lessening of inhibitions, significant reduction in muscular coordination, and transactional amnesia."

"I'm not familiar with that last term," the older voice said as it seemed to come closer, but stubbornly remained outside of Megan's view.

The man in green handed a piece of paper toward the voice. "It works on the neuro-perceptors, causing everything viewed while under its influence to be seen as unreal. It all seems like dream or hallucination, therefore the brain decides the experience must be a dream. So, like most dreams, the brain rejects the memory.''

"I see." The older voice came still closer. "Since my time, I'm afraid."

The woman in green checked Megan's pulse. Megan smiled pleasantly up at her. "It was developed as an interrogation aid initially. Something midway between scopolamine and LSD. Now I think they sell it as a sleeping pill in South America."

"And at a buck a pill to frats looking to spike the punch of coeds, I hear." The man in green pulled up what looked like an EKG strip, beginning to study it.

"I know I don't drink anything around here unless I pour it myself," the woman in green laughed.

"Indeed," the older voice said sadly. Then a pause. "Is she ready yet?"

The man in green looked over at him. "Almost."

"And she has been completely searched."

The woman in green nodded. "We sent her clothes over to X ray to be sure. Then we did a full cavity search. There's nothing."

The man in green seemed to be looking at some piece of equipment on the other side of the table.

"Hi," Megan said pleasantly to him, as she wondered if she was wearing the right amount of makeup for the occasion.

"She's ready."

"Thank you, Doctor," the older voice said quietly. "Would you and your staff please wait in the outer area? Thank you."

The people in green left Megan's field of view as a bright operating room light was switched on above her. She felt, more than saw, a large form move next to her, just outside the halo of light.

"Is the recorder running, Paul?"

"Yes, Mr. Kilbourne."

The older voice, now so close, seemed to spark a memory in Megan. A buried thing, but its bare recollection sent a shiver through her body.

"Is your name Megan Turner?" the older voice said after long seconds of silence.

"You talking to me?" Megan chirped.

"I am. Is your name Megan Turner?"

"Sure it is. What should it be, huh?" She giggled.

"Are you a producer for the Wilkins International Network?"

"Bunch of cheap bastards."

"Are you a producer for the Wilkins International Network?"

"Didn't I just say so," she said in a little girl's annoyed voice. "Try and pay attention, huh?"

The barest chuckle, from the form beside her. "I will. Are you researching a story on a military convoy in the Southwest?"

"The convoy . . . yes." Something about that word, convoy, sent warning signals to Megan. But she had no idea why.

"How did you discover the story about the convoy?"

"I don't think I'll tell you." Childish obstinacy filled her voice.

"How did you discover the story about the convoy?"

"I'm not going to . . . I'm not going to tell . . . I'm not . . ."

"How did you discover the story about the convoy?"

"I . . . *Arizona Republic* articles. Old articles. Yellow, crumbling . . ."

"Who did you talk to about the story?"

"Tracy."

"Who is Tracy?"

"You don't know Tracy?" She laughed. "I thought she knew everybody."

"Who is Tracy?"

"My assistant."

"Who did you talk to about the convoy other than Tracy? People other than your staff. People outside the network."

"Sheriffs."

"Who else?"

"Cops."

"Who else?"

"The major." She paused, a confused expression coming across her face. "Who's the major?"

"What did the major tell you?"

"Uh, did he tell me something?" A pause. "That's right. Something about the men from the telexes."

The older voice suddenly changed, becoming lower, slightly more threatening.

"What men from the telexes?"

"Joe and Max Gray, silly. But he didn't say much. Just kinda mentioned them."

"Shut the tape, Paul."

"It's off, sir."

The voice seemed to have moved to the very edge of the halo of light. She could see the form more clearly, but still couldn't make out any features.

"Who are Joe and Max Gray?" the older voice now demanded.

"From the convoy."

"Who are Joe and Max Gray?"

"From the convoy. He says they *are* the convoy."

"Who says?"

She seemed suddenly reluctant.

"Who says?" the older voice demanded in an even stronger tone.

"Just a voice on the phone," Megan slurred out, almost against her will. "He calls me sometimes." She laughed. "Like an obscene caller."

"Who belongs to the voice on the phone?"

Megan turned her head away from the voice, closing her eyes.

"Who belongs to the voice on the phone?"

"I don't feel so good," she slurred out.

"Paul?"

Her head was grabbed by a large hand, forced back around to face the form.

"What did the voice on the phone tell you? What did he say?"

"I don't want to play this . . . anymore. Leave me . . . alone."

"What did the voice on the phone tell you? Did it say where to find Joe and Max? Did it say anything about—"

"Forty-seven," she interrupted the growing angrier voice with her slurred answer. "Said the answers were all . . . were all in 1947. Where the whatsit called started and where it . . . What is it?"

"The convoy?"

She smiled, rolling her head as sleep began to come over her. "Thass it. The convoy. The answers are where the, uh, convoy ended up. Where it started. Never says anything straight. It's really annoying." She seemed to drift off for a moment. "Can you talk to him about how he talks to me?" She sounded hopeful, like a little girl checking on her letter to Santa.

"I would like to talk to him very much. Can you help me talk to him?"

"Okay."

"What is the name of the voice on the phone?"

"Never said, but . . ."

"Yes?"

"Hello," she said happily.

The voice paused. "You were going to tell me about the voice on the phone."

"No," she said petulantly. "I was going to tell you about the convoy."

Another pause.

"Tell me about the convoy."

"What do you want to know?" she said happily.

"Where did the voice on the phone say the convoy ended up?" The older voice was suddenly caressing.

"Didn't say. Don't know. Maybe someplace in California."

"Where did the voice on the phone say the convoy started from?"

"What?"

"Where did the voice on the phone say the convoy started from? You can tell me."

"Don't like you, I think."

"Where did the convoy start?"

"Won't . . . tell . . ."

A hand reached out, gently stroking her cheek.

"Where did the voice on the phone say the convoy started from? You can tell me. You can trust me."

"I can?" Again, a little girl's voice. "Really?"

"Of course." The voice was filled with smiles and sunshine. "I promise I won't tell anyone. It'll just be our little secret."

"Well . . ."

"Where did the voice on the phone say the convoy started from?"

"Didn't, exactly. But I think . . ."

"Yes?"

"I think it was somewhere in New Mexico."

A long pause.

"New Mexico?"

"Uh-huh." Megan closed her eyes again.

"We're losing her, sir."

Megan felt a light pat on her cheek. "What? I'm tired."

"Did the voice on the phone," the older voice said in a near whisper, "ever say where in New Mexico?"

"Where? Like a place or somethin'?"

"Where in New Mexico did the convoy start from?"

"No, uh, yes. Uh, you mean like a place or somethin'?"

Although her eyes were closed, she felt a face come very close to hers. Could smell the mint-scented breath. Felt a single drop of sweat fall onto her face.

Then the older voice spoke again. "Where in New Mexico did the convoy start from?"

But she was already asleep.

Kilbourne stood over her for a full minute. Looking down at the sleeping woman, as if trying to divine answers from the regular rise and fall of her chest or the look of occasionally interrupted repose on her face. Finally he reached up, flipped off the light, then headed out of the examination room.

His driver/assistant, Paul, followed him out, carrying the cassette from the recorder. He was immediately approached by a uniformed man who handed him a slip of paper.

"Doctor," Kilbourne said as he approached the man in green, "how soon before we can begin again?"

The man checked a wall clock. "We'll start bringing her up right away." He paused. "Maybe forty minutes. An hour to play safe."

"Administer another dose in forty minutes."

The doctor nodded, then started for the examining room.

"And Doctor?"

"Yes."

"How many times may we repeat the process before she develops a tolerance?"

The doctor smiled grimly. "Toxemia will set in long before that happens. Five, maybe six more sessions at the outside."

"Thank you, Doctor."

Kilbourne sat at a nearby desk, beginning to sort through the contents of Megan's briefcase for the third time.

Paul stepped over to him. "There's a problem, sir."

Kilbourne looked up, not saying a word. Just waiting.

The young man looked uncomfortable. "Sir, well . . ."

"What is it, Paul?" The old man's tone demanded an instant reply.

"The bodies have been discovered."

Kilbourne looked at his watch, then nodded. "To be expected. A fire like that draws attention." The look of discomfort on the younger man's face immediately got his attention. "There *was* a fire, wasn't there?"

Paul shifted his weight from foot to foot. "They discovered four bodies, sir. The major, his daughter-in-law, as well as the two men we left to, uh, clean up things."

Kilbourne slowly stood, walking to within inches of the uncomfortable young man. "The fools got caught in their own fire? It got out of hand?" His voice was challenging.

"Uh, well, it seems that the news crew returned about the same time as the woman's son." He was trying not to stare into Kilbourne's demanding, fiery eyes. "They found the McCutcheons, apparently our men *did* take them out."

"And?"

"They also found our men. It seems they were shot to death. After a struggle, the police seem to think."

"McCutcheon put up a fight perhaps? They got to squabbling between themselves over some foolishness with the woman?"

He was silent for an incredibly long minute.

"Maybe God caused thunderbolts to strike them down for their *evil deeds?*" He stopped, the anger flowing off him in waves. "Pick one!" His voice was low and deadly.

Paul took a deep breath. "The police believe they were killed sometime after the McCutcheons. Sir, uh, the police have the scene completely cordoned off. They've called for assistance from the Illinois State Police as well as the McHenry and Boone County Sheriff's Offices." He paused, looking anywhere but at Kilbourne. "There's no way we can get in there now, sir."

Kilbourne's mind was racing. The possibilities were extremely limited, but each one spelled disaster.

1. There was a second team somewhere out there, cleaning up any loose ends that Kilbourne had left behind.

2. It was a random occurrence, some home invasion burglary that had run into his men with unfortunate, tragic results.

3. Burglary. One burglar in particular.

The first possibility was negligible. This late in the game not even the paranoid button pushers in their corner offices would risk compromising everything. Certainly not with some sloppy hits that left bodies behind.

Along with possibly incriminating evidence.

And if there had been a home invasion, his men surveilling the property would have seen it happen.

Which left only . . .

But that seemed impossible on the face of it. Why would a man who was wanted by the police, who was being pursued by the police and many others nationwide, risk contacting a man he could never have known about in the first place?

The answer, he thought, might lie in a note he read over a burning, demolished beach house.

"Nobody's safe," he whispered.

"Excuse me, sir?" The younger man hoped the phrase didn't mean what he thought it might.

"Maintain full coverage on the site," Kilbourne said as he turned back to the desk. "Find out who we have in Illinois law enforcement, then get them on this immediately. With the media involvement, we won't be able to just make this go away." He was quiet for a moment. "Maybe we can sell them organized crime involvement. Say that McCutcheon was involved with the black market during the war. Diverting convoys of supplies to the Mafia and the like. Maybe say that Turner had the story when the Italians intervened."

He paused, smiling spasmodically. "Coordinate that with MJ-7."

"Yes, sir. Right away, sir."

"Also heighten security around here. Set condition two if you have to."

"Consider it done, Mr. Kilbourne."

"And, Paul?"

"Sir?"

"That was shoddy work. Don't let it happen again. Disposing of an old man and a woman shouldn't be such a chore, should it?"

"No, sir."

"I mean, I don't expect perfection, but a little stand-to efficiency would be a nice change." He began concentrating again on the things on the desk.

The young man hurried to the door, then stopped suddenly. He held up the cassette from the first interrogation session. "Shall I send this on, sir?" From now on, he was going to be the most efficient aide Kilbourne ever had. Being fully conscious of what his fate might have been.

Kilbourne looked up, then returned to reading Megan's appointment book. "Have it transcribed here first. I'll want it for the next session."

"Right away, sir." The man headed for a door on the opposite side of the room.

"When is the next session, Paul?" Kilbourne said without looking up.

"In about a half hour." He opened the door.

"Paul?"

"Yes, sir?"

Kilbourne turned to him, a curious expression on his face. "Do they really use that pill on college campuses? To commit rapes, I mean."

The young man nodded. "So they say on the news. They say it's fairly common in the Southwest; Texas, Arkansas, Oklahoma I mean. I also think I heard of a case at UCLA."

"Thank you, Paul."

As his driver/assistant left the room, Kilbourne returned to the appointment book.

"Sick bastards," he muttered beneath his breath.

The first rule of searching an unknown building is that true power always rises to the top—as represented by most corporations; or hides in the bottom—such as the White House Situation Room, in the famous building's subbasement.

Because walking down stairs is faster and easier than walking up, Greg started from the top.

The third floor contained darkened offices. Administrative settings for bureaucrats, clerks, paper people whose most deadly weapons were pens and memos.

Not a single piece of paper lay exposed on a desktop. No files lying around, Rolodexes open, or even scratch pads with doodles. Not even a single piece of trash in the twin wastebaskets at each desk marked "Burn" and "Normal."

But the offices had better-than-average locks on the doors, some requiring card keys, which Greg easily bypassed (using his ATM card and the wrapper from Juicy Fruit chewing gum).

But the secrets in their well-designed safes would have to wait. The third floor didn't have what he was looking for.

The second floor seemed to be a series of conference halls, labs, almost an academic setting. File cabinets labeled "Solubility Ratings Through Gamma Seven" or "Tensile Comparison Testing As Relates to All Weather Capabilities."

Here the locks were even better. Government-issue Banhams or even top-of-the-line Yales. Card keys were supplemented with digital keypads beside them. But even these more formidable obstacles didn't slow Greg down much.

Rather than try to bypass the alarms and barely hidden triggers, he simply used a heat sensor the size of a cigarette pack to determine if anyone was in any of these more secured rooms.

No one was.

On both floors, all the computers were off-line, apparently centrally controlled. Probably powered down after a certain hour to ensure information security.

Nowhere could he find any facility directories, tables of organization, letterhead; any of the things you'd expect to find in an office.

Even a heavily secured office.

Checking his watch, he finished his pass-through, then left.

He was on an unamendable schedule, forced to move at twice or three times the pace he would've liked.

Avoiding the elevators, most likely controlled by a central security station at this hour, Greg headed for the north stairwell and the first basement level.

In his first moments in the building, he'd realized that the ground floor was mostly for show. Rooms where elaborate machines were set up to demonstrate new agricultural techniques. Video display rooms with farming statistics going back to the 1780s.

All of it a fraud. A blind to sell this facility as a supersecret agricultural test station.

A cheap clown on black velvet, hung over a safe that contained millions.

What it really was, now that was another matter.

From what he'd seen so far, Greg was sure that this was a highly secret testing facility. Most of the labs seemed to deal with various forms of metallurgy. Although some seemed to deal with aviation, with wind tunnels and the like.

But he hadn't taken the time to open the combination-locked file cabinets to look further.

He was running out of time.

There was less than fifteen minutes left before he had to turn around and head for the extraction point. Assuming that he could find his way to the "crash" exit he'd created, without alerting security. Assuming that Foss would be able to carry out his part. That Deo would be there on time with what was needed.

Assuming he found the girl.

He hurried down the unsecured fire stairs, constantly on the look-out for hidden alarms, intrusive cameras, or guards trying to catch a smoke or a nap. But so far, nothing.

In a way, it was disappointing. But not terribly surprising.

Many times in the past, Greg had seen this kind of mind-set. Spend thousands on the most sophisticated security systems possible around a building. Hire big, mean, well-armed and -trained men, put them at the access points. Then nothing, or next to nothing, inside.

Why spend the money? the mind-set went. *No one could break in any-way, right?*

He grimaced as he started down to the first basement level, hop-ing there was something there more interesting than water pipes and heaters.

He stopped cold. His hope fulfilled.

The door in front of him was metal, not pressed wood like the others. Not hinged, but set into the wall; no handle, no seams around the edges, no intercom, keypad, or card key port. Just a small sign glued flush to its middle.

No Access Beyond This Point!
Majic Series 300 or Below
Only!

But also no indication of any kind how to open it.

Greg stood perfectly still, only his eyes moving, examining, search-ing every inch of the polished surface. He checked the walls, the ceiling, the floor. It apparently was a door that couldn't be opened. At least not from the stairwell side.

"Something new, eh, Linus? Well"—he paused as he glanced up the stairs to make sure he was completely alone—"I'll try not to disappoint you."

He pulled off his pack, beginning the usual sensor runs. It was clearly an electrically operated door, the power signatures were clear. There was an alarm, or what looked vaguely like an alarm, hooked into the same source as the power signatures. It probably deactivated automatically when the door was opened correctly.

But how?

He sat down on the bottom step facing the door, his head sup-ported in his hands, eyes locked on the door.

The clock was running, he was where he had to be, he was at least sure of that much. But stuck, dead in his tracks.

By a door! That was the truly insulting thing about it.

"Think, you stupid son of a bitch. How do you open a door that has no doorknob, latch, or accessible locking mechanism? How do you . . ."

And he smiled.

"If you can't open it, why put a sign up forbidding entry?"

He stepped forward, after digging in his pack, examining the small sign under a black light/magnifying glass combination.

"They're sneaky bastards, Linus. I'll give them that."

Using a plastic screwdriver (to prevent activating any undetected heat, impedance, or other alarms), he pressed the slight impressions in the sign that the black light had revealed.

Nothing.

"Been staying up nights planning this one, have you, Linus?" He studied the impressions, then began again. "Well, I'll try not to disappoint you."

Humming to himself, he pulled out two more plastic tools. His options had become severely limited by this unexpected challenge. He could try pressing all the impressions at the same time, or pressing them in sequence. But what sequence? Pick wrong . . . and die.

Carefully, almost prayerfully, he simultaneously pressed the *N* in No, the *A* in Access, and the *M* in Majic.

A vibration, followed by a slight whirring sound, as the door slowly slid open.

A uniformed guard, writing the time in a log at a desk just inside the door, glanced up. Too late to stop a black-clad figure from rushing at him. He lost consciousness moments later from the steady, unrelenting pressure around his throat.

Two minutes later, wearing parts of the uniform of the guard, Greg wandered casually out to a lightly populated corridor just past the entry alcove. Following the directions on the wall to Secure Examination Room B-3.

The room that "Umbra 12/MJ-096, escorts and female detainee" had been logged into.

As she tried to blink her eyes into focus, as kaleidoscopic, indistinct images assailed her brain, as the reality, or unreality, of her situation became clearer, Megan began to scream. Not for long, or with all that much intensity, but it seemed like a start.

The people milling about the far end of the room glanced over, then returned to their discussion, unimpressed.

"Where am I?" she demanded. "Who are you? What am I doing here? What are you doing to me?"

The people ignored her as they silently filed out of the room.

"Think, damn it!"

But the act was futile. She could remember talking to Betty McCutcheon, going in to see the major, then . . . What happened?

She tried to sit up, suddenly realizing that she was strapped onto what appeared to be an operating table. Both legs, arms, and her chest were tied down with heavy leather straps. An IV was running into her left arm, which was outstretched, tied down to a board. She could turn her head to either side, but only with difficulty.

She closed her eyes, fighting to calm herself.

What *had* happened?

A friendly, older voice spoke to her from deep inside her head.

You can trust me.

With the voice came sudden memories of fear, pain, and the terror of the garage.

Megan turned her head to the right as a security guard slowly opened a door at the far end of the room, then peeked in.

Apparently curious, but not wanting to be caught looking, he carefully looked all around the room before entering. Oddly he carried a backpack in his hand. The man walked over to her; his eyes not on her, but on the door on the opposite side of the room.

"Who are you?" she said in a voice between panic and fury. "Why are you doing this to me? I demand . . ."

"Will you shut the hell up?" He began loosening the straps. "I'm a friend. I'm going to try to get you out of here, but you've got to be quiet, damn it."

She felt her legs come free.

"Who . . . How . . ."

"Later," he said as he freed her arms, then started on the chest strap. He glanced up at the large digital clock on the wall. Less than five minutes to go before Foss executed the next part of the plan. "I'll explain everything later, okay? Right now I don't trust my luck and their incompetence to hold that much longer." She was finally free. He turned to the door he'd come from. "You coming?"

She didn't know who he was; for all she knew he was some other part of whatever all this was. But a glance down at the red marks on her wrists and ankles from the straps decided her.

"Where are we going?" she asked as she pulled on surgical pants and a shirt that were folded on a nearby table. "What's going on? Who are these guys?"

Greg shook his head. "My luck, I get stuck rescuing a reporter," he mumbled as he led her toward the far door.

"About a minute ago, Mr. Kilbourne," a voice said from the other door. "I'll see that everything's . . ." Paul froze in midstep as he saw Greg grab Megan by the arms.

"Struggle," Greg whispered. "Make it look real."

He needn't have told her.

As confused as she thought she'd ever be, Megan began screaming, writhing around, trying to kick, claw, or head-butt her way free.

"What, who the hell, what's going on?" The driver/assistant rushed forward.

"Someone let her go, sir," Greg said as he held both her wrists in one hand, working his other arm around her throat. "If you'll give me a hand . . ."

Paul grabbed her legs, helping to carry her back to the table.

"Damn it," he said as he held her down, waiting for the guard to strap her in. "Nothing's going right today!"

"Too right," Greg said softly as he wormed his arm around the man's throat. Grabbing that arm's fist with his other, he squeezed and turned until the man fell limp in his arms.

"I'm going crazy," Megan mumbled as she sat up on the table.

"God, I hope not." Greg quickly searched the man, taking his gun, and a card key that hung from a chain around his neck. He helped her down, and again they headed for the door.

"Mr. Kilbourne!"

Greg froze as the voice behind him screamed out, followed by two other voices, yelling "Freeze!"

"Turn around!" another voice demanded.

Less than five feet from the door, Greg and Megan slowly turned around, looking into the angry eyes of two security men in front of three of the medical staff.

Their guns leveled at the fleeing couple's heads.

For a long moment, both sides just stood there, staring at each other. Then there was a pushing from the back of the small knot of people, with Kilbourne eventually emerging in the front.

"No," he said quietly in a voice that demanded that this all be a bad dream. "It can't be."

"We've got them, Mr. Kilbourne," one of the gunmen said, mistaking the look on the old man's face for concern.

"Kilbourne, huh?" Greg said casually, watching the seconds tick off on the clock in front of him. "That's an improvement on 'Smith.' "

"Who are you?" the lead gunman demanded. "How the hell did you get past my security?"

Greg looked Kilbourne in the eye. "Tell the man."

Kilbourne nodded, without realizing it.

"It—it's what he does."

Megan looked at Kilbourne, the terrors of the McCutcheon garage, the struggle in the car after, flooding back.

She still didn't know who the man next to her was, but from the look on Kilbourne's face, she knew he was the old man's enemy.

For the time being, at least, that was enough.

"In a way, I'm sorry to see you here, Mr. Picaro."

Greg actually managed a laugh. "Not half as sorry as I am."

Kilbourne barely nodded. "Indeed." The old man seemed to be regaining his balance.

The burglar shrugged as he took a half-step forward. "So do I get to know what this is all about before we get started?" He looked, not at Kilbourne, but at the thick pile of papers held together by large binder clips in his hand. The pages were old, yellowed, some of them seemed to be crumbling.

Kilbourne smiled, a genuine act of friendship toward this brazen man.

With a hundred such over the last forty years, he thought, *the world's history might have been very different.*

"Is this the point where the villain, overconfident of his position, reveals everything to the young stalwart and his lady?"

Greg nodded comfortably as he watched the clock, tensing the muscles in his legs. "Pretty much, yeah."

"Sorry to disappoint you. But I suggest that *you* consider making the confessions. Not me."

"Look," Megan said in an authentically angry voice, "I don't know what's going on, but you'll never get away with kidnapping a member of the media. The press'll be all over you and this place in hours."

Kilbourne ignored her. "You'll forgive me, Mr. Picaro. But I have some business to finish with the young lady. We'll talk later."

It was almost exactly an hour since Greg had last talked to Foss.

The dark night was growing colder. A light wind blew off the small lake, chilling Foss to the bone.

But he stayed nonetheless.

He watched the red LED countdown clock as it moved inexorably toward zero. He double-checked the connections that led from the timer to the detonator, exactly the way Greg had shown him several times over the years. Then he checked his watch.

If he didn't hear from Greg in the next twenty seconds, he would arm the device, then, as Greg had instructed, "run like hell!"

Fifteen seconds.

Five seconds.

Taking a deep breath, watching the timer count down to one minute, he pressed the arming buttons in sequence, then took off at a dead run. Never once looking back at the huge aluminum and steel electrical tower that channeled 95 percent of all the electricity for the nearby town of Friesburg.

As well as all the power needs of the mysterious facility less than a half mile away.

He counted down in his head as he ran, praying to make it far enough away before . . .

The blast picked him up, throwing him twenty feet in the air.

Bouncing twice, then rolling halfway down a hillside, Foss painfully got back to his feet, looking back at the tower.

Deep black, orange-highlighted smoke roiled up the side of the light girder construct. Then a moaning, almost human groaning came from the sixty-foot-high power structure. Slowly, like a stripper with arthritis, it seemed to bump, grind, then fold in on itself.

Bright blue sparks leaped up into the night sky as the first wires touched the ground. A few seconds later, a deep booming sound echoed toward Foss as the four transformers blew up.

An acrid taste filled the air as the PCBs in the transformers mixed with the burning smoke and toxic gases from the overheating metal.

Foss broke into a hurried jog, trying not to breathe in too many of the carcinogens he was sure he'd just released. But despite the fear, a deep, growing, emotional panic from the rigors and demands of the night, he also smiled.

As he watched the faraway lights of Friesburg begin to blink out seconds after the facility itself went black.

The lights in the examining room flickered, faded to brown, then went out entirely.

"What?"

"Blackout!"

"Somebody get some flashlights!"

Then the sound of something old and heavy being slammed into by a younger object.

As the lights had first flickered then gone out entirely, Megan found herself in the most complete darkness she'd ever known. Then, almost at the same instant, she felt herself being roughly shoved backward. She fell over, hitting herself in the side with what she discovered was a doorknob.

The sounds of anger, confusion, and frustration were everywhere. People moved around in the total blackness, stumbling over each other and into things.

Suddenly a shot rang out. The flash from the barrel lighting up the room for a millisecond.

"Stop shooting," Kilbourne yelled, as if he was in pain. "You're going to hit one of us!"

Then Megan screamed as a hand reached out, grabbing her around the wrist. "No!" she yelled as she tried to pull away.

"Will you shut the hell up," the strange man's voice called out to her in a near whisper. "Come with me."

"I can't see," she whispered back.

"I can. Now be quiet, damn it!"

She allowed herself to be led from the room.

It was worse than being blindfolded.

There was the barest perception of people moving around her, but nothing could be made out. As they slowly moved, along a corridor she thought, there would be occasional flashes of a lighter or matches burning; small oases in the midnight landscape. But otherwise, just scared mutterings in the dark.

After only two minutes they stopped, as the lights began to flicker, then come on very low.

"Emergency generator's kicking on," Greg said.

For the first time, she saw the night-vision goggles strapped around his head.

"What now?" was all she could think to say.

"Now," he said as he tossed the goggles aside in the growing light, "we walk casually down that corridor. As if you owned the place, right?"

She took a deep breath. "Right."

When the lights came back on in the exam room, Kilbourne immediately saw the open door.

"After them," he shouted. "Lock down the facility. Now!"

Paul, who'd just been regaining consciousness when the lights went out, quickly helped the old man up.

"Ahhh!" Kilbourne screamed in pain as his left leg refused to support his weight.

With a glance down, the young man helped Kilbourne to a nearby chair. "I think it's broken," Paul said.

"Forget that," Kilbourne screamed as he waved the man away. "Find them!"

Ignoring the throbbing in his leg, Kilbourne began to give orders. Within three minutes of the lights coming back on, the facility was on condition one.

Uniformed armed patrols covered every inch of the now-floodlit grounds. Plainclothes agents searched the building floor by floor, room by room. A helicopter was called for to search the surrounding countryside.

But, so far, there was no sign of anyone.

"Grey from Black."

Greg's voice was so quiet that Deo had to turn up the volume on his radio. "Grey by."

"You ready?"

"On your signal."

There was a pause, and Deo thought he could hear an engine starting in the background.

"Do it."

Deo shut the radio, put the big truck in gear, then steered it toward the spot in the fence that had been agreed on. He rode its bouncing, bladder-rattling course at maximum speed, praying that the explosives lashed to the fuel tanks wouldn't go off prematurely.

The driver had stolen virtually every type of car there was. Had performed expert getaways in most four-wheeled vehicles known to man.

But this was the first time he'd ever put down a score in a garbage truck.

He rounded the bend in the road, then pulled the wheel as hard to the left as possible. The truck jumped the curb, began racing toward the onrushing fence at close to fifty miles an hour.

He straightened the course, locked the wheel and gas pedal in place, then opened the door. At the last possible moment, he jumped.

He instantly rolled to his feet, running as fast as he could to where he hoped Foss and the utility company van would be waiting.

Guards jumped out of the way as the truck plowed through the first fence without slowing; raised thousands of sparks as it smashed the inner, electrified fence, then seemed to rise up on its rear wheels. It rolled over onto its side, like a beached dinosaur.

Sliding halfway across the lawn, it finally came to a stop, instantly surrounded by all the guards in the front of the complex.

None of them noticing a green staff car start slowly down the driveway toward the gate.

"Careful," a guard called out. "There might still be . . ." He never finished his thought as a loud explosion seemed to mushroom from under the truck. It lifted the multiton vehicle three feet in the air, sending metal fragments, like bullets, flying across the lawn.

Completely covering the sound of the staff car smashing through the gate.

Ten minutes later, Megan finally got up from the floor.

"Are we safe?" She was out of breath, completely exhausted from the chaos of the blackout, running up the stairwell, jumping out a second-floor window (that Greg had removed earlier) into a nearby Dumpster.

Greg glanced up at his rearview mirror. "For the moment."

He pulled off onto an access road marked "Fox Lake Dam Cross Through—Authorized Personnel Only." The gate lay unlocked and open ahead of him.

"We've got to get to the police," Megan said as she tried to catch her breath. "Maybe the FBI. Somebody from the government."

"I don't think so." Greg concentrated on the increasingly narrow, slippery road. "Lady, in case you hadn't noticed, that was the government that was hosting you back there." His voice was calm, serious, decided.

Megan thought for a moment. "Get me to a phone. Whoever they are, I'll make them the lead story on the morning news tomorrow."

Greg navigated the car through an even narrower, open gate.

"Do what you like, if you think they can protect you. Me, I have other plans."

"I don't get any of this," Megan said as she threw up her hands in frustration. "All I was doing was trying to research a story on . . ."

Greg stopped the car abruptly, just before it reached the one-lane road that ran along the top of the dam. He leaned past her, opening her door. "Have a good life. What's left of it anyway."

She started to get out, then stopped.

"Whoever you are, thank you. I think you may have saved my life back there." She held out her hand to him.

Greg shrugged. "Just keep me out of your story." He paused. "I've had enough press lately." He sounded tense and bitter as he turned back to the road. "I'll give your regards to the Grays."

She was halfway out of the car when she stopped as if she'd forgotten to take off her seat belt. "What did you say?"

Greg continued to stare down the narrow path over the top of the dam.

"You know who . . . where they are?" she asked.

A pair of headlights pulled up on the other side of the dam, stopping as far off it as the staff car was. Greg took a deep breath.

"You stayin' or goin'?" His voice was heavy with physical and emotional pain.

For long seconds Megan stood, half in, half out of the car. Then she decided, closing the door with a stronger slam than she'd meant to.

Greg pulled his pack from under his seat, the sheaf of papers he'd torn from Kilbourne's hands half hanging out of it. "Hang on to these."

He put the car in gear, gunning it forward onto the dam, just as the headlights opposite began to move toward him.

Several hours later, in the same examining room where he'd questioned Megan and confronted Greg, Kilbourne faced the doctor.

"Well?"

"It's definitely broken, sir. I'd like to schedule surgery to set it, maybe put in a pin."

"Can you do it here?" Kilbourne signed a clipboard a staffer put in front of him.

The doctor was more than hesitant. "I'd rather have you moved to Boone County General."

"Then it'll have to wait. Thank you, Doctor." He winced as he shifted in his chair.

The doctor reluctantly nodded, standing to leave. "Call if the pain gets worse." He quietly left the room.

Kilbourne read over the damage report again, ignoring the spasms in his leg. He tried to concentrate, but there was no way.

The image of the young burglar, tough, smart, seemingly fearless, kept getting in the way.

He knew he shouldn't, but he smiled.

Picaro was so much the man that he had once been. Then the smile melted away, replaced by two tears born of pain.

Physical, from his ruined leg; and psychic, from his ruined life.

"Mr. Kilbourne? Mr. Kilbourne? We've got them!"

"What?"

Paul nodded enthusiastically.

"Seems they tried to avoid our roadblocks by cutting over the dam access way. They had a head-on with a public utility van, both vehicles going over the side." The man was jubilant.

"Is it confirmed?"

"Absolutely! They've recovered both vehicles from the dam's spillways. They're completely smashed. No question about it."

"Bodies?" Kilbourne said in a partially skeptical tone. "What about the bodies?"

The young man shrugged as his cell phone began to ring. "The dam people say they've unquestionably been sucked into the spillways' filtration system. Reduced to hamburger in seconds." He turned away as he answered his phone. "Yeah?"

Kilbourne closed his eyes, then began rubbing his forehead.

"Mr. Kilbourne, they want to know what happened to McCutcheon's papers. Especially the ones he was going to give the reporter." The young man's voice was suddenly somber.

Kilbourne never opened his eyes. "Tell them they were lost during the incident. Tell them not to worry."

"Yes, sir." He turned, then whispered into the phone.

Kilbourne began to rub his temples. His spasming leg, his exhaustion, his years, all bore down upon him with the weight of twenty worlds.

"Mr. Kilbourne?" Paul's voice was choked with emotion, almost tearful.

"Yes, Paul?" He swiveled in his chair to see his emotional young assistant pointing his .45 at Kilbourne's head. The old man never flinched. "You've received your orders, then."

"Yes, sir," the young man said reluctantly. "A message from MJ-1." He seemed unwilling to continue.

"Go on, Paul."

"Yes, sir. MJ-1 requests either your retirement"—he thumbed back the hammer on the unswerving gun—"or your immediate presence at Habitat." Another pause, this one more puzzled than anything else. "Completely your choice, sir, he said to say."

Something within the injured old man shouted for death. Screamed to be finally and irrevocably released from the clutches of the lunatics and psychotics who had shit on the world he'd dedicated his life to preserving. To finally close his eyes and leave it to the amoral *others* to clean up after the elephants.

But, in the end, they *knew* he wouldn't, *couldn't*, take that easiest of paths.

The job lay undone. Joe and Max still precariously close to exposure. The work of a lifetime, the *faith* of a lifetime, hanging in the balance.

"When do we leave, Paul?" he asked simply, quietly.

"As soon as your leg is set, sir."

Kilbourne nodded. "How decent of them." He waved Paul's gun away. "How very—" He paused. "How very *human* of them."

PART THREE

THE CREW

As a teen, young Victor knew little more peace of mind than in the turbulent years before.

Thanks largely to his instinctive talents and unsettled mind, the locksmith's business had grown from a small family operation into a national franchise. The locksmith was universally praised for his innovative security systems, newly patented locking mechanisms, unconventional (seemingly unbeatable) security plans.

Young Victor didn't mind if he didn't get the credit (or the patents). At least, not very much. He was satisfied with having a purpose, a reason for getting out of bed in the morning.

School had been a nightmare for him. He either didn't or couldn't figure out what everyone else was smiling about. The world, at least the world he'd known, just wasn't this sparkling glittery place that all the other children seemed to inhabit.

He would try to mimic their ease, their awkwardness, their unfettered/clumsy dance through the days. He forced himself to be with others (whether he cared for or understood them or not), hoping to pick up the carefree contagion they seemed to carry.

But in the end, he would retreat to his adoptive father's workroom. Losing himself in the intricacies of some new pin-tumbler-slider configuration.

For reasons he didn't, couldn't understand, they came to him, always in the conflicted nights. He saw the complex circuitry in his head. Understood natively the mysterious interrelationships among tachyons, ions, charged particles, and microwaves. Saw security zones as living things with needs, desires, weaknesses, and strengths. Easily divined how to construct, bypass, nurture, or reinforce those system zones. To a point where even he couldn't see a way around them.

Followed by utter exhaustion and a troubled sleep.

Then, there were the other nights. The nights when the work, the

myopic concentration, wouldn't drive away the pain. Nights he
would sneak away, vanishing into the few dark streets of the otherwise middle-class town. Merging with the pimps and the whores; the
dealers, users, and used.

His adoptive mother openly worried about "his contaminating
our real ones."

The locksmith was openly disinterested . . . so long as the work,
the innovations, kept coming.

And the people at his school, the well-meaning, well-trained counselors, teachers, coaches, and would-be mentors, just shook their
heads. Not willing to commit "that kind of energy to a borderline
kid who's in the system already."

Once a month, the social worker came. Once a month, she in-
spected his room, the house, talked with his teachers and adoptive
family. Once a month, she would write a virtual carbon of every
other month's report.

"Victor seems less socially developed than others his age. He
shows an inability to communicate his true feelings, even within a
strong, loving family structure. He is bright, has tested out at well
above genius level. But his grades are barely acceptable, all of his
instructors in agreement that he is markedly underperforming. He
gets angry very easily, explodes at the slightest intrusion into what
he perceives as his personal space. Can become remote, detached,
automatonish when under stress. Several have recommended therapy or the exploration of developmental guidance programs for the
boy."

But no one ever got around to it.

Shortly after his eighteenth birthday, on the anniversary of his
ninth year with the locksmith's family—never (in any real sense) *his*
family—the little boy, grown into young man, took it out of all their
hands.

And disappeared.

To try to find the truth or lie of the question that haunted him in
nights of half-sleep. Nights when memories of Gravesend Avenue
would merge with images of suburbia in a psychotic, psychedelic,
painful montage. With the question shouted out by faceless creatures who he knew, deep down, were mere reflections of himself.

"Who am I?" they would scream. "Why am I alone?"

NINE

THE SETTING couldn't have been more perfect if it was staged on a Hollywood back lot.

The senator leaned against the aged fence post, obviously comfortable in his well-worn jeans, faded flannel shirt, red, white, and blue bandanna. A rolling green field with a few black and white cows grazing completed the easily captioned picture.

It all said . . .

America!

Van Ness patted his horse's neck as it stuck its head into the picture.

"Guess he wants to be on the TV," he said easily. "Takes after his lord and master, I guess."

Van Ness smiled, not at the joke it had taken an animal trainer most of the week to get the animal to learn. But rather at the basic naiveté that most of the press still had.

"He a Democrat or Republican?" one of the press pool called out.

"He look like there's any elephant in him?"

The five reporters with their camera operators laughed lightly.

"Well," Van Ness said after a deep breath, "let's get to it."

"Have you decided on a running mate yet?"

Van Ness raised his eyebrows. "Got to have a little something to liven up the convention."

"The president called your proposed tax plan laughable. Any response?"

"Considering the only taxes that man knows about are 'A'-tax—attacks on the middle-income and poor folk of this country—I'm willing to take his comments in the spirit they were intended. A dumb-ass attempt to attack new ideas that weren't hatched by his Wall Street cronies."

"Any comment on the Kerry investigation or the closing of the case?"

Van Ness paused, suddenly becoming somber, introspective . . . presidential-looking. "I'm glad you brought that up."

He hesitated, straightening as the camera pushed in on him. "As you know, this campaign has been dedicated to the spirit of Jack Kerry. To his memory and to his belief that the best days of America lie, not behind us, but ahead. Somewhere, a shining place, almost within our reach.

"With the death of that monster, the Mafioso hit man Picaro, those of us who knew Jack can finally begin the process of closure. I only regret that the authorities were not able to catch up to the man before he claimed more victims. Innocents like Betty and Lewis McCutcheon, like that brave television producer Megan Turner. That they had to die, be slaughtered by this product of organized crime, is the ultimate indictment of our system."

As the camera pushed in on the flint jaw, the set expression, the single tear rolling, unnoticed, down his cheek, Roman Peterkezs muted the sound on the television behind his counter.

"Bastard," he muttered beneath his breath as he turned back to the radio that lay open in a tangle of circuits and wires before him. "Republicans, Democrats, always the same." He looked over at a close-up of the likely presidential nominee, seemed to intensely study, or perhaps judge, the man as he spoke of meaningless images, unclear goals, and granite nothings.

"Bastard," Roman said again with an air of finality as he turned back to his work.

"You don't like the man, Papa?" The little boy looked up from the floor of the appliance shop where he was playing with some action figures.

"He's gadj, Tomascke." He paused, smiling down at the little boy. "Who are we?"

"Romany Polska," the boy instantly replied as he mirrored his father's smile.

"And who do we fear?"

The little boy, no more than six or seven, jumped to his feet. "We fear none but God," he said in his most adult voice.

"And who do we trust?"

"None but God," Tomascke said as he struck an aggressive pose. "God and the Romany; who God has placed on earth to pay homage to his son, Jesus."

Roman nodded. "Then why did God create so many of the gadj?"

Tomascke's serious look melted into an ear-to-ear grin. "God created the gadja so that his most faithful servant, the Gypsy, would never go hungry."

Roman stared seriously into his son's eager eyes, then suddenly spread his arms. The small boy squealed as he leaped into the strong hug by the huge arms.

"Tomascke?" a woman's voice called from the back of the shop. "Where are you? Grandmother needs you under the table."

Malika Peterkezs walked into the front of the shop. When she saw her son and husband playing behind the counter, she set her hands on her hips, with a stern look on her face.

"Tomascke! Go help Grandmother."

The boy looked at his mother, then up at his father. "Do I have to, Papa?"

One look at his wife was all Roman needed.

"Maybe we are also a little afraid of Mama," he said as he put the boy down. He swatted him lightly on the butt. "Go get under the table for Grandmother."

"Okay, Papa." He happily scampered off.

Malika didn't move, just continued to stare angrily at her husband as he turned back to the radio.

"I know that look," Roman said as he pretended to concentrate on the job.

"What look? You aren't even looking at me."

Roman shook his head. "Do I have to look at the sky to know that it's blue?"

"You're spoiling him." It was getting hard for her to maintain the angry tone.

"He's my son," Roman shrugged.

Malika sighed. "There's no arguing with you."

Roman raised his eyebrows. "But you do it so well."

She gave up, walking in front of the counter to get a better look at what he was doing. "How's it coming?"

Roman grunted. "They make these things so you can listen to the police calls, then they make it so you can't tune to the really important frequencies or the surveillance nets." He paused. "It's very inconvenient."

She smiled. "You'll make it work."

He nodded. "Eventually." He put aside the screwdriver, leaning over to give his wife a kiss. "Mama got someone?"

"In a few minutes. A full reading. That's why she needs your little friend. To make the table noises."

Roman laughed. "Long Island money or city secretary?"

"Neither. Strange guy, actually."

"Strange how?"

Malika walked around the counter, taking a broom to start sweeping up. "Sent over by Madame Ferzics."

"Really?" Roman looked over at her. "Why?"

"The guy wants a full read. Real traditional phases-of-the-moon, birth-to-death thing." She shrugged. "Ferzics won't do that thing, you know? She didn't like the spirits around this guy anyway. Didn't want to get into it. So she recommended Mama."

"Out of the goodness of her heart? Come on!"

Malika laughed. "That, and a tenth of the take before blessings or spells. A fifth after."

Roman nodded. "More like it." He returned to the work for the moment, then stopped. "Phases of the moon, huh? Probably only Mama and half a dozen others in this country do that today." A strange look came over him. "If this guy's got the dark spirits, maybe somebody ought to look after things, huh?"

"My brother Lazslo's in the watching room with the sawed-off and a hangover."

Roman smiled. "After, maybe you and me can go into the watching room, eh?"

Malika laughed. "After nine years, you still act like a—" She was interrupted by three short buzzes.

"He's here," she said quietly.

Deep within the house, behind the appliance shop, a parlor had been darkened with scarves over lamps and windows. Candles burned on several tables. The sweet smell of incense rose into the air.

Grandmother Peterkezs arranged her scarves and skirts for maximum effect as she waited for the new client to be escorted into the parlor.

Her crystal ball sat on its stand on a small table to her right. Three decks of tarot cards, each wrapped in a different-colored kerchief, sat on the table in front of her. Three unlit candles seemed to stand sentry by each deck.

"Enter," she said as the beaded curtain parted. "Enter and be at ease with the universe."

"May I take your coat, sir?" the teenage girl said to the man.

He nodded, handing the coat to her.

The girl casually ran her hands along it, then barely shook her head. There was nothing in the pockets, so there would be nothing she could tell her grandmother about the man. She silently left.

For a more thorough search.

As the man sat in the indicated chair, across the table from the old woman, she carefully studied him from behind a harmless smile.

In his mid-thirties, the man was dark, in both complexion and aspect. He was tall, in excellent physical condition. This much was evident to her trained eye despite the cheap, baggy, off-the-rack, nondescript clothes he wore. His long hair and beard seemed unkempt, but in a practiced way.

He is someone who does not want to call attention to himself, the old woman thought. *But also someone who does not want to be recognized if someone does look his way. His watch and jewelry are expensive, his manner loose, relaxed, but his eyes miss nothing in the room.*

She busied herself placing two boxes of matches on the table, in precise positions, either side of the candles.

This one has the gift of stillness, she reflected. *He has a confidence, almost an arrogance, but there is something hunted in his eyes. The look of the* Loup Blanc *as the Romany Français call it. The White Wolf, the feared one. The one who hunts alone but is hunted in turn . . . by man—out of fear.*

And the dark spirits seemed to circle just beyond the man's aura. Threatening to consume him, yet held at bay by some force deep within.

Confounded by the man's manufactured blankness, as well as intrigued by it, she began.

"We call the peace and guidance of God, and the son he sent to our world, Jesus who is the Christ, into this room. We beseech him to look with favor upon we few here, that we may share in his insights. Ask for his protection from the dark ones who would seek to pervert his words. Look to his light to brighten us with wisdom."

She looked up, into the sunglasses-covered eyes. "What shall you be called?"

The man seemed to hesitate.

"Linus," he finally said. His voice was flat, without intonation or accent.

"What offering will you make, Linus?" She hoped for a hundred dollars for this first time out. Then, in future sessions, the cost would slowly escalate as she convinced him of the need for various spells and potions.

The man placed five one-hundred-dollar bills on the table.

For the first time in her adult life, Grandmother Peterkezs was stunned into inaction.

"What . . . I . . ." She quickly pulled herself together, eyes locked on the money, but refused to touch it. "I will not invoke the dark ones," she said in a strong tone. "I will not bring them here for any money or cause." She sounded firm, although her heart wasn't really in it.

"All I want," the man said flatly, "is a full reading. Old style, phases of the moon, the fringe to the center." He stared at her from behind those darkened lenses. "One reading, one time. I seek . . . knowledge."

"It is a rare thing you seek. The phases of the moon can be unforgiving. The tell may not be pleasant."

Somehow she needed to draw the man out. Discover something that she could hold on to. A thing, however small, that would give her the direction she needed before going to the cards.

"Perhaps your family's powers aren't up to it. There are few left in this country that can do it." He put his hand on the money, as if about to take it back.

"The House of Peterkezs has been doing this reading for seven generations of fifth daughters," she said in legitimate indignation.

The man seemed to stiffen.

"This *is* the House of Peterkezs," he said softly. He pulled back his hand. "Then do the reading."

Hesitantly, understanding now why Ferzics had been frightened of this man, the old woman gathered in the money.

"Select a match from one of the boxes in front of you, then light one of the candles. One match, one candle only."

The man nodded.

Slowly he reached out, holding his hand over the first box of matches, then turning the box parallel to the candles. He turned to the second box, seemed to study it, then slammed his clenched fist down on it.

The sound echoed through the small room.

After a long moment, he lifted his fist, using his other hand to remove the match that had stuck to his skin. In front of the wide-eyed, nearly trembling old woman, he lit the one candle that had remained standing.

"Benci Joska," she whispered in an instinctive invocation of "God's Blessed Grace."

"Jonka," the man replied quietly in the traditional way.

In the walk-in closet with the two-way mirror, looking out into the parlor, Lazslo leveled his sawed-off twelve-gauge at the figure less than fifteen feet away. Then he pressed a button on the floor with his foot.

"Czigany?" Grandmother Peterkezs asked in a cautious tone.

"Arpad Czigany," the man said after considering her question. "In a roundabout way."

Roman let himself into the watching room, a loaded and cocked .45 in his hand. "What's going on?"

Lazslo never took his eyes off the man in the next room. "This Linus, he threw the fist." His voice was soft but edgy.

Roman studied the man through the glass. "He doesn't look Gypsy."

Lazslo had both hammers back on the lethal weapon. "Grandmother challenged him. He called himself a wanderer."

Roman moved closer to the hidden door that separated the two rooms. "You think he's from Sascha's bunch?"

Lazslo shrugged as he fingered the trigger.

"Remember," Roman said in a near whisper, "aim high. Tomascke's under the table."

Lazslo nodded.

"Who are you?" Grandmother Peterkezs asked in a strong, almost insolent voice.

The man remained silent as he swept two of the decks off the table with his forearm. He unwrapped the third, then began to shuffle.

"Ask the cards."

He rewrapped the cards, placed them on the table, then turned them diagonally, so that one of their corners pointed at the old woman, the other at him. He slowly slid them across the table.

Muttering an almost silent prayer, the old woman unwrapped the cards, then began to deal them out, facedown, in the ancient pattern.

"When you were born, Linus?"

"In the new moon."

A low moan seemed to rise up in the room, coming from everywhere and nowhere.

The man barely smiled, looking down at the table.

Grandmother Peterkezs began to turn over the cards, starting from the upper right corner of the pattern.

"You have come a long way. But you have a further way to travel."

"Yes."

"You are born without a father's name, but have shed the name you were given. You have, in its stead, taken another name; with it . . . another life." She paused. "The name is *not* Linus."

The man seemed to smile, for just a fraction of a second. "Go on."

"You have been with evil men, done evil things in their name. I see death and pain as your constant companions." Another pause. "You were an assassin?"

"No"—a pause—"not exactly."

Lazslo started to get to his feet, only to feel Roman's restraining hand on his shoulder. He was trying to stare through the man's tangled mop of hair and uncombed beard. To pierce the deeply darkened sunglasses.

"Wait," Roman said softly.

Grandmother Peterkezs turned over three cards at the bottom of the pattern.

"This is your present," she said as she studied the cards. "You have been wronged. But you bear some blame for this. As if your lesser evil caused a greater one to be drawn to you. Others—two, no, three others—look to you for strength in this ordeal."

She looked up at him, an almost sympathetic look.

"There are great forces arrayed against you." She seemed momentarily confused. "But they no longer see you as a threat." Another hesitation. "They are wrong."

She turned over another card. "For two moons"—she turned over another—"two moons and a crescent, perhaps ten weeks, no more, you have been running." She passed her hands over the faceup cards. "Not from fear. From caution?"

The man nodded.

"There is one close to you, a man not a father but still a father, who is ill. This time has not been good for him."

She looked up at the man.

"This man who is not your father, the cards say he is dying slowly, but by his own hand. Can this be true?"

"It can."

"Especially if he's a junkie," Roman whispered in the watching room.

Grandmother Peterkezs shook her head. "I pray to God for his mercy and healing love for your . . . friend."

She returned to the cards. "There is another, perhaps, yes, a woman."

"There is."

She nodded. "A fire burns within this one. She cares not for justice, vengeance, or equity. She seeks only"—Grandmother Peterkezs turned over another card—"acclaim. For that, for the barest possibility of that, she has attached herself to you."

Just the hint of a smile from the man. "And the third one?"

"A friend. A man you may trust. A man from the East who lives for the chase beyond all else."

Roman smiled as he lowered the hammer on his gun, then gestured for Lazslo to relax.

"Deo Hartounian," he said. Again with the barest hint of a smile.

The man who called himself Linus gestured at the center of the pattern. "What about my future?"

She turned to the cards in the center of the table, turning over the card to the left of center.

"The Eye of Egypt. Upright." She paused. "There is deception, a great deception. A dangerous thing you are compelled to confront."

She studied the card and its relation to the others.

"One you would confront alone." She looked him in the eye.

"But know this, you must not. To do this thing, whatever it may be, will require all you have. And more still."

"Why I'm here," the man mumbled.

She hesitantly turned over the card to the right of center.

"The King of Cups." She looked up at him. "It is bad place for this card. It means that your fate, your life force, is bound to another."

Almost fearfully, she turned over the card in the center of the pattern.

"Benci Joska!" Her face turned white.

"Jonka. What is it?" The man's voice was calm but intense.

"The Magician lying on his right side," she said breathlessly. "On his side is no good. On his right side is very no good."

She shook her head as if she was suddenly deeply confused. "Have never seen this card in position to others. Is very bad but . . . very strange also."

"What does it mean?"

She continued to study the lay of the cards for long minutes.

"It has no sense. Cannot be, but . . ." Her voice dropped to a near whisper. "Your fortune lies not in this world. Not in next world. But in *different* world. Very strange. Have never seen cards . . ." She looked over at him. "There is other thing here."

"Go on."

She pointed while she talked.

"The Magician's head touches the Eye of Egypt. Have never seen this before, but . . ." She held up a warning finger. "Message for you is clear, even if make no sense." She took a deep breath.

"You seek a justice; and through that justice, peace." She shook her head. "But you will find no peace until . . . this maybe has meaning to you, for sure not me."

She paused, her voice dropping into an ominous whisper. "No peace until you face the Magic Eyes."

The man nodded, appearing to withdraw into himself.

"May I ask a question?" He seemed suddenly relaxed, as if the odd fortune read from the cards had somehow confirmed something. Some *thing* that was buried deep within himself.

The old woman gathered herself, then glanced down at the cards. "Up to four," she said in a recovered tone. But her eyes never left the strange alignment of the cards.

"One will do."

"Speak."

He took off his sunglasses as he turned toward the mirror. "Where can I find Roman Peterkezs?"

Roman stepped through the hidden door into the parlor. "You're supposed to be a dead Mafia hit man," he said lightly.

Greg grimaced. "Who said that?"

"Gadj politician."

Greg stood up, shrugged, then took a step toward the bigger man. "Well," he said lightly, "you just can't trust the gadja."

The two men suddenly embraced, to the surprise of the old woman and the curious expression of the young boy peeking out from under the tablecloth.

Just across the river from the neighborhood appliance shop, in a four-block area of Paterson, New Jersey, known as "the Hole," a yellow taxi cruised the dark, burned-out streets.

"Why do I have to be here?" Megan was slumped in the front passenger seat.

Deo's expression never changed. "Greg says not to leave you alone."

"Come on with this! You let *him* out alone."

"Foss is committing a Class A felony in this state. Maybe federal weight." He checked the street around them. "That's the one risk we don't share."

After two and a half months with these men, Megan still wasn't sure if she liked them or not. But there was one thing she *was* sure of.

It would all have been worth it if everything happened the way she hoped it would.

She would return from the dead, with a story that was undeniably the scoop of the century. Maybe of any century in the past or yet to come! It would be a story that would bring in untold millions, instant international fame, awards. Recognition at a level that would have made Cronkite, Murrow, Rather, and Sevareid green with envy.

And all she had to do to get it was, well, survive.

A thought that hadn't occurred to her when she made the impetuous decision on that night almost three months ago.

The smell of the shooting was still in her nose; the sounds of Betty McCutcheon's struggles still in her ears. The feeling of her own fear in each drop of the sweat that had soaked the hospital greens despite the night's chill.

She'd gone with them, helped them fake the accident on top of the dam, because, at the time, she hadn't seen any other choice.

Hours later, after reading through McCutcheon's mimeographed copies of Majestic Twelve (Majic 12) documents in a seedy Illinois roadside motel, the choice didn't seem quite as clear.

The story contained in those papers seemed to confirm most of what she'd suspected. That an ongoing cover-up had been perpetrated against the American people for almost fifty years. That this cover-up was still going on today was evidenced by what she'd been through in the last twenty-four hours. In addition to the other deaths that the burglar had told her about.

Her first instinct had been to get it on the air immediately. To go public with the documents and her own eyewitness testimony. To get on a satellite link at the nearest WIN affiliate and broadcast the facts to the world!

But the noon newscast the next day had changed all that.

The story of Mafia hit men trying to cover up half-century-old scandals was so absurd, so obviously contrived, that it came as a body blow when she saw it receiving universal acceptance.

Even WIN was saying that the Mafia in World War II was "the main focus of Ms. Turner's upcoming special. A special which will go on, now dedicated to a woman who believed that the scourge of organized crime must be made to pay. For their crimes today, as well as their atrocities of the past."

"Well, damn it," she'd almost yelled at the TV, "they can't deny *me!* Not when I show up in the flesh."

"Can't they?"

Greg had been watching her from another part of the room. "Do you really think that after all this killing, after McCutcheon, Kerry, and who knows how many others, they'll just let you show up and bring them down?" He laughed bitterly. "Lady, they'll squash you like a bug on the windshield."

"But if I'm actually there, in person . . ."

"Tell it to Oswald."

He flipped a copy of the documents over to her. "Read that again. To protect all that, they'll do anything. If they don't kill you, they'll have prominent, high-integrity professionals declare you insane, then lock you up."

Megan had shaken her head. "My people will believe me. Especially with these." She held up the papers.

This time Greg laughed openly. "Papers, copies of copies of papers I mean."

Megan thought about that for a moment. "I could take them
to . . ."

"The agricultural station? Go ahead, I'm sure that's all it'll be by
the time anyone gets inside. You'll just be consigned with all the
others; people who spend their days connecting leaves, like dots, to
make out 'badge man' on the grassy knoll."

He was quiet for a moment, looking down at the floor, seeming to
concentrate intensely. "Then, there's the other thing."

"What's that?" she said sadly.

He looked up, seemed to be studying her.

"If you show up, alive and well, then the same people that'll stop
you will figure out I'm probably still out here." He walked over to
her. "I'm not sure I can allow that."

For the first time, Megan felt afraid of the man who'd rescued
her.

"So what am I supposed to do?" she'd said weakly.

Then a strange thing happened. A completely unexpected moment in a seemingly endless string of surprises.

Greg smiled.

"When you do, finally, resurrect yourself," he said with a hint of
laughter in his voice, "do it right."

"What do you mean?"

"Come back from the dead," he said slowly, definitely. "Show
them the documents, give them your testimony. Then give them Joe
and Max."

She'd been quiet for a long time before she barely whispered her
response. "It's not possible."

Greg had shrugged.

"That's to find out," he said simply. "But you decide now."

"What do you need me for?"

"Well," Greg said, "you know how this all started, maybe other
things I need to know. And Joe and Max, such as they are, are only
leverage. *Will be* leverage. As such, I'll need the right platform to"—
he seemed to search for the word—"I'll need some public forum to
negotiate from. Or threaten to negotiate from."

He seemed about to say more, then stopped himself.

"Regardless," his voice grew low and deadly, a younger version of Cold Man's, "you have two choices. Come with us. Help us." He pulled a gun from his waistband, cocking and leveling it at her head. "Or die here, now."

She had stared at the large barrel of the gun, at the cold, emotionless eyes behind it. She knew she was scared, but after the events of the last twelve hours, what was one more fright?

No.

The overriding emotion in her at that moment had not been fear, but a near-electric thrill! A native understanding that no matter what happened; if they found the Grays or if they didn't (making the story one of living on the edge with public enemy number one, as she was sure this man in front of her must be); either way, hers would be the story of the year, the decade.

The possibilities were almost more frightening than the burglar with the gun.

If she survived.

She agreed immediately.

After that, they'd moved every night. Traveling random distances and directions for the first six weeks.

"Just to be sure we're alone," Greg had said.

Then they'd started moving east.

This travel was more directed, with stops arranged to begin what Megan was beginning to understand as the accumulating of the mountains of data required to "pull off the score."

All of this had led them to Paterson.

"A safe place to work New York from," Greg had said.

But there was now a problem.

At various points on their cross-country trip, it had been difficult or impossible for Foss to find an adequate supply of heroin. Since they'd been avoiding the larger cities and towns, he would often have to buy in large quantities in order to see him through the "dry" towns.

But, as Megan had learned in a special she'd done on drug abuse, addicts seldom, if ever, learn to hoard their drugs. A junkie with a large supply simply uses more, needs more, craves more.

The old man had been no exception. His habit, until recently fairly moderate as those things go, had exploded out of control. Foss would go days without eating. Suffered massive mood swings, lost weight, seemed to be in a constant daze.

But it was clearly not a subject that anyone could bring up with Greg.

Until now.

Foss had failed to return from a drug-buying trip to this New Jersey sinkhole. So, after talking to Greg over the phone, Deo and Megan had set out in search of him.

Deo pulled the car over to the curb in front of an abandoned storefront. "Go ahead."

She looked at the driver with all the anger she could muster. Which by now had grown to a considerable amount. "Why don't *you* ever go?"

"I stay in the car," was his flattened answer.

Shaking her head, she got out. "Great."

Looking around the empty street, she slowly went up to the door, then knocked.

"Yeah," a groggy voice said from the other side.

"I'm looking for a friend."

After a moment, the door opened.

Two obviously stoned men looked her over.

"I'll be your friend, bitch."

She stepped back from them.

"He's around fifty but looks older," she said as both men came toward her.

"TV? That you?" Foss's voice came from somewhere back in the dark.

"It's me! Now get the hell out here!"

The men looked back into the dark, then back at Megan. The sound of Foss's shuffling came toward them.

"He still owes us, bitch."

"Yeah," the other said as he reached out for her open windbreaker. "Course, you could always settle up for . . ."

The man suddenly froze.

"Move your ass, old man," Deo shouted from just behind Megan, where he held a raincoat over the barely protruding gaping barrel of an automatic weapon. Leveled at the men's stomachs.

As Foss emerged from the dark, Megan put her arm around him, helping him to the car.

Deo backed away from the men, allowing them to dash back inside, throwing the heavy door shut behind them. He rushed into the car.

"I thought you never held . . . anything?" Megan said as he opened the driver's door.

Deo tossed her the raincoat, which she pulled back to reveal just the barrel of the weapon. No body, no gun, just a foot-and-a-half length of barrel.

Megan looked confused.

Deo raised his eyebrows as he dropped the cab into gear. "All right. Sometimes I get out of the car. But I *never* hold."

Greg, Roman, and Lazslo sat around the kitchen table, sipping their thick, steamy, Hungarian coffee.

"So how does a smooth operator like you get in trouble with the G?" Roman lit a new cigarette off of Lazslo's. "Last I heard, you were putting down six-figure scores in overpriced cribs."

Greg's eyes shifted over to Lazslo, then back to Roman.

Roman smiled, gesturing with his cigarette. "My brother-in-law. He won't shop you. If he does, I'll cut his throat," he said lightly. "Okay, brother?"

"Of course, sure," Lazslo said casually as he added his fifth spoon of sugar to his glass.

Malika put a bowl of chickpeas and a plate of brown bread with garlic butter on the table.

"Enjoy," she said lightly as she started out of the kitchen. "Come, Tomascke."

But the boy stood his ground, staring at the stranger. "Papa, I thought you said we don't trust the gadja. Never."

"Tomascke!" Malika hurried back, an embarrassed look on her face. Roman waved her away.

"It's a fair question." He lifted his son onto his lap. "Vic . . ." He paused. "It isn't really Linus now, is it?" He sounded worried.

"Greg, these days. Gregory Picaro."

Roman seemed to consider it for a moment. Then he nodded in approval before returning to his eager son.

"Picaro here may not have been born Czigany, but he's as good a one as I am."

"I don't understand, Papa. How?"

Roman paused, locking eyes with Greg. "You don't have to, little one. Not now." His voice was growing soft. "All you need to know is that years ago, before you were born, he did a deed for our tribe that we can never repay. For that, he is forever Czigany Romany Polska.''

"But, Papa.''

"Enough with you.'' Roman handed him to Malika, who quickly left the room.

Greg stared into his coffee glass. "How's your back?''

Roman shrugged it off. "How can I help you?''

"I had a helluva time finding you. Then I remembered what you told me about your mother.''

Roman ignored him. "How can I help you?''

"That Ferzics woman was about the fifth . . .''

Roman reached out, touching Greg's tightly clasped hands. "You've found me now. How can I help you, brother?''

Greg took a deep breath, then leaned forward, followed by the other men. "You've heard about my problems?'' Roman nodded. "I have a plan to get out from under, but I need help.''

"Sure. From Mama's reading I know this. Whatever I can do, I will,'' Roman said.

"You'd better wait before you say anything. We're talking high risk.'' He paused. "Higher than anything any of us have ever played for.''

Lazslo smiled. "Listen, Picaro. From what Roman's told me, if it wasn't for you, he wouldn't have lived to marry my sister. So she'd still be a big pain to me. For that alone, I am with Roman on this.''

They all laughed. Tightly, tensely.

"I'm going to need more than just you two.'' Greg looked up, making sure they were alone. "I need a crew.''

"A full crew?''

Greg nodded.

Roman shook his head. "I haven't worked a full crew in . . .'' He thought hard. "Ten, maybe twelve years. It was a dying art then.''

Greg looked concerned. "But you can get the people, right?''

Lazslo held up his hands in a gesture of futility. "To get the people is not the problem. To get the *right* people, that's the problem.''

Roman agreed. "It's not like the old days in Paris, my friend.'' He laughed. "In Paris, I could get you a crew. But here . . .''

"Going to cost a loaf too. Maybe more,'' Lazslo added.

"He's right. Lazslo and me, we come for *you*.'' Roman smiled. "To get the kind of people you need, at least five hundred a week a head and expenses." The smile turned unsure. "Long time, short time, a lot of loaves and fishes."

"What kind of mark, if it may be told at this time?" Lazslo asked as he lit another cigarette. "It may affect the price."

"Yeah, well," Greg delayed. "It's a secured government facility."

Roman broke out laughing. "I knew one day you'd try for Fort Knox!" His laughing trailed off when he saw the look in his friend's eyes. "It isn't Fort Knox, is it?"

"Maybe something just as hard." Greg reached into his pocket, pulling out a small velvet sack. He handed it to Roman. "You used to be into stones. Think that'll cover the deposit?"

Roman dumped the perfectly round stone into his hand.

"Glass marble?" Lazslo said in surprise.

Roman rolled the stone in his hand as he looked into Greg's eyes. Then he held the stone up to the light.

His expression froze between awe and disbelief.

"It's not a joke?" he asked softly.

"No joke."

Roman studied the stone again, then handed it to Lazslo. "Show it to Mama."

The younger man shrugged as he headed for the living room.

When he was gone, Roman leaned close to his old friend. "You got more?"

"Lots more."

Roman leaned back, thinking. A smile slowly came over his entire face. "Lots more," he mumbled. He handed Greg a long cigar from his vest pocket.

The two men sat quietly, waiting for Lazslo to return. Ten minutes later, he came in shaking his head.

"I think Mama going to have a heart attack when she looked at this." He handed the stone back to Roman. Reluctantly.

"What did she say?"

Lazslo took a deep breath. "Twenty-five, maybe thirty years. Maybe more. Whole family in silk and gold."

Roman pictured the money that twenty-five or thirty years' high-end income added up to. All from one little round stone.

"What's the crew's end?" he asked while he was thinking.

Greg straightened in his chair. "For the crew, one stone, split equally. For your family, one stone as the leaders."

Both Gypsies' cigarettes dropped from their mouths at the same moment.

"Where is this 'government facility'? Behind the gates of Hell?" Roman asked in an awestruck voice.

"Who cares?" Lazslo added almost immediately as he stared down at the stone. "For that price, I'd 'Chicago shuffle' Old Nick himself." He spit over his left shoulder.

"You may be right, brother." Roman looked up at Greg. "Go on, Picaro."

Greg looked deeply into Roman's eyes, seeing not only the natural greed; not only the dedication of a man who had sworn to stand by Greg. But also that fatalistic, almost fanatical belief of most Gypsies. That one day, somehow, somewhere, they will stumble into that one, perfect moment when blind luck delivers to them their ultimate reward.

He pulled a folded sheaf of papers from his jacket pocket. "Read this before you decide."

Roman took the papers, reluctantly handing the stone back to Greg. He glanced down at the words stamped across the top of each sheet.

TOP SECRET/
MAJIC EYES ONLY

"Majic eyes," he muttered as he settled back to begin to read.

TEN

"WELCOME TO FREEDOM RIDGE."
A small group of people stood around their guide, looking out at the unforgiving desert terrain below.

"Up until 1948, everything you see out there was open territory for prospecting, mining, development, recreation. Then, in the middle of that year, the central one hundred acres was purchased by the air force and redesignated as Gunnery Test Range Areas 43 through 55."

The sun was well on its way down, turning the sky an orange-streaked blue against the western hills behind them. But the heat still formed false rivers on the scrub-dotted sand flats the man pointed at. The temperature had dropped ten degrees, but was still well over one hundred. The air was dry and bitter.

But it didn't matter.

The people who came to this place, who seemed drawn to this place, couldn't have cared less about the conditions.

Because they were here to see and believe.

"Gradually," the guide continued with all the emphasis his two years of drama in college could muster, "over the years, the air force expanded their holdings in the valley below. They said that with more sophisticated weapons of greater destructive capabilities, they needed the land as a buffer to protect any civilians wandering in the area from danger."

The disdain and disbelief in his voice matched his expression as he looked them each in the eye.

"This despite the fact that no one has ever seen anything even resembling gunnery practice take place here."

There were knowing nods, a few smiles, and a few overserious expressions. They all knew the story, the story that had brought them to this otherwise forgotten piece of desert near Rachel, Nevada, in the first place. But actually hearing it from a man who *knew* was different. A man with hands-on experience, an acknowledged expert.

Even if no one was exactly sure who acknowledged the guide as an expert.

"Then, beginning in 1966, massive construction was observed in the valley below us, in Area 51 of the so-called Range. No one was allowed close enough to see exactly what was being done, requests to the government for information were met with steady denials that anything *was* being built. But every night the mysterious, unmarked cargo planes came, leaving before dawn.

"By the beginning of 1967, a runway, believed to be the longest in the world, was observed. Then a series of hangars and other buildings. Security increased. Government denials increased. But whatever was going on there was clearly getting bigger, more complex . . . darker."

The guide started down the trail followed by the group. They rounded a bend in the trail, suddenly confronted by several poles with bright red signs on them.

A middle-aged couple in matching walking shorts took turns standing next to the signs, taking each other's picture, asking others to take pictures of the two of them by the signs.

The young couple wearing the "Where no one has gone before" T-shirts held their arms up toward the sky, as if beckoning some spirit to reveal itself to them.

Several people stared through binoculars at the barely visible installation across the shimmering sand, while others rolled their camcorders at maximum zoom, hoping to see something, anything, even a hint of anything, that they could show their friends when they returned from vacation.

But two men and a woman hung back from the rest, carefully reading the messages on the signs.

NELLIS BOMBING AND GUNNERY RANGE
RESTRICTED AREA
NO TRESPASSING
BEYOND THIS POINT

Warning
This Is a U.S. Air Force Installation
Photography Is Prohibited!

WARNING
U.S. Air Force Installation
It is unlawful to enter this area without
permission of the Installation Commander
Section 21 Internal Security Act 1950; 50 USC 797
While on this installation all personnel and
the property under their control are subject
to search
USE OF DEADLY FORCE AUTHORIZED

PHOTOGRAPHY
OF THIS AREA
IS STRICTLY PROHIBITED
50 USC 795

"Seems a bit unfriendly," Roman said casually. The tension in his voice belying the casualness of the comment.

Greg barely shrugged as he wandered closer to the guide, who was continuing his patter.

"Those of us in the Freedom Ridge Society," the guide said in a serious tone, "have filed papers in federal court to attempt to block the air force's acquisition of this hillside. Along with several local ranchers, we've argued that there is no reason, consistent with a democratic government, to bar people from this last place in the valley that is not completely under air force control. The last place from which their mysterious installation can be seen.

"We believe that America, being the home of freedom and democracy, cannot tolerate 'black projects' like this one. It is our steadfast belief that the American people have a right to know what is down there, what they've been doing for the last thirty years, and why it has been kept secret for so long."

He paused, mustering all the drama he could.

"Failing that, we believe the Constitution demands that we be allowed to maintain our monitoring of whatever dark secrets they so tightly protect down there."

His assistant started handing out flyers to the people.

"We urge you all to sign this letter to the governor of Nevada, to our senators, the secretary of defense, and the president, demanding that these cosmic secrets be revealed to a waiting world." He paused. "I'll be happy to answer your questions."

As the tourists' questions began, Greg pulled what appeared to be an old-fashioned video camera from his bag, the kind attached by a cable to a battery pack in the camera case. He pointed it across the desert, not at the installation, but at the grounds between it and him.

"What do *you* think is going on there?" one of the tourists asked eagerly.

"I have my own thoughts, seen some things and all." The guide smiled enigmatically. "But the essence of the Freedom Ridge Society's argument is that monitoring from this hillside is the most inefficient means for answering those questions." He gestured across the desert at the barely seen shimmer of a base. "The answers are over there. From here, we can only watch and wonder."

"Why don't you just drive over there?" the woman asked with genuine curiosity. "It doesn't seem that far."

The guide chuckled. "First, you can't get permission from the installation commander, like it says on the signs, because the air force denies that the place exists."

"But I can see it," someone said.

The guide shrugged. "Apparently the air force can't. Second, no one's ever gotten very far beyond this point without being intercepted by security." He looked around for something behind the tourists. A few moments later, he smiled. "As I was saying . . ." He pointed at a nearby ridge.

A white Jeep Cherokee was parked there, seemingly watching them. Two men in camouflage fatigues clearly staring at them from behind the tinted windshield.

"This is still public land. For the moment, at least." He paused. "Despite that, there are motion detectors and other stuff all over the place. I've never been up here when they, whoever they are exactly, didn't show up eventually. Sometimes in the Jeeps, sometimes on foot. I've even seen them patrolling in helicopter gunships."

As everyone snapped pictures, a woman wandered over to the guide. She was in her twenties, wearing a button-down-the-front miniskirt and mostly unbuttoned top over a bronzed, firm, disturbing body.

"Are we in any danger?" she asked breathlessly.

The guide wiped his forehead as he tried to peek down her blouse. "As long as we stay here, uh, we're fine. I've seen all this and a lot more besides before."

The girl smiled, moving closer to him. "I bet there's a lot of things you've seen."

"Yeah."

She walked past, brushing against him as she did. "And all from way up here?"

"Well . . . some nights there are ways down partway into the valley."

"Really?" She sounded excited. "God, that sounds really dangerous. And exciting," she added.

Roman glanced at the girl, smiled, then walked over to Greg.

"Magda will know everything he knows soon enough." He laughed. "Probably before we get down from this filthy hot mountain. I told you she was worth bringing in from Cleveland."

Greg put the camera away, seeming to fiddle with something in the camera bag as he did. "I hope so."

Roman moved between the rest of the tour group and the bag. Screening anyone from seeing the sensors hidden within. "What's wrong?"

As he straightened, Greg nodded out at the desert below them. "There's a damned forest of plug-nasties down there."

"Such as?"

Greg shrugged. "I'll have to run the telemetry through Foss's computer to be sure, but I saw signatures for motion detectors, microwave sensors, ammonia sniffers, and a few things even I haven't seen before."

The experienced Gypsy thief shook his head. "You lost me with the ammonia sniffers."

Greg was studying the men in the Jeep. "Very nasty stuff. Almost no way to beat them." He shouldered the bag, beginning to stroll back toward the group. "Only three animals in the world secrete ammonia. Vampire bats, monkeys, and man. Out here, I think you can safely eliminate monkeys. Vampire bats have never gotten this far north that I know of. So if the sniffers get a hit . . ." His voice trailed off as the same picture flashed before both men. "These sniffers can probably spot a man from twenty meters out. Just from his sweat."

Roman shook his head. "Someone does not want us coming through the front door."

Greg nodded. "Happens," he mumbled as he walked away.

As the tour started back down the hill a half hour later, Magda almost wrapped around the happy guide, Greg trailed behind. He stopped after everyone else had gone around the bend of the trail, then turned back toward the installation that could barely be seen in the distance amid the failing light.

"Linus, Linus, Linus," he said softly. "This one, even you'd be proud of."

Several hours later, Roman pulled the car to a stop outside a run-down warehouse in South Las Vegas. A young man in jeans and a UNLV T-shirt wandered over to them. He glanced in the car, then leaned in the driver's window.

"Got a light, friend?"

Roman shook his head. "Don't smoke."

The man shrugged. "What about the car lighter?"

"It's broken."

The man nodded, turned, walking away as casually as he'd come.

A moment after he disappeared around the corner, the large metal overhead door to the warehouse opened.

Roman shut his lights as he pulled into the darkened entrance. As soon as the door closed behind him, there was a popping sound as the large overhead lights were turned back on.

The large, main bay of the warehouse had been divided into three sections.

By the door, there were five other vehicles of various types. All older, battered, nondescript. All being gone over by Deo with two other men in tow.

The middle section was divided into cubicles, work areas, improvised conference rooms with maps spread across them, an area with hundreds of photographs of various places being pored over. All filled with ten or more people, men and women, busily studying, explaining, planning, rehearsing.

The final, smallest section had been converted into an impromptu living area where old women prepared meals, sewed clothes, watched the children. All the while making sure that the occupants of the men's and women's sides made it to the "proper" sleeping areas, whenever they came in to rest.

It had taken the better part of a month for Roman to put together this crew of Gypsy specialists. The call had gone out to New York, Cleveland, Detroit, Chicago, Milwaukee, Los Angeles, and San Jose, the major Gypsy population centers in America. Specialists in forgery, con games, second-story break-ins, pickpocketing, seducing, planning, were all contacted.

But only people personally known by someone in the family Peterkezs. Then, only after Grandmother Peterkezs had checked the cards on them. Finally, after passing interviews by Lazslo and Roman, and after Malika had checked their palms, they were told where to be and when.

No one ever asked to know more, either. It was enough to know the huge amount they were being paid. That, in and of itself, told them the two things they needed to know most of all.

The risk in this *game* was immense.

And any act of disloyalty would be repaid upon their families.

So seventeen people had come, along with their most immediate families, to this warehouse in Las Vegas.

"Praise be the Lord in bringing you back to me, my love." Malika smiled as she came over to Roman as he got out of the car. "For your return as well, Gregory," she added casually after embracing her husband.

She held out two baskets to them. They emptied their pockets into them, Gypsy style. A Gypsy on the play keeps his pockets empty whenever not actually in the play.

A police raid is easier dealt with if nothing is found on you.

She handed the baskets to a preteen girl standing beside her. The girl hurried away with them.

Greg walked around, opening the trunk. Malika snapped her fingers and another girl came hurrying up. Greg handed her his camera bag.

"Think you can carry it?"

She smiled up at him. "Of course, sir."

He smiled back. "Take it to Mr. Fosselis."

"Immediate, sir." The girl almost raced away to a steel staircase that led up to an office suite suspended from the ceiling.

"You should've seen her work, my love," Roman said as he put his arm around his wife. They walked back toward the living area. "Magda is a thing of beauty to behold."

Malika laughed. "Make sure you behold her from afar, my love."

Greg watched them go, then turned, heading for the work area. He found Lazslo, his feet up on a card table, smoking his ever-present cigarette. He raised his eyebrows when he saw Greg.

"It went well?"

"It went. How 'bout here?" Greg looked around, then sat on a soft love seat that had materialized from nowhere a day after the furnishing of the warehouse had been completed, and this area assigned as Lazslo's.

Lazslo handed a carefully drawn map of the streets of Nellis Air Force Base to Greg.

"A very open place," Lazslo said, giving voice for the first time to the thought he'd had in his mind since his three visits to the base in the last two days. "Except maybe the flight line. MPs are there. Not too many, not too smart from their looks, but two at each turnoff to the airstrip and the hangars. But this is only the main part of the main base. I hear that the other bases have better security."

"How many other bases?"

Lazslo shrugged. "The best we tell now, there are maybe eight, nine other bases attached to the main base. Each secret, or discreet anyway. The main base is wide open—like a prostitute on a cold Saturday night. Other places, they're *very* serious about strangers. Some have checkpoints on roads, others you can only reach by flying."

Greg handed him back the map. "What do we have inside?"

"It's early days yet," Lazslo said as he checked a clipboard. "Right now, we have a flower truck, package delivery truck. Aliz starts in the main base beauty shop today. Khrizta in"—he shuffled through some papers on the table—"Enlisted Social and Recreational Services Society, starting tomorrow." He paused. "By the end of the week maybe four, maybe six people inside." He smiled. "Like I said, early days."

Greg stood, patted Lazslo on the back, then headed toward the back of the work area.

"Mr. Gregory?" A youngish man—late teens, early twenties—came hurrying up.

"Uh, Lukacs, right?"

The young man beamed. "Yes, sir. Lukacs Mosognli."

"What do you need?"

"My question for you, Mr. Gregory. Anything you want, anything you need, just ask for Lukey." He paused, apparently uncomfortable. "That's what they call me." The not yet man/no longer boy seemed open, enthusiastic, energetic.

"What's your thing, Lukacs?"

The boy beamed when Greg called him by his full name. "Crib man," he said with genuine pride. "Second stories, lockboxes, safes, just like you." He paused, a look of sudden embarrassment flying across his face. "Well, not like you," he said softly. "But I think I could be. If you'd let me apprentice to you," he said with unintended emphasis. He stiffened, as if expecting Greg to slap him down.

Greg looked into the young Gypsy's eager eyes, saw his pride, his belief in himself, his certain knowledge that the world was his for the taking.

"Come on," he said as he started off again. Lukacs fell into step alongside. "What's your job here?"

They started up the steel staircase.

"So far just commercial break-ins. Cracker boxes like the State Department of Unemployment to plant our people's records; then Nevada State Department of Justice, Las Vegas Annex to get the right computer codes so Mr. Fosselis could place the security clearances." He paused. "Nothing challenging."

Greg used his key to let them into the upstairs office suite. Megan looked up, then smiled at him.

"If I had a staff like this back at WIN, we'd have blown *60 Minutes* off the air years ago," she said in a cheery voice. "They're smart, fast, never let up, ask when they don't know something; there's even a couple of college degrees among them!"

"So you're making progress?"

She gestured at the bank of four televisions mounted on the wall behind her. "They've found six videos on the area already. Even one *I* did and forgot about." She leaned close to him. "I've learned not to ask where they got them."

"And?"

"We'll be ready in about ten days. A week if I stay out of their way." She hurried away to oversee the installation of a sophisticated video mixing board that had mysteriously appeared four hours after she'd complained about its lack.

Greg gestured at Lukacs, who had stepped back discreetly during the conversation. They walked through a door at the end of the room.

Foss, gulping down large mugs of heavily sugared coffee, glanced up, then turned back to his computer monitor.

"Too soon. I need another hour, maybe two," he grunted as he took a CD from an assistant.

Greg shook his head at the man's pallor, at his trembling hands, then led Lukacs into the last office.

It was largely empty, a worktable with tools spread across it on one side, a large desk on the other.

"You know what a 'pop' is, Lukacs?"

The boy pulled himself away from a wide-eyed inspection of the specialized tools. "Sure. It's using a high-powered magnet with a soft plastic probe to fool an electronically controlled tumbler system into thinking the right key has been turned."

Greg nodded approvingly. "Ever do one?"

The young man shook his head. "No. I run across the situation a couple of times, but I never did it."

"Why not?"

"Didn't have the equipment," the young man said hurriedly. "Besides," he added in a quieter voice, "I'm not sure I know how, so I didn't want to take the risk of setting off an alarm." He looked down at the floor, speaking in a low, sad voice. "I passed on the marks instead."

Greg studied him intensely for nearly a minute. "Hand me that blue pack."

Lukacs did as he was told.

"How are your reading skills?" Greg asked as he rummaged through the gym bag.

"I was in and out of school through twelfth grade. And I sat in on some college classes."

Greg finally found what he was looking for. He tossed a beat-up, old, dog-eared pamphlet and a thin book across the desk.

"*Universal Principles in Lock, Tumbler, and Driver Systemology* by Linus Yale, Jr.," the boy read. "And *Nobody's Safe: A 21st-Century Guide to the Vulnerabilities of 20th-Century Locking Technologies* by Victor Hadeon." He looked up at Greg. "Yale I know. But who's Victor Hadeon?"

Greg was busy looking at some U.S. Geological Survey terrain maps that lay on his desk. "Read them." His tone was clearly dismissive.

"Thanks, Mr. Gregory." He turned to leave.

"Hey, kid?"

"Yes, sir?"

Greg never looked up. "Stay available."

Three hours later, changed into jeans and a loose sweatshirt, Magda, Roman, and Lazslo sat in Greg's office sipping coffee or tea and reviewing the results of the day.

"The flight comes from someplace called Nellis North Field once a week," Magda said confidently. "It arrives at the installation sometime before dawn, lets off about twenty-five men and women, then takes off again. It comes back about an hour or so after sundown on the same day to pick them up."

"Who are they?" Roman asked.

"Mostly maintenance people. Byron, my horny little expert from the Freedom Ridge Society, thinks they also use the flight to rotate base personnel."

"Procedures?"

"At North Field, he claims to have seen them go through triple security and credential checks before boarding. Same thing when they get off at the installation. But next to nothing when they leave. Just in a hurry to load their stuff and get out."

Lazslo shook his head. "He must've missed something. You check going, you check coming, no?"

Greg shrugged. "It's the system. Set up to keep people out, not in."

Magda sipped her tea. "Whatever. One thing's certain. No one who's not supposed to is gonna get on that plane in North Field or off at the installation."

"We could go for maintenance," Roman offered. "Start from the main base, then maybe . . ."

Lazslo shook his head again. "Our people couldn't pass that level of security checking."

"Take too long anyway," Greg added.

"We try anyway," Roman said while Magda checked the notes she'd made in her car after leaving the sleeping tour guide. "Maybe also try to ID some of these 'occasionals' too."

Greg only grunted as he returned his concentration to a spot on the wall.

"The installation itself," Magda continued, "is approximately thirteen miles due east of Freedom Ridge. It's made up of eight buildings, six hangars, and two runways. The long one, which is on a northwest to southeast access, and a shorter one that crosses it a third of the way up from the southeast end. The building with the, uh"—she suddenly looked uncomfortable—"uh . . . our mark is the middle-sized one, third from the south fence. Or so he says. I don't know."

She was quiet for a long time. "The guy's off in the ozone sometimes, talking about stuff like 'Spaceship Earth' and all, but he's got photos, maps, authentic-looking documents that seem to give him some credibility. I shot three rolls of film after he gave out. Goran's developing them now."

For not the first time in the meeting, Roman and Lazslo openly admired the Gypsy seducer, sympathizing with (and slightly envying) the innocent young man who had so easily given up his innermost secrets to Magda's "talents."

But Greg just stared at the wall. "What else?"

Magda shrugged. "He also thinks there's underground facilities connecting the surface buildings."

"Thinks or knows?" This from Lazslo.

She shrugged. "He says 'I know' so much it loses a lot of its meaning. My guess? It's a suspicion."

"Swell," Greg said beneath his breath.

Magda nodded. "The little walking erection is an asshole, no question. But he sure does talk a good game about this stuff, I'll give him that."

Greg waved for her to continue.

"Well, except for the pictures, that's about it. Oh, one more thing. I'm not sure if it's important or not, but the little guy kept whispering something about how he had a way to get closer to the installation sometimes."

Greg appeared bored. "What'd he say?"

She finished her tea, then put the large glass down. "He said something about new moons and broken ladders." She shrugged in response to the skeptical expressions on the Gypsy men's faces. "Might have been the beers."

"Or he's trying to get you out on the desert at night to get into your pants," Roman offered.

"Could be." She paused. "Could be something else. You want me to follow up? I mean the guy's harmless and all."

Roman glanced at Greg, who was looking through the papers on his desk. "How'd you leave him?"

Magda smiled. "Happy."

Roman looked back at Greg, who was now studying one of the terrain maps.

"We'll let you know," Roman said as she stood to leave.

"Were those his exact words?" Greg asked without looking up.

"Which?" Magda said from the door.

"The thing about broken ladders."

She thought for a moment, then took a step back into the room. "It might have been something like 'broken ladders' or 'ladders that break' or . . ."

"*Lateral* Break?" For the first time Greg looked up, and the fire in his eyes froze everyone in the room.

"It could've been," she said slowly.

Greg circled something on the map. "When's the next new moon?"

"Twelve days," all three Gypsies answered at once.

Greg nodded, then leaned back in his chair.

Roman dismissed Magda, made sure the door was secured, then he and Lazslo walked over to the desk.

"You have something." Roman's words were a statement of fact, not a question.

Greg turned the map to face the men. "You guys read a topographical map?"

The men leaned over, studying the confusing jumble of swirls, arcs, and broken lines of the blue and white map.

Greg closed his eyes. "Start at Freedom Ridge."

"Right."

"Follow that first canyon to the north."

"White Sides," Lazslo said. "I see it."

"It intersects another geographic depression about two and a half kilometers to the north. A six-to-twelve-foot-deep depression that cuts into the desert, for almost four and a half kilometers."

"So?" both men said as they looked up.

"What's it called?"

They ran their fingers along the jagged line until they saw the small print of the name.

"You have the luck of Saint Michael himself, old friend," Roman said after looking into the equally surprised eyes of his brother-in-law.

"But won't they have their machines there also?"

Greg seemed to ignore him, beginning to make notes on a pad. "An unstable geologic fissure or break that runs below the line of sight of any camera or sniffer, too unstable for motion detectors, and probably invisible under the new moon." He paused. "No. They'd start their electronic minefield at the mouth of the fault; maybe even a little distance away to play safe."

He glanced up at the calendar. "We go on the twenty-third. The new moon, twelve days from now."

Lazslo shook his head as he hurried out to set in motion the complicated steps that had already been agreed on.

"*Benci Joska,*" he muttered as he left.

"*Jonka,*" Roman said as he picked up the phone and dialed an extension. "Sasha? Roman. Aerial photographs and anything else you can get on coordinates"—he checked the map in front of him—"217-928-175, page 4,356."

He listened as the coordinates were read back to him.

"That's right. Lateral Break, Nevada." He hung up the phone, staring down at Greg until he looked up.

"Yes?"

"You are very lucky, my brother."

Greg locked eyes with him, slowly stood, walking to a heavily curtained window. He parted the curtains, staring out at the slight pinkish blue line that would soon be the sunrise.

"Let's hope I stay that way."

Early morning in Las Vegas is the strangest time of the day. It's as if the entire town agrees to take a pause. A brief moment out of time to take its breath, straighten its gaudy clothing—then prepare for the young joggers, the seniors at the slots, the power brunchers, and the morning-afterers.

A well-worn Japanese compact slowly moved down the empty streets of the city's East Side, seemingly the only waking creature in this forgotten, dirty part of Las Vegas. It pulled to a stop half a block away from a coffee shop that looked more abandoned than anything else.

"Ten minutes, kid," Foss said as he started to get out of the car.

The nineteen-year-old Gypsy driver looked worried. "You got important meeting soon, Mr. Fosselis. Maybe you should . . ."

Foss smiled. "We'll be back in plenty of time. Besides, I gotta get some breakfast, right?" His face took on a look of deep worry. "No way to tell when I might get another chance." He got out, slamming the door closed.

The driver hesitated, then grabbed his jacket from the backseat as he climbed out. "I go with you, then, okay?" He forced cheeriness into his voice. "For the walk, okay?"

His orders had been clear. Foss was to be protected. From everything except himself.

"Forget it, kid," the old man said without turning around. "My friends are only expecting *me*." He headed down the street toward the coffee shop.

The driver watched him go, rubbing his chin as he tried to figure out what to do. Finally, deciding that the letter as well as the spirit of his instructions were the same in this case, he let Foss go.

Pulling on his jacket against the morning's damp, he walked back to the trunk of the car, opened it, then reached into the rimless spare tire. He pulled out a Russian Tokarev semiautomatic pistol.

Jacking a round into the chamber, he thumbed down the hammer, then wandered over to a nearby doorway, settling in to wait for the drug transaction to be completed. His eyes never leaving the coffee shop's door after Foss stepped through it.

Checking his watch to be sure exactly when ten minutes would be up.

Foss stopped just inside the door. The waitress and cook barely looked up at him.

"I'm looking for Mikey D," he said in a whisper to the waitress.

She nodded toward the booth, then walked back to the kitchen, followed by the cook.

One of the men in the booth stood, turning to face the old man. "Whachu want, Gramps?"

Foss looked into the young, angry, soulless eyes. "Tambo sent me."

The young man seemed skeptical as he patted Foss down for weapons or a wire. "Tambo, yo? How you know Tambo?"

"A guy I know from shaky."

Foss noticed that the other man from the booth never turned around, just kept playing with the straw in his drink.

"Who you know in shaky, old man? Gimme some tags," he demanded.

"TNT Washington. Flatman Corinth. Mustafa Sixty-nine."

The hostile young man studied him closely, then the angry stare was replaced by a smile.

"Yo! Mighty Mikey D! Gramps is cool." He stepped out of Foss's way. "Take a seat, Gramps."

Foss moved past the man and sat in the booth opposite the other man. He watched while the first man moved to the coffee shop's door, checked the street, then coughed in an obvious signal.

The man across the table was older, better dressed, seemed more impressive than the first man. He was in his twenties, face impassive, clothes and jewelry expensive but sedate.

"I don't do hits, old man," he said in a bored voice. "You want to deal with me, we talkin' ounces or better."

"That's no problem," Foss said as he kept his hands on the table.

The man was clearly studying him. "Okay," he said after a couple of minutes. "What you need?"

"Straight shit."

"I got Pale Horse, Special D, Free Man, and Homicide right now. You want to wait, I can special-order some Dead Man in less than a day. Of course that's got a special surcharge on the order."

"Tell me about the Special D."

The man raised his eyebrows. "A man with taste. I like that." He leaned forward. "Three hundred fifty an ounce, and I guarantee it ain't stepped on more than four times. Break maybe another two, maybe three times an' not lose no edge."

Foss thought about it.

An ounce of chemically synthetic heroin, more potent than the regular with a longer high and fewer aftereffects. Cut four times, it would be too lethal. But cut another four . . . and it would last him maybe a week.

"Let's have a taste," he finally said.

The man held up two fingers to his assistant, who left the front door and disappeared into the men's room. "How much we talking, old man?"

"Let's say a half to start. If the shit's good, we'll start talking pounds."

Foss had no intention of ever buying from the young dealer again, but there was no reason for him to know that. Ounces of the special heroin were hard enough to find as is.

"Twenty-eight." The dealer paused. "But we get tight, we might be able to work a discount for bulk."

Foss politely joined in the man's light laughter.

Out on the street, nine minutes had passed.

The young driver checked his watch a final time, checked that the automatic was securely in his waistband, then started to step out of the storefront.

Instantly he froze.

Whether he'd heard something, seen some movement out of the corner of his eye, or if it was just the instincts of a man raised from birth to feel such things, he might never know. But he knew that there were others on the street around him.

A careful look around confirmed that men in black outfits were stealthily moving down the street toward the coffee shop. Men carrying large ugly weapons, shields, radios. Men whose identity was made clear by the lettering on their jackets.

When he was sure their attention was riveted on the coffee shop, he slipped out of the storefront, melting away in the early morning light, to watch from a safer distance.

Forty-five minutes later, Roman lightly knocked on Greg's office door.

ELEVEN

T HE ROOM WAS like much of the rest of Las Vegas. Far too
clean for Foss's taste.

An interrogation room should be dimly lit, maybe by a single,
unshaded bulb hanging from a bare wire. There should be vulgar
graffiti scratched on the walls; peeling paint; uncomfortable wooden
chairs. Maybe the smell of puke and piss choking off whatever humanity there might be in the room.

Not *clean*.

But the recessed fluorescent lighting amid the acoustical tile ceiling gave the room an almost cheery feeling. The table was new, or
new-looking; chrome and plasticine, with three comfortable, padded chairs around it.

Foss closed his eyes, trying to force the image from his brain,
concentrating on how his body was steadily falling apart.

It had been just over three hours since the police had killed
Mighty Mikey D and arrested his assistant. Three long hours of refusing to answer questions, of asking for a lawyer, of trying to ignore
the growing ravages of the withdrawal that fought him for possession of his body.

He was drenched in sweat, his shirt plastered to his trembling
body. His hands shook as he gulped the Styrofoam cup of coffee
with five sugars the detectives had given him. A crust was forming
around his lips and eyes, while a muscle in his cheek was beginning
to twitch erratically.

And the pounding in his head sounded like cannon fire.

The interrogation room door opened, and an older detective walked into the room carrying a file.

"Take a break, Jimmy," he said quietly.

Reluctantly the younger detective who'd spent the last twenty minutes screaming at Foss to "give it up or we'll make sure you *never* fix again" straightened, stared daggers at the quivering silent man in the chair, then left. He slammed the door to the tiny room loud enough to make Foss jump.

The older detective settled into the seat across from Foss, spreading a file out in front of him. "Jimmy's young," the man said easily. "Seen too many Steven Segal movies. Can I get you another cup?"

"No. Thank you."

Although his vision was clouded, and sound hallucinations played at the corners of his consciousness, Foss suddenly steadied himself. This new man sounded . . . dangerous.

"Well," the man continued in a casual manner, "let's see what we've got."

He moved some papers around, adjusted the file folder, then cleaned his glasses with the collar of his shirt. "Well, your name is Robert Thomas Fosselis. You were born in 1935, graduated high school in 1952, college in 1956, then four years in the army through ROTC."

He looked directly at Foss for the first time. A pleasant, noncommittal smile on his face. "Marvelous things, computers. But then, you'd know all about that, wouldn't you, Foss? They call you Foss, don't they?"

"I'm sick. I need a doctor." Foss looked all around the room. Anywhere but into those calm, steady eyes.

"Yeah, I know." He returned to the file. "Well, it says here that you do the Internet thing for a high-roller, crib man named Gregory Picaro. Help him set up scores, get around alarms, whatever. You seen your old friend lately?" the detective said in an innocent tone without looking up.

"He's dead," Foss grunted as he tried to blink the sweat from his eyes.

The detective nodded amiably. "That's what it says here. Picaro, Gregory. Deceased about six months ago." He suddenly looked confused. "But you see my problem, Foss, is that this says you're dead too."

Foss froze.

"You a ghost, Foss?"

No answer.

"It was *another* Robert Thomas Fosselis, born on your birthday, that went to your high school and college, Foss?"

Again, no answer.

The detective shrugged. "Be that way. I've got all morning."

There was a knock on the door, then the first detective came in, followed by another young man, this one in a better suit than the first.

"Denying my client his constitutional rights, Dominguez?"

The older detective stood up. "Just passing the time of day, counselor."

The new man shook his head, then stepped past the detectives. "John Gavilan. I'm with the Public Defender's Office. I'll be defending you." He pressed a card into Foss's hand. "How long ago did you ask for a lawyer?"

Foss wiped his face with an offered tissue from a box in Gavilan's briefcase. "Don't know. They took my watch."

Gavilan pulled out a legal pad, began to write, then stopped. "You guys still here?" he said without looking around.

The older detective scooped up his file, then half pushed the younger one out, closing the door behind them.

"Okay, let's get down to basics. Did you tell the detectives anything?"

"No."

"Smart. Don't. They are *not* your friends. They want to talk to you from this point on, you tell them to call me. And don't say anything if I'm not there, right?"

"Okay."

Gavilan began to write. As he wrote, he referred to his copy of the booking slip. After three minutes, he looked up. "You're being charged with five counts of possession of a controlled narcotic and possession of said narcotic with intent to sell. Said narcotic being synthetic heroin. Do you understand that?"

Foss shivered as he nodded.

"We'll get you a doctor," the lawyer said with a touch of genuine sympathy. "But we have to get through this first." He handed Foss his coffee. "Do you have your own attorney, or would you like someone else to defend you?"

"No."

"What about family or friends? Is there anyone you'd like notified?"

Foss stiffened, thoughts of Greg, of the Gypsies, of the warehouse, pounding against his brain, demanding voice. Demanding to get someone here *now*! Someone who knew what was going on, who would get him out.

"No. There's nobody." He fought off another paroxysm of pain. "I'm alone."

Two hours later, after three more defendant intakes, Gavilan returned to his cramped office. Although it was only a little after noon, he was already exhausted.

Physically and mentally.

His intern/assistant came hurrying up almost as soon as he saw him. "That bad?" he asked as Gavilan took off his jacket to change his shirt.

Gavilan rolled his eyes. "Four, three of them junkies. One of them jonesing like you can't believe." He pulled off his sweat-soaked shirt, taking another out of the file cabinet's bottom drawer. "Had to find a bed at Valley for him."

His assistant took the files out of the briefcase.

"Any appearances?"

Gavilan nodded. "Payne on a DUI and Kerellan on an assault back-to-back at three-thirty. Samarino wants to plead out; and Smith, the joneser, D.A.'s putting off charging until he decides about going federal."

"Full day," the assistant said as he sorted the files, "and I hate to make it worse. But . . ."

Gavilan froze, his shirt halfway buttoned. "What?"

"Prof wants to see you."

"When?"

"Yesterday."

Gavilan took a deep breath. "Shit."

He tucked in his shirt, grabbing his jacket in the same motion, as he headed out the door at a trot.

"Prof" was Senior Assistant Public Defender Linwood Capers. A bleeding-from-the-heart McGovern liberal, the man believed no one was ever guilty of anything. Only the police were the bad guys in their "constant trampling of John Q. Public's civil rights!"

A former prize-winning academic, Capers had joined the P.D.'s office out of "a moral responsibility to stop teaching and start do-ing."

Translation: he'd lost his tenure.

As a former favorite professor for the chief public defender, he'd immediately been given the senior job.

A job that would otherwise have been Gavilan's.

Gavilan knocked on the door, then let himself into the corner office. "You wanted to see me, Lin?"

Capers waved him in.

"Come in, John. Mr. Kilbourne, APD Gavilan."

For the first time, Gavilan noticed the man sitting in the corner of the office. He was old, expressionless, with his left leg extended stiffly in front of him and a heavy teak cane to the side of his chair. He seemed to be staring through the office windows, concentrating intently on the gray, somewhat stormy clouds.

A description that somehow also described what was going on behind the coldest eyes Gavilan had ever seen.

"Did you do an intake this morning on an addict arrested in a raid on the East Side?" Capers seemed to hang on the answer.

"Yeah," Gavilan answered cautiously as he studied the old man. "He was in bad shape, so the riding ADA agreed to put him in detox before arraignment."

Capers wrote it all down. "Anything unusual?"

Gavilan shook his head. "Something on the guy's ID turned up funny. Metro's running a double check on it. What's your interest in this, Mr. Kilbourne?" he asked the old man without pause.

"Mr. Kilbourne's with the Nuclear Regulatory Commission, Domestic Counterintelligence Investigations Division," Capers said flatly. Adding venom to each word as if the sound itself made him ill. "He has an offer for us."

"Yeah?"

Kilbourne smiled a meaningless smile. "Gentlemen," he began in a raspy voice, "I'm here for the benefit of your client, I assure you. The government just wants to help a valued employee out of a difficult situation."

"As the government is so well known for doing," Capers added sarcastically.

Gavilan ignored him. "I don't even know all the facts of the case yet. So how did you get here before me?"

"That's what they do," Capers said quickly.

Kilbourne looked at the man behind the desk, then back to the young lawyer. "Perhaps, Mr. Gavilan, we shouldn't take up your superior's time with so trivial a matter."

Gavilan studied the nonexpressive face, then nodded. "My office is down the hall. Number 2394."

Kilbourne stood, nodding at Capers. "Thank you for your time, sir." He limped out of the office, leaning heavily on the cane.

Gavilan looked at his boss, shrugged, then stood to leave.

"John?"

"Yeah."

Capers walked out from behind his desk. "You cut any deals, I want three copies, approved by me, before it goes in front of a judge." He looked out at the man waiting in the hall. "I'll also send over the wiretap sweepers as soon as they get through in here."

Gavilan sighed. Capers saw government plots in the changing of the weather. He shook his head, then left. He led Kilbourne down to his office.

"You never answered my question," he said as they sat down.

"Which question was that?" Kilbourne said quietly. He arranged himself in the uncomfortably small chair.

"How'd you get here?"

"That's not terribly important, is it, sir?" He smiled—a broken thing that stopped at his mouth and wasn't reflected in the dead eyes. "That I *am* here, and prepared to help, is."

The public defender might not see government plots where his boss did, but he recognized bullshit when he heard it. "Whatever that means. What's your interest in Smith?"

"Fosselis, actually."

"Whatever."

Kilbourne handed a personnel file across the desk, marked "Fosselis, R. T." "Mr. Fosselis is a computer researcher for the NRC's Sandia, New Mexico, facility. A brilliant, if somewhat troubled, man. Several months ago, he disappeared, we now realize because of his unfortunate addiction. He has apparently been suffering from delusions, drug-induced psychoses, and other severe mental defects."

He paused, intently watching Gavilan flip through the file. "He also was quite brilliant in his work and continues to be in possession of several, shall we say, highly classified pieces of information. As a result, we at the NRC would like to see Mr. Fosselis in a federal treatment program rather than a state penitentiary." A brief, concerned pause. "I'm sure you understand."

Gavilan continued reading. "Cops say he's an associate of a known burglar."

The older man smiled spasmodically. A thing that may or may not have happened. "They are quite mistaken, Mr. Gavilan." The briefest of pauses. "I'm sure if you check with them again, they will now support the government's view of Mr. Fosselis."

Gavilan put the file aside, beginning to wonder if his boss's paranoia was contagious. "Assuming what you say can be verified . . ."

"I assure you it can."

"I can just imagine." Gavilan pulled over a pad and began to write. "What's your offer?"

"We will see that all state charges pending against Mr. Fosselis are dropped; that the remaining federal charges are held in abeyance, anticipating dismissal, while Mr. Fosselis undergoes evaluation/treatment at a federal treatment facility here in Nevada." He handed a glossy brochure across the desk. "We have rather a nice one right here, at Nellis Air Force Base, North Field. Arrangements have been made."

Something smelled wrong. About the offer, about the story, about Kilbourne. But the offer was better than any Gavilan could expect from the D.A.

"I'll run it past my client," he said as he began looking at the brochure.

"I was hoping we might avoid that, Mr. Gavilan."

"Why?" He put the brochure down, folded his hands on top of the desk, and waited.

"It is the hope of my superiors—shared, I'm certain, by the police and District Attorney's Office—that this could be dealt with between the two of us and the judge. The assistant district attorney will move for the evaluation, you concur, and Mr. Fosselis ceases to be of any concern."

Beyond the patent violation of process that the suggestion contained, there was something chilling about the tone of those words.

"Move without Fosselis's informed consent?" Gavilan leaned back in his chair. "Are you serious?"

Kilbourne winced as he leaned forward. "You've seen him. Do you really think he's competent to deal with any of this? Let us deal with him, Mr. Gavilan. For his sake."

A silence settled between them. Kilbourne stared expressionlessly, while Gavilan went over it all in his mind, searching for the most minute loophole.

"I'll want the offer in writing," he finally said. "In triplicate, by end of business today if possible. Signed off on by the U.S. Attorney for the Southern District and a reachable official from the NRC."

Again the spasmodic smile. "That presents no difficulties."

Gavilan felt a chill go through him. "In the meantime, I'll talk to Fosselis again, as well as the attending physician."

"Agreed," Kilbourne said stiffly, then rose, nodded at the younger man, and limped away.

After he'd gone, before leaving for his first court appearance of the day (then a visit to Foss in the hospital), Gavilan stuck his head in his boss's office.

Just to ask when the wiretap sweepers were coming.

Valley Hospital on the edge of western Las Vegas is one of the most state-of-the-art medical centers in the country. Which you'd never suspect by looking at it. The art deco, low-slung buildings gathered together in the almost desert setting, to suggest a retirement community, or maybe a shopping mall. Anything but a thousand-bed hospital for the residents of the gambling capital.

Half an hour after Foss's arraignment had been postponed—on the motion of a pale, sweating, *very senior* assistant district attorney—Gavilan pulled into a doctor's space, then headed inside.

A yellow taxi seemed to hesitate just outside the parking lot, then let out its passenger as soon as Gavilan had gone inside.

The drug treatment wing with its detoxification center was on the third floor to the rear of a side building. After identifying himself, then going through two locked doors, Gavilan was shown to the senior attending physician.

"I need an update on the condition of Robert Fosselis."

The doctor checked through a stack of charts. "Right. Metro P.D. hold." He read through the chart, then closed it with a snap. "He's a junkie."

Gavilan wasn't smiling. "Doctor, please."

"Look, I've got thirty-two other people here right now in a facility designed to hold twenty-five. He's a junkie, and he's deep into withdrawal. Other than that . . ."

"Can I talk to him?"

The doctor shrugged. "Sure. Why not? But don't expect any answers."

"You dope him up?"

The doctor shook his head. "Not the way you think." He reopened the chart. "Your Mr. Fosselis is a man in his sixties, easily thirty-five pounds underweight, with one massive addiction to heroin. The veins in both arms are mostly collapsed, his legs aren't much better either. His withdrawal had reached a point where we felt that methadone stabilizing was dangerous. So we gave him a mild tranq, some anticonvulsants, and check on him every twenty minutes or so. That's about all we can do, until the junk in his system works its way out."

"Can he talk? Reason rationally?"

Again, the irritating shrug. "What's rational? He's in 198, why don't you find out for yourself."

After making some notes, Gavilan wandered down the hall to Foss's room.

A male nurse was reading a betting tip sheet in a chair by the man's bed. "Can I help you?" he said without looking up.

"I'm his lawyer." Gavilan looked down on the barely conscious man in the bed, then over to the nurse. "I didn't know this ward had private nursing."

The man shrugged. "It doesn't. Mr. Kilbourne thought—"

"Get out," Gavilan interrupted in a strong voice that was matched by a look of severe annoyance. "Kilbourne's got no deal yet. Until he does, I expect my client's privacy to be protected."

The nurse put down the sheet, slowly stood up, his every move suggesting a tightly held-back threat. "I'll have to call Mr. Kilbourne," the man said in a low tone.

"You do that. And tell him he tries a stunt like this again, all deals are off." He closed the door in the nurse's face. Finally, after several deep, cleansing breaths, he turned back to the man in the bed.

Foss was dressed in clean hospital pajamas, his hair was combed back, and he'd been shaved. But his arms were secured to his sides by a strap across his chest. His wrists in leather shackles tied to the bed's railing, his ankles similarly secured, with a strap across his legs.

Despite the air-conditioning in the room, he was sweating fiercely, his eyebrows twitched, the veins on the sides of his neck stood out, and his eyes were bloodshot, weepy, and crusted. They had a painfully stoned look in them.

Gavilan pulled the nurse's chair over by the head of the bed. "Mr. Fosselis?" No answer. "Mr. Fosselis? Foss?"

The man in the bed slowly turned his head to face the public defender.

"Do you know who I am, Foss?"

"Lawyer," Foss said in a subwhisper.

"Good. That's right. I'm your lawyer. Do you remember when we met this morning?"

"Cops. Wouldn't get me . . . doctor."

Gavilan took out a pad. "Stay with me, Mr. Fosselis. I have to ask you some questions."

"Not supposed to . . ." He seemed to drift off.

"I'm your lawyer, remember? Mr. Fosselis? Foss!"

He opened his eyes again. Barely. "Questions," he mumbled.

Gavilan took a deep breath, then began. "Is your true name Robert Thomas Fosselis?"

"Foss. Everybody . . . calls me . . . Foss."

"Were you born in 1935?"

"Yes," Foss said in a dreamy sort of way.

"Are you an employee of the Nuclear Regulatory Commission?"

Foss barely shook his head.

"Are you an expert in computers?"

A thin nod.

"What *do* you do?" Foss closed his eyes, so Gavilan reached out, tapping him lightly on the cheek. "What do you do, Mr. Fosselis? For a living, what do you do?"

"Fuck up, mostly."

Gavilan suppressed a laugh, then tried again. "What do you do with computers?"

There was a long pause, during which Foss seemed to be trying to focus on the young lawyer. "They'll do anything to find us, Greg says."

Gavilan made some notes. "Who's Greg? Who's looking for you?"

"Government."

"You mean the NRC? Is Greg with the NRC?"

"Tell Greg, tell him . . . I'm sorry?"

Gavilan stood, leaning over the semiconscious man. "Who's Greg? Do you want me to contact him?" No answer. "Mr. Fosselis, who's Greg?"

"The best," was all he said before slipping under the influence of his pained, poison-racked body, and the hospital's tranquilizers.

Gavilan sat again, making notes for about ten minutes before repacking his briefcase. At the last minute, he pulled out the copy of the plea agreement that had arrived at his office less than an hour after his meeting with Kilbourne.

He read, then reread, the four-page document that was signed by the local assistant United States Attorney and the head of the Nuclear Regulatory Commission's Las Vegas office. All was in order, exactly as Kilbourne had laid it out in the office. But it all seemed too pat, too easy somehow. Everything too easily set aside and forgotten.

But the reality of the old man in the bed before him was all the argument he really needed. There was no way this frail, burned-out wreck of a man could survive a long prison term. And, at the moment, that seemed the only alternative.

He closed his case, then headed for the door. Halfway there, he stopped, turned around, then carefully pulled up the blanket around the sick old man before leaving.

Two minutes later, the male nurse slipped into the room.

He walked to the night table, reached under it, pulling out a small cassette recorder. He plugged in an earphone, then played it back, all the while looking down on the fitfully sleeping man.

He replaced it beneath the night table, then turned to the addict. "Foss? Come on, Foss! Wake-up time."

No response, so the nurse slapped him hard on each cheek.

Foss groaned, then turned his head the other way.

The nurse bit his lower lip, checked that no one could see through the small window on the room's door, then pulled a syringe out of his pocket. A moment later, he pulled the needle out of Foss's neck.

At first, nothing seemed to happen. Then gradually, the color seemed to return to the old man's face. He moaned in pain, his head snapped back, his eyes opening and closing rapidly. He tried to focus, but the world was cotton wool, fog, and pain.

"Foss!"

"Who?" he wheezed out.

"It's your lawyer, Foss," the nurse said in a deliberately lowered voice. "Remember? Your lawyer?"

"Lawyer." He felt a warmth course through his body, a happily familiar sensation that his fevered brain instantly recognized. "Thank you," he said in a near whimper.

"No problem, Foss. I'm your friend, right? You can trust friends to help you."

"Friend."

"That's right, Foss. I'm your friend. You even gave me a message for Greg, remember? You gave your friend a message for Greg."

Foss licked his dry, cracking lips. "For Greg."

"But you didn't tell me where he is. Foss! Where's Greg? I can't give him the message unless you tell me where he is."

Foss barely nodded. "That's right," he said as his body relaxed for the first time in hours. "You need . . . know where he is. Sorry."

"That's okay, buddy," the nurse said as he took out a pad. "Just tell me where he is and I'll give him the message. I'll make sure he gets it."

Gavilan took off his jacket, then threw it in the trunk of his car along with his briefcase. When he slammed it shut, he flinched as he saw someone standing just behind it.

She was in her twenties, dressed subtle sexy in tight jeans and a tank top with a lightweight jacket.

And she was smiling invitingly at the lawyer from just three feet away. "Hi!"

"Hi," he replied as he pulled himself together.

"You're John Gavilan, right?"

He smiled. "Most of the time. Do I know . . ."

"I saw you in court today. You were very impressive."

Something felt wrong. Nothing he could put his finger on, but there nonetheless. "Is there something I can help you with?"

The woman moved around him, putting her arm through his.

"If I told you that my friend over there behind the light pole had a gun pointed at you, would you come with me, John?"

Gavilan followed her gaze to a man in a hat pulled low, with an overcoat cradled in his arms. Apparently pointed at him. "I don't have much money," he said sullenly.

The woman laughed loosely, with no concern. "Of course not, John," she said as she began to lead him across the parking lot. "You're a public defender." The man with the overcoat in his arms seemed to track with them. "But I won't hold that against you."

A gray van pulled up alongside them, its side door open.

"Go ahead, John." She smiled warmly. "Please."

Taking a deep breath, he stepped into the van.

Instantly he was pulled down onto the floor, strong arms pinning his neck and arms, while others searched him.

"Listen, I told the girl . . ."

"John," the woman said easily from somewhere in the van, "this will be a whole lot easier if you just stay quiet, don't look up, and do what you're told."

He heard a car's trunk open and close, then felt the van start to move.

"I'm not resisting," he said quietly as he stared at the shag carpeting an inch from his face.

He could hear movement around him. No words, but the definite impression of more than two people. Then he heard the familiar sound of his briefcase's clasps snapping open.

Papers rustled, seemed to be passed back and forth, felt the van turning corners. Time seemed to stand still while that iron grip still held him in place.

"John," the woman said after some time, "if we let go of you, you're not going to be a problem, are you?"

"No."

The grips were released.

"Now, John, a friend of mine is going to ask you some questions. Will you be a love and answer them truthfully and fully?"

Panic growing in him from the frightening calmness of the woman's voice, Gavilan nodded slowly.

"Describe Fosselis's condition." A man's voice.

"He's in pretty bad shape. Semiconscious, semicoherent."

"Where's he being held?"

"Third-floor detox."

"Beyond your notes, what has he said to you?"

"Nothing. It's all there."

"Beyond your notes, what has he said to you?" The voice sounded firmer than before.

"I told you, nothing. That's it."

A foot was pressed up against his neck.

"Beyond your notes, what has he said to you?"

"Nothing. Just, just that he was a—a fuckup!" More pressure from the foot. "I swear!"

"Have you or anyone in your office ever heard of this Kilbourne before today?"

Curiosity began to replace Gavilan's fear. "No. In fact, my boss thinks he's part of some government plot or something."

Urgent, indecipherable whispers.

"What kind of plot?"

Despite his position, Gavilan shrugged. "Who knows? It's the way the guy thinks."

Another pause of whispering.

"What does it mean, your note 'Who is Greg?' "

"Just a name the old man mentioned. Something about telling Greg he was sorry."

The pressure from the foot was instantly released.

"Describe the physical layout of the detox ward."

"Uh, I'm not sure."

"John, darling," the woman said in a cautionary tone, "be sure."

Twenty minutes later, the van pulled to a stop. The side door was opened, people got out, then the door was slammed shut.

"You can get up now," the woman said sweetly. "But no sudden movements or foolishness, or my friends outside will have to, well, deal with it. You understand, darling?"

Gavilan nodded, then felt her help him up. He sat down on a bench along the side of the van.

"Can I ask what's going on here?" he said as he rubbed his neck.

The woman was opening a thermos. "You're a lawyer, darling. I'm sure you can ask all sorts of questions." She poured him a cup of clear golden liquid from the thermos.

He sniffed at it, then took a cautious sip. It was a strong, sweet tea. "Who are you people? What's all this interest in Fosselis?"

The woman shrugged. "Just looking after a friend of the family, you might say."

"Or you might not." He took another sip of tea. "How long are we going to be here?"

She smiled. "You'll be released as soon as my friends get back." She paused. "You don't like the company?" she asked in a playfully annoyed voice.

Despite the situation, all he'd been through in the last half hour, Gavilan actually managed to laugh. "Frankly you play a little rough for my tastes."

The woman laughed. "Tastes can change." She tossed an envelope to him.

He thumbed it open, staring at the wad of hundred-dollar bills inside. He slowly looked up at the woman.

"What's this? A bribe?" His voice was choked with confusion.

The woman shook her head. "Just compensation. Call it a private consulting fee. For your time and inconvenience."

"And my silence."

She smiled, a natural, winning smile. "I've always been attracted to intelligent, charming men."

The nurse in Foss's room once again had his head buried in the betting sheet, never noticing as the door was slowly pushed inward. By the time he looked up, it was too late. A man in hospital whites almost flew across the room at him, slamming his head against the wall.

The nurse was quickly and quietly stored in the room's closet.

Foss blinked his eyes open as he felt himself being lifted from the bed.

"Wha . . . What's going on?"

"Shut the hell up, you old pain in the ass," Greg whispered. He helped Lukacs strap Foss into a wheelchair.

The young Gypsy thief cracked the door, peeked through, then nodded. They casually wheeled Foss out into the corridor, toward the inner locked door.

Ten minutes later, Foss and Greg were headed down the highway in their yellow cab. Foss was drinking heavily sugared coffee directly from a thermos Greg had given him, while Greg stared straight ahead. Concentrating not on the road, but on something deep within him.

"Where is everyone?"

Greg kept his eyes straight ahead, his expression one of deep concentration. "Letting your lawyer go, then heading back to the safe house."

Foss studied the intensity of the barely suppressed emotions in his old friend.

"Where we going?" he said weakly.

Greg just continued to drive out into the desert, as if the setting sun was his eventual destination.

□ □ □

Traffic had been stopped for three blocks on all sides of the North Las Vegas warehouse that served as Greg's secret headquarters. Not all at once, but gradually so that nothing would be noticed by the hideout's occupants.

Men in black uniforms, complete with black face masks, came with the sunset. They meticulously moved into the area around the old building, their shoulder-slung MP-5K automatic weapons carrying double banana clips, with flash-bang grenades attached to the straps.

A jail bus with military police guards was parked a block away, waiting for the inevitable prisoners.

A muffled helicopter moved in on the roof of the building, dangling four black-robed commandos forty feet below on ropes. They alighted noiselessly on the roof of the building and moved toward the access points.

Finally, at precisely ten minutes after eight at night, the power was cut to the entire city block.

Almost instantly, explosions seemed to tear through the building. Their obscene vulgarities screaming off the walls of the other nearby concrete and steel structures.

Twenty heavily armed men simultaneously poured into the building. Automatic-weapons fire could be heard raking the inside. The pop/gush of the flash-bangs punctuated the shooting, as smoke began to pour out of the holes that had been blown in the old warehouse's sides.

Three minutes after it began, it was all over. Power was restored and lights flashed on inside the partially burning hulk.

It was empty.

Even emptier than when Roman Peterkezs had first leased it.

Not a stick of furniture, a sheet of paper; not so much as a thread of fabric or gum wrapper was in sight. There were holes in the walls where equipment had been hastily torn out, drag marks in the few carpets that couldn't be easily removed, but no usable sign of who the occupants had been or where they'd disappeared to.

Kilbourne was slowly, painfully helped along the inside of the deserted building, shaking his head as he viewed the signs of the hurried exit. In the upstairs offices, he traced his fingers over the pinholes in the walls where obviously a great many things had been posted for study.

"Nothing, sir," the commander of the assault team reported to him. "Place's picked clean. But neighbors say they were here as recently as six hours ago."

"Thank you, Major." Kilbourne pulled his cell phone out and dialed a number. "We'll bring in Mr. Fosselis and see if he can enlighten us further."

He held the phone close to his ear, listening to ring after ring. On the tenth ring, he held the phone out at arm's length, staring at the compact machine, seeming to will an answer from the other end. Then, from somewhere within himself, sensing the answer.

He hung up.

"Picaro," he said in a bare whisper; then angrily flung the phone across the empty room with enough force for it to lodge in the plasterboard wall.

"Picaro."

TWELVE

THE NEVADA DESERT can be an empty, forbidding place. A place where the most spectacular things can seem lost in nature's vastness.

Or so the man on the Gulfstream Executive jet might have thought had he looked out his window during the day on the seven-minute flight.

But it was the middle of the night. And the man in the wheel-chair, locked in place behind the small conference table, had better things to do than gaze philosophically at the landscape. Now or ever.

Especially now.

He considered the entire flight silly. Using an expensive-to-operate exec-jet to travel the twenty-four miles was just another example of the mind-set of a bloated federal bureaucracy.

A bureaucracy he'd helped bloat.

But he was older now, beginning to see things the way they were, not the way he wanted to. In fact, that was rapidly becoming his curse.

The Secretary reached beneath the table for the oxygen mask he knew would be there. He took long, deep pulls at the life-preserving gas as he tried to steady himself for the meeting ahead.

"Mr. Secretary?" His aide had returned from the cockpit.

"Yes, Paul."

"North Field reports that call sign Kilbourne has arrived, and is standing by."

"Thank you, Paul."

The aide nodded, then turned back toward the front of the plane.

"Paul?"

The man turned around, his practiced but still believable smile instantly on display. "Sir?"

The Secretary took another deep pull on the O^2, then put the mask away. "Stow this thing somewhere after we land. No need for Kilbourne to . . ."

"I'll see to it right away, Mr. Secretary."

"Thank you, Paul."

As he felt the jet bank on its approach to Nellis Air Force Base's North Field, he picked up the file he'd only received minutes before leaving Habitat. The file he hoped would answer at least some of the questions that plagued him.

Five minutes after the jet had parked at the foot of a runway built for aircraft twenty times its size; after it had been surrounded by combat-hardened, heavily armed security troops, the door opened. The Secretary's aide stepped out, walking up to the man who stood by the captain of the guard.

"Mr. Kilbourne."

"How are you, Paul?"

The upwardly mobile aide smiled professionally. "Well, sir." He looked at the obviously braced leg and the heavy cane. "I was pleased to hear the surgery went well."

Kilbourne just stared unemotionally into the young eyes of his former assistant.

"He's cleared," Paul said after an uncomfortable few moments of silence. He helped Kilbourne up the four steps, then closed the door behind him.

The interior of the jet had a few traditional seats up front, but the rest was set up like a small conference room. An oblong table with two chairs on either side, one at either end.

"So they're alive," the Secretary said without preamble as he indicated a wide, comfortable seat for Kilbourne.

"So it would appear."

A steward brought a footrest and helped Kilbourne raise his leg onto it. After each man was served a drink, the steward disappeared into the front of the plane—leaving a pained silence behind.

"To us," the Secretary said, raising his glass.

Kilbourne remained still.

The Secretary smiled at the man's open disrespect. Governments might come and go, politics swing left and right, but Tom Kilbourne remained the same.

And it made the dying old man glad.

"To fallen comrades, then," the Secretary offered.

Kilbourne looked up from the floor, nodded sharply, then raised his glass. "Fallen comrades."

They both emptied their glasses.

"You know, Tom," the Secretary began, "as I get older, things seem to become so much clearer."

"Indeed?"

The Secretary nodded. "Very much so. Naked guesses become dogma. Desperate actions become considered realities. Stumbling steps—history. It's all very comforting."

Kilbourne slowly shook his head. "I'm afraid I don't share your certainties, Mr. Secretary." He laughed bitterly. "In fact I haven't felt certain of a great deal in the last few months." He looked directly into his creator's eyes. "I don't know if I envy or pity you your clarity."

Suddenly a chill swept over the Secretary. The slightest touch of final judgment and mortality. And, as he looked into those cool, emotionless eyes, he had a sudden desire for this meeting to end.

"Report," he said after a full minute of silence.

"Well," Kilbourne began as he massaged his leg, "after Picaro rescued Fosselis, we issued a Wanted bulletin in all the western states."

"On what pretext?"

Kilbourne actually smiled. "Mr. Picaro and Ms. Turner are now accused of having aided in the escape of a dangerous felon . . . Mr. Fosselis."

"I hate bringing them back to life. If the media gets ahold of it . . ."

Kilbourne interrupted the Secretary with his tone as well as his words. "Why am I still here, Michael? This is a job done better by any of your . . . *people.*" He spit out the word. "Let me go or kill me now!"

The Secretary nodded. "I should have killed you many years ago."

"There are a great many things you *should have* done years ago."

"Tom," the Secretary said after a long, deep breath, "nothing much has changed in the last fifty years. The things that bound us together then still bind us now. We are inextricably linked, like a hunter and his hound."

Kilbourne returned to staring at the floor. "Dogs turn on their masters."

The Secretary nodded seriously. "But would you turn on Joe and Max? Leave them naked and exposed in a world that could never comprehend them?" He hesitated. "Would you leave the world naked and exposed . . . to them?"

For five long, seemingly endless minutes the two men sat silently. Two warriors who each perceived a different enemy; that neither could reach or define.

But that each believed in with their souls.

"What do you want from me, Michael?" Kilbourne's voice seemed more dead than the barely animate corpse across from him.

In answer, the Secretary slid a file across the table. "Tell me how to stop him."

Kilbourne looked down at the stenciling on the beige folder with the bright red classified stripe running across it.

Hadeon, Victor. Believed deceased July 1987

As he opened the file and began to read, Kilbourne spoke so softly that the Secretary had to lean forward to hear. "Nobody's safe, Michael."

The Secretary nodded. "The monument we've dedicated our lives to."

Other parts of the Nevada desert appear crowded. Sheer rock walls suddenly rise up out of endless sand plains. Cutting you off. Forcing you 'round. Threatening, by their very presence, to crush all you are.

Or ever can be.

The two men, thief and addict, had driven for hours. First on the superhighway that connected Las Vegas to L.A.; then on a series of unimproved side roads out into the desert. Eventually they pulled over next to a shale cliff that cast its imposing shadow over them from the half-moon above.

"What's out here?" Foss's voice was more normal, stronger than a few hours earlier. The nurse's shot, the coffee, the adrenaline of the experience, all propped him up.

At least for the moment.

Greg ignored him as he got out of the car. He looked around, went about ten meters in all directions to make sure they were alone, then returned to the car and a watchful Foss.

"Get out."

For a reason even he didn't understand, Foss hesitated.

Greg's face was a frozen mask of nothingness. "You too sick? You need help?"

Foss slowly climbed out of the car. "What's going on?" His voice reflected the uncertainty written across his face.

Greg started to walk alongside the cliff. After a few seconds, Foss fell in with him.

"I'm sorry, Greg. I can't tell you how much."

Greg nodded casually. "You got that right."

They followed the curve of the cliffside for five minutes in silence. Then, when they were out of sight of the car, Greg suddenly stopped.

"We've got a problem, you and I."

"I know."

"Do you?" Greg's voice was just beyond sarcastic. "Why don't you tell me about it, then?"

Foss couldn't look him in the eye. "I didn't mean for this to happen."

"You never do."

"I—I don't know what to say." He paused as Greg took a few steps away from him. "I shouldn't have . . ."

He never finished the sentence.

Greg spun around with a .45 automatic held rock-steady at arm's length. Leveled at the old man's eyes.

"You shouldn't have? That's what you have to say for yourself? You shouldn't have? You're going to have to do better than that, old man," he said as his voice dropped into a low, dark tone.

"Greg, I . . ."

"No!"

Foss froze as Greg thumbed back the big gun's hammer.

"What you did," Greg spit out through almost clenched teeth, "is more than you can possibly imagine."

He took a few steps forward.

"They know you're alive," he said as he took another step toward the visibly shaking man. "Because of that, they'll know Megan's alive." Another step. "They'll know *I'm* alive," he almost growled.

He shoved the barrel of the gun into Foss's eye.

"They'll find the warehouse, if you haven't already told them about it."

"Greg! I wouldn't . . . ," he lied badly.

In an act of almost savage affection and feral hatred combined, Greg reached out with his free hand, throwing Foss back against the cliffside. He fell, shale flakes raining down on him, as Greg tumbled down on top of him.

The gun was jammed under the unresisting man's chin, forcing his head back. His eyes locked with the almost mythically furious man above him.

"Don't talk!"

Greg was breathing heavily, sweat dripping off his contorted face.

"Everybody, and I mean everybody, told me to get rid of you. For years, I've heard it. 'He's a junkie, Greg.' 'He's unreliable, Greg.' 'You can't trust him, Greg!' But I always defended you. I always . . . *I believed in you!*"

Foss closed his eyes, feeling the pressure of the gun. Wondering whether he would hear or feel the shot as the bullet entered his brain.

What he felt instead was the not-quite-gentle touch of Greg's hand on his trembling cheek.

"Oh, Foss," Greg mumbled in an exhausted voice. He fell back, collapsing on the sand in front of the shaking old man.

Foss straightened, sliding back until he could use the side of the cliff for a backrest. After two minutes of silence, Foss finally spoke up. In a tone Greg had never heard before.

"Nobody can save nobody," he said in an almost completely sober, normal voice. "It's every man for himself. Save yourself or else."

"You're right." The younger man nodded resolutely.

Greg stood, wiped some sand from the hammer and side of the gun, then leveled it at the calm man in front of him. When he spoke, it was in a . . . committed voice.

"Forget about me. Forget about the score. You put Megan at risk. Deo. You put Roman and his family at risk. You put all of them— men, women, their children—at risk."

His finger wrapped itself around the trigger. "They could all go to prison because of you," he said calmly. "Have their children taken away from them and raised by strangers because of you."

Foss saw him begin to squeeze the trigger.

"They could all be dead because of you." Greg swallowed hard. "Because of me." He stepped toward Foss. "I can't, I won't allow that to happen again."

Foss looked up at the man in front of him, knew the truth of his words, then nodded.

"I understand," he said as he prepared himself for the inevitable.

Again, the nothingness that came surprised him.

Greg remained motionless in front of him. His sweating had stopped; his expression firm, committed. The gun held in the vise of his hand, aiming directly between the old man's eyes.

"You have two options, old man. For old times' sake, if you like. One"—he paused briefly—"I can kill you here, now.

"Two. Grandmother Peterkezs says there's an old Gypsy way. A ceremony, she called it. Guaranteed to cure . . ." His voice trailed off. "Or kill."

Foss studied the man in front of him, his commitment, his decision, clear in his every fiber. He *would* pull the trigger. There was no doubt of that. It would haunt him in the nightmares that seemed to come more and more regularly since this larger nightmare had begun, but Greg would learn to live with it.

Foss thought about his own, long-lost children. A son and a daughter who had long ago given up on him, denied him. He thought of his mostly wasted life. The promises lost, the potential never fully realized.

And he thought of Greg.

A stranger. A man who had found him, tried to save him; forgiven him and started again. Over and over and over. A son, not by blood, but by heart.

And he thought of the one last thing he could do for him.

He held out his hand. "Give it to me."

"What?"

Foss shook his head. "There's no cure. No hope for someone like me." He took a deep breath, then pressed his open hand farther out.

Greg hesitated, nodded, then handed the man the gun. He turned, walking steadfastly back to the car. "Bye, Foss."

"Bye, Greg."

Foss fingered the gun, heavier than he'd expected. He held it with both hands, wrapped both fingers around the thin trigger, then put the barrel halfway into his mouth.

Greg had turned the car around. Was sitting, listening to the radio, when he heard the sound. He waited for the passenger-side door to close, then started back up the dark road.

"I'm sorry, Greg."

The young thief looked at the old addict with undisguised animosity. "You're weak," he said as if it were the ultimate obscenity.

"Cure or kill, huh?" Foss couldn't look him in the eye as he put the gun in the glove compartment.

"That's what she said."

"Okay."

The silence settled back around them.

"Did anyone get hurt because of me?"

Greg shook his head. "We were out of the warehouse two hours after we heard."

Foss looked deeply relieved. "I'm glad."

As they pulled back onto the interstate, Foss began to look around. "Where we going?"

For the first time, Greg smiled. Just for a moment, then it vanished. Stored away in favor of a severe, reproving look.

But Foss has seen it and was glad.

Three hours later, the car slowed to a stop outside a cinder block wall with a heavy steel gate.

They were near the old Vegas rail yards. A place seldom used today except by the occasional Hollywood film crew. There were no businesses, no homes or stores, no nothing.

Except for deserted rail track and whatever lay behind. A young man in jeans and a windbreaker wandered over to them, glanced inside, then leaned in the driver's window.

"You know where Talbot Street is?" the young man asked.

"Couple of blocks south, I think."

"You're not sure?"

Greg raised his eyebrows in response.

The man shrugged, then wandered away. Thirty seconds later, the gate slid open.

Greg pulled to a stop just past the gate. Another young man came, driving the car away as soon as Foss was clear of it.

They were standing on the edge of what old-time Las Vegans called the Neon Morgue. Lying on their sides, some stacked on top of each other, others towering forty feet or so above them, were spectacular, unlit, neon signs.

One proclaimed "The Flamingo Spa," another "El Rancho Vegas Welcomes You to Paradiseville!" It was surreal, standing there among a hundred or more signs that were dully screaming out their once bright messages to nobody. Easily the strangest junkyard in the world.

"How'd you know about this place?" Foss asked as he followed Greg deeper into the bizarre yard.

"Roman knew about it. Gypos on the fly used to crash here in the old days when they could hobo the trains."

They continued deeper into the yard, toward four Quonset huts with barely any light escaping from them.

He nodded toward the huts. "Those used to be repair shops used by the railroad. When the hotels bought this land in the fifties, they just left them rather than spend the money to tear them down."

"Sounds comfortable."

Greg stopped a few meters from the nearest hut. "Roofs are good, we hung blankets over the broken windows, there are good electrical hookups. And each hut can hold up to forty people."

He started to point at each hut.

"Dorm's in one. Command and control in two. Computer and photo labs in three. Logistics, machine and auto shop in four."

Greg stopped as three people approached from out of the dark.

"Thanks be to God for your safe return, my brother." Roman glanced over at Foss. "You're *still* alive."

The old man suddenly felt ashamed, facing the people he had so easily betrayed. He stared down at the ground.

"Anything happening?" Greg asked quietly.

Roman ignored him, staring instead at Foss. "You'll go with these men. If you try to get drugs, try to leave, try to contact the outside, they will stop you." He paused, anger coming off him in waves. "Do anything that might endanger our children again, either during or at any time after the cure—if you survive the cure . . ." He paused, moving within inches of Foss. ". . . and I'll kill you myself."

The two big men stepped forward, starting to lead Foss into the stacks of dead signs.

"Greg?"

But his friend kept his back to him.

After they had disappeared among the signs, Greg turned to Roman.

"I'll need him in five days at the max."

"We'll know by then." Roman gestured toward hut 2. "A lot has happened."

Greg followed him in.

Deo looked up. His face a picture of deep concern.

Greg looked at him, nodded, then Deo returned to studying the maps on the table.

Partitions had been set up in the back of the large aluminum hut to segregate Greg's office from the rest. Lazslo and Megan were sitting at a card table as they came in.

"How is he?"

Megan looked pale. Of the crew, she had taken the sudden move the worst. As if in the unspoken threat, the controlled chaos of the evacuation, all the memories of Kilbourne and the McCutcheons had returned.

"He's . . . fine." Greg nodded toward the outer, noisy part of the divided single room. "Would you excuse us for a minute?"

"I've got to check on the new video equipment anyway," she said as she started out. "I was praying for him," she whispered as she passed.

When they were alone, Greg collapsed on a small sofa. "What's happening?"

Lazslo glanced down at a pad on the table. "They took down the warehouse a few hours ago. Many men, many guns. Very, uh, *loud.*"

Roman picked up from there. "We are about seventy-five percent operational now. Everything will be up to speed in"—he checked his watch—"two hours at the most."

"Everyone is very happy," Lazslo added. "The place is no palace, but when did Gypsies need palace?" Then something changed in him. His eyes became set, his manner firm. "But there is one other thing."

Roman held up a restraining hand, but Greg waved it away.

"Go ahead."

Lazslo looked down at him. "You should have killed the man in the desert."

"I know."

"It's not too late. If you don't want to do it"—he shrugged—"I'll see that it's done."

"No."

"It is a foolish, unacceptable risk."

Greg rubbed his bloodshot eyes. "I *need* that man. The things he can do on a computer can save me weeks, if not longer. Gives me a massively better chance of success. Hell. Without him, this might not even be possible."

Roman nodded. "We understand all this. But he'll have less than a week before we go, by the time he comes out of it. Assuming he comes out of it." He spread his hands in a gesture of frustration. "What can he do in a week? If, and that is a very real word here, *if* he survives, he will be extraordinarily weakened, perhaps not thinking clearly."

"You should get another computer person. We can find . . ." Lazslo was interrupted by a completely washed-out-sounding Greg.

"I'm going to wait," he said as if that was the final word on the topic.

"I will not trust my family's fate to that pathetic, sick gadja's fortunes."

Looking up into the committed, dangerous man's eyes, Greg slowly stood. "You're not."

"No?"

Greg never looked away, never blinked. "You're trusting it to mine."

Lazslo stared into the tired, pained, but unblinking eyes, then nodded.

"May God's graces protect us."

Across the bizarre junkyard, the same prayer was being silently uttered.

Surrounded on three sides by thirty-foot-high dead neon signs from the old Landmark Hotel, isolated from the other buildings, stood a large, colorful tent. With a blue roof, patchwork green and blue sides, it appeared to belong more in a circus than this center of high-tech thievery.

But Grandmother Peterkezs, who had invoked those same graces several times in the past hour, had insisted that the ceremony could not be done in the hangarlike aluminum and plywood buildings.

So the tent had been found.

The two men who were guarding Foss sat outside the tent's only entrance, smoking, stargazing, anything to take their minds off what was happening inside. They were young men, born and raised in Michigan. Men who proudly boasted of putting the old ways behind them. Of being "Gypsies to the core, but Gypsies for today."

But they crossed themselves, kissing their talisman as they heard the ceremony begin just beyond the tent flap.

Foss lay on a camp bed covered with rubber sheets. He was naked, every inch of exposed skin covered by a semiclear greenish gel. His wrists were wrapped in sheep's wool, then tied with scarves above his head. His ankles were also tied. He lay motionless, both curious and fearful of what would come next.

Grandmother Peterkezs had been frighteningly blunt when he'd been brought to her.

"It will be greatest test you have ever undertook," she said as he undressed. "Demons have haved you for so long"—she shook her head sadly—"they will fight to keep you."

"What—what do I have to do?"

The old woman had begun walking around him, seeming to study his skin, his bone structure. She seemed to be looking into his very being. When she came around in front of him, she paused, staring up into his frightened eyes.

"Want to live," she said in a strong voice. "You must want to live, to beat off demons that will come. That live inside you."

"How do I . . ."

"Trust in God," was all she had said.

Now, using a red powder, she was tracing patterns onto the gel, muttering, half singing to herself as she went about her work.

Foss was hotter than he felt was possible. He wanted to leap up, run out of the tent, find a pool or lake to jump into. He even tested the knots on his limbs, but they didn't give as much as an inch. The gel, the smell and feel of it, made him more claustrophobic than at any other time in his life and he felt the first pulls of withdrawal creeping into him.

But he had given himself over to these people. People who Greg had often called "the healers of souls." The one and only time Foss had ever heard the aloof man talk like that.

"Mr. Fosselis, you are ready to live?"

As strange as the question sounded to the prone man, he recognized the truth of it.

"I'm not sure," he said, swallowing a tear.

Grandmother Peterkezs nodded solemnly. "Is first step."

She walked over to a small table, picking up two objects, then returning to the bed.

"God in your heaven," she began in a singsong voice, "hear this your humblest servant. I do beseech you come to this place to look down and protect these dwellers from the dark ones who do now gather."

She held a Star of David in one hand, a simple wooden cross in the other, as she raised her arms.

"Faith of this man, symbol of David the King, come down this place at this the time of your believer's greatest peril. Faith of this woman, symbol of Jesus who is the Christ, come down this place at this the time of your believer's greatest peril."

She pushed the Star of David into the gel on Foss's forehead. She tied the cross to the foot of the bed.

"You are ready for this?"

Foss took a deep breath, then nodded.

The old woman inserted a large strip of leather into Foss's mouth. He bit down hard on it as he had been instructed.

"Benci Joska," she mumbled as she took a lit candle and touched the flame to the gel on the old man's torso.

It exploded into bright blue, orange, red, and green flames. Crackling, spitting, it sent a foul-smelling dark cloud toward the tent's roof, which combined with the flames to completely obscure Foss from sight.

Foss's moans could be heard by the men standing guard outside, who shifted nervously on their feet.

Then, as suddenly as it had begun, the flame was out.

Foss lay still on the bed, an unmoving form covered in a dark black gunk.

Grandmother Peterkezs stood next to him, praying, watching the blackened form for any sign, any reaction, at all. After what felt like an eternity, the man's chest slowly rose and fell.

"Jonka," she said as she picked up a towel to begin to clean him off in preparation for the next treatment.

It took most of an hour to finish wiping the burned ooze off him.

Then another hour spent checking him for burns, tending to the few, minor ones. Then she began reapplying the homemade gel.

"Be strong," she said. "We will defeat the evil ones yet. Rest, for the trials ahead."

A thought echoing through the mind of a man in a room on a base that didn't exist; in a part of the Nevada desert that some thought filled with the secrets of the universe.

Kilbourne lay on a thick, soft couch, his leg brace removed, a state-of-the-art electronic stimulator working the muscles gently. Kneading the old, battered limb, deadening the pain.

Contents from the Hadeon file lay strewn across the coffee table, across his lap, a disorganized blanket of information on top of, as well as around, the old man. Each having been read thrice, having been analyzed, disputed, discussed in a series of phone calls to many of those involved.

Now analysis was over. It was time for contemplation.

Of Victor Yale Hadeon.

After a sip of the drink, the veteran of many wars (secret, public, and many in between) allowed his mind to drift.

Born almost forty years ago, Victor Hadeon had been raised by his unmarried mother in the slums of many of the major cities in America.

The woman who begat the problem that had solely occupied Kilbourne's thinking for the last few months died young. Leaving Victor alone, abandoned first by his junkie father and then his deceased junkie mother to the vagaries of the state.

Interesting, he thought, *how often abandonment slides into our lives. Hadeon by his parents. McCutcheon by his country. Joe and Max by their . . . the others. Me by God.*

Early on, young Victor had shown an affinity for what would become his life's work. For no reason perhaps than a fascination with the man he shared a name with, the young boy soon displayed his natural talents.

He read incessantly. Everything there was on Linus Yale, Jr., on the history of lockmaking, on security systems of the past, the present, and the future. By his late teens, Victor had already developed a reputation for brilliance within the international security industry. But for one other thing as well.

To his adoptive father it was simply . . . "genius."

To others, charged with overseeing the young man's care, it was something far more disturbing.

Whatever, it grew and festered within the young man. There was talk of therapy, "programs," institutionalizing him.

So in his early teens, Victor disappeared.

He turned up in Paris. Arrested by the Sûreté after a series of daring break-ins to some of the finest homes in the Bois de Bologne, Victor was almost instantly approached by recruiters from NATO Intelligence. Their offer was simple enough, and he quickly accepted.

Thus began his "officially sanctioned" career.

Kilbourne put down the papers he'd been absently reading, allowing the thoughts to drift and shift before his closed eyes. Forming random pictures of a life.

There was no embassy, no consulate, foreign ministry office, or military base that could keep the budding young thief out. His skills, previously talented but unrefined, blossomed under the tutelage of the West's best spymasters. He was considered a phenomenon of nature by the time he was recruited by the National Command Authority Directorate.

But something went wrong.

Outwardly Victor was as he'd always been. Calm, quiet, intense. He flawlessly assisted the operatives of America's most secret intelligence organization in their missions.

A notorious terrorist assassinated behind the walls of his heavily secured Bavarian chateau.

A deposed African head of state found shot to death in his own, impenetrable vault room.

An American expatriate stock swindler silently gunned down in a walled estate protected by the world's best, most sophisticated, high-security company.

But after these triumphs, Victor would disappear into the back streets of Europe. Vanish from sight, only to appear again when the proper personal advertisement would be placed in the *Paris Afternoon Gazetteer*.

Supervisors wrote reports commenting on Victor's "innate iciness on the job, but lack of tolerance for any intrusion in his private life whatever." Or they would say that "he continues to grow more remote from the teams."

But this was the world of black ops, where personality failings and bad attitudes weren't considered important.

As long as the jobs were getting done.

Then, one day, Victor didn't respond to the advertised call to duty. Searches were mounted, orders to apprehend were issued, people were questioned.

But Victor had gone, taking with him virtually all the files that had been kept on him. Emptying sophisticated computers of their files on him. Removing all recent photographs of the man.

Kilbourne opened his eyes, then pushed a button on the table. A moment later, Paul entered the room.

"Sir?"

"Ah, Paul. Would you get me the phone number for the *Las Vegas Sun*, classifieds. Personals column, please."

"Right away, sir."

The man picked up a local Vegas directory while the old man on the couch checked a document for the proper form for the contact ad that had been used in Paris.

He took the number from his aide, nodding his dismissal, then dialed the number on his cell.

"*Sun* Classified."

"Yes, can I still get a personal ad in today's paper?"

The voice on the other end hesitated. "Sorry. That edition closed two hours ago."

"Very well. I'd like this to run beginning tomorrow. To run continuously until further notice."

After giving the paper a "safe" credit card number on a phony name, Kilbourne began to dictate.

LINUS!
Master Yale Banham's Presence Is Requested
Upon Your Earliest Convenience.
Object: Reconciliation
702-929-1929

That it was probably a futile act, Kilbourne had no doubt. There was no guarantee that Victor Hadeon would read the *Sun;* or that if he did, he would read the classifieds. It had been over ten years since the man had last responded to such an advertisement.

Hadeon might well be miles away by now. Should be, anyway.

But no approach, no possible gambit or tactic, could afford to be overlooked in protecting this secret that had been buried for over half a century.

That now seemed almost laid bare, hiding behind a flimsy door with a nickel-and-dime lock.

With a human key standing on the very threshold.

PART FOUR

THE SCORE

THIRTEEN

G UARD!"
     "I see him."

Greg looked over at the young Gypsy, then smiled without realizing it. Lukacs's voice might be tight, filled with tension; but his body looked completely relaxed. Like he was aware of the danger but didn't give it more importance than it deserved.

The young man's eyes stayed locked on the guard as he passed within ten feet of their hiding place.

The heavily armed man casually looked around the underground parking lot, then moved to his key station. He took the small aluminum key from its little box by the exit, put it in his watch clock, then turned it sharply. He returned it to its box in the same motion as he opened the door and stepped through.

The two thieves moved instantly.

They raced across the floor to a small chain-link-enclosed area at the far end of the garage. Lukacs started to reach for the simple padlock on the gate but felt Greg's strong hand grab his wrist.

"Always by the numbers. Even when there's no way there's a trap." He stared at the Gypsy. "Especially then."

Lukacs nodded, unclipping the multisensor from his belt. He flipped it on, then held it up to the gate.

"Talk to me."

Lukacs spoke as his eyes followed the small glowing readouts. "Starting with the broadbands. Nothing. Extreme high width . . . nothing. Extreme low width . . . noth—what's that?"

Greg's voice was casual, almost soothing. "Just read it."

"Uh"—Lukacs licked his lips—".758 amps in the sub-one-ohm range. That's a . . ."

"Forget about the numbers," Greg coaxed and coached. "See it."

"I'm not sure."

"Just relax. Picture it. Picture the tachyons and ions flashing. See their fire, the colors. Feel the heat from each micro-explosion. Close your eyes, become part of it."

Lukacs did as he was told, his face tensing from the concentration.

"Now," Greg whispered after a moment, "take that picture, freeze it in your mind, then open your eyes."

The boy's eyes flashed open.

"What do you see?" Greg's question was more important, with deeper implications than the talented Gypsy thief could possibly know. "What do you see?"

Lukacs looked at the sparkling chain-link, at the cabinets mounted on the walls behind it. At the power conduits running from the cabinets, at the seemingly bare cement flooring.

"Gate's clear," he said a moment later.

"Why?"

"Signature dispersion would look different if the current was in the fence."

"What *would* it look like?"

Lukacs thought for a moment, then shrugged. "Don't know. But it'd be different."

Greg patted him on the back. "Now let's see what you can do with a standard Master Series 22 padlock."

The basic lock gave itself up after a few seconds of gentle probing.

Ten minutes later, they were done, quickly letting themselves out through an alarmed (bypassed) fire exit. Just as quickly picked up by Deo in a stolen used car. Less than an hour later, they were back at the junkyard.

"So?" Lazslo seemed anxious for news.

As he changed his clothes, Greg waived the man's anxieties away. "He'll do."

Lazslo exhaled deeply, as if he'd been holding his breath for the hours the thieves had been away.

"I was never concerned," he said casually as he opened the door.

"See you at the meeting." And he muttered a silent prayer of thanks as he went.

Greg nodded, then returned, physically at least, to dressing. But his mind was racing, over what was needed for the next five days. Over all that had happened in the last seven.

That the boy had passed this last, functional test was good. A help. One less thing to worry about. Of course, the expected challenges they would face out in the desert (not to mention the unknown ones in the installation) would be considerably tougher. But then, nothing could ever prepare Lukacs, or anyone else for that matter, for those.

As he walked to building 2, he allowed his mind to drift from point to point in the plan that had taken shape in the last week. It was a combination of calculated daring and improvised caution. While its form was dictated by the conditions in the desert, the plan held several . . . *options* that Greg had created as unconventional alternatives to the conventional thinking he expected to encounter.

And above all other things, it depended on divine intervention on either the twenty-second or the twenty-third.

The back half of the command and control building had been cleared. Three of the biggest, toughest members of the crew stood guard at the partition that separated the building in half. They nodded to Greg as he walked past, noticing his frown as *he* noticed the guns in their waistbands.

The first crisis of the past week.

"Damn it!" Roman had screamed. "I was there! I *saw* them!" He held up a pile of eight-by-ten photos. "Look for yourself. They are heavily armed, most probably military or paramilitary."

He paused as Greg looked at the pictures of the raid on the warehouse.

"I am responsible for these people," Roman continued as he had gestured out at the main room. "They came because I gave them my word they would be paid and that they would be protected!"

"I don't like guns," Greg had said as he tossed the photos down. "And I don't like them associated with my business."

Roman picked up the .45 that had been retrieved from Greg's car. "Then what is this, please?"

"That was different. Personal." He walked to a blanket-covered window, peeking out at the glow from the tent in the distance. "A matter of personal honor."

Roman had nodded.

"Yes. *This* is personal. *This* is a matter of honor."

The two men had been quiet for a time after that. Eventually Greg turned back to his old friend.

"Keep them to a minimum. Low-key, concealed, and only in the hands of the most stable people you have."

And it had been on to the next crisis.

Greg walked past the guards, into the improvised conference room, nodding his greeting at the people already there.

Megan sat to the side of the table, playing with a multifunction remote control, cueing up tapes on the projection TV at the end of the room.

Lazslo and Roman were going over two clipboards of lists. Muttering to each other, to themselves, as the final personnel and equipment decisions were being made for the imminent attempt.

And Foss—well, Foss sat off by himself, at a computer station to the back of the room. Looking like a combination of Yul Brynner and Oliver Hardy. His shaved (partially bandaged) head, pink and fleshy; sporting a five-day growth of a bare, brush mustache.

His eyes reflecting a calm that Greg had never seen there before. As well as a seared image of unimaginable pains.

"Deo back yet?" Greg asked as he came up behind the busy man.

Foss never looked up. In fact, it seemed to Greg, hadn't looked anyone straight in the eye since he'd rejoined the group less than a week ago.

"Just pulled in." His voice was flat, weak. But it lacked its usual slurred or animated tones (depending on what state of his addiction he was experiencing). "You going to want the field projections?"

"Yeah," Greg said after a short silence. Foss was so changed, so different from anytime he'd ever known before. Gone was the sarcasm, the chiding, the bad jokes and mother hen worry.

The man Greg had come to know and love.

For a moment, the least definable increment of time possible, Greg wondered if in curing the man, he'd lost his friend. Wondered whether or not this flat, worn-out old man who sat hunched at the keyboard occasionally sipping a diet soda *was* his friend. Or if his friend was the personality Foss had found in partially filled syringes.

Embarrassed, he turned away; taking his seat at the large oblong table.

As he glanced through some notes, charts, and diagrams, he sneaked glances at his friend. The man who sighed a lot, constantly rolling his fingers as if they no longer quite understood what he wanted them to do.

"The demons are goned in him," Grandmother Peterkezs had told Greg. "The poisons in his body are exorcised. The cobwebs burnt away from the brain."

"Thank God," Greg had whispered.

The old woman nodded.

"Yes. That is what you should do."

Greg had glanced into the tent, seeing several of the Gypsy women bandaging Foss's few burns, feeding him some thin soup. He seemed older than Greg could imagine. He quickly turned away from the oddly disturbing scene.

"When can he get back to work?"

The old woman was silent for a long time. When at last she did speak, it was in an ominous tone.

"You are Romany, Gregory. Not by birth, but by actions; which have more meaning than accident of birth. You live in the gadja world, but respect and understand our ways. I speak to you now, as I speak to Roman or his brothers I carried in my body.

"You are Romany, Gregory. Your friend is not. Demons, poisons are goned. He is"—she seemed to search for the word—"*delivered?*"

"Released."

The old woman nodded. "Yes. He is released from their power over him." She looked up into the tall man's eyes. "But he is still gadj. Still without faith, for certain of God's love for him."

The old woman sighed deeply. "A life like that," she had said with a tone of enormous pity, "who can say how long he can resist the demons' calls to him in the night."

"I understand," Greg said quietly. "I thank you for everything you've done."

He started into the tent but a surprisingly strong grasp from the old woman stopped him.

"Once, long ago, you gave back my son to me. While I live I will keep your friend in the light." She smiled. "Long time I have hoped for this, to repay what cannot be repaid."

Greg started to interrupt, but she put her hand gently across his lips.

"No. Truth is truth." She looked into the tent just as Foss was being helped to his feet. "But what I do means nothing"—she nodded at the impossibly weak man in front of them—"if he no *want* to live."

Greg caught himself staring at Foss, so quickly looked away.

"Hey?" Deo smiled down at Greg. "Sorry to bring you back from wherever, but I thought you could use a piece of good news."

Greg smiled weakly as he leaned back in his chair. "You know it."

Deo perched on the table. "I talked to the man."

Greg instantly lost the look of worry that had clouded his eyes for days. "And?"

"The man says he got no problem so long as you stay with what you said. And there's no fee. He says if you pull off what you said, he'd be interested in anything he could do for you after."

Greg nodded seriously. "That's a break."

Deo agreed. "Amen. By the way, just how much did you tell him?"

While the best, most sophisticated branch of U.S. intelligence had still not found the improvised Gypsy camp, the same could not be said for the local Mafia. Less than twenty-four hours after they'd moved into the old junkyard, the boss of the crew that worked the Vegas rail yards had come calling.

It hadn't been a surprise, really. This was, after all, Las Vegas. A town that appears more and more corporatized, more and more a family tourist resort, but at its dark heart still rests the demon that created the city.

Deo had served as an intermediary. In his two meetings with the crew boss, he'd made it clear that they were prepared to pay any reasonable "courtesy fee" to continue to operate out of the junkyard. And the Mafia's man had no problem allowing the Gypsies to work. Hell, the Gypsies and the Italians had worked together for years.

But the young tough had recognized from the size and complexity of what little of the operation he was allowed to see that this was not a decision for him. A meeting had soon been arranged.

On a ranch just south of Vegas, Greg had been searched, then brought in to meet "the man."

"I heard you were dead," the casually dressed eighty-year-old man had said.

Greg shrugged. "I've heard the same thing about you from time to time."

The man smiled. "Okay." He gestured at the door, leading Greg out for a walk around the pastures of the comfortable ranch. "So what do you want?"

"Permission."

That stopped the man in his tracks. "I didn't think young people today cared about the niceties."

"I wouldn't have if your men hadn't found us."

The man studied Greg closely. "I heard there was no bullshit in you." He paused as Greg stood there, his face a complete blank. "What's the score?"

"My business."

"Not true," the man said easily as he put on sunglasses. "I need to know how much you got to pay, and that's got to do with what you think you'll get from the score."

Greg remained completely still. "My business," he said slowly, "will not infringe on any of yours. Will not impact any businesses under your protection or patronage. We'll remain at the junkyard for two more weeks at the most, then be gone."

The man shrugged. "Not enough."

"It's all you're going to get."

The man stared into Greg's blank stare, his open defiance of the man's authority, politely wrapped in the courtesies of tradition.

"I need more," he finally said. "The where, at the very least, right?"

Greg hesitated, thought about the man, his reputation, his convictions, then leaned very close to the old man, whispering in his ear for long minutes.

The man's face became impassive, nodding at some point or other for the five minutes or so that Greg whispered. Then, slowly, a smile appeared, growing quickly to an ear-to-ear grin. When Greg pulled back, the man took a few steps away. Obviously deep in thought.

Finally he turned back to the thief he'd heard described as "a serious individual." One of the old mob's highest endorsements of a man and his character.

"You wouldn't bullshit an old man?"

Greg's set, committed expression was his answer.

The man chuckled as he shook his head. "I always knew you couldn't trust the fucking G. But this!"

"So your answer is . . ."

The man paused, the seriousness, the risks of Greg's plan outweighing the man's humorous view of it. "You'll have my answer in a few days."

"What about his watchdogs?" Greg asked Deo as the man sat down across from him.

"Still there," the driver shrugged. "But very low-key about it. They got their orders: 'Look, but don't touch.' No problem."

Megan watched the two men talking in low tones, wondering just when the secrecy would end.

If it would ever end.

It was strange just how easily she'd adapted to the rest of it, though. How simple it had been to drop off the face of the planet.

There was no close family to worry about—her mother, one of life's perpetual victims, had died two years earlier. Her father, well, he was as cold as the scientific journals he edited. They hadn't spoken since the funeral. Hell, he'd probably find fault with her posture when she broke this amazing story.

There were no close friends to ask questions; and she'd long ago admitted to herself how dead-ended her job had become.

Still, she missed the routine of her life.

The certainty of waking up in the same bed every morning. Of knowing that the worst danger of the day would be the commute to work. The greatest challenge, staying awake in the staff meetings.

But, she thought as she finished cueing up her tapes, it wasn't all on the downside.

In the last four and a half months, she'd lived, really lived, more than at any time in her life. As chaotic as life underground might be, there was a constant electricity around them. An almost palpable living presence that came from the precautions, the safeguards, and the always present danger.

The Gypsies called it *kat vicuska,* pure life. Enjoying every minute, every moment of the day as if it were your last. As it might well be.

For in that delicious mixture of fear and joy, hope and despair, you were forced to throw away all the garbage, all the crap that you built up around your life as a protective shield. Forced to come to terms with who you are, for good or bad, to find a way to make the best out of it.

To Megan's surprise, she liked what she'd found.

Always goal-oriented, hard-driven, task-myopic—in these most dangerous days of hiding she'd managed to find time to play with some of the many children of the Gypsy families. To completely lose herself in a game of jacks, rocking a baby to sleep, or helping teach some of the children to read or write.

For years, her driving ambition had forced down any sense of humor or whimsy that she might have had. She'd always thought of herself (not critically either) as a humorless, somewhat priggish individual. Now she routinely joined in the never-ending series of dark practical jokes that seemed to sweep through the camp.

As for romance, well, she'd never considered herself particularly sexy, certainly not attractive and constantly battling her waistline. She'd always been the first to reject, turning down men before they could, would, be disappointed in her.

But in the Gypsy camp, things were different somehow. The men seemed to care less about "the perfect body." Treated the women, more or less, as equals. Actually seeming to prefer the women to take an active, sometimes dominant role in the relationship.

Several had openly and quite frankly approached her, not being even a little put off by her usual games and defenses. Even in the sex (she'd drifted into the first truly casual affair of her life) she found herself more open, more giving, more demanding. Feeling she could ignore all the rules of "proper" behavior that had been drummed into her over the years.

And to her surprise, her work hadn't suffered because of it.

It was a contradiction that—instead of being liberating—made her very nervous.

Megan had always been about direction. Straight ahead, no deviations or distractions! And all of that in the relatively stress-free life of feature producing.

Yet now, on the run and in constant danger, she took time off. Allowed herself daydreams and fantasies. With the possibility of exposure and destruction looming around every corner, she was stunned to find herself worrying about the men, women, and children who had become like a communal hug to her, rather than *getting the job done.*

Constantly she reprimanded herself. This was all about *the story,* not about a baby cutting a new tooth or an old lady learning to read. This was about the cover-up of the century exposed by—she was certain—the thief of the century. Nothing more! And whether the story could be completely proved true or not (if it *was* really true or not), it was about grabbing that brass ring that was now within a fingertip's reach.

But she would think the thought while rocking a baby to sleep, joining in with the constant games of cards that were epidemic in the improvised camp, or while sneaking away to the sweet caresses of a man who cared nothing about the professional . . . only the woman.

And the work *hadn't* suffered.

The young Gypsies that made up her staff proved themselves to be sharp, bright, and ingenious in their ability to improvise. In the last week alone, they'd acquired, reviewed, edited, then reedited enough material to paralyze a network newsmagazine's staff for three months.

All the while laughing, joking, smiling through crises that would have reduced Megan to a screaming wreck (eating tranquilizers like popcorn) a few months earlier. All while not ignoring the threat, the all-too-real dangers, that lay just beyond the junkyard's walls.

Kat vicuska.

Pure life.

A thing she hoped she could hold on to some part of when this bizarre nightmare/fantasy existence ended.

If it ended.

She pulled herself back from her reveries as everyone started to settle around the table.

"Okay," Roman began simply, "where are we?"

Lazslo lit another of the never-ending chain of cigarettes, each lit from the stub of the last. "There, I suppose."

"You suppose?"

The logistics man shrugged. "We have enough on the base to do the job. No question. I *would* like more, but as God wills." He checked a sheet from a folder in front of him. "Everyone will be in place by 0430 on the twenty-second. Also the twenty-third if needed. No problems."

"What about the safe zones?" Greg asked from his seat. He never looked at the logistics chief, rather asking the question while watching the pretty landscapes and desert scenes displayed by the Weather Channel on the TV to his side.

"From 0430 to 0600 base beauty salon," Lazslo said from memory, "0600 to 1830 Warehouse North 156, and 1830 to 0600 Auxiliary Administration Building 34. Office of Enlisted and Noncommissioned Officers family welfare. No sweat."

Greg nodded as he continued watching the broadcast of temperatures, barometric readings, and flash flood warnings. "Go ahead."

"Equipment?" Roman asked, looking down the table at Deo.

"In place, checked and double-checked. Vehicles were on their final shakedown this afternoon. It went perfectly. Final tech on the electronics is an hour after this meeting, but no problems are anticipated. Everything's ready except the blanket."

Greg looked up at that.

"What is the problem?" Roman asked before Greg could.

"No problem," the driver said casually, "it's just not ready yet. It should be later today or early tonight. Your mother put four more women on it."

"How's it look?" Greg turned back to the TV as he asked.

"Better than the real thing."

Greg smiled as he returned to the weather broadcast.

If Greg was satisfied, Roman was too. "Megan?"

"We've combined preexisting footage with stuff we shot," she said. "I can give you a detailed look at all the terrain between Freedom Ridge and the outer fence whenever you want it. Also some of the patrol movements. As well as computer-enhanced close-ups of any patch of desert you want."

"Foss?" Roman studied the man who was so changed since coming through the ceremony.

"Well, uh." Foss cleared his voice, then took a sip of tea before continuing in a barely audible voice. "We've done every kind of analysis we can think of on the data we've received. And, uh, well, we've been able to identify three different kinds of devices. Along with establishing the existence of a fourth, unknown type."

"What?"

"I can't hear him."

Greg muted the TV, then turned to face his friend. "Hey, Foss." He smiled. "Just talk to me, man."

The older man continued having trouble looking Greg in the eye. "I, uh, think . . ."

"Don't tell me what you *think,* old man. Just tell me what you know." Greg's voice was demanding, but in its own way also supportive.

For the first time in days, Foss looked directly at him. "The fault line looks clear—uh, *is* clear."

Again, the supportive smile. "Talk to me, Foss."

Foss glanced down at his notes, then locked eyes with Greg. The younger man seemingly willing the older man out of his shell.

"Talk to me."

Foss took a deep breath, not at all sure of himself, if he could trust any of the conclusions he'd made since he'd begun the computer plot of the telemetry from the desert in front of the mystery base. But he knew Greg needed to trust them.

To trust him.

"Okay," he began in a forced stronger voice. "Here's the way it is." He called up a computer-enhanced rendering of the desert in front of the installation on the projection TV at the end of the room. "The red dots indicate probable motion detectors; blue are seismic devices; yellow are the ammonia sniffers." He paused. "The black dots I got no idea."

While the others stared at the multicolored images that seemed to crowd the desert floor, Greg stood, then walked close to the TV. "What's their impedance?"

"Don't know."

"Active or passive scans?"

"Don't know."

"Power signatures?"

"Indistinct from this range." Foss paused. "Maybe you can get some clearer readings when you're closer to them."

Greg bit his lower lip. "Swell."

Foss shrugged, a seemingly forced mannerism. "You want it should be easy?"

Greg suddenly turned around, grinning at the old man. "No pain . . . ," he said as he watched his old friend start to relax.

". . . is the only way to go," Foss finished.

Greg turned back to the screen, tracing the narrow Lateral Break on the lower edge of the picture.

"Ten and a half miles once we come out." He studied the terrain in front of the Break. "Not too bad for the first few miles."

Roman shook his head. "I count between fifteen and twenty motion detectors in that area alone."

Greg started back to his seat. "What's the return on them?"

Foss checked a printout. "Thirty in thirty-one."

Greg sat down, then unmuted the TV. An anchor was talking about "seasonal, brief downpours."

"No sweat," Greg said as he again turned his attention to the weather broadcast.

Roman looked worried. "What is this thirty in thirty-one?"

Since Greg seemed engrossed in the weather, Foss turned to the Gypsy leader. "That's the timing on the thing. It sets off its alarm if anything moves past its sweep faster than thirty feet in thirty-one seconds."

"Is that slow?" Megan seemed confused. "I mean how fast is normal?"

Foss glanced at Greg, who seemed completely unconcerned. "Normal is approximately a hundred and fourteen feet in thirty-one seconds."

"Jesus!" Megan gasped. "You're talking about less than a third of normal! At that rate it'll take you . . ."

"Fourteen hours and fifty-three minutes to get across," Greg said calmly.

"You can't make it in one night," Lazslo said in a stunned tone. "And to be caught in the middle of that desert at daybreak . . ."

Greg smiled briefly. "I'll think of something."

Roman shook his head, but other than that almost instinctive act, he allowed none of the misgivings he so deeply felt to show in his voice or his face.

"We will move on." He turned to Megan. "Have you prepared your, what is it?"

Megan laughed. "Damned if I know what to call it. Actually, I've prepared three . . . statements I guess. One if we're successful. One if we're not." There was too long a pause after that. Long enough for dark, hideous images to flash into everyone's mind. "The last one is mostly blank for some contingency in between," she rushed out.

"When you gonna tape them?" Greg asked without looking up.

"Just before you go. Either Saturday or Sunday."

"Right."

Roman looked over at him. "Which brings us to the final thing." He paused, almost unwilling to ask the question. "When will you do this thing?"

"Just a second, I want to hear this." He turned up the volume on the TV.

"Five-day forecast for the eastern deserts now," the cute blond weather anchor was saying as numbers were projected behind her. "Beginning tonight, we should see our usual pattern of hot and sticky during the day, with increasing thunderstorm activity at night through Monday evening. If the Pacific cutoff low continues to hold out through the week, as I expect it to, you can expect the most severe storms on Sunday and Monday evening."

Greg shut the set, then turned toward the worried faces around the table. "We go on Sunday."

It might as well have been a dismissal, since everybody immediately stood up and left the room. Foss and Greg stayed behind.

"How'd it go today?"

Greg nodded seriously. "Boy's quick, smart, can think on his feet. He'll be all right."

"You're going to need more than 'all right' behind you out in the sand."

"I've put down three scores with him in the last five days. He's got the talent and the touch. He'll be fine."

"It's not him I'm worried about."

Greg smiled spasmodically. "Glad to have you back, Mother Fosselis."

Foss grunted, turning back to his keyboard, bringing up a heavily secured program. "You know this is a seriously dumb thing to do."

"Yup."

"It could compromise the whole operation."

"Not if you can do what you can do," Greg said in a confident tone.

"I'll do my job," Foss said with confidence that he didn't truly feel. "Provided you didn't fuck up the installation while playing commando with that kid." He paused to manipulate the complex-looking program. "It'll take a few minutes."

Greg picked up a phone receiver that was hardwired into the computer.

"Whenever you're ready, Mr. Bell."

□ □ □

At the heart of arguably the most secured (electronically as well as physically) facility in North America, in its most secret depths, a dying man sat with a ghost from his past.

"Yes?" the Secretary asked at the knock on the door.

His assistant opened the door but remained outside. "Sir?"

"It's all right, Paul."

The young man walked in, nodding at a phone to the Secretary's side. "It's the dedicated line, sir. I've had it transferred here."

The Secretary looked down at the flashing light, then held up a hand to stop his assistant from leaving the room. He looked over at Kilbourne.

They both picked up conjoined receivers, hesitated, then Kilbourne punched the flashing button.

"This is one-nine-two-nine," he said simply.

"Do I really have to introduce myself?" the voice on the other end said without inflection.

Kilbourne had received so many crank calls since the ad had first appeared in the Vegas papers that he didn't get excited. "Perhaps. Just a little. To establish your credentials, let's say."

There was a long silence.

"Are you Smith or Kilbourne today?" the voice asked.

The Secretary froze, then immediately gave the hand signal for his assistant to start the trace.

"What should *I* call *you*?" Kilbourne said after stretching his silence for as long as he dared.

"Names aren't important."

The Secretary's eyes flashed back and forth as his assistant's fingers almost flew over a computer keyboard and his old "attack dog" made notes.

"They are to me."

"Don't bother with the delaying tactics," the voice said in an amused tone. "I've removed the tracer tone from this line."

The assistant nodded.

"Very well." Kilbourne took a deep breath. "I thought, perhaps, we might reach an accommodation before things spiral out of control."

"Things seem to be spinning pretty good right now."

"I'd like to stop that. But I need your help."

"Our history suggests otherwise," the voice said bitterly.

"Mistakes were made. Neither of us can change the past, but maybe we can do something about the future."

"And the present?"

The Secretary watched as a map of Las Vegas suddenly appeared on his assistant's monitor. A vertical and horizontal line sliding back and forth over it, seeming to search for an intersection. He glanced over at Kilbourne, who was concentrating too intensely to notice anything but the phone in his hand.

"What will it take for you to stop whatever it is you're doing?" Kilbourne prompted.

The voice was quiet for almost a minute. "Give me back my life," it finally said.

"Done," the old man said quickly. "All you have to do is come in. With Ms. Turner of course."

"Really?" The voice sounded unconvinced. "Aren't we a little old for fairy tales?"

Kilbourne shrugged without realizing it. "You understand the game, Mr. . . . sir. You come in, get debriefed, and sign a National Security oath that you'll not divulge any secrets you may have learned. Then we have no reason to harm you."

"And the check's in the mail."

The lines settled on a spot on the map. The Secretary quickly scrawled a note and held it up to Kilbourne.

"This offer expires with the end of this call," he said flatly. "I suggest you take a moment to think it over." He paused. "Choose life, sir."

Paul was on a phone, urgently whispering instructions.

"I think I will," the voice said after a brief pause. "So I'll reject your offer."

The Secretary seemed uncomfortable with the flatness of the man's voice. He wrote out another note for his effigy.

"Then give me your word, on your honor, sir," Kilbourne read, "that you will desist from any future attacks or forays into areas better left alone. Do that, and I promise to scale back my efforts at the very least. Then, with time, end them altogether."

As the silence on the line began to fill the darkened room, Paul hung up his phone, a forlorn expression on his face. The old men ignored it as they waited for an answer.

"How," the voice said softly, "how do you know you can trust me to keep my end of the deal?"

Sensing a break in the man, Kilbourne lowered his voice to what he hoped was a comforting tone.

"I know I can trust you, for the same reason you can trust me." He hesitated. "Because we are the same man, sir. You and I. Dinosaurs perhaps, but honorable dinosaurs at the very least."

Another pause on the line. Then: "You're very good. You almost had me with that one." The man's voice sounded firmer, resigned, resolved.

The Secretary decided to try one last gambit, and spoke into the phone for the first time. "Nobody's safe, Mr. Hadeon. Not even you."

A long silence on the other end resulted.

"Best regards to Joe and Max," the voice said as the connection was suddenly terminated.

Kilbourne looked at the receiver in his hand, unwilling to put it down. But the Secretary had no such hesitations.

"You got him?" he demanded of his assistant.

Paul looked ill. "He was better than we expected. The tracer tone was scrambled, so we had to do a voice-only search. We could only search during those moments when he was actually talking."

"But you *did* get him?"

The assistant shifted nervously on his feet. "He piggybacked the lines. Must've used some kind of microwave relay system."

The Secretary now knew what was coming. "Go on."

"We traced his end as far as we could. To the originating relay. The first in the sequence. But we couldn't go beyond that."

The Secretary was shaking his head. Not at his assistant's ineptitude, although the younger man thought that was the cause. Rather at his own underestimation of the abilities of the thief.

"Where was the first relay?" he asked calmly.

His assistant took a deep breath. "A phone trunk line that serves a bank of five pay phones. In the parking lot of North Field's Intelligence Annex."

A blank stare came across the old man's face. Almost instantly replaced by a look of grave concern. "Double the guard at North Field Terminal. No one, and I mean no one, gets on a transport without quadruple check."

"Sir!"

"Brief our men in the field. Tell the jackasses they have twenty-four hours to find Hadeon and/or Turner—or suffer the consequences!''

"Sir!''

"First take Habitat to condition one; augmented security checks to be in place within the hour!''

"Sir!'' His assistant executed a crisp about-face, then hurried from the room.

As he stared at the empty door, the Secretary's angry, twisted face slowly turned to Kilbourne. *What now?*''

Kilbourne finally hung up his receiver, shook his head, then—oddly—smiled. "Now?'' He exhaled deeply as if in an attempt to cleanse himself of what had happened.

Now, and in the last half century.

"Now,'' he said sadly, "now . . . he's coming.''

FOURTEEN

P SYCH 301."
    "Psych 301 by."
"Psych 301, Dreamland. Report status."
"Psych 301. Holding beta pattern in grid five one Baker. Fuel five zero, stores full. All systems functioning five by. Uh, we still have that mobile home on 168 but they're on the wrong side of the ridge for anything and, uh, in a nonsecured area."

"301, roger. Be aware, Dreamland, weather reports possible unstable air mass bearing zero eight six at seven five miles. Velocity two niner kph."

"Psych 301. Copy, Dreamland. Uh, we can see the thunderheads. But so far things have been very calm."

"301, roger. Cleared to continue patrol. How will you proceed, sir?"

"Psych 301. We'll continue moving into forty group and, uh, guess we'll stay out for as long as we can, Dreamland. Would appreciate your keeping those weather updates coming though."

"301, roger. Will update you in ten, sir."

"Thank you, Dreamland."

"Dreamland clear."

"Psych 301 on patrol."

The jet-black, heavily armed Apache helicopter gunship banked sharply to its right, then moved off across the desert. Keeping Freedom Ridge on its left, it skimmed just under two hundred feet above the broken ground, back toward the open desert.

And in the near pitch-black of a nine-foot-wide, twelve-foot-deep natural fissure in the earth's crust, two men breathed deep sighs of relief.

"Too close," Lukacks sighed. "Too damn close."

He couldn't clearly see Greg, a few feet ahead, but he sensed him begin to move again.

"Let's make time," the experienced thief whispered in a calm voice. A tone that masked his rapid heart rate as well as the tightened lips that reflected his inner worry.

Everything about this score required precision, both in timing and in execution. The circling of the patrol helicopter had cost them fifteen crucial minutes. Fifteen minutes spent standing stock-still, praying that the sensors on the hovering surveillance platform couldn't pick them up.

Now they needed to make up the time. Although they were less than a thousand meters from the end of Lateral Break, Greg estimated they would have used up most of the cushion he had built into this part of the score's schedule by the time they got there. The going had been so slow, so difficult, that critical minutes had been lost climbing around boulders, open pits, narrowings of the way. And the helicopter.

But they pressed on.

Each man was dressed in a dirty tan coverall, specifically sewn for them. They wore lightweight climbing boots, tan knit hoods that completely covered their faces and necks, tan work gloves. Not an inch of skin was visible, only two bare slots for their eyes, and two small holes to breathe through at the nose and mouth. And beneath all that, each man wore a one-piece (bottom of the feet to the top of the head) black wet suit.

It was beyond uncomfortable. Combined with their twenty-five-pound backpacks, seven-pound chest packs, and two-pound waist packs, the coverings provided as much of an obstacle as the terrain. More, because they could only stay dressed that way for a limited time. Six hours at the outside, taking into account the night's dropping temperatures. Then would come heat exhaustion, dehydration, oxygen starvation, incoherence, muscular failure, unconsciousness, then death.

Six hours and counting.

Six hours to cross undetected the sandy ocean of mantraps that lay ahead of them. Once they crawled out of the Break and into the desert proper.

An hour and fifteen minutes after they first stepped down into the Break, almost an hour and a half since they had put on the cumbersome outfits, they arrived at the end of the Break.

A planned ten-minute rest.

Both men were breathing heavily as they slouched against the gently rising edge of the Break. Neither said a word, neither moved. They just prayed to their gods that the way ahead would be easier than what they'd just come through.

Taking a deep breath, Greg unclipped one of the sensors on his belt, holding it above his head. The device, held upside down so Greg could see the barely glowing readouts from below, was moved slowly from side to side. Each slight tick of a needle or move of a digital readout was carefully scrutinized. Carefully analyzed.

"Looks okay," he said quietly. "What d'you get?"

Lukacs repeated the process with one of his matching sensors from his side of the fissure. "I get a .003 amp return in the low zone."

Greg took a sip of the potassium-laced energy drink in his canteen. "That's me. My toys. You can discount that right on through."

It had been five minutes since they'd stopped.

"Let's get to it," Greg said as he sluffed off his backpack.

Lukacs nodded as he dropped his pack.

They worked quickly, quietly, in well-rehearsed movements.

First, a series of interlocking hollow plastic tubes were pulled out, then assembled into a framework measuring seven feet long by six feet wide. Then four three-foot-long fiberglass boards were clicked together, making two skis which snapped into the framework. Finally each man pulled out a fourteen-square-foot heavy burlap blanket. Using Velcro attachments, it was secured to the framework.

They worked more quickly now, each man realizing they were taking longer than in practice. Both of them grabbed a side of the contraption, carefully lifting it above their heads and onto the desert floor just beyond.

Lukacs crossed himself.

Greg took a final sensor reading.

Then both men climbed up, out of the Lateral Break, immediately crawling under the flattened tent on skis they'd constructed.

Not a word passed between them as they continued working.

Lukacs checking that the blanket completely hid them from overhead detection; Greg attaching sensors in front and to the sides of
the blind. After two more minutes, there suddenly seemed nothing
left to do.

They looked at each other, tired, blank expressions on their faces.

"Ready?" Greg asked softly.

Lukacs took a deep breath, then closed his eyes.

"Two others also," he whispered, "who were robbers, were led
away to be put to death with him. There they were crucified, one on
the right and one on the left. The thief on the left cried out, 'Are
you not the Christ! Save yourself and us!' "

The young man's breathing slowed, his body relaxed.

"But the one on the Lord's right rebuked him, saying, 'Do you
not fear God, since you are under the same sentence of condemna-
tion? And we indeed justly; for we are receiving the due reward of
our deeds; but this man has done nothing wrong.' And he said,
'Jesus, remember me when you come into your kingdom.' And the
Lord said to him, 'Truly, I say to you, today you will be with me in
Paradise.' "

Another brief pause.

"My Lord, Jesus who is the Christ, please remember and watch
over this unworthy child of the Gypsy who sits by your right hand in
Paradise. Amen."

"Omein," Greg whispered, then looked up at a sensor. "Clear
right."

"Clear left," Lukacs said, looking at a sensor.

Greg checked the sensors hanging in front of him. "Clear
ahead." He reached down, pushing a button on the small transmitter on his belt three times. Then he put one hand on the front bar
of the framework, the other on the sand beneath him. He dug the
toes of his boots in, then nodded at Lukacs.

In a planned, arrhythmic, uneven motion they began to crawl
forward, bringing their carefully painted desert blind with them.

4 Hours 27 Minutes Remaining

In a mobile home parked on the side of State Highway 168, three
miles from Freedom Ridge, the three soft beeps seemed to drive
straight through the occupants. Silence reigned. Several crossed
themselves. Foss closed his eyes in an expression of pure anxiety.

Roman sighed.

"Inform the others," he said in a monotone. "They have reached the Sinai."

One of the Gypsy women picked up a cellular phone and began the calls.

After checking with the men and women monitoring the police, state, and federal authorities frequencies, on the scanners that were mounted on the walls, Roman walked over to Foss. "Where are they?"

Foss looked down at the central of the three monitors in front of him. There, a computer-processed reproduction of the desert terrain (taken from Megan's videos) was displayed. Superimposed on it was a computer simulation of the desert blind that the two men were crawling under.

"They should be about there," Foss said in a tense voice. "Maybe sixty, seventy feet from where they came out of the Break."

Roman nodded. "How long before they hit the heart of the sensor field?"

"An hour. Maybe a little longer." His eyes never left the computer simulation.

Roman patted the old man on the back, feeling his tension through his shirt and windbreaker. "You should get some rest before then. Maybe take a walk, get some air, no?"

Foss shook his head. "I'll be fine," he rushed out through clenched teeth.

"Okay." Roman started for the door, tapping one of the other men on the shoulder as he passed. "Watch him," he whispered.

Glancing over at Foss, who was busy with his computer, Roman turned, then stepped out into the rapidly cooling night.

The outside was set up like any other campground. A barbecue stood off to the side where a man casually turned almost done hamburgers. Children, including his own, played in the growing darkness, city kids reveling in the strange desert environment. Women sat in lawn furniture, gossiping.

A carefully orchestrated, well-rehearsed tableau arranged to give the casual (or not so casual) observer one simple message.

"Ignore us! There's nothing special here!"

Malika came up behind her husband, wrapping her arms around his spreading middle. "So?"

He didn't move, just stared off into the darkness in the general direction of Lateral Break.

"They're in the desert." Roman's voice still held that odd monotone.

"So soon?"

"Three minutes late, actually," he sighed.

"That's not so bad," she said encouragingly.

He pulled her hands up to his lips, kissing them gently.

"Three minutes in the first ninety." He pulled away from her, actually taking a couple steps toward that place he saw in his mind. "In six hours that's twelve minutes. Twelve minutes." He paused. "In those suits, six hours was already a gamble. Twelve minutes could make all the difference."

Malika came up beside him. "You wanted to go with him."

He nodded solemnly. "Lukacs is more qualified. More right."

"But you wanted it anyway."

Roman laughed sharply at his wife's insight as he turned to her. "You should tell fortunes, you know?"

Malika laughed in turn. "You don't need the gift to know that. It's written across your face."

Roman nodded. "I suppose." He turned to her. "I have not seen the man in ten years. Didn't know if he was alive or dead. But when he asks, I come. And for what? A chance to help him kill himself, maybe get the rest of us killed along with him? All to see . . ." He laughed bitterly. "It's all too comical."

Malika walked over to him. "What's wrong, my love?"

Roman hesitated. When he spoke, his voice seemed far away, as if the words came from another place or time.

"I'm standing here, not sure whether or not I'll ever see the man again, and I still don't know why he did it."

"You mean Paris?"

"Paris, yes." He seemed to drift off, then caught himself. He smiled down at his wife. "I never knew why, you know? Why he took such a risk to help a perfect stranger."

"You never asked him?"

For the first time, a genuine smile floated across his face. "That's just the point. When I came to, a month later, when I found all this out, I did ask him." He actually laughed. "You know what he said?"

Malika shook her head.

"All he said was 'I don't like inequities.' Very matter-of-factly too. 'I don't like inequities.' Can you believe that? If it had been only one or two of them, he might never have helped me. I was actually saved by being completely outnumbered." He continued to laugh, then turned back toward the nearby mountain range. "Imagine that."

Malika hugged him, then kissed him on the cheek. "I do," she said softly with deep emotion, "I do and I thank God for his being there every night."

Roman continued to stare off into the night. "I should be there," he muttered.

"What will you do?" Malika asked after a long silence.

Roman never turned away from his . . . vigil.

"About what?"

"What will you do if he does not come back?" She held her breath as she waited for the answer.

"Avenge him," came the answer she was afraid to hear.

"Why?"

Roman turned to his wife, sighed, then shrugged.

"Because . . . he does not like inequities."

4 Hours 13 Minutes Remaining

In the desert, the going had been easier than they'd expected. So far, no seismic detectors, only a few motion detectors and ammonia sniffers. The sniffers were defeated by the two men's almost complete body covering of neoprene and fabric; while their arrhythmic, slow movements along the sand had fooled the motion detectors. As they would any seismic sensors.

But so far the detection devices had been few and far between. A state that Greg's sensors were saying had just come to an end.

"It's almost off the scale to our left," Lukacs whispered. "All band lengths and widths. I've never seen anything like it!"

Greg ignored him, concentrating instead on the sensor display hanging in front of him.

"Don't move," he mumbled. "Don't change your position in any way at all."

Lukacs froze, lying half on his stomach, half on his side. "What is it?"

"Damned if I know."

Moving his hand slower than the boy next to him thought possible, Greg pushed some buttons on the nearest sensor. Without moving his head, he peered at the readouts that were displayed a moment later. "Interesting."

"What is it?" Lukacs asked again, this time in a calmer voice.

"One of Foss's little black dots. Now be quiet, and don't move, damn it!"

Using his index finger, Greg cleared the sweat from his eyes under the hood.

"Show me the magic," he muttered to himself. "Come on, little fellow, show me the magic."

The display momentarily flickered from .00271 ohm to .00341, then immediately back again.

"Ah, Linus. Something new to play with, then?"

Again, the momentary readout change, then back to the earlier steady reading. A less-than-a-second change of .0007 ohm. Greg watched the sequence repeat itself three more times, then closed his eyes.

Lukacs watched as the thief relaxed, almost as if he was asleep.

"Nine-tenths-of-a-second burst of .0007 ohm in the ultralow-band spectrum. Nine-tenths-of-a-second burst of . . . Ahh." He sounded satisfied as he opened his eyes.

He turned, very slightly, toward Lukacs. "When you answer me, don't move. Just answer me."

"Okay."

"Do you know where the 3K sender is?"

Lukacs thought for a moment. "Small of my back. Right side."

Greg took a deep breath. "Okay. I'll count you down like this: three, two, one, zero. On zero, reach back with your right hand and grab it. But don't, do not try to unclip it. Understand?"

Two weeks of working with the thief had taught the Gypsy to do exactly what Greg told him to. No more, no less.

"Right."

"Then I'll give you another countdown. On that zero, unclip it and bring it forward, right?"

"Right."

"Then I'll give you a third countdown. On that zero, put the sender in my left hand, then grab the bar by my hand. Don't try to pull your hand back, right?"

"Right."

Greg checked the readouts again. "Okay, tell me when you're ready."

Lukacs took several deep breaths, went through the three movements in his mind, then barely nodded. "I'm ready."

"Right," Greg whispered. "Here we go." He studied the sensor's readout, waiting for the momentary burst to register. "Stand by."

The burst!

"Three, two, one," another burst, "zero!"

The young Gypsy's nimble fingers flashed back and grabbed onto the long microwave-sending device.

"Three, two, one," another burst, "zero!"

His hand flew forward, almost tearing his belt as he clawed the device free, burying his hand slightly in the sand by his ear.

"Three, two, one," another burst, "zero!"

Lukacs slapped the machine into Greg's waiting left hand, then instantly grabbed the front bar of the blind.

"Good hands, kid," Greg said calmly as if he'd expected nothing less. With one eye watching for the bursts, he began manipulating the machine's control pad with only the fingers of his left hand.

Almost trembling from gripping the bar so tightly, Lukacs watched Greg closely.

"You know what it is?"

Greg nodded, barely. "Not really."

"Then . . ."

"I may not know what it is," Greg mumbled as he continued playing with the sender's settings. "But I know how it works."

A moment after the next burst, he hung the sender on the front bar next to his sensor, its tiny dish sender/receiver pushing the blanket up about six or seven inches.

"Whatever that is out there, it transmits extremely low frequency microwave bursts. Since there's no return signature, it doesn't work like radar. So there must be a passive receiver somewhere behind us. Maybe, probably, ten or twelve for the entire sensor field." He paused as he concentrated on the readouts. "Damned efficient way to make a spiderweb."

Lukacs tried to picture the several hundred microwaves forming an impenetrable, invisible electronic web across the desert. With all lines of the net ending at hidden receivers.

Disturb any of the strands, even barely . . . Well, it wasn't spiders Lukacs was afraid of.

"How do we turn it off?"

Greg grimaced. "We don't." He watched as with each burst, the readings on the sender started to come closer to those on the sensor. "Interrupt the signal with any moving organic material, like us," he added almost as an afterthought, "and the receiver sends off an alarm that the impedance from a given sender has stopped. That's when the guys with guns come raining down on us."

"But if you can't turn it off . . ."

"We misdirect it. Our sender intercepts the original signal, like a magnet pulling in metal filings; then sends a cloned, duplicate signal over our heads to the receiving unit."

Lukacs thought about it for a moment. "Like a prism bending light," he mumbled.

"Very good." Greg grit his teeth. "Now let's see if theory and fact intersect. Three. Two. One. Now!" He pressed a button on the sender, then waited.

For two endless minutes, the men lay on their stomachs, watching the signals from the sensors as well as the sender, seemingly perfectly matched.

Finally Greg nodded. "Okay," he said, exhaling deeply. "Let's get going. Clear right."

Lukacs blinked the sweat out of his eyes. "Will all the senders have the same frequency?"

For the first time since the young man had met him, Greg seemed unsure of himself. "I think so." He checked his sensors again. "Clear right."

"Clear left," Lukacs mumbled self-consciously.

"Clear ahead," Greg said as he regripped the front bar. "One, two, three!"

They began inching their way across the desert floor again.

Five minutes later, as they continued to push/crawl their way across the sand, Lukacs turned to the man he was beginning to think of as "the Magician."

"How did you know that would work?"

Greg shrugged as he pushed forward. "I didn't. I don't."

"But what . . . How? How do we know if you're right?"

Greg paused, taking another sip of his energy drink. "If we get shot," he said matter-of-factly, "I was wrong."

3 Hours 3 Minutes Remaining

The junkyard had taken on the feel of an armed camp.

Outside, on all four sides of the place, men sat in careful concealment. Armed with handguns and radios, they kept their eyes on anyone that came within a city block of the compound.

Just inside the fence, the small-caliber handguns that Greg had insisted on were gone. Replaced by sawed-off shotguns (the preferred weapon of the Gypsy), augmented with recently "liberated" Ingram submachine guns from Nellis Air Force Base.

Deeper inside, around building 2 (the command and control center) guards stood by every entrance. Cars with drivers behind the wheels stood at the ready. One at each of the three doors.

The men warmed up their engines for five minutes each half hour as Deo had trained them. With their reinforced grilles and trunks, perfectly tuned big engines, solid rubber tires, the cars would be used, if necessary, to crash through any and all obstacles to make a successful getaway.

Inside, Megan supervised the loading of every map, every photograph, every piece of paper or diagram, into four suitcases. Her personal bodyguard never more than five feet away.

When she was finished, after making a final trip around the large, strangely empty room, she turned to Magda.

"You're sure they can take care of the rest?"

The attractive woman smiled. "If there's one thing we know how to do, it's move." She noticed the tension, the eyes red from not crying, then put a reassuring arm around her. "All will be taken care of. I promise you."

Megan laughed, embarrassed. "I didn't think it was that obvious."

"Why shouldn't it be, these are dangerous times. Fear is a fitting companion."

Megan stepped away, her footsteps making hollow sounds in the empty, hangarlike building. "I don't think I ever really thought it would get this far."

"No?" Magda seemed surprised. "Why not? The plan is a good one."

This time a nervous laugh.

"It's not the plan. It's me. It was all a game to me, you see. Before any of this started even."

"How?" The experienced Gypsy seducer was honestly interested.

Megan lifted her eyebrows while cocking her head to the side. An expression of . . . saddened disbelief.

"When I was first on the story, I figured 'Hey! Here's a way to get on the map.' A way to get around the jerks who didn't believe in me. But it was all in the abstract, you know? I never saw it as anything but an interesting trip down some old mystery. A game of hide-and-seek.''

Magda laughed. "Then you became *it.*" She smiled. "The best part of any game."

Megan nodded sadly. "It was terrifying. But also somehow . . . exhilarating. Like some bizarre game of tag. Running, hiding, everything with Greg, with all of you. It never seemed real somehow. Just like some kind of weird game of dress-up."

She paused, wiping her lightly tearing eyes with a tissue.

"I mean I knew it had to end at some point, but I never rationally contemplated what it would be like, you know?"

Magda shook her head, walked a few paces away, then started to laugh. A full-throated, from-the-heart-and-soul belly laugh.

"My God, girl! How is it you could spend so much time with us, eat with us, laugh with us"—she paused and smiled—"sleep with us? How could you do all that and not understand us?"

Megan seemed confused. "Wha—what are you talking about?"

Magda lifted herself onto a table, dangling her legs like a little girl as she talked.

"It *is* a game, Megan. A wild, no-holds-barred, no-rules-but-those-you-make-yourself game. That's our way, dum-dum," she chirped as her laugh wound down to a light chuckle. "In all the time you've been with us, have you ever heard anyone even mention work?"

Megan thought, then shook her head.

"Of course not, my gadja princess. We make everything a game. Planning this score was a game called 'can we beat the system?' Gathering the information we needed was a game called 'what can we know that they don't want us to?' Emile there," she said, nodding at Megan's bodyguard, "even he's playing a game."

Megan turned to the big man.

He nodded with a smile. "Am I stronger, tougher, smarter than bastards who try hurt you?" he said as he fingered the Ingram on a strap around his neck and shoulder.

Magda hopped down. "To the Gypsy, all life is a game. It must be." Her eyes grew clouded, her expression dark. "For to face it any other way is unbearable."

For a moment, the barest moment, Megan thought she saw incredible pain just beneath the surface of the girl she'd come to know as a happy-go-lucky, take-it-as-it-comes comet of light.

Then it was gone.

"So we play, darling!" Magda grinned, then kissed Megan on the cheek. "To play is to live. You should try it sometime."

Shaking her head, thinking she might never understand these people her fate had become inextricably linked with, Megan followed the girl out to the waiting car.

2 Hours 57 Minutes Remaining

The nondescript van slowed as it pulled up to the brightly lit, heavily guarded gate.

"Smooth like a baby's ass." Lazslo whispered his warning from the passenger's seat.

"It's greased," the driver whispered back as he smiled at the approaching guard.

"State your business."

"Cleaning carpets. NCO club, building 238," the driver said as he handed his work order, driver's license, and proof of insurance to the guard.

"Wait here."

"Sure, sure."

The military policeman carried the work order back to his guard shack, checking it against a list on a clipboard. Then he picked up the phone.

"Problem?" Lazslo shifted in his seat to get a better look at the guard shack.

"Relax, this is normal," the driver said. "In a minute he'll come back and say"—he lowered his voice to a rough equivalent of the guard's—" 'Y'all drive safely now. Keep it under fifteen an' park in da green slots.' Routine," he said with a smile as the guard started back to them.

He slapped a sticker to the front of the windshield. "Y'all drive safely an' keep it under fifteen miles an hour, right? Y'all can park in any of the green slots."

The driver saluted the guard, then drove through the raised gate.

Lazslo shook his head. "I am properly impressed." He looked out the window at passing soldiers and airmen. "Of course now comes the hard part."

The driver snorted. "Ha! You sit, wait, maybe take on the whole U.S. of America army. Me? I got to clean the fucking carpets!"

Lazslo, along with the three men who were hidden in the back of the van, broke into laughter as the van threaded its way deeper into the base.

2 Hours 49 Minutes Remaining

It had been a long day, a boring night, and it was time to think about sleep.

Gavilan put aside the brief he'd been working on, polished off the last of his drink, then reached for the table lamp. A knock at his door stopped him.

Looking at his watch (it was after midnight), Gavilan muttered the most vulgar epithet he could think of as he walked to the door.

"It'd better be freaking important for you to . . ." He froze. Stunned into silence by the smiling woman leaning against his doorway. "You're not going to kidnap me again, are you?" he asked in an exasperated voice.

Magda kissed him lightly on the cheek, then slid past him into the house.

"Would I do something like that?" she said in her most innocent tone.

"What do you want? Or is it the same as last time?"

Magda nodded approvingly at the living room, then tossed the wary man a thick envelope as she made herself a drink at the bar.

"Ten thousand dollars for an hour of your time, darling." She smiled seductively. "Be smart and there may be more in it for you."

He thumbed open the envelope, tossed it in a drawer, then walked over to her. He took her drink, then sat down in a nearby chair.

"I'm listening."

Magda smiled as she made herself another drink.

Half an hour later, Gavilan looked over the six pages of notes he'd made, then nodded at Magda. She checked that the video camera was running and in focus.

"Okay," she whispered.

Gavilan took a breath, then began. "My name is John Gavilan. I am an attorney licensed to practice in the state of Nevada. Bar card number J-0926-85. I am witnessing the statement that is about to be made in my presence. I assert and avow that these statements are being made freely and with no coercion that I am aware of. I have spoken with the attester and am convinced of the soundness of her mental state. A written transcript of this tape will be made this eve-ning, placed in a file with supporting documentation, then signed by me. It will be stored in a safe location."

He turned to his left, then nodded to the woman beside him. Magda moved the camera to her right.

"My name is Megan Turner," she said in a firm voice. "As you can plainly see, I am not dead!"

2 Hours 9 Minutes Remaining

"Psych 301."

"Psych 301 by."

"Psych 301, Dreamland. Report status."

"Psych 301. Initiating gamma pattern in grid four seven Kilo. Fuel at two five, stores full. All systems functioning five by. No rattles or shakes in current patrol area."

"301, roger. Be aware, Dreamland, weather reports unstable air mass now bearing zero eight three at nine miles. Velocity three two kph."

"Psych 301. Copy, Dreamland. We've been having a real interest-ing ride the last few minutes. Can you advise on ceiling and dura-tion?"

"301, roger. Dreamland, weather reports ceiling at Angels three seven, winds at core in excess of six four kph with shear. Advises probable duration unknown due to mountain effect."

"Psych 301. Copy, Dreamland. What do you advise?"

"Uh, 301, Dreamland. We've already started losing the field north and east of Dreamland due to high winds, heavy downpour, inter-mittent hail. And, uh, it's bearing down on your area now, sir. Dreamland advises that you make for North Field Alternate, weather the storm, refuel, then continue patrol when the instability passes."

"Psych 301. Uh, control? Any idea how long we're gonna be down?"

"301, roger. Dreamland, weather estimates niner zero minutes for the storm to pass you by. We'd like you in the air as soon as possible after that, sir. We've recalled all Cherokees and it's gonna take us a while to reboot the system. So we'll need your eyes as soon as you're good to go."

"Psych 301. Roger that, Dreamland. Request vector to North Field Alternate."

"301, roger. Turn left to two four seven. Contact North Field Control on zero four six point three. Have a safe trip, sir."

"Psych 301. Copy, Dreamland. Turning left to two four seven. Contacting North Field Control at zero four six point three. Back to you soonest, Dreamland."

"301, roger. We'll be waiting. Dreamland clear."

"Psych 301 outbound."

2 Hours 7 Minutes Remaining

Even under the heavy blanket of the blind, the two thieves could feel the fury of the rapidly approaching storm. The wind tore at it, the first waves of rain began to soak it. All as the temperature seemed to be dropping by the second.

Both men concentrated on the sensors around them. Movement became almost impossible as the rain grew heavier, starting to soak the sand around them. Finally Greg signaled for them to stop.

"Now?" Lukacs had to almost yell to be heard above the wind as it howled through the blind.

Greg shook his head. "Field's still active!" he shouted. "We have to wait!"

Their world was lit up by sheet lightning. Greg immediately began to count.

"One! Two! Three! Four! Five! Six! Seven! Eight! Nine! Ten! Eleven! Twel—"

A roar of thunder washed over their exposed position.

"Two point four miles," Greg called out. "You get the next one! I'm going to do a full-spectrum check!"

"Okay!" Lukacs barely lifted the front edge of the blanket as he prayed that the sensors on the framework wouldn't attract the lightning.

A jagged flash cut across the horizon, momentarily lighting up the desert floor.

"One! Two! Three! Four! Five! Six! Seven! Eight! Nine! Te—"

A cannon shot of thunder shook him to his bones.

"I humble myself in the presence of my Lord," he mumbled, then did the math. "One point nine miles!"

Greg shook his head, a look of disgust in his eyes. "The jerks still have the field on full intensity. They don't start shutting down systems quick, they could lose the whole damn thing!"

Another lightning burst, this one seeming to silhouette something on the desert floor several miles ahead of them.

"I saw it!" Lukacs shouted as he pointed. "Maybe three, four miles at one o'clock!"

Greg nodded. "Five! Six! Seven!" Then the thunder. "One point four miles!"

Something began pounding on the blind from above. Like a boy with a stick striking erratically at a suspected snake.

Lukacs flinched as something hard hit him on the back of the neck. "Ow! What is . . ." He looked to the side of his head, seeing the golf-ball-sized hailstones. Almost at that same moment the sound of popcorn furiously popping reached them.

"Cover your head," Greg yelled as the wave of hail moved across the desert floor toward them.

The blanket was being torn to pieces by the wind, the rain, now the large, heavy hail. The two men protected themselves as best they could, sneaking glances at their hanging sensors.

"Seismic and motion sensors are gonna overload if they don't . . ." Greg paused as the hail and rain suddenly stopped.

Lukacs started to raise his head. "What?" he said in the odd silence.

Greg grabbed the boy, forcing his head down. *"Cover!"*

His shout was almost lost a second later as a jagged lightning bolt hissed through the storm, impacting on the desert floor less than a thousand yards away. A shower of orange and blue sparks seemed to explode into the air, followed three seconds later by a bone-rattling explosion of sound and air.

"You alive?" Greg shouted as soon as he'd recovered from the body blow.

"I think so." Lukacs's voice sounded slurred. By the shock of the too-close thunder, by the adrenaline rush of the storm. By heat exhaustion from the suits they'd been too long in.

"Hey?" Greg shouted at the boy who was looking around in a vaguely disoriented way. "Hey? What's your name?"

"My name?"

"What's your name? Come on!"

Greg waited anxiously for ten long seconds.

"Lukacs."

Another jagged tooth of nature's power tore at the ground

around them. Another explosion of sparks. Another teeth-rattling shot of thunder followed two seconds later.

"How far was that, Lukacs? Luke? How far?"

"Um, less than half a mile," he said in a slightly stronger voice.

Greg grimaced. "They've lost two of the microwave web senders. They don't shut down the system right now, they're gonna lose maybe half a million dollars' worth of hardware!"

Both men ducked as three lightning strikes, with almost instant thunder, came down at them.

"And if they don't?" Lukacs said in an almost fully recovered voice.

"We take our chances out there! Hope they'll mistake us for rain, hail, and wind."

Lukacs momentarily raised his mask to wipe his face. He looked pale, either from dehydration or fear of having to run through an active sensor field.

Maybe both.

Suddenly the lights on the sensors around them turned from orange to green.

"Wait," Greg said softly. "Wait."

He took one of the sensors, holding it in his hand as he checked a full 360 degrees around the blind.

"Son of a bitch," he whispered. "Son of a bitch! They've shut the field down!"

Both men cheered as though they'd just seen the winning run in the seventh game of the World Series.

A moment later, they grabbed the sensors off the bars of the blind's framework, then cast the blanket and frame away. They crouched on the desert floor, squinting against the driving rain, trying to ignore the painful hits of the hail.

"How long do we have?" Lukacs asked as he readjusted his backpack.

Greg peered through the lessening lightning flashes at what he hoped was the outer fence of the installation.

"Half hour. Maybe more." He paused. "At least fifteen minutes after all this ends, anyway." He pointed slightly to their right. "I make it about four and a half miles, maybe five."

"Can we make it?"

Greg shrugged, checked again with his sensor in a full circle, then stood up. "Let's find out."

With the next lightning flash, they were off at a quick jog.

1 Hour 58 Minutes Remaining

As the digital clock above Foss's computer banks in the mobile home began to wind down, the people grew quiet.

For fifteen minutes now, they had begun to gather in the cramped quarters. Nobody talking. Nobody working. Just nine men and women sitting or standing. Alternately watching the clock and the computer simulation of the blind's expected movements.

When the thunderstorm broke around the mobile home, the simulation showed the blind 5.3 miles from the outer perimeter of the installation.

As the clock counted down below 1:00, Malika came in, putting her hand in her husband's.

At 0:30, Foss put his glass of tea aside, plugged in a set of headphones, beginning to listen intently to dead air.

At 0:05 remaining, Roman put the receiver on the loudspeaker so that the group (now grown to fourteen) could hear the empty sputtering static.

0:03.

0:02.

0:01.

With nobody breathing, with everybody praying, the clock rolled down to zero.

Foss leaned forward, holding the headphones tightly to his ears.

Malika looked into her husband's eyes, which were locked on the closest speaker, then slipped her arm around him.

Roman shook his head, muttering "twelve minutes" beneath his breath.

A soft, clear beep echoed through the room.

Everyone straightened.

A pause, seeming to last a year, then three more of the beautiful sounds filled the room of now-cheering people.

Roman crossed himself, then turned to the women working the cell phones.

"Inform the others," he said in a barely recognizable, choked voice. "Tell them the Magician has reached . . ." He paused, locking eyes with an exhausted but smiling Foss. ". . . the Promised Land."

FIFTEEN

IT WAS LATE.

Or maybe it was early. Depending on your point of view.

To the heavily armed, scowling guard, it was neither.

It was just cold.

It had been a night of shivering in the cramped guard post. Of watching a string of thunderstorms tear across the desert, almost blacking out the entire Dreamland installation. Of responding to the constant false alarms from the outer fence. Alarms caused by the heavily ionized atmosphere of the storm. Each necessitating a long, pointless trip through the driving rain to confirm the alarm's malfunction. Then trying to get back to the relative dryness of the post before he got drenched.

It was nights like this that sometimes caused the man to question his commitment to his job.

Sometimes.

But all in all, bad weather notwithstanding, he liked what he did, who he was . . . a member of the most elite multiservice security corps in the world.

Drawn from all the armed services, that corps took only the best of the best. The finest shots, the toughest men and women, the most loyal, dedicated, and committed that the military had to offer. Even then, there were eighteen months of training before being accepted for assignment.

Only a third of those accepted for the training made it through. Most of those being assigned to outlying facilities or one of the eight

Dreamland annexes. But the cream of the crop, those few who were found worthy of the task ahead, made it to this place. The secret heart of the government's most classified, heavily secured facility.

Dreamland Base.

Actually four large underground facilities made up the base. Each with its own cryptic code name: Majic Ops, Labyrinth, Blinder Control, and Vortex. When it had first been proposed, the facility had been called Prairie Dog, a concession that there was to be over forty times the floor space belowground as there was above it.

At its height, it contained underground facilities and laboratories for the Atomic Energy Commission, the Department of Defense, the CIA, and the National Command Authority Directorate. But that had been thirty years ago.

Now only two of the vast, secret burrows were still in use.

The National Command Authority still controlled its original underground space, and had expanded halfway into another, adjoining space, formerly belonging to the AEC. The DoD's space across the field was now the home to—well, maybe fifteen people outside of Labyrinth knew what.

Despite their proximity, despite the occasional chance meetings between the staffs of the two secret projects, they knew very little of each other's work. Which is how the authorities wanted it. Compartmentalization, they called it. Need to know. Mutually blind coexistence.

The final touch had been the security corps: 225 men and women dedicated to preserving the secrecy of the two projects, neither of which they had any real concept of. Which isn't to say they didn't speculate.

Eight years after he first stepped off the transport from Nellis North Field, the guard knew very little more about Dreamland Base than he did on that first day.

But he had *seen* some things.

Bizarre things that he'd never questioned, couldn't explain or begin to understand, but knew he had to protect.

Because his country had told him he must.

So he smiled with a knowing look when he saw the documentaries. Laughed as he heard the earnest academics discuss the possibilities. Shook his head at the inevitable futility of lefties like the Freedom Ridge Society.

All the while denying to himself the truth of his own experience.

He might have seen more than the others, might be able to name some names or give thin half-explanations for some of the things. But in his heart of hearts, he realized that he actually knew less than the outsiders.

And it made him sad that his government had not seen fit to confide "the great truth" to him.

But he was satisfied that there *was* a great truth and that was enough.

Keeping his head down against the light rain, the last vestige of the stormy night, he continued to the site of the last fence alarm signal. A thin strip of dark red-blue shone across the eastern sky, and he could feel the morning wind begin as he reached the spot.

"Dreamland Field three seven at scene," he said into his headset.

"Dreamland Field three seven, roger." The voice on the other end sounded as tired as the guard felt. The storm had made for a hard night on everybody.

Looking through the inner wall of doubled chain-link fence that surrounded the sprawling facility, he could already see three of the white Cherokees heading out across the desert, checking on damaged or nonfunctional sensors. Although he couldn't see it yet, he looked in the direction where he knew the patrol copter would be. He took a deep breath as he tried to remember when his next patrol outside the fence would begin.

Finally he turned to his inspection of the fence.

The light rain turned to drizzle. Large drops forming on each of the chain-link squares. The fence seemed slightly bowed in, probably from the force of the high winds of the night. The sand beyond was beaten and churned; again, most likely from rain, hail, and winds. But in all other respects everything was as it should be.

As the barest edge of flaming globe began to clear the eastern mountains behind him, the guard keyed his headset. "Dreamland Field three seven."

"Dreamland Field three seven, Central by."

"Three seven. Central, I'm at frame 14692 slash Whiskey. Everything seems okay here."

"Dreamland Field three seven, Central by. How would you like to log this response?"

The guard reached out, grabbing the inner fence near one of its support poles. It pulled away from the pole easily. A surprised look came over the man as he tried again. Pulling far enough inward to leave a gap of about two feet from the ground.

"Three seven, Central. Looks like the rings that hold the thing to the pole got bent out in the wind last night. Log it . . ." Something on one of the bottom points of the fence caught his attention. ". . . storm damage," he finished as he bent to inspect the tiny whatever it was.

"Dreamland Field three seven, roger. Logged 'storm damage.' Stand by until field maintenance arrives on scene."

"Three seven, copy, Central," he said quietly as he reached out, pulling the small thing loose from the fence.

It was a piece of rubber or pseudo-rubber, less than a half inch across. He pulled one of his gloves off with his teeth, then rubbed the piece with his bare fingers. He held it up to his nose, smelling the acrid rubber smell.

It was a nothing, just an insignificant *piece* of nothing. Blown halfway across the desert from some distant campground or hiking trail. Had probably been blowing around the sand and rocks for weeks before the storm drove it up against the fence for him to find.

Nothing.

He put it in a jacket pocket, regloved, then started to turn away. Then, without knowing why, he stopped. "Dreamland Field three seven," he called in.

"Dreamland Field three seven, Central by."

"Three seven. Uh, Central? What's the ETA on that field maintenance response?"

"Dreamland Field three seven. ETA three five minutes. Sorry, but you're third on the list." When the guard didn't respond in the required three seconds, Central came back on. "Dreamland Field three seven. Do you wish us to expedite, sir?"

"Three seven. Negative. Uh, just checking, Central. Thank you."

"Central by."

It was silly, really. Probably a by-product of all those years in the desert where security was not just job one, but life itself. There was no reason to even think once about a tiny piece of black rubber found among all the garbage that the desert tended to collect. All of which eventually found itself tangled in a sensor or against the security fence.

But he spent the next thirty-two minutes studying the desert beyond the fence through his high-powered binoculars. Then, when relieved by the maintenance team, rather than returning to the meager comforts of his guard post, he made a full patrol of his sector on the base's apron.

And logged the rubber shard into his shift report when he was relieved an hour later.

A little before ten that morning, Gavilan knocked lightly on his boss's door.

"Come on in, John."

"Got some time?"

The man nodded. "Always for my staff," Capers said in his professorial tone. "What do you need?"

Gavilan looked around the office, then closed the door behind him.

Since Capers always made an elaborate point of keeping his door open during all but the most sensitive meetings, he immediately came to attention. "What's going on?"

"You ever have those antibugging people in?" Gavilan spoke in a near whisper, not taking the chair that his boss gestured at.

"Uh, last week." Capers began writing on a pad as he talked. "Had them do all the suites while they were here." He held up a pad.

GO SOMEPLACE ELSE???

Gavilan nodded to the man whose paranoia he was just beginning to understand. "I was just wondering," he said casually as he wrote a message on the pad.

Capers read the message, then nodded his agreement. "Was there anything else?" he said casually.

"No," Gavilan said as he opened the door. "I got what I came for."

Twenty minutes later, the two men met at a bench by the noisy construction site across the street.

"What's wrong, John?" Capers said without preamble. "You get another visit from Kilbourne?"

"You ever find out anything about him?"

Capers shook his head. "Only the most reluctant, perfunctory confirmation of his ID from the NRC. And they were none too happy about my calling either." He laughed, but was surprised when Gavilan just continued watching the passing traffic.

Gavilan took a deep breath. "I, well, I've taken on something that I'm . . . let's say *unsure* of."

Capers leaned back, studying the man in front of him. "Can you discuss the details?" The constitutional law professor that he most truly was began coming out in every syllable of his speech. "Without divulging confidences, of course."

"It's sort of an immigration case."

"Uh-huh."

"I've been approached by a—a group that has documentation that some, uh, aliens have been detained by the federal government."

"Pending deportation?"

Gavilan sat down next to Capers. "Not exactly. These documents seem to indicate that these aliens have been held in special custody for a long period of time, in order to obtain—well, intelligence information is probably the best way to put it."

"Go on." Capers closed his eyes as he leaned back on the bench. His usual way of concentrating on a student's brief.

"Well, these *aliens* have allegedly been held for a number of years, been denied counsel; were never brought before any federal magistrate; were never allowed to communicate with their, uh, place of origin. The group that brought this case to me believes that these aliens are in danger now that knowledge of their existence has leaked out."

Gavilan paused before getting to the really hard part. "Also, this group has alleged that a government agency has conspired or participated in a minimum of four killings, possibly many more. All with the avowed goal of maintaining the secret of these custodies."

Capers nodded but kept his eyes shut. "Three questions," he said in a semidreamy voice. "What are the people like in this group who've come to you?"

Gavilan never hesitated. "Career criminals, probably. I've personally witnessed several well-thought-out, well-executed criminal acts. But in each case they went to great lengths to avoid violence, and never threatened me to get my cooperation or silence. Also"—now he did pause, wondering how far he should go—"also there is an individual who was previously known to me as a media reporter or producer. This individual alleges having been kidnapped by a government group, then fled their hands to live underground."

"Interesting." Capers seemed to think it over. "How much did they pay you for your cooperation?'' He smiled as he opened his eyes.

Gavilan returned the smile, however strained it might've been. ''Enough for me to take them seriously.''

''Next question. What does this group plan to do about these aliens?''

Gavilan took a deep breath. ''Since they believe that public exposure of their existence would result in the execution of the aliens, they intend to free them themselves. Only failing that would they go public.''

Capers had closed his eyes again, reassuming his concentration. ''Last question. Are these legal or illegal aliens we're talking about?''

Gavilan paused, thinking about it. ''That they entered U.S. territories without permission is clear. But only by accident, and they have never been given the opportunity to return to their point of origin.''

Capers nodded. ''What do they want you to do, this group that's contacted you?''

Gavilan got up, starting to pace. ''That's the problem. They want me to represent their rights in a federal court. Both the group's and the aliens'.''

Capers seemed to be deep in thought. After almost two minutes, he opened his eyes. ''Okay,'' he said firmly.

Gavilan sat down beside him, opened his briefcase, then handed a file of yellowed, aging documents to him.

''I've been led to believe these are originals, taken from the personal archives of one of the murder victims.''

For the next fifty minutes, Capers read each document, sometimes cross-referencing between several. Shaking his head, clucking his tongue, as the time passed, his expression became one of something between deep concentration and animal fury.

Finally he was done.

He gently straightened the documents, returning them to their file, then Gavilan. Again, he closed his eyes, allowing a silence punctuated by the rattle and cacophony of the construction site to fill in the twenty-minute gap. When at last he opened his eyes, his expression seemed far away. He gestured at Gavilan's briefcase.

''The implications of what you have in those papers, if *half* true, are truly frightening.'' He shook his head. ''Hell, forget the government for the moment, forget their breaking God knows how many laws and statutes, trampling the Constitution into the ground and all. That's just for starters."

He turned to the younger lawyer. "Every religion, every orthodoxy or belief system we have, will feel threatened. Every man, woman, and child on the planet will lose their sense of security. Think of it."

He shook his head. "This could make the Second Coming look like a carnival sideshow." He looked Gavilan in the eyes, with a deeply probing intensity. "How good are these people that brought this to you?"

"I've been representing criminals in this state for almost fifteen years, and they're the best I've ever seen."

"They better be." He paused, thinking. "How far have they gotten with their plan?"

"I've been led to believe it's currently under way."

Unconsciously Capers looked at his watch. "When will you know something?"

Gavilan shrugged. "I'm not sure. Sometime tonight or tomorrow night, I think."

Capers seemed suddenly energized. "What are you going to do?" he asked with a genuine curiosity.

"Do I make it a private or an office case?"

"Aliens are usually indigent. What the hell. Why not? Assuming there's some substantial proof of their positions. Over and above these documents." He paused. "What do you need?"

Gavilan pulled a rough brief from his case, handing it to his growingly enthused superior. The man quickly read through the fifteen-page document.

"You really think you're going to get a U.S. district court judge to hear this?"

"Why not? It falls under their jurisdiction."

"Technically," Capers said as he flipped back a few pages.

"Law, by definition, is a series of technicalities."

Capers ignored him. "The moment you file this with any federal court, these Majic 12 people will be climbing all over your ass. You'll never get it to hearing."

For the first time, Gavilan smiled an open, easy smile. "You got the Langley manuscript case to trial. You always said you had to fight off the CIA, Defense Department, and half the City of Chicago Police Department."

"I argued that the public safety was at stake," Capers mumbled. "I convinced the court to hold an immediate . . ." He stopped, snapping his head up. "Tell me you're not thinking of . . ." His voice trailed off in disbelief.

"You'd be making law again," Gavilan said quickly. "Not defending druggies, pushers, or sociopaths. Not shuffling papers and deciding on the color for the third-floor ladies' room." Gavilan's voice was seductive. "Second-chair me. Handle the constitutional points. Everything else, I'll take care of."

Gavilan saw a spark growing into a fire behind the old man's eyes.

"I haven't been in a courtroom in years." But Capers's voice was less convincing than his words.

"Think of it, the ultimate test of the most sacred constitutional principles. Do they apply to everybody or not? Universal application of personal freedoms, regardless of race, religion, color, creed, gender, or point of origin."

Capers seemed to be looking off into a murky future. But his eyes were blazing.

"A *universality doctrine*," he almost whispered. He pulled back from his vision, locking eyes with Gavilan. "Are you that good with your street crime cases?"

Gavilan laughed. "Better."

Capers got up, took a few steps away, then turned back. "I'll need to meet your people," he said in a committed voice.

Gavilan pointed at a van down the block, which started its engine at the lawyer's gesture.

"Transportation provided free of charge," he said as he led his boss down the block.

Capers shook his head, then followed. "Angels, Ministers of Grace," he mumbled, "and Gene Rodenberry protect us."

Two ladders seemed to stretch downward forever. On either side of a nine-foot tube, the aluminum rungs were barely visible in the dim light of the place. Only by each access hatch, at each level, was there enough light to see where you were or what you were doing.

So far, the men had soundlessly moved down maybe 120 feet. Less than halfway down the escape tube. They moved slowly, constantly monitoring for the slightest indication of an alarm, a camera, any device or system that might betray their presence to the occupants.

At each level's entry hatch, they'd paused. Sometimes for just a few minutes, sometimes for as much as half an hour. Checking, testing, guessing whether or not that was the hatchway that led them to whatever they were looking for. So far, after five of the access points, they'd moved on again.

"Clear ten feet down," Lukacs whispered as he checked his sensor readings.

"Concur. Proceed." Greg started down. "We'll rest at the next level."

A nod from Lukacs as he carefully worked his way down his side of the tube. "I can use it."

Just after they'd first climbed down into the escape tube, they'd hooked up for their first rest. Hooking their climber's webbing to the ladders, they'd leaned back over the daunting drop, held in place by the nylon and titanium device. Allowing the exhaustion of the previous night's work to overwhelm them.

Lukacs had almost immediately drifted off. The aftereffects of adrenaline overload, muscles stretched raw, and naked fear taking their toll.

Greg, however, just hung there, motionless. He used binoculars to check out the length of the three-hundred-foot-long tube. To examine the access hatches that appeared to be about twenty-five feet apart. As he lay back, suspended over the chasm as it were, he allowed his pained body to recover, while working his mind overtime.

An hour later, they began their descent.

"What are we looking for?" Lukacs had asked when Greg rejected the first two hatchways.

"Tells. Something that screams '*Stay out!*' Preferably in bright pink letters."

"But each of the hatches was alarmed."

Greg had shaken his head. "Basic stuff. Simple contact like what we bypassed upstairs. Just to let security know if a door's been opened. Nothing more than that."

So they moved to the next one.

Greg took advantage of this latest rest to wipe his face with a soft cloth.

The neoprene suits were gone, buried outside the fence. Except for the gloves, which they continued to wear. But whatever inconvenience they were, it was more than made up for by the lightweight khaki jumpsuits they'd donned as soon as they'd penetrated the installation. Gone was the feeling of suffocation, of drowning in your own sweat. Both men felt reinvigorated and revived.

Greg glanced over at the young thief across from him. Lukacs's eyes were closed, his breathing settling into a steadily relaxing rhythm. The climb down had been especially hard on the young man, not being used to fighting gravity on a narrow ladder while monitoring for detectors.

Odd, Greg thought, that anybody could get used to such things.

Checking again that the surprisingly steady young man was resting, Greg glanced at his monitor, then unhooked himself, continuing down the ladder.

Twenty minutes later, he gently reached up, touching Lukacs on the foot.

"Wha . . . What's going . . ." He stopped himself, looking down at Greg, who had apparently swung across to his ladder, just below him.

"What's going on?"

Greg smiled grimly up at him. "I've found it."

"What? Where?"

"About sixty feet down, on your side." He glanced down. "And it's something special." Greg started down the ladder, followed a moment later by Lukacs.

For the most part, the hatch looked like all the others. Labeled with a stenciled, two-foot-tall number 7, it was stainless steel with a gear-like latching mechanism. But it was the sign that was attached to the wall beside it that caught Lukacs's attention.

ATTENTION!
RESTRICTED AREA
NO PERSONNEL ALLOWED
BEYOND THIS POINT
WITHOUT HABITAT CLEARED ESCORT
DEADLY FORCE
WILL BE USED!
ATTENTION!

Below it was a smaller, less angry-looking sign.

Emergency Access
For Level Seven (7)
Through Opposite Portal Only

Greg hung to the side of the ladder to make room for Lukacs to drop level with the hatch.

"Check it out," he said with a grim smile.

The young man held up his sensors, which were instantly driven off the scale. "Bright pink letters," he whispered.

Greg nodded as he hooked himself to the ladder, then pulled off his backpack, hanging it on the ladder just level with his waist. Lukacs mirrored his movements.

"How do we start?"

Greg never took his eyes off the hatch. "Lock's simple enough. We can beat it with an EM package."

His voice was flat, emotionless as he studied the readouts on his sensor. Shaking his head, he reduced its sensitivity as far as he could, then gave up, reclipping it to his belt. "Take a straight reading."

Lukacs pulled a voltmeter from his pack, placing its sensitive probe less than a quarter of an inch from the wall, then the hatch frame, then the hatch itself.

"Five hundred cgs on the hatch. Looks like three fifty on the frame, maybe one sixty on the wall."

Greg continued to stare at the door. "Check the ion dispersal."

After wiping the suddenly appearing sweat from his forehead, Lukacs pulled out a digital meter, slowly repeating the process. "Wall and frame are clear. Hatch lock shows a spike in zone 24, high-width, four-ohm band."

Although he wasn't sure what the readings meant, from Greg's expression Lukacs knew it wasn't good.

Slowly, painstakingly, Greg held one of his special sensors, the ones he'd never allowed Lukacs to see, over the hatchway. It took him the better part of twenty minutes, but he made sure that every inch of the stainless steel had been covered. Then he leaned back, reviewing the playback of its readings.

"Shit," he said quietly after another ten minutes.

"What's wrong?"

Greg ignored him, again seeming to concentrate on the hatchway to the exclusion of all else. Staring at it, through it, inside of it.

Finally he turned to his young partner, a grim expression on his face. "Okay," he began in a quiet, almost academic way. "This is going to be hard, but we can do it. So long as we remain calm, stay patient, and keep our cool. Right?"

Lukacs heard the *we* but understood what the experienced thief was saying.

If *he*, Lukacs, kept his cool.

"I'm with you," he said with forced confidence.

"Right." Greg took a deep breath. "We've got two active and one passive system on the hatch. The galvanic reader we can take out with a simple signal absorber and avoiding contact between any of the metal and anything conductive on our bodies." He forced a smile. "Now you know why we kept the neoprene gloves."

Lukacs just nodded. Afraid to interrupt.

"Next problem is an infrared or ultraviolet-light web. Receivers on the top and left of the hatch, senders on the bottom and right." He studied the hatch again. "Easy enough to deal with if we knew which kind it was, but there's no way to tell from this side.

"Last problem, a mercury switch, probably on the inside locking mechanism. Undoubtedly hardwired into a simple trigger mechanism. Easiest to beat, if you can get to it." He paused. "Which we can't."

"So? What do we do?"

Greg looked into the young man's eager face, then shrugged. "Damned if I know."

They hung there, suspended by the ladder, staring in silence at the seemingly impenetrable steel door.

"Set up the absorber," Greg suddenly said in a firm voice.

Lukacs pulled out the small machine, attaching its suction cups to the points on the door that Greg indicated. "You have a plan?"

"More like a guess. You remember how it works?"

Lukacs nodded. "Just like the fence. I keep the needle in the middle of the dial, compensating for any changes in polarity or modulation."

Greg pulled out an electric drill, selected a sixteenth-of-an-inch bit, then screwed it firmly into place. "Keep your eyes on it," he said as he positioned the drill just above a spot between the suction cups. " 'Cause when I start, it's gonna buck like hell!"

"What about the light beams? Or the mercury switch?" Lukacs asked nervously as Greg bumped the drill's engine.

"Beams need a straight line, so I drill between the gear's supports," he said as he gently laid the bit on the hatch's surface.

The signal jumped on Lukacs's meter but was almost instantly corrected for by the nimble-fingered boy.

"As for the mercury switch—" He glanced at Lukacs, then smiled. "I'll try to be gentle." He started the drill.

Four minutes later, he was through and the drill removed.

"How's the readings?"

Lukacs grunted. "Steadier than I feel," he said in a whisper.

Greg reached into his sack. "I'm going after the mercury switch now."

He threaded a thin cord into the tiny hole, then attached it to a small penlight-type attachment with what looked like a jeweler's loupe at the end. He stared through the device while manipulating the fiber-optic cable with two fingers.

"Where'd they put it, Linus? Where would you have put the little . . ."

"You say something?" Lukacs said with some concern.

Greg ignored him. "Where are . . . ah."

He pulled out the cable, then threaded a small tube in its place. He attached the tube to a small spray can. "Okay, last step. And Lukacs?"

"Yes?"

Greg stared through the young man, sending a shiver through his bones. "We have got to do this next part together. If either of us hesitates, pauses, does anything other than exactly what's needed, it's all over. Right?"

Lukacs swallowed hard.

"If you have any doubts," Greg continued, "any at all, now's the time to tell me. Maybe I can think of another way."

For a full minute, the Gypsy thief thought about those words. Thought about all he'd learned, what they'd been through in the last fourteen hours. About the dangers that lay just inside that gleaming hatch.

"I'm ready."

Greg stared at him for a minute more. "Right." He handed him the elaborate electromagnetic package still encased in a cigarette carton. "Here's how it goes. One: I freeze the mercury switch with liquid hydrogen. That'll give us thirty seconds to open the door and deactivate all three systems.

"Two: you use the EM package to throw the bolts while I spin the lock. The door pushes in and to my left.

"Three: I take out the light web, you take out the galvanic reader with UV light under its casing, right onto its CPU. You remember how to do that."

Lukacs nodded tensely. "Where is it, exactly?" he forced from between clenched teeth.

Greg cocked his head uncertainly. "Should be directly above the door. But wherever it is, find it and take it the hell out. Don't worry about being neat, 'cause you'll have less than twenty seconds at that point. Just wait for me to take out the light web, then go like hell, right?"

"Right." He was already reaching for the tools he would be using.

"While you're doing that," Greg said as he also reached for certain tools, "I'll go for the mercury switch."

They both positioned their tools exactly where they wanted them. Then Greg waited as Lukacs positioned the EM package on the hatch, flipping the switch, watching it hug the door. Manipulating the signal absorber almost at the same moment.

"Ready," Lukacs said in a committed voice as he wiped his face. Ignoring the images of what would happen if either of them was as little as a second late in their tasks. He crossed himself, whispering a near-silent prayer.

"Okay," Greg said. "We go in three, right?"

Lukacs nodded, put the UV projector in his mouth, then grabbed the cigarette carton with both gloved hands.

With his right hand on the lock mechanism, wire clips and plastic spacers in his ungloved left hand, Greg took a deep breath.

"See you on the other side," he said in the tensest voice that Lukacs thought he would ever hear.

"One.

"Two.

"Three!"

SIXTEEN

SILENCE, either ominous or relieving, wrapped itself around the two men as they lay in the dark, just beyond the hatchway.

Lukacs thought his heart would never stop racing, that he'd never catch his breath. He didn't dare move, barely breathed despite his lungs' urgent demands, as he waited.

Hopefully, for nothing to happen.

For the first time, he realized how heavily he was sweating, at the same time knowing it wasn't because of how hot the room they'd broken into was. Although the room seemed to be as bad as a sauna. Rather, it was because of how close they'd come to complete disaster.

He looked up at the aluminum plate that had covered the alarm he'd had to deactivate. Half torn, bent angrily out in his fury to get to the central processing unit. Stained red from the ignored angry gash in his hand. An injury that he hadn't noticed until the ultraviolet-light projector had disabled the machine's microchip brain.

Now he held his hand close to his eyes, checking it with a penlight. Grateful that the less-than-an-inch cut was all he had to worry about.

For the moment, at least.

Greg lay on his back, letting his eyes adjust to the strange darkness inside the hatch. Everything about this place seemed strange to him. Completely unexpected. Instead of a polished, sterile, brightly lit laboratory or office complex, there was nothing but this infuriat-ingly hot, dark nothingness.

The air felt artificially heated, there was a bitter or sharp taste to it. Then, there was the movement of the air, almost like a contained breeze. But there was no sound, no random gusts or noise. Yet no sense of the air being machine-forced either. Just silence . . . ex-cept for the labored breathing of the Gypsy on the floor to his right.

Sensing that their entry had gone undetected, Greg rose to his knees. A quick check of all three alarms confirmed that they were bypassed or out of action. A more detailed check showed that their being off-line hadn't been noticed. But there was no telling how long that would last.

He slowly stood up. "Stay here," he whispered. "I'm gonna look around."

Lukacs waved weakly at the seemingly unflappable man, wonder-ing if he would ever develop nerves like that. Then he turned to bandaging his wounded hand.

Greg moved down what he discovered was a very narrow corridor. Too narrow, actually. Not enough room for two people to walk side by side.

There were no doors, no windows, no lights of any kind. The wall on the outer, hatch side seemed to be reinforced concrete. The other made of some lightweight material, either fiber-form or dry-wall.

Through the weak light of his penlight he couldn't make out a ceiling, just darkness and walls disappearing up into a dark forever above.

After exploring for over a hundred meters in each direction, he returned to the hatchway and a kneeling Lukacs.

"We got a problem."

Lukacs shrugged, a resigned expression crossing his dark looks. "The novelty of that is wearing off."

Greg seemed pleased at the reaction. "We could wander around in here for days. This corridor probably runs for a quarter or more of the base's length. I think"—he tapped lightly on the inner wall—"I think it was put up to disguise this hatchway. Making this corridor a nonfunctional one. So I don't think what we're looking for is at either end of it." He hesitated. "Problem is we don't have time to test my hunch. We got to start out of here in"—he checked his watch—"four and a half hours."

"So?"

Greg shined his light on the wall. "We could break through real easy."

Lukacs looked at the small circle of light on the inner wall, then back to Greg.

"You're kidding, yes?" Greg's expression was his answer. "So far, okay," Lukacs said in a hurry. "Nothing we've done is noticed or can't be explained away. I understand that." He stood up, reaching out to the wall. "But somebody is going to notice a hole in their wall!" He stared into the master thief's calm eyes. "Assuming we don't walk into somebody's office or a lunch room or something."

Greg unbuttoned the top of his jumpsuit, lifting the Lucite-covered thing he'd worn since taking it from Kerry's safe to wipe at the sweat that was rising from the over-ninety-degree heat.

"So we look first. That's why God created fiber optics, right?" He paused, stopped by the skeptical expression on his protégé's face. "Hey, I'm wide open to alternatives."

Five minutes later, Lukacs held Greg's echo locator over the wall, listening for weak spots. "It seems uniform," he said nervously. "Maybe a half inch thick. Starting three feet up."

"Under that?"

Lukacs shook his head. "Sounds scattered but mostly solid."

Greg put away a listening device. "Silent as a morgue in there."

"Could you pick better descriptions, please?"

Greg took the offered drill. Working well above eye level, he quickly had his hole, then threaded the compact viewing system through.

"Let's see," he said as he took a deep breath. "Damn."

"What is it?"

"Hang on." He manipulated the thin cable to give a view of everything in sight. Five minutes later, shaking his head, he repeated the process.

"What's there?" Lukacs asked again as he adjusted the jumpsuit that was beginning to stick to his body.

Greg oddly shook his head as he handed the eyepiece to the anxious young man.

It took Lukacs a moment to focus, then he began to pan the thirty-second-of-an-inch lens around.

Sand, nearly white, seemingly windblown, piling up in dunes. Little recognizable vegetation, but some kind of sparse trees and

bushes. All clumped together by what appeared to be a deep, bab-
bling stream of almost royal blue.

"We've broken through to the outside?"

Greg shook his head as he concentrated on what he'd seen.
"We're over a hundred and fifty feet underground." He unconsciously glanced up. "Check the ceiling and the walls."

Lukacs carefully manipulated the cable.

The ceiling, some thirty feet or more up, was painted a light iri-
descent orange, with gray, fluffy (for lack of a better word), cloud-
like things attached irregularly across it. The strong yellow-orange
light that filled the room seemed to come from those weird
"clouds."

The walls, at least the one they'd drilled into (the others were too
far away to see clearly), were the same color as the sand. Possibly
textured with the stuff.

"What is this place?"

"Check out—up and to the left," Greg said in a cautious voice.

More manipulating of the fiber-optic view piece, more focusing,
then . . .

"Mirrors? Why are—"

"It's a terrarium," Greg interrupted. "An artificially manufactured environment made to look like the natural environment
of"—his voice dropped low—"something. To keep things alive, in
good shape, comfortable. Locked up." A nasty expression shaded
his eyes. "All for the sake of science." The man's voice had taken on
a tone of dark menace. "Think of it as a glorified fish tank."

Lukacs couldn't pull himself away from the viewfinder. "Sounds
like jail to me."

Greg nodded as he dug in Lukacs's backpack. "Me too." He
pulled out a small battery-powered saw. "Watch the mirrors."

It took over fifteen minutes to cut through the pressed wood and
fiberglass wall. Fifteen minutes of start and stop. Of "Is that a light
flare in the mirrors?" Of cleaning tiny grains of the white silica out
of the saw's motor. Finally a square, three feet across, was finished.

While Greg held it in place, Lukacs used duct tape in three places
across the top cut. When he was finished, both men stepped back,
examining their impromptu "doggy door."

Greg began buttoning his sweat-stained jumpsuit. "Mask up."

Lukacs wiped the layer of heavy sweat off his chest, then reluctantly closed his jumpsuit. As he pulled on a same-colored ski mask,

he chuckled. "I crawl across a bastard desert, to break into a bastard desert." He shook his head.

Greg remained stone-faced.

He pushed the panel far enough inward for him to slide through, hesitated, then rolled through to a crouching position, looking more animal than man.

He stayed there, completely still. Eyes searching, ears straining. Every muscle taut, coiled, pantherlike; ready for an instant leap back through the panel to the only possible escape route.

He remained there for what seemed like hours, actually a little over five minutes. Motionless. Tense. Ready.

Finally, as slowly as he could move, he looked in a 180-degree arc. Then turned to the mirrors.

He stared up at them, studying their brilliantly reflective surface. He had no doubts that they were two-way glass. Was equally sure that if anybody was up there, they would've already spotted him in his desert-beige jumpsuit. It might've been a perfect match for the Nevada desert, but in this odd, white oasis, he stood out like a bloodstain on white velvet.

After five more minutes, with no signs of speeding guards or sounds of alarms, he pulled out his ion sensor, taking a reading of the place.

There were indications, suggestions of significant telemetry hiding in the walls, the ceiling, even under the sand. But it all seemed to be in a passive or inactive mode. There if needed, but not currently in use.

Satisfied by instinct, more than by anything he saw or didn't see in the readouts, Greg put the sensor away. Taking a last look around, satisfying himself that he was alone and unseen, he reached back, knocking once on the panel. A moment later, Lukacs was crouched next to him.

After giving him two minutes to get used to the strange, hot, oddly lit environment, Greg tapped him on the shoulder.

"Work your way around to the right," he said, pointing to the side. "Find the eastern wall, then head north along it." Greg checked his wrist compass. "I'll do the same to the west. We'll meet at the midpoint of the north wall."

Reluctantly Lukacs nodded, checked his compass, then started off over the surprisingly firm sand. Suddenly he stopped.

"Uh, Greg?"

"What?" Greg turned back to him.

Lukacs looked concerned. "What happens if I run into, uh, the residents?"

The experienced thief thought about that, something he'd been doing quite a lot of lately. That's why they were here, to contact the residents, then hopefully come away with proof of their existence. Possibly to come away with the residents themselves.

But, somehow, he'd never quite figured out how to pull it off. In truth, he never really thought they'd get this far in the first place. Hoped, sure. Prayed, planned, created contingencies, but all in the abstract.

And this white, sandy, desert scene was no abstract.

He finally shrugged.

"If you see anything, *anyone*," he quickly corrected himself, "make a friend. Then call for help." It was all he could think to say.

"Thanks," Lukacs said, shaking his head. "That's really helpful." His sarcasm was tinged with fear. "I'll be sure to tell them this was all your idea."

The two men started off again.

"Uh, Greg?"

Exasperated by the suddenly frightened boy, Greg turned back to him. "What now?"

"I've made a friend . . . I hope."

Greg looked at the suddenly motionless man.

Lukacs was balancing on one foot, the other frozen in midstep. He didn't move, didn't seem to be breathing, just standing statue-like in the middle of the sand.

"What is it?" Greg whispered as he came over. "What's the . . ." He froze as he came up to the spot.

The sand in front of them seemed to be undulating. It was almost as if something was swimming just below the surface, moving back and forth in gentle gliding motions. Like the bottomless, triangular pressure waves made when a whale is coming to the surface of the ocean.

And two large, oval eyes stared up at them from just under a thin layer of the sand.

Greg was the first to recover.

"Take a step back," he said in a quiet, calming voice. "Nothing sudden, jerky, or violent, right?"

All Lukacs could do was look down into those nonblinking eyes and nod.

He stepped back, then crossed himself. "Jesus who is the Christ, stand with me," he whispered.

Greg ignored him, staring instead into the eyes that moved, ever so slightly, between the two men.

They were large, maybe three inches long by two inches high. The pupils were black, all black. With no white showing, and a slightly darker center. There wasn't any eyelid that he could see, but the sand seemed to have no effect on the eyes at all. No skin was visible around the apparently deep sockets.

"Make friends, I think you said," Lukacs mumbled.

"Yeah," Greg said uncertainly.

Both men were silent for several minutes while whatever it was continued to study them.

"Keep your voice calm and all your motions slow and obvious. We don't want to frighten him," Greg said as he slowly loosened his backpack.

"Frighten *him?*" But the Gypsy's voice remained steady in a calm tone. He took off his pack as Greg did.

Slowly, as if he was stuck in a gel, Greg crouched to get nearer the eyes.

Suddenly they were gone. In an instant as if someone had turned off a switch.

"Damn it," Greg whispered. "Don't move. Just look around. Slowly."

"There."

Greg turned slightly to his left, to see the undulating sand and the eyes again looking up at him. Slowly, carefully, he held up his hands, making sure they could be seen. Spreading the fingers to show that they were empty.

The eyes followed every movement.

"Hello."

No reaction.

"I'm a friend," Greg said in what he hoped was a friendly voice. "Friend. You know, friend?"

"Uh, Greg?"

"Not now," he said while smiling at the eyes.

"Uh, yes now," Lukacs said in a jumpy voice. "He's *got* a friend."

Greg glanced behind him, where another, identical set of eyes was studying Lukacs.

Greg sighed, his mind rushing with options, then he carefully sat down on the hot sand.

"Sit down. Smile. Let him see in your body language that you're not here to harm him."

As he complied, Lukacs whispered back to him. "Can we say the same about them?"

A thought that had crossed Greg's mind. "Can you speak?" he said to his set of eyes. "English, Française, Deutsch?"

Lukacs stiffened. "What the hell was that?"

"Be quiet!" Greg leaned closer to where he thought the mouth of the eyes should be. "Can you speak to me? Understand me?"

A series of high-pitched squeals, clicks, and guttural noises came up to him from the sand.

"I—I don't understand. Are you talking to me? Is that how you talk? Do you . . ."

And the undulations were off, gliding across the sand field, two even rows of half-foot-high sand berms stopping maybe fifty feet away.

"Something you said?"

"I hope to hell not." Greg slowly stood up, followed by Lukacs, both men watching the undulating, almost vibrating intersections of the two paths. "Take a reading," he said as he continued to watch.

"All clear," was his answer a minute later.

Greg nodded. "You think we ought to go over to them?"

Lukacs shook his head. "It is always better to let the *pavosti* and *nebashti* come to you. Bad luck to go to them." He paused. "We should wait." He sounded sure of himself.

Greg would've smiled in any other circumstance as he remembered the legends Roman had told him years ago. "You think these are spirits of the earth and water? Pixies?"

"You have maybe a better explanation?"

Greg shook his head. "No, but I'm sure they're not from . . . Look."

One of the tracks of sand berms headed off into the distance at high speed, while the other came back toward them.

They sat down again, in front of the expressionless pair of eyes in the sand.

"How big do you think he is?"

Lukacs shrugged as he studied the moving sand pile by his feet. "Hard to tell, maybe four, four and a half feet. Maybe bigger."

They sat there, the men and the sand thing, contemplating each other in silence after that. Greg tried drawing some letters in the sand, but that only served to make the sand thing recoil from them. After a few minutes, it came close again.

"Here comes the other one." Lukacs nodded in the direction of the approaching berm.

"Let's hope he didn't bring anyone with him."

"What do we do if we can't talk to them?"

Greg checked his watch. "I don't know," he said as the approaching creature slowed, then settled in by the first one. "We're running out of time."

Suddenly there was an eruption of sand from between the creatures. Both men jumped, then quickly recovered, seeing that a device of some kind had been expelled from the sand in front of them.

Slowly Greg picked it up. "Some kind of handheld VDT."

"What?"

"Video display terminal." He pressed some buttons, but nothing seemed to happen. "If only I could figure out how to turn it on."

CODE PRESS 070347///

Greg showed the message to Lukacs.

"You think they . . . ," the boy started to ask.

Greg took a deep breath, then began entering the code on the small keypad.

"What if," Lukacs said softly, "what if that sets off some kind of alarm?"

Greg stopped just before entering the last digit. "Then we're screwed." He looked Lukacs in the eyes. "You got any other options?"

After a long moment, the boy shook his head, and Greg finished entering the sequence.

"Can you understand me now?" he said to both sets of eyes.

UNDERSTAND///

"That's progress." He paused, looking at both sets of eyes in front of him.

"Now what?" Lukacs asked.

Greg studied the small monitor as he thought. "We could try telling them the situation. Ask them to help."

Lukacs looked skeptical. "Just like that? Maybe we should go slow." He paused, staring into the sand eyes. "I don't know." A strange aura seemed to be settling over this young, *modern* Gypsy.

Greg shrugged. "We're here to help you," he said to the eyes.

WHY///

"We would like to help you be free."

FREE WHAT IS///

"Free is not being confined."

That got their attention.

Their eyes blinked rapidly, then they disappeared off into the distance, rapidly going in circles just under the sand. And the sands around them swelled, mixed, boiled.

"What'd I say?" Greg whispered nervously.

The monitor blinked to life.

DO NOT PLEASE///
INFORMATION GIVE YOU IF NO FREE///
FROM OUR BODIES DO NOT FREE US///
PLEASE///

"They think free means kill," Lukacs whispered in a stunned tone.

In the distance, the sand things seemed to be calming, slowly moving back toward them.

Greg bit his lower lip. "So how do we get through to them? Get their trust? With all the possible misunderstandings, we'll be here till we're old men." He checked his watch. "If we live that long."

The eyes reappeared by their feet.

"Can I try?" Lukacs was smiling at the nearest pair of eyes. The new mood or aura having seemed to strengthen his resolve for the task at hand.

"How?"

The young man crossed his legs, held his hands in front of him as if holding a baby. "The Gypsy way."

Greg hesitated, then nodded, taking the monitor from him. "Try it."

"My name is Lukacs Mosognli of the Romany Hongrois."

JOE///
MAX///

Lukacs's smile couldn't be warmer or more sincere. "We have come as friends, in God's graces, to extend our friendship to you."

FRIENDS KNOW WE///
FRIENDS HEAR WE OFTEN///
FRIENDS MEAN PAIN///

Something in the eyes that regarded them so steadily from just beneath the sands seemed to change. Suspicion, anger perhaps, entered into the otherwise flat looks.

KNOW WE WHAT FRIENDS MEAN/ARE///

"I think we've got another problem," Lukacs said in worried tones without the smile on his face varying a millimeter.

Greg ignored him. He looked into the eyes nearest him, then nodded solemnly. "My name is Picaro."

PICARO///

"I know *friends* also." His voice was cold, steel-hard and unforgiving. "Friends make you weak, vulnerable, exposed. Friends can betray you, hurt you"—his voice took on an anguished tone—*"change you."*

AND///

"I *do not* want to be your friend," he said in the coldest voice Lukacs had ever heard. "I want to *hurt* your friends. I want to be your"—he searched for the word—"ally."

YOU ARE WITH FRIENDS///
YES///

"No."

The strange eyes beneath the sand and the hard eyes from within the thief's soul locked for a long time.

WITH WHO YOU ARE///

"I'm not *with* anyone. I'm alone."

The eyes disappeared for a moment, then a message slowly began to display on the small monitor.

ALONE///
KNOW WE ALONE///

Both sets of eyes focused on him.

KEEP YOU FROM FREEING HOW///

"Freeing?"

Lukacs nodded appreciatively. "They mean dying." He paused. "I think they have Gypsy souls."

Greg looked at his young colleague as if he'd lost his mind. "Who are you?" he asked as he turned back to the eyes.

JOE///
MAX///

"I mean, *what* are you?"

YOU LIKE///

Greg looked from one pair of eyes to the other, trying to understand how these things thought. Trying to think alien.

"I don't understand, what is it you're trying to say?"

SIMPLE///
IN ENGLISH PLAIN///

"I'm getting a headache."

LIVE WE///
LIKE YOU///
ENOUGH IS///

Greg checked his watch. There were limits to how far he would press his luck standing so painfully exposed beneath those ominous mirrors.

"Can you live away from this place?"

DID///
YEARS MANY BEFORE HERE BROUGHT///

Lukacs's head snapped up from a brief inspection of his monitors. "Reading just jumped to point ninety-six amps."

"Which way?"

"North, a little bit west." He pointed up at the mirrors near the far end of the habitat.

"Shit." Greg checked the readings. "Looks like a mainframe powering up." He quickly turned back to the eyes, a look of near desperation on his face.

"Do you know who is behind all this? For your being here?"

A delay that seemed like hours.

NOW NOT///
BEGIN KNOW///
BEGIN HATE///
NOTHING CAN DO///
THEN///

Lukacs casually moved his arms—as if stretching—reassuredly feeling the tiny lump of the LWS Seecamp minigun in the small of his back. "I'm not sure I like the sound of that."

Greg ignored him. "Who was it? In the beginning?" If he couldn't get *them*, he would get what they knew.

He hoped.

Lukacs checked his monitor again as the eyes retreated beneath the sand. "Signal's fading."

"Thank God."

The young thief checked a full circle. "We're clear now." He put away his sensor. "That was damned lucky."

Greg mopped his face and neck. "Something we're running out of fast." He checked his watch. "Ten minutes and we're out of here."

"No matter what?"

Greg looked down as the eyes returned. "No matter what."

NAME///
ON PROTECTIVE COVERING WAS///

Greg pulled at the top of his jumpsuit.

"You saw a name on a shirt? On a uniform, like this?"

WAS NAME VANNESS///

"Vanness," Lukacs repeated. "Shouldn't be too hard to find a guy with a name like that." He paused to write it down. "Sounds Belgian, maybe Dutch. Lazslo shouldn't have any trouble finding him."

Greg took a deep breath, then shook his head sadly. "No. Not hard at all," he said softly before returning to the eyes in the sand.

He wiped the sweat from under his mask as he tried to think of a way to get across to these sand things what he needed from them.

"If you come with us, we'll get you out of here. That will hurt the *friends*. That will hurt them very badly."

More excited churning of the sand.

WILL FREE THEM///

"No," Greg said with just a touch of disappointment in his voice. "It won't kill them."

NOT ENOUGH THINK WE///

He looked down at them. "All we want from you is the chance to take you from this place. To try to get you back again with your . . . kind."

He took his hand off his chest, holding it out toward them. "That is something I would really like to do with you."

Another explosion of sand! This one from both of the things. So sudden, so violent, that it knocked both men backward.

"You okay?"

Lukacs groaned as he rolled over to a semisitting position, the Seecamp in his hand, hammer depressed. "What'd we do now?" He looked over where the sand was settling. *"Benci Joska!"* he almost screamed.

"Jonka," Greg mouthed in an awestruck whisper as he looked at the two creatures, standing on the sand in front of them.

Serenely contemplating the two prone men.

SEVENTEEN

DON'T MOVE," the older thief whispered.

"Believe it," the younger thief replied in a stunned voice.

The sand things stood about three feet in front of the fallen men, clicking and whistling to each other. Seemingly calm, collected, both with their big eyes staring at Greg's chest.

GET THAT WHERE///

"What?"

The one to Greg's left raised his arm, pointing at the Lucite block on the chain around the thief's neck.

ZERO COMPONENT///

GET THAT WHERE///

Now both sand things were pointing at the token.

Lukacs looked from the newly exposed aliens to the thing around his patron's neck.

"What is it?" he asked out of the side of his mouth. "What the hell's a zero component?"

Greg barely shrugged as he tried to study the "expression" on the alien faces.

The face was unlike anything Greg had ever seen before. Set as it was on a completely unfamiliar head.

It was as if someone had taken a perfectly round ball, cut out the lower quarter, and replaced that section with a small rectangle. The large eyes were the dominant feature, maybe two inches below where the hairline should have been.

But there was no hair. Instead, tiny serrated ridges ran across the top of the head from left to right, as well as from the middle of the face where you'd expect a nose (none was evident) to the back of the head. The ridges were also visible along the back of the hands and wrists.

Their mouths were imperfectly round, set in the small, lower rectangle part of the front of the head. No lips; rather, thick ridges which opened and closed side to side instead of top to bottom whenever they spoke. Two dark, bony protuberances flashed on either side of the ridges whenever they opened to produce their sounds.

Each was wearing a singlet, barely covering the apparently flat groin, tiny waist, and barrel chest. What could only be described as half a long sleeve came down the outside of each arm from the shoulder. Held to the thin arms in no way that Greg could tell.

Greg noticed that their skin was gradually changing from the exact color of the sand to a midgray tone. He lifted the Lucite block. "You want to know where I got this?"

He watched as all six thin fingers on the hand of the alien to his left worked over a tiny keypad worn around his neck. The alien never looking down at the keypad as he worked it.

YES///

"Okay. Then we share information, right?"
There was a painfully long pause.

SHARE///

Greg nodded, then turned to Lukacs.
"Be casual about it, but see if you can get your camera out of your pack. Then try to get some pictures." His voice was barely audible, his lips barely moving.

Lukacs nodded, reluctantly putting the gun away as Greg turned back to the aliens.

"Which of you is Joe and which is Max?"

GET THAT WHERE///

And a strange hand was held out in either a pointing or threatening gesture. Greg wouldn't have bet on which.

Lukacs had the tiny spy camera out, cradled lightly in his hand. As the aliens focused on Greg, he (literally) tried to focus on them.

Greg hesitated, trying to decide how honest to be with his reply. "From a man."

More clicking, whistling, and unpleasant glimpses inside that weird-looking mouth.

WHERE MAN GET///

Greg took the chain from around his neck, holding it up to them. The light shined off the small engraved metal tube he'd taken from the envelope in Kerry's safe.

"What is a zero component?"

PIECE SMALL LARGER THING IS///

TOGETHER PUT ALL DOES TEAM GROUND///

FIND DOES TEAM AIR///

Lukacs shook his head. "That doesn't sound good."

"It's part of some kind of a rescue beacon. I think." Greg took a step toward Joe. "Here." He handed it to the alien. "Take it."

Lukacs held out a restraining hand. "Are you really sure you want them to, uh, *phone home* just now?"

Greg held his hand out, rock-steady, to the aliens. "One step at a time," he said as he locked his confident eyes with the now-questioning eyes of the sand things.

ENOUGH NOT IS///

"Take it." He paused, steadily holding it out to him. "You'll need it when we find the rest."

WE///

Greg nodded. "We."

Joe slowly reached out, lightly gripping the Lucite container, allowing his suddenly trembling fingers to barely touch Greg's.

He took it, quickly turning to Max, who lowered his hand.

Both of them gripped the sides of the Lucite, bending it down until it suddenly snapped.

Max caught the small tube thing in his hand in one smooth, speed-blurred sweep of his arm.

Both aliens took turns closely examining it before Max stowed it beneath his singlet. Then, there was a long muffled conversation between them.

Finally Joe typed out a message.

GO///

Greg looked confused. "We were sharing. We need to keep . . ."

GO///

"But I thought you were beginning to understand," Greg said in a mixture of frustration, confusion, and the slightest touch of fear as the aliens stood straighter, stronger, more aggressive.

GO NOW///

Max typed. Then Joe finished his thought.

GO WE YOU///
FRIENDS AGAINST///
ALLIES WE YOU///

And there was a brief pause as the readout cleared and was slowly replaced by a new message.

FOR NOW///

They both turned, starting to waddle over toward the spot in the wall where the thieves had cut their improvised door.

Lukacs shrugged, smiled, then followed them over.

Greg watched them for a moment, glanced up at the mirrors, at what he knew lay behind them, with an expression caught between fiercesome anger and deep concern. Then, slowly, he fell into step behind.

Less than ten minutes later, the Secretary wiped his eyes, took a deep drink of the long medically forbidden coffee, then opened the curtains to look down at the sand dunes that were Habitat.

From his seat behind the mirrors, he'd watched with deep intensity over the years the various moods (playful, stubborn, intransigent) of the aliens. Listening through the hidden microphones, reading the printouts from the language processors. Drawing his own private conclusions about the two.

Throughout the years, his face always remained blank, a cipher. A mask that revealed nothing of the torment that churned within him.

This was a man whose very existence had been made up of duty. For his entire adult life, the words of General Douglas MacArthur, perma-plaqued on his desk, emblazoned on his soul, had been his life's blood.

"Duty! Honor! Country!"

His duty to his country had always been clear and resolute. It was his job to protect it from the truly evil men who lay in wait to destroy it. A duty he had fulfilled admirably. There was no question in his mind that he would, on his death, leave America a stronger, safer place.

But there was one thing still undone. A final brick to be laid before the edifice of his legacy would be complete. Before his country's future and his immortality would be assured.

A thing that he had waited decades for the right opportunity at the right time to attempt.

Years before—the clear-eyed time, as he thought of it—the thing had seemed simple enough. The Russians were racing to get the bomb. They had taken Eastern Europe, were agitating in the Caribbean, daily pressed the Western alliance back on all fronts. The American people were shit-in-the-pants scared and there was no discussion necessary for anyone on the initial assessment team to understand the panic that the truth of Roswell would've created.

To say nothing of the *possibilities* the aliens suggested. Possibilities that their advanced technologies might well thrust the U.S. decades ahead of the Russians. Maybe even provide a *surgical* means of eliminating their threat entirely.

But those were heady days, now long past. Too many secrets, and too many lies, too much . . . time passed. The conspiracy had continued under its own momentum as *great goals* and *patriotic fervor* had eroded to a bloated bureaucracy doing whatever it had to, to preserve its own existence.

But now, thanks in part to the bungling of many of the dark men that had helped the dying old man assemble this dark world, a chance was here. An opportunity, the *slimmest* of possibilities, that in a single act of blood and violence he could secure his country's future. To ensure that long after he was gone, America (his America controlled by *his* inheritor) would continue. To leave a statement—carved in a medium as lasting as Rushmore—that it *did* all have meaning once. That the meaning, the reason, *the cause,* was no less valid, no less *vital,* than it had been half a century before! And he wouldn't miss that opportunity, that double-edged opportunity, for anything.

Now, with a brutish surgical efficiency, almost all of them, those who had planned the obscenity/crusade along with the original crew that had carried it out, were dead. Eliminated by the Secretary's avenging angel, Kilbourne, in his pursuit of Turner's source.

Megan Turner had become the Judas goat to point Kilbourne like the weapon that he'd been, that he became again. To clean up the garbage of Majestic Twelve.

To pave the way for the final act of the drama that he had been director of for over fifty years.

But even as the bodies began to pile up like cordwood, the Secretary had despaired of being able to accomplish the most important part of the final act. The one final masterstroke that would assure that his life had not been spent in vain pursuit of an empty promise.

An act that the thief Hadeon/Picaro was making as simple as picking up a phone.

After taking a long pull on the ever-present oxygen mask, the Secretary signaled for his aide.

"Sir?" The man stood in the doorway less than fifteen seconds after being called.

"Paul," the Secretary said in an exhausted, thin, weak voice, "do you have those reports yet?"

The young, tough aide-de-camp handed him a file. "All incident reports from the last twelve hours, sir."

The Secretary nodded. "Very well." He took another hit of oxygen and began sifting through the few papers. "In the morning, Paul, I want staff to begin a full inspection of the Habitat. With an eye toward the, uh, *fragile health* of our subjects."

"Sir. I understand, sir."

The Secretary tried to lift himself from the console chair to his wheelchair but almost fainted from the effort. Paul immediately rushed over; gently lifting the ninety-pound man in his arms, placing him even more gently in the motorized chair.

"Thank you, Paul," the old man said in a thin voice. "I think I'll have dinner in my . . ." He stopped short as he looked down at a small piece of black rubber that had fallen from one of the reports.

"What's that?"

As his aide bent down, handing him the small shard, the Secretary scanned the report it had fallen from.

"I'll have your dinner sent up immediately, sir," Paul said as he began to wheel the Secretary from the room.

The old man, a veteran of so many battles, both real and imagined, who had always survived by trusting his instincts implicitly, looked at the small *nothing* in his hand, looked out at the sand dunes below, hesitated, then held up his hand.

"Now, Paul."

"Sir?"

"Do it now! Get them in there now!"

The young man looked shocked at the legend's sudden change in demeanor. "Sir! Yes, sir!" He almost leaped for the telephone.

The Secretary never heard the younger man's shouted orders into the phone. Never saw the covert looks of worry from the man whose time with Kilbourne had led to his promotion as the Secretary's aide. He was too busy.

Staring with the intensity of a zealot at the empty, blowing dunes below him.

Across thirteen miles of desert, on the *wrong* side of Freedom Ridge, the mobile home site was brimming with activity. Six or seven children were playing "find the buried treasure." Their mothers worked on improvised picnic tables setting up for an early dinner. Around the three portable barbecues, the men prompted each other on how to grill the perfect lamb or skewer the perfect kabob.

But inside the trailer/command post, a silence, an odd stillness, had descended hours ago. Showing no signs of letting up anytime soon.

And the big, digital clock remained the dominant feature of the scene.

+12:34

"Not long now," Foss said in an artificially cheery voice.

Roman grimaced. For the last twelve and a half hours Foss had refused to leave the trailer. Refused to move, except for two occasions when he'd stood (next to his computers, of course) to stretch his rapidly cramping legs. Roman had brought him a meal, some occasional strong tea, but that was it.

All while the man's former addiction played across his face, seeking the narrowest opportunity to reassert itself.

"Two hours twenty-six minutes," Roman said with a forced casualness. "Then we must settle in for the night."

Foss nodded. "Less even. It'll take at least forty-five minutes to
pull it all together from our end."

"We'll do it in less if the need is such," Roman said in a reassuring voice.

"I hope so," Foss said in a distracted voice.

"And if we get the signal?" Roman quickly corrected himself as
Foss shot an alarmed look at him. *"When* we get the signal, can you
do this thing?" He nodded at one of the dark computers.

Foss looked unsure of himself. "I think so. The theory's perfectly
sound, anyway."

"But the security?"

Foss leaned back in his chair, seeming to enjoy a memory. "Greg
once said that the secret to beating any security system is to *not be*
whatever it's defending against." He raised his eyebrows. "So we
don't attack." He turned on one of the dark monitors, then the
attached CPU. "Their computers are all set up to defeat any attack
from the outside world. To keep hackers, kids, spies, from being
able to read their mail, so to speak."

"So you go through a—what's it called? A back door?"

Foss shook his head as he called up a program, then routed it
through his modem. "Back doors in this system? Shame on them if
there are any." He shook his head. "No. No back doors, side doors,
front or trap doors on that system."

The monitor went blank, then a series of random symbols started
playing across it, filling the large screen with gibberish.

"No."

The symbols slowly began to clear, leaving a clear message in their
place.

"We attack a system that talks to a system"—he punched in a
code that cleared the remaining symbols away—"that talks to our
real target."

They looked at the message displayed on the monitor.

Welcome
You have logged onto the
United States Air Force
Foreign Technologies Division
Wright Patterson Air Force Base

Routing Terminus

Please Enter Your Authorization Now

Foss entered the series of numbers, letters, and words he'd spent the bulk of the last week trying to hack.

"What now?"

Foss ignored the other man as he concentrated on the monitor's next message.

Access Accepted

Releasing a long-held deep breath, the old man turned to Roman with an expression equal parts triumph and relief.

"Now?" He looked up at the clock. "Now we wait."

Twenty-five miles away, Deo leaned against a beat-up sedan as he lit a cigarette.

"Which one?" he asked casually.

Megan tried not to lean out the car's window as she focused her binoculars on the TV station's parking lot.

"White ones," she whispered, despite their being alone, except for their Gypsy driver. "Blue vans are minicams. They can only transmit to the repeater. We need a satellite truck."

Deo studied two of the trucks across the lot, behind a four-foot-high chain-link fence.

"No problem." He leaned into the car for his windbreaker. "If they pull out, we'll play 'em on the fly."

Megan nodded grimly. "How much longer now?"

He checked his watch. "Couple of hours. Maybe less. Then we stand down for the night." He looked around the busy city street. "You want to try that Thai place if it aborts?"

Megan allowed herself to look the way she felt. Furious!

"How can you even think about that? My God, don't you know what it'll mean if we, if *they*, have to wait another day!"

"Sure," the professional driver said calmly. "It means I'll have to eat dinner tonight, and Greg'll have to find another way out tomorrow." He shrugged. "Whatever."

The casualness of his voice came as a slap in the producer's face. Particularly since she suddenly realized that she cared more about the safety of these people, who had at some point shifted from subjects to friends to something more, than she did for the story.

The realization silenced her for a chilling moment. All the bull-shit, all the ambition, all the fantasies about world acclaim and tak-ing over *60 Minutes,* vanished in the blink of an eye. She no longer cared about government corruption, cover-ups, lost aliens, or con-spiracy theories.

She cared only for, prayed silently for, a camp of Gypsies that were in it for the gain and *the game.* For an old, half-poisoned man who was functioning only on pure love for another. And, most espe-cially, for two men far across a painful desert who were battling greater odds than a more generous God would have allowed.

"How—how can you be like that?" she mumbled as she realized the silence and the stare from the driver next to her. "He's your friend."

Another noncommittal shrug. "You think I should get therapy?" It sounded like a genuine, honest question, but the lie (and the understanding) was put to it by the twinkle in his eye.

Megan shook her head. "I'll never understand you people." Al-though she stayed in the car, she slid closer to where Deo leaned. "I mean you're a smart guy."

"Thank you."

"You're good with cars, with engines and mechanical things."

Deo shook his head. "Not good." He paused. "Great."

"So what are you doing living like this?"

Deo didn't seem to have heard her. "You can work that thing?" he asked, nodding at the large trucks.

"You didn't answer my question."

"Didn't I?" He took a long drag on his cigarette. "You sure there's a satellite up there you can hit with that thing?"

"Three. Two with windows of about two and a half hours each; one synchronous."

"Each of the networks has one?"

Megan sighed. "Each of the major ones, yeah."

Deo nodded, suitably impressed. "The government just gave these satellites to the networks, did they?"

"Of course not. They paid hundreds of millions of dollars to build them, get them into space, to maintain them around the clock." She shook her head in exasperation. "It's complicated," she finally said in a dismissive voice.

"So the satellites are there," Deo said as if he was working to understand the concept, "because the networks spent a lot of money on them. To be sure they'd be there, in top condition, for them when they were needed, right?''

"Right."

Deo nodded sagely. "Just like me."

Megan suddenly sat up straight. "What did you say?"

Deo smiled as he reached into the car for a bottle of water. "Did I say something?"

She looked deep into the eyes of the casually smiling man.

"You're saying you'd do all this, take all these risks, for anyone who could pay your rates?"

"That's me." He pocketed his sunglasses as the sun dropped below the upper floors of the TV station.

"Liar."

"Said the fugitive to the car thief," he mumbled happily. "Maybe we'll go Italian."

As the sun continued to turn the sky from pale blue to darker shades of orange, at a spot nearby (but isolated from) the mobile home's campsite, Grandmother Peterkezs sat by herself. She stared down at a large flat rock she'd turned into a table.

"In name of Lord God, in name of Jesus who is de Christ his son; in name of de Most Holy Mother and of him who sits on right hand of God, I do beseech ye. Open mine eyes to your truths. Give unto me de wisdom to see your plan in dis, our hour of darkest peril."

She picked up a small pail, swished the contents (chicken entrails, chicken blood, small lamb's bones, tea leaves, and a lock of Greg's hair she'd asked him for), then poured it over the rock at the moment she judged as midsunset. Carefully she examined the carmine for any indications.

Ten minutes later, her hands stained, covered with the goo, she froze.

"Ah!" she said happily. "All my thanks to you, my God."

Somewhere in the middle of a triangle made up by Deo's parked car, the high-tech RV, and Dreamland Base, Lazslo wandered down a lightly trafficked street, taking large, messy bites out of a hot dog. He turned to a Gypsy comrade who walked alongside him.

"Sometimes hiding is such pain," he said as he smiled at two heavily armed MPs coming in the other direction.

They passed the Gypsies by.

"Se rappeler asseoir un camp Russe?"

"Sure I remember. Tough as a German virgin to get inside that bastard Russian barracks. But soft, like a French girl, after. We stole some horses that night, heh?" He laughed at the memory. "Even took some piece of shit Zil truck to carry off everything we took there."

They turned a corner, casually appearing to pay no attention to the men with automatic weapons patrolling a double steel-barred gate at the end of the street.

A gate under a sign that read simply "North Field Access Only."

"You see the lines?"

"Oui."

They continued on, away from the gate. Lazslo slowly shaking his head. "Getting in here easy-easy compared to that Russian barracks."

His partner nodded gravely as they headed for the nearby empty warehouse that had become their watcher's nest. *"N'y pas aller par quatre chemins . . ."*

"I know, I know. This place will be harder than Satan's ass to crawl out of if they open their eyes to see what's happening."

The thought chilled both men as they let themselves into the warehouse. They retook their previous positions by a mostly covered window that looked out on the road that led to the North Field.

Five minutes later, their cellular phone rang.

"Magyarovar," Lazslo answered with the approved "all is well" code word. The name of a Gypsy safe haven in Hungary for the last 250 years. "This is Caravan."

"Stand by, Caravan," a woman's voice said.

Lazslo could hear another connection being made.

"Magyarovar," he heard a young Gypsy answer. A moment later, he heard Megan come on the line.

"This is Tapestry."

"Stand by, Tapestry."

Another connection.

"Magyarovar. This is Esmeralda with Counselor," Magda's voice said.

Two more connections were made, then confirmed.

"All units stand by for Vagabond."

Less than a minute later, Roman's voice came across the static-filled connection.

"All units," he said slowly, clearly, taking great care to be certain he was understood. "All units. Stand by for a go/no-go message."

Static filled the tied-in lines for long seconds, while prayers, hopes, and dreams begged the semisilence.

"All units," Roman said just over a minute later, "the Magician is on the fly. Repeating. The Magician is on the fly."

A long pause that froze all the instantly electrified listeners.

"Begin the dance."

Before the next minute had fully passed:

An old, battered, computer expert began hacking into one of the air force's most secured databases;

A man casually hopped the fence of a TV station's parking lot, wandering over toward the satellite trucks;

Two lawyers and a Gypsy woman pulled away from a private home, heading for the Las Vegas Justice Center;

Two Gypsy men, their knives drawn, melted into the shadows of the approaching night on a secret military base;

And two thieves crouched in a shed, in a place that wasn't supposed to exist, trying to explain their "game" to two impossible beings.

PART FIVE

THE PAYOFF

It was in Paris, amid the dark, dangerous arrondissement of the Rive Droit, that the little boy/angry teen became a man.

It had been a gentle thing, unfelt, unnoticed. But it had happened with a profound silence and power.

He'd run away from the locksmith and his family at eighteen and stolen his way across America. A car here, contents of a pawnshop's safe there. A constant, if directionless, journey of bare survival.

In no way could it be called living.

His skills were growing exponentially. Money raised from the scores used almost exclusively to buy the components of the equipment he saw so clearly in his head. Small amounts put aside for food and lodging, the rest spent on travel, research, outs.

Never knowing how it was that he could do the things he could. All the time knowing he did it better than anyone else.

But that was never enough.

On the East Coast, he'd drifted north.

Four pawnshops in Brooklyn. A series of check-cashing offices in Albany. A small thrift in Montreal. Four banks in Newfoundland.

But throughout the jobs, for all the money and exhilaration he gained with each score, each greater challenge conquered, there were still no answers to the unclear questions that plagued him.

By the time the police of North America began to become aware of him, he was gone again.

England was a bore. The pickings too easy, too unchallenging. Ireland, Scotland, and Wales were even worse.

Finally, more out of a deep-seeded ennui than for any other reason, he ended up in Paris.

Six months of learning the language, establishing a base, learning the city while he lived off the last of his nest egg, resulted in the first of a series of headline-grabbing break-ins. All concentrated in one of the most fashionable upper-crust sections of the French capital.

The private safes of the richest of the city fell open to the young thief as if by magic. The most sophisticated alarms went silent. And the cry that was raised by these most influential of Parisians was so delayed, so after-the-fact, that there seemed little or no chance of his being caught.

All because of a brief friendship with a dying fence.

The man at one time had been one of the last of the great cat burglars in Europe. Virtually a legend in criminal circles. But his age had combined with three packs of cigarettes a day to leave him nearly blind, riddled with cancer, dependent on other thieves bringing him their modest swag for fifteen cents on the dollar.

And in the young, strong, clear-eyed, steady-handed American, he saw his immortality.

For hours on end, the old man would speak, the young thief would absorb. Finding direction and purpose in the daily, some-times hourly, lessons. Seeing for the first time a path, however dimly lit, that his life might intentionally (instead of randomly) follow.

The old man would teach to his acolyte the mysteries of the yeggmen. That most private fraternity of European and American thieves who stole only the best! Who lived by nobody's rules! Who were forces unto themselves conceding nothing to anyone!

Who were now almost all dead.

Or dying.

"The yeggman takes only some, never all," the former thief would say. "Never uses force unless force is completely unavoidable; and always sufficient force to end *all* arguments there and then. He leaves no one and nothing behind that might bring about a future reckoning.

"A yeggman never leaves any signs of his entry or exit. Never defaces, profanes, or vandalizes a score. He is there only to steal a *thing*, not the owner's complete peace of mind or sense of safety.

"The true yeggman, the best of the best of the best . . . uses the tools of the trade, true enough. But what sets him apart, what distin-guishes him from all other thieves, is his instincts. And these, he relies on beyond all else."

For years, the sophistication and style of the American thief grew in leaps and bounds. At the direction of the fence, Greg took col-lege courses in art, literature, philosophy. Attended cotillion in Paris's finest etiquette training salons.

Made alliances with the Corsican Union in the dark, nightmare streets of Toulon, where he acquired a reputation for toughness that even the most feared members of the Brotherhood came to respect.

And the word began circulating throughout Europe that that most elite corps of criminals, the yeggmen—which traced their roots back to turn-of-the-century Boston, where safes were known as "eggs" (pronounced *yeggs*)—had a new member.

And he was loose on the streets of Paris.

Then one day, the day after the retired yeggman died (in his sleep from a pillow mercifully held over his choking form), a hand slipped; an alarm not previously noticed, triggered.

He lay in a Paris jail cell for weeks.

Although this was his first significant time in any adult jail, the experience didn't seem to affect him. The little boy/angry teen/wanderer/thief had always lived within whatever his circumstances demanded. In a thousand-dollar-a-night suite at the Georges Cinq or in a dark alley, it didn't really matter. Years ago, he'd learned to take whatever came, however it came, with equanimity.

Or disdain.

They came to see him on the forty-third day.

Blank men with meaningless names and plastic cards. Bureaucracy pervs, he'd thought, without the guts or the talent to execute the actual perversions themselves. For that, they needed robots.

Like him.

Of course he'd accepted their offer. Hell, all they'd asked him to do was what he was already doing. Only this time he'd do it for their purpose . . . whatever that might be. And it was markedly more appealing than the long prison term he faced as the alternative.

And there was one other reason.

His time in the Paris jail had taught him that whatever one did, there was no way you could completely hide from the system. Completely beat it. But perhaps you could use the system, hide within it, learn its frequencies, its patterns, its tendencies.

And with that knowledge . . .

In the following days, months, years (he would lose track of time), he followed their orders, broke into the assigned targets. Let the killers into wherever, to kill whoever. All with about as much emotional or patriotic commitment as a grain of sand felt toward its desert.

But the day-care bombing had changed that.

Images of the dismembered tiny arm would come to him at unexpected times. Break his concentration on jobs. Disrupting his sleep and life.

For a man who had spent his life in almost complete denial of any moral code save self-preservation, it was a psyche-altering experience.

Finally, after days without sleep and years without a life that he could truly call his own, he'd left them all behind. And, hopefully, the images of the arm along with them. But this time, there was nothing aimless in his flight. Far from it.

Days later, when they broke down the door to his secret apartment, the one he'd expected them to find days earlier, they found three blank walls, no furnishings or possessions, and a short note pinned to the fourth wall.

From my weary limbs honor is cudgeled.
Well, bawd I'll turn, and something lean to cutpurse of quick hand.
Away will I steal, and there . . . I'll steal!

EIGHTEEN

"Y OU THINK THEY got the signal?" Lukacs whispered as he
pulled on the first pair of dress suit pants he'd ever owned.

"Don't know." Greg was trying to tie his necktie while keeping an
eye out through the barely open door of the equipment/escape
shed.

"You think everybody's in place?"

"Don't know."

"You think Foss can get into their database?"

"Don't know."

Lukacs studied the strangely calm man for a long, curious moment. "What *do* you know?" he asked with a half-smile that tried
(and failed) to hide his barely held-together nerves.

Greg turned away from the door. "I know this is the only way out
of here. So there's not much point in worrying about the things we
can't control. We got enough to worry about from just our end.
Don't you think?" His voice was unintentionally hard.

Lukacs just shook his head while tying the shiny black shoes.
"Craziness," he mumbled.

Greg nodded, then looked over at two four-and-a-half-foot-high
duffel bags that seemed to be undulating. "You all right in there?"

GO///

"Maybe we should punch out some airholes or something?"
Lukacs looked at the nearest bag. "Can you breathe okay in there?"

GO NOW///

The young Gypsy sighed deeply. "I'm never gonna get used to this." He pulled a brightly colored tie under his collar.

Greg turned from hiding their equipment packs behind an air shaft outlet, to the duffel bags. "Now, you remember what to do?"

COURSE OF///

"If anything bad happens, if you hear gunshots, or one of us running; or if you hear either of us say 'We give up,' you jump out of the bags and run for the nearest fence."

Lukacs finished with his tie.

"If you can get to the desert, you'll be safe. People from my tribe will be waiting across the sand at the crack in the ground, right?"

There was nothing on the monitors at first, but considerable chatter between the two concealed aliens.

WHEN GO///

"Okay," Lukacs mumbled as he pulled on his jacket. He took several deep breaths, then turned to Greg. "I'm ready, I guess."

Greg smoothed back his hair, then checked out the Gypsy thief in the five-hundred-dollar suit. "You clean up good, kid."

"Thanks." He glanced at the equipment they were leaving behind, half hidden under a tarp. "You sure we're not going to need some of that?"

Greg looked longingly at the expensive, unique electronics.

"No choice, really. We've got enough to carry." He pulled the tarp farther down on the pile. Then he turned determinedly toward the door. "From this point on, until we make contact with one of the rescue teams, we have to survive on bluff, bluster, and our good looks." He clipped a photo ID card to his jacket's lapel. "Ten minutes, kid. If you ain't on the plane"—he paused, looking deeply worried—"I don't even want to think about it."

Lukacs shrugged, then clipped on his laminated high-tech forgery of hopefully the right organization's credentials.

"The Gypsy way," he said with a voice that nearly hid his grave doubts. He lifted the nearest duffel containing a surprisingly light alien. "Let's go."

Greg checked the door, then quickly opened it. Lukacs walked through without looking back. The door was instantly closed behind him.

After testing the weight and bulk of the concealed interplanetary visitor, after he was sure more than two minutes had passed, Greg opened the door again and stepped onto the dark tarmac.

"Keep an eye out, Linus. Just this once."

He wandered off into the darkness, in a different direction from Lukacs.

Ten minutes later, a small crowd stood on the edge of the one brightly lit area of the field. Fifteen people standing in the humid, early evening air of the Nevada desert, waiting to be processed by the guards in front of them. Waiting to board the military transport that was beginning to warm up its engines.

Greg approached the group from the rear, careful to keep his speed not too fast, not too slow. To blend in as much as possible. So far his ID had only undergone a cursory inspection, he'd been given a processing number, no one had asked to inspect his duffel. Things were going the way he'd predicted back in the warehouse when they'd first conceived the plan.

Greg had no idea how much time they had. Had no way of knowing when Joe and Max's disappearance would be discovered and a general alarm issued. All he *really* knew was that their life expectancies were measured in moments, and the sight of the idling transport was the most beautiful thing he'd ever seen.

But, as the time passed, as the group waiting to board the plane thinned, he began to stare off into the darkness in a near panic over Lukacs's absence. Then, with just six people other than himself left, the Gypsy thief showed up.

Lukacs's duffel was on a handcart, a cup of coffee in his hand, and an attractive young woman in uniform smiling at his side.

He made the barest gesture with the cup toward Greg, smiled, then continued his animated conversation with the woman. Moments later, Greg heard his processing number called.

He closed his eyes, steadied himself, then lifted the duffel as he walked toward the processing desk.

"Name?" the older gunnery sergeant demanded as two heavily armed subordinates looked on.

"Valentine. James Valentine." Greg handed over his ID the way he'd seen the others do.

The sergeant ran his finger down a page on his clipboard, then the second and third pages. A confused expression began to spread across his face.

"Valentine," he mumbled. "Valentine . . ." The expression was changing from confusion to suspicion.

Greg casually dropped his hand down to the top of the duffel, preparing to throw it open.

"Valen . . . You're not on my—" He turned to the final page. "Oh. Here you are." He shook his head angrily. "Damned last-minute update." He turned the clipboard around for Greg to sign next to his name.

As he bent over the clipboard, Greg tried not to notice one of the guards approach his bag.

"Lance Corporal!"

"Yes, Gunnery Sergeant!" the twenty-year-old marine shouted as he straightened in response to the challenge from the gunnery ser-geant.

The sergeant shook his head, then almost tore the clipboard from Greg's hands. "Did I tell you to search this man's things?"

The boy stood at ramrod attention, frozen by discipline and fear. "Gunnery Sergeant! No, Gunnery Sergeant!"

The sergeant held the clipboard an inch from the lance corpo-ral's eyes. "And tell me what that says, next to Mr. Valentine's name; if you can read, that is, Lance Corporal?"

The boy's eyes moved back and forth, but his head remained still, as he read from the document titled:

URGENT!
FLIGHT MANIFEST UPDATE
FOR IMMEDIATE EXECUTION!

"Gunnery Sergeant! It says, 'Subject Valentine is carrying confi-dential classified parcel that is not to be interfered with in any way,' Gunnery Sergeant!"

"Then back off, Lance Corporal!"

"Gunnery Sergeant! Yes, Gunnery Sergeant!" Then he stepped back to his earlier position, eyes locked straight ahead.

The sergeant turned back to Greg. "I'm sorry, sir. This is his first rotation here. He's a good marine though. He'll get it." He paused, seeming to be suddenly uncomfortable. "But if you wish to report his . . ."

Greg smiled, lifted the duffel, then walked past the sergeant. "Report what, Gunnery Sergeant?"

"Thank you, sir." He turned back to his small processing table and picked up the microphone. "One one seven!"

Without a backward glance, the thief carrying the alien boarded the rumbling transport.

After strapping the duffel into the seat beside him (the urgent flight manifest update had included orders to the flight crew to that effect) Greg stared out the window or busied himself writing meaningless notes in a pad.

Then, two excruciatingly long minutes later, allowed himself to relax, just a little, when Lukacs settled into a seat three rows in front of him.

Five minutes later, they were airborne.

"Clearing Majic 10811, Majic 10815, Majic 10829 into Habitat," a guard said as he entered a code on a digital keypad. The techs gossiped among themselves as they waited for the heavy vault door to open and let them into the desert habitat of Joe and Max.

The Gypsies lay on their stomachs, each in their own carefully chosen hiding place, waiting.

They'd seen the guards at the gate to North Field respond to the double ringing telephone, then immediately heighten their vigilance.

They'd heard (or thought they'd heard) a plane come in for a landing somewhere to the north.

They'd seen a large bus thoroughly searched (inside, outside, underneath) before being passed through the gate.

They saw a small group of people arrive in cars at the bus kiosk a quarter mile down the road from the gate.

But so far (due either to a merciful God, their own native abilities, or a combination of the two) *they* hadn't been seen.

Lazslo looked down the road to the secret airfield from his place of concealment, less than four feet from the guard shack.

It had taken over half an hour to slide noiselessly on his stomach around the blooming desert bushes, to the base of the scraggly tree. He was hidden from the road by the beginning of a concrete barrier, from the guard shack by the thick growth of the thorny bushes, from the north by the tree itself. The natural camouflage also blocked most of his view.

Except for the one view he needed.

He pictured his partner, the French Gypsy assassin, who also looked up at the shack, from the opposite side, at the two young soldiers guarding the gate.

Both men lightly fingered their ten-inch, double-edged knives; silently praying that they wouldn't have to kill those brave young men. They prayed that by sheer brass alone (if all else failed) Greg and Lukacs would make it through the checkpoint.

But either way, they *would* make it through.

The sound of a bus approaching from the north caused him to shift to his left side, to watch the headlights of the heavy bus come bouncing up the barely improved road.

The bus slowed to a stop just on the other side of the electronically controlled gate. Air hissed through the still night as the door was popped open. One of the guards slung his weapon over his shoulder, grabbed a printout from the guard shack, then boarded the bus.

Without noticing that the phone lines on either side of the gate had fallen limply to the ground.

The other guard, MP-5K automatic assault rifle cocked, held at full combat ready, stood with his back to Lazslo's position, carefully watching the windows of the bus.

The cold-blooded assassin crept inches closer, deciding that at the slightest discordant note, the man would die. Instantly. Painlessly. Without a sound or the slightest note of alarm. Lazslo calculated the angle, the distance, tensed his muscles . . . and waited.

He was too low to follow the other guard's progress through the bus, so he concentrated on the guard in front of him. For five endless minutes he analyzed every move, every shift of weight, every slight tic, for any indication. Anything that would make his decision for him.

Then the other guard stepped off the bus, nodding at the second guard. "Clear," the first guard called out in a strong voice. "Pass them through."

The second guard nodded, returning to the guard shack, pressing the button for the gate to slide open.

Completely unaware of the relieved venomous shadows that melted back into the undergrowth behind him.

□ □ □

Five minutes later, Greg and Lukacs stood by themselves at the bus kiosk.

"I think we can breathe again."

Lukacs shook his head. "When we're off this place, then I'll breathe, if you don't mind."

Greg nervously checked his watch. "Five minutes, then we try for the first safe zone on our own."

Lukacs nodded. "At this time"—he, too, had begun checking his watch and looking around every few minutes—"that would be Auxiliary Administration Building number 34."

"Right."

Greg pulled his VDT from his pocket, then walked back to the duffels they'd hidden behind the kiosk. "You still all right?"

COLD WE ARE///

BUT COLD TOLERABLE///

"We'll get you warm as soon as we can," Lukacs said.

Greg was growling under his breath as he paced. "Where in the hell is that son of a . . ."

"Always be careful how you speak of someone's mother," Lazslo said easily as he stepped out from behind the kiosk. He was grinning ear-to-ear. "You never can tell how they might react." He threw his arms around Greg. "Praise be to God that you have come through well."

Lukacs, showing the same relieved look a condemned man might have if the governor's call came through, walked over.

"So you're alive too, little Lukey?" Lazslo said in an amazed voice. "Who would believe it?" The big man paused, shook his head, then his hands exploded forward, grabbing the labels of the expensive jacket, pulling the boy into a rib-crushing bear hug.

Embarrassed by the man kissing him on both cheeks, Lukacs pulled away.

"Little Lukey no more," Lazslo proclaimed in a serious but happy voice. "From now on you will be Lukacs *Pisti*, the victorious one. And let no Czigany say otherwise or he will have Lazslo Pisti Arapazic of the Peterkezs to deal with!"

Despite the dark, the tension, the fear, Greg could see the young man swell with pride.

Lazslo suddenly looked around. "We should be leaving this

place.'' He seemed to notice the duffels for the first time. ''You got what you needed? Some proof?'' He stepped out into the street, looked around, then waved twice.

Greg and Lukacs brought the bags to the curb.

''Better,'' Greg said as they saw a truck flash its lights, then start in their direction. ''I got *them.*''

Lazslo helped lift the first of the bags into the back of the truck. ''Their bodies?''

''And they're still using them,'' Lukacs added as he climbed into the back, then took the next duffel from Lazslo.

The big Gypsy looked up into the truck, then stroked his chin.

''Really?'' He paused, seeming to think very hard about it for a moment. ''And how do they feel about coming with us?'' He looked self-consciously up into the starry night. ''They are not expecting, well, are there any other . . .''

Greg climbed up into the truck. ''Can you get us out of here or will we have to wait at a safe zone?''

Lazslo kept looking up at the stars, then shook himself loose. Physically, as well as away from the visions that were welling up inside of him.

''We leave now,'' he said forcefully. ''Take pictures, take papers, take things even, the gadj probably don't find out for hours or days. But this . . .'' He fastened the back gate of the truck, pulling the canvas cover over the open space. ''Something like this they are going to miss.'' He started for the passenger door. ''So we change the plan. We don't sit on ice,'' he said as he slammed the door shut, then looked into the back of the truck. ''Now we run like hell!''

His partner dropped the truck in gear.

''Any trouble at main gate,'' Lazslo said quietly, ''and you know what to do.''

The man nodded, reaching down to loosen the gun in his boot as he drove through the dark, deserted base.

''That's just *not possible!*'' a Habitat tech shouted at the three-man inspection team in front of him. ''They're playing one of their games, they're being difficult, gone deep and such. They're . . .''

''Gone,'' one of the team said in a bare whisper as he nervously glanced up at the mirrored windows.

''Should we tell him?''

The sound of glass breaking in one of the mirrored-off rooms above them was quickly followed by a high-decibel klaxon sounding throughout the facility.

"I don't think we have to."

Twenty minutes later, inside the crowded, noisy mobile home, Roman jumped when his personal cell phone clattered to life.

The room instantly silenced.

"Magyarovar. This is Vagabond."

A long pause.

"Magician."

Roman exhaled deeply. "Praise be to God for bringing you through."

"Yeah," the tense voice said quickly. "Where are we at?"

"The base was just closed off to all outside traffic. All personnel, civilian and military, restricted to the base area until further notice." He worked hard to keep his raw emotions out of his voice.

There was a long silence on the other end of the line.

"Anything specific?" Greg finally said.

"They're calling it a drill. So far, nothing more than that."

Again, the pained silence filled the trailer.

"What else?"

Roman looked up at a white board that listed all the elements of the plan, the personnel assigned, their state of readiness, and so forth. "Everything is in position, waiting only for your orders."

Another long pause.

"Go with—" He paused. "Tell all units to go with Unveiling. Repeat, Unveiling."

"Understood," Roman said as he wrote the word on a paper plate in front of him. "Unveiling."

"Good, now give me the old man."

As he handed the cell phone to Foss, Roman began issuing orders to the communications team.

Foss's hand trembled as he held the phone close. "Hello?"

"You straight, old man?"

A spasmodic smile played across the dry, cracked lips. "Yeah," he almost whispered. "I'm straight. You okay?"

"For the moment. At least no one's shooting at me this time." A brief pause. "At least so far. We cleared the gates ten minutes ago without incident."

"Thank God."

"As soon as I have the time. Right now, I need you to do something for me with your magic, if aging, fingers."

"And where would you be without those aging fingers, smart-ass?" For the first time since the detoxification ceremony, Foss was beginning to sound like his old self. He swiveled to the nearest computer. "Go."

"Set up a search, all databases, anything you can think of, especially the government."

The old man began calling up menus. "What am I looking for?"

"Any references to something called a zero component."

Foss entered the words, then ordered his computers to begin their elaborate search. "What's that?"

"Just let me know, right?"

"As soon as I do."

There was another, longish pause on the line.

"Hey, Foss?"

Surprised by his friend using his name on an open line, the old computer expert turned away from his terminals. "Yeah?"

"Everything you did, all the stuff you built, everything you guessed . . ." The voice trailed off for a moment, then came back in a strong but soft, emotionally charged tone. "Thanks, man. It all worked, every bit of it. We wouldn't have made it without you."

"I, I . . ."

Greg chuckled on the other end. "I know," he said softly. "I know."

Then the line went dead.

Foss turned back to his terminals, checked that the searches were well under way, then stood, heading for the door.

Roman patted him in celebration as he passed. "Fantastic job, Foss!"

The old man just nodded, then let himself out of the mobile home.

The women and children were quickly packing up the campsite. Beginning their next move with the combination of joy and alacrity that their people had been known for, for centuries. Foss ignored them, wandering out into the darkness until he found himself completely alone.

He wiped the tears from his eyes, took a deep breath, then looked up into the starry night.

"Thank you," he said so quietly he could barely hear it himself. "Thank you."

Deep in the Nevada desert, twenty miles off the main highway on a barely paved narrow road, five people swarmed around the stolen satellite truck. Two men checked that the supports that lifted the truck off its tires onto four heavy steel stanchions were properly in place, leveled, and locked.

On their okay, two women climbed inside, instantly bringing the mobile studio to life. They carefully powered up, then positioned the large dish antenna, checked that the VTRs were running up to speed, then brought the two external cameras on-line.

Megan nodded as she shut her cell phone, then walked over to Deo's car. A lighted mirror had been set up on the roof, where she checked her hair and makeup. In the mirror, she saw Deo talking on his cell phone, then hang up.

"So, we on?"

Deo nodded. "The boy and the"—he paused—"are on their way," he rushed out.

"What about Greg?"

Deo seemed grim. "I'm meeting him."

Megan had long ago learned that there were some questions that wouldn't be answered, so it was pointless to ask them. She took a deep breath, then continued to work on her hair.

"I can't believe all of this is going to end tonight."

Deo didn't seem to have heard her.

She stopped, then turned to him. "Something wrong?" Her expression was frozen.

Deo bit his lip. "They're on their way," he mumbled.

"What is it?" she said softly. "What's happened?"

"What? Oh." He smiled sheepishly. "Sorry. No. Nothing's wrong. I was just thinking about the implications of your broadcast."

Exasperated, Megan turned back to the mirror. "What implications?"

"I got to be somewhere," he said distractedly as he climbed in, then started the engine. He let the engine warm up for a few seconds before dropping it into gear. And he was gone in a small cloud of dust.

Megan stood there, watching the car disappear into the night.

"What implications?" She started toward the satellite truck, hesitated, then stopped to look down the now-deserted desert road.

"Shit."

Sandwiched between neon-blazing casinos, art deco hotels, and shoulder-to-shoulder pedestrian traffic, the Las Vegas Justice Center seemed completely out of place. With its clean lines, rough pink granite walls, softly lit plaza, it appeared totally at odds with its surroundings.

Much as United States District Court Judge Antoinette Alexander felt that concepts of right and justice were at odds with the moral foundations of the gambling Mecca.

And she was annoyed at having to leave the best French restaurant in town, not to mention one of the most sought-after dates, to come in to hear an emergency petition.

"This better be about the Second Coming or an invasion from Mars, Mr. Capers." She settled behind her desk, waiting.

Capers and Gavilan exchanged nervous looks, then turned back to the annoyed jurist.

"Mr. Gavilan will make our initial presentation, your honor," Capers said in a weaker voice than he'd intended.

"Make it worth my time, Mr. Gavilan."

Gavilan smiled his most charming smile, taking the offered envelope from Magda. "Your honor, may we go on the record at this time?"

The judge glanced at the court reporter, who nodded. "Very well. We're on the record in the matter of . . ." She paused to check the docket sheet on her desk. "In the matter of Joe Gray and Max Gray. Present are Mr. Linwood Capers and Mr. John Gavilan of the Clark County Public Defender's Office. As well as Ms.—" She paused again, looking at Magda.

"Jane Smith," Magda said casually. "Mr. Gavilan's assistant."

"Very well. Your serve, Mr. Gavilan."

Gavilan handed a copy of a file across the desk. "Thank you, your honor. I am presenting your honor with a document labeled Petitioners' One for identification. It is an emergency petition asking for an immediate temporary restraining order against all organs of the United States federal government. Said order asking that the government be prohibited from contacting two individuals, Joe and Max Gray of Las Vegas, Nevada; also prohibiting any of the government's agents or representatives from coming closer than one hundred fifty feet to said named individuals.

"I am presenting to your honor a document labeled Petitioners' Two for identification. It is a request for an immediate court order compelling the federal government to release all files, classified or otherwise, as they relate to the named individuals in Petitioners' One.

"I am presenting to your honor a document labeled Petitioners' Three for identification. It is a request for an immediate injunction against the federal government to prevent them from arresting or detaining in any way the named individuals in Petitioners' One. As well as three additional individuals: Gregory Picaro, Robert Fosselis, and Megan Turner, all of Los Angeles, California.

"I am presenting to your honor a document labeled Petitioners' Four for identification. It is a request for your honor to grant transactional immunity from prosecution to the individuals named in Petitioners' One and Three so that they might come forward and testify in any on-the-record hearings your honor might wish to conduct.

"I am presenting to your honor a document labeled Supporting Information. Petitioners' Five for identification." He paused to help Magda put two small stationery boxes on the judge's desk. "Said document consisting of an index to copies and originals of federal government documents dating from 5 July 1947 to 26 November 1979, contained in Petitioners' Five A for identification. As well as sworn depositions, statements, and additional supporting material contained in Petitioners' Five B for identification."

The judge quickly read through the first four petitions, then glanced through the index.

"Care to give me the abridged version, gentlemen?"

Both lawyers looked at each other throughout a long, nervous silence.

"Mr. Gavilan?"

He hesitated.

"Mr. Capers?"

Capers took a deep breath, then slowly straightened in his chair. "Your honor?"

"Mr. Capers?"

He took a deep breath, then jumped off his burning bridge. "Your honor, it is our allegation that for a little more than the last half century, an organ of the federal government calling itself Majestic Twelve has illegally held two beings from another planet in close custody.''

He hesitated as the judge's annoyed expression subtly started to shift toward angry.

"We further allege that they have lied under oath before Congress and other duly authorized investigative bodies in denial of these facts. That they have subjected these beings to treatment, mistreatment actually, in violation of the constitutional rights protecting them as visitors to our nation. That they have conspired to commit a series of felonies in the last six months, ranging from breaking and entering to kidnap and murder, in order to perpetuate this continuing fraud and illegal detention.''

He paused as Gavilan whispered in his ear.

"Further, your honor," Capers began again, "we allege that the actions enumerated in the supporting papers indicate a pattern of behavior that falls well within the definition of racketeering; therefore we inform this court that we will be seeking redress through the civil statutes of the RICO Act, as well as your honor's good offices.''

"Your honor?''

Antoinette slowly swiveled to face Gavilan. "Yes?'' Her voice was cold, furious. Her eyes burned through him.

Gavilan self-consciously straightened his tie. "To make it completely clear to your honor, we have been informed within the past hour that these extraterrestrial beings, assisted by the three individuals named in Petitioners' Three, have escaped the custody of Majestic Twelve at a secret military base here in Nevada. It is our deep concern that this out-of-control, fundamentally criminal organ of the federal government is at this moment pursuing them. And will, with deadly force, take any actions it can to cover up these living proofs of their culpability. It is because of this that we appear before you to seek these emergency reliefs.''

"Are you finished?'' Antoinette's voice was completely without emotion. Cold, flat, tingling with suppressed energy.

"Yes, your honor.''

"Mr. Capers?''

"Yes, your honor.''

She was quiet for a full minute. "Gentlemen," she said with her rage barely controlled. "I'm going to read through your presentations. We're all going to sit here, if it takes the rest of the night, while I read. And I hope, for your sakes, that this isn't all some bizarre, *deeply unwise,* practical joke. Because when I'm done"—she opened the nearest box of documents—"someone's ass is going to be in my jail."

Then she began to read.

One of the Gypsy technicians checked the order of the cue cards he held as they waited for the "go" from the truck.

"You sure this is going to work?"

Megan hoped she sounded more confident than she felt.

"Piece of cake. Bounce the signal off the B channel of the WIN satellite and the picture goes into each of their eighty-seven news-rooms across the country. It won't go right on the air, they control that at each station, but, yeah. I think it'll work."

The man nodded as he got the one-minute signal over his head-set. He held up the cue cards, lowered them until Megan nodded, then began to count.

"In . . . five. Four. Three. Two. One. On the air."

"Attention, WIN affiliate! Attention, WIN affiliate! This is a special purpose transmission. This is a special purpose transmission. I am Megan Turner, an executive producer in the WIN News Division. Many of you know me, and I ask those of you who do, to go live with this broadcast. I assure you that this is not a trick or a hoax. I will explain it all in my feed. To the rest of you, I ask that you please begin recording this feed for later transmission after consideration. We will transmit color bars while you code in."

Megan glanced at the monitor by her feet. A test pattern was displayed.

Nervously shifting her weight, glancing up and down the road, at the satellite truck, she waited for some confirmation from her technicians in the truck.

Eight minutes later, her impromptu Gypsy floor manager looked up as he listened to his headphones.

"We have twenty-one stations on-line," he said. "Twenty-five. Twenty-seven on-line. Eight of them going live. Including the Vegas affiliate."

Megan wet her lips, took a deep breath. "Go for it."

The other technician flipped on the high-intensity lights that turned the desert around Megan into bright, sharply illuminated relief. The test pattern disappeared, replaced by her picture.

"Slug the broadcast Turner One." She paused, gathering her thoughts, focusing on the cards, trying to picture the puzzled expressions on the news directors' faces around the country.

"In three, two, one. This is Megan Turner, WIN News, coming to you from somewhere deep in the Nevada desert." She paused, to steady herself, rather than for effect.

"Mark Twain once said that reports of his death had been greatly exaggerated. In his case, it was due to the accidental publication of his obituary."

This time, the pause was for effect.

"In mine, the reports come from an elaborate, evil conspiracy of men without faces. Of men who would go to any lengths to preserve the dark secret they have kept from the American people since the end of World War II."

The camera pushed in close on her stern, committed face.

"A secret that WIN will reveal to you tonight."

In the heart of Majestic Operations, Paul stood before a closed door, wiping the sweat from his face, his palms, from every square inch of revealed skin. He'd awakened that morning knowing that his future was assured. That his rise from field operative to Kilbourne's assistant to chief personal aide to a legend had been made possible by his skill, intelligence, and commitment to the ideals that the men he served exemplified. And he had known that his future was bright, upward, and guaranteed.

But it was no longer morning.

In a moment the door would open. He would have to walk through, ending at the very least his *professional* life in disgrace. Knowing that he'd failed the decades-old responsibility that had been entrusted to him. Knowing that he'd failed his country in as grievous a way as was possible.

The door slid noiselessly open and he stepped through.

The Secretary was half lying on the couch, watching a woman who seemed to be doing some kind of broadcast from a desert. Kilbourne sat in a swivel chair, shaking his head and frowning.

"Yes, Paul?" the Secretary said without taking his eyes off the TV.

"Sir. I must report to you that, uh, sir, we've completed the search of Habitat, the open areas above, as well as heard from Security Ops at all other Dreamland sites including North Field."

The Secretary continued to watch the broadcast as Kilbourne responded. "And?"

"Sir," Paul said while holding himself at the straightest, stiffest attention he ever had. "We have a problem."

For the first time, Kilbourne looked up from the TV, swiveled to face the panicked man who had once been on the verge of murdering him. "Paul . . ."

"Yes, sir?"

Kilbourne glanced at Megan on the television, then back to Paul. "Son, you have no idea."

NINETEEN

STAND BY, one zero nine. Routing you now.''

Molly shifted the receiver to her other hand, then shakily poured herself a water glass of vodka.

The door to the luxury suite opened and Senator Van Ness walked in, laughing with some aides. Van Ness took one look at his wife's expression, the plate of food that had obviously been bounced off the TV, his wife's shaking hands, then hustled the aides away.

"What in the hell is going on here?" he asked as soon as the suite was empty. His voice was soft but firm. "They called me out of a meeting with the Campaign Finance Committee for crissake." He checked his watch. "And I'm due with the transition planning staff in . . . now, actually."

Molly rubbed her forehead. "We may not need the damned transition staff." Her voice was half an octave higher with her shattered emotions.

Van Ness took a hesitant step toward her. "What's happened?"

She put down her drink, then unmuted the set, gesturing with the remote.

Megan still stood in the Nevada desert, talking into the camera, as document after highlighted document was displayed on a split screen.

"These papers detail the organization and staffing of that illegal, corrupt organization that calls itself by the self-deluding name of *Majestic* Twelve. They set out in microscopic detail their plans to conceal the facts of these alien landings from Congress and the

American people. How they anticipated, even in 1947, that, and I'm reading now from the document on the screen before you: 'We must be ever vigilant, ever prepared to deal with any threats to our internal security. We must implement these preparations ruthlessly, whether the response required is a dismissive chuckle, a knowing wink, or cold-blooded murder.' "

She paused as the camera pushed in on her, as well as the high-lighted passages.

"And, ladies and gentlemen, I have personally witnessed two of these ruthless, cold-blooded murders firsthand. And would've been a third victim myself if not for the actions of some brave individuals who were likewise sickened by the insane arrogance Majestic Twelve has displayed throughout the last five decades.

"Copies or originals of these documents, as well as considerably more, have been delivered within the last half hour to the custody of United States District Court Judge Antoinette Alexander in her chambers, here in Las Vegas.

"There, Judge Alexander is being presented with the facts of this brutal, far-reaching conspiracy, as she is asked to issue federal judicial orders to protect more innocent victims and bring this dark, sordid secret finally to the light of day."

Molly remuted the TV. "Does that answer your question?"

Van Ness stood frozen, staring at the screen. "We're through," he said in a defeated voice. "Twelve days away and we're all through."

"We are if your name's in any of those documents," Molly said as she tried to psychically force the phone connection through.

Van Ness shook his head as he half collapsed onto the arm of the couch. "We have to do something. Gotta figure out how to get on top of this. We have to . . ." He suddenly seemed to regain himself. "We have to call the Secretary!"

Molly shook her head as though dealing with an idiot child. "Who do you think I'm trying to get through to?"

Van Ness rushed over. "What's the problem?"

Molly swallowed half her drink. "Majic bullshit. They're sweeping the line now."

For two minutes, the two people who were closer political allies than they'd ever been as man and wife stood holding the receiver between them. Neither having the nerve to unmute the accusing woman on the TV.

Nor the strength to turn it off.

"Majic one zero nine?" It was a different voice on the other end.

"Yes? I'm here." They both leaned closer to the receiver.

"Stand by for Majic 1."

Clicks and whistles filled the line, then suddenly cleared.

"Molly," the Secretary said in a cheery voice, "it's been far too long."

"Mr. Secretary, do you have any idea what's going on? It's a disaster!"

"A disaster?" he said in an easy, slightly confused voice. "Oh, you mean the girl on the TV." He paused. "Yes. That is unfortunate. But hardly a disaster." He sounded more disappointed than angry or fearful.

"Unfortunate? That's the woman who was with McCutcheon, right? The woman who escaped from the Majic Annex, right? The woman who *died* when the McCutcheon papers were destroyed, *right?*"

There was a long silence on the line. "I'll admit this does present a bit of a complication but—"

"You told us she was *dead!*" Molly screamed into the phone. "You promised me that they were all dead! That the papers had been destroyed along with the bodies! What in the hell is happening?"

"Do try and calm yourself, dear," the Secretary said lightly. "You won't help anyone by making yourself sick over this."

Molly laughed spasmodically, bitterly. "Calm myself? Is that what you said? Calm myself? If you think I'm loud now, just you wait until . . ."

She never finished the sentence as her husband took the phone from her, pushing her back. He spoke quietly into the phone.

"Mr. Secretary, Jesse James Van Ness here, sir."

"Good evening, Senator."

"Sir, could you hold the line for a moment?"

"Of course, Senator."

Van Ness punched the hold button as he turned to his steaming wife. "Go over and monitor what that bitch on TV is saying."

"What did you just say to me?"

"Goddammit!" he said between clenched teeth. "You know how the old bastard gets when he's pushed, so shut the hell up and see what Turner's saying."

She started to protest, but the look in his eyes stopped her cold.

Reluctantly she turned on the sound, then took a pad over to the TV.

Van Ness turned back to the phone, took several deep breaths, then pressed the blinking line button. "Mr. Secretary, what can you tell us?"

"About what, specifically, Senator?" There was just a hint of sarcasm in the distant man's voice.

The tone was familiar to the presidential candidate. It was one he'd heard fifty years before whenever he'd seen the great man under maximum stress.

Fake calm disregard, the man had taught him, *and most people will believe you and therefore remain calm as well.*

So, from the depth of the calm on the other end of the line, this crisis must be of epic proportions.

"What does the girl have, what does she know?"

"Oh, well, she seems to have the broad strokes down pretty well. As well as some of the more ancient history."

"Anything that can hurt us?" Van Ness tried to force the same calm into his own voice.

"Nothing *on paper* can hurt us, Jess. You know I took care of all that years ago."

Van Ness knew the Secretary had said he'd removed all written references to him years ago. But the chasm between what the man might say and what he might do was . . . "Do you have any idea where she got this stuff?"

"Mostly from Jack Kerry's safe, I imagine. Also some other things. Possibly some of the Muroc stuff, from McCutcheon." He paused. "Wasn't McCutcheon with you at Muroc?"

He sounded as though he was passing the time of day in a neighborhood barbershop.

"Muroc could be a problem, don't you think?" Van Ness was trying desperately to gauge the other man's voice. "There might be pictures, supporting witnesses. There were a lot of people there."

"That was over forty years ago, Senator. If you haven't been recognized by now, I should think you're in the clear on that score."

"Nobody's been looking until now."

There was a long, ominous pause. "If you'll excuse me, Senator, I seem to have the White House calling on the other line."

"Of course, Mr. Secretary. You'll keep us informed?"

"As often as I can. And good luck with the election." Another ominous pause. "We're all counting on you, Jess."

The line went dead.

Molly muted the TV, then turned to look at her husband, who had hung up but still stared down at the now-quiet phone. "What'd he say?" she asked in a subdued tone caused by the strange expression on Van Ness's face.

"He wished me luck with the election."

Molly slowly shook her head. "We're going to need it." She turned the volume up on the TV.

Megan's voice talked over an enhanced copy of one of the documents.

". . . in the past eight months. These twelve murder victims, seemingly disconnected, seemingly unrelated in any way, did, however, share one fatal link. From 1947 until 1954, they served as a form of palace guard for the extraterrestrials. They kept the uninitiated, the uninvited, the 'no need to knows' far away. They guarded the doors physically as well as through disinformation programs aimed at the public."

Judge Alexander compared her original to the document being displayed on the television. Then she shut the TV. "And your point is, Mr. Gavilan?"

"Simply, your honor, that you must realize now that from the form, content, designations, and other obvious indicators, the documents before you are genuine. Combined with the extraordinary steps taken by Ms. Turner, we believe their bona fides have been fully established."

The judge flipped through some of the documents she'd just finished reading. "You know television, Mr. Gavilan. The things they can do today, the realism they can put in movies—fantasy or otherwise—borders on the miraculous." She hesitated. "I can see why one *might* believe in the authenticity of these documents, but frankly you're still far short of crossing the threshold of proof I'll require before I'll act."

"But your honor . . ." Gavilan was interrupted by the phone on the desk.

"Excuse me, gentlemen. We'll go off the record at this point," she said to the court reporter. "Hello? . . . Speaking." She stiff-

ened in her chair. "Yes, I recognize the voice. But could you tell me
. . . Yes, sir. I do remember. How are you?"

The lawyers looked at each other as Antoinette began making
notes as she talked.

"Yes, sir." A long pause, while she seemed to be concentrating
very hard on the muffled, angry voice on the other end.

"I do understand your position, sir. But you need to understand
mine. These things need to be dealt with in an orderly . . . I see.
But the law also is clear on this. When emergency remediation is
prayed for . . . No, I completely understand what you mean."

Another pause, while she made some notes. "Yes, sir. That would
be fine. Thank you . . . Oh, yes sir, I'll wait. Good night, sir." She
hung up, then pressed a button under her desk. A moment later, a
bailiff appeared.

"Billy, how many marshals in the building right now?"

The man thought for a moment. "Five. Maybe six."

She never hesitated. "Call the Marshal's Service, then county
sheriff, then Metro." She wrote a note on a small piece of paper. "I
want this building sealed off. Now! I want marshals on each entrance to my chambers and courtroom. And only the names on this
list get into either."

"Right away, your honor." The marshal rushed from the office.

"Your honor," Gavilan asked, "has something happened?"

Antoinette nodded at the court reporter, who began again. "Back
on the record in the matter of Joe Gray and Max Gray. Counsel for
the petitioners are present. Before I hear further arguments, gentlemen, I'd like to put into the record some new information which
bears on the petitions before me. If there is no objection."

Both men remained in cautious silence.

"Hearing no objection. The court has just been contacted tele-
phonically by the attorney general of the United States. He has
asked me to hold all actions relating to this matter in abeyance until
his representative can arrive. He has assured me that said representative is en route, due to arrive within the next ninety minutes.
Accordingly, he has asked me to put off any actions the court may
be considering until the government can present their side of the
issues at hand."

"Your honor?"

"May we be heard?"

The two lawyers spoke over each other in almost panicked calls for attention.

"Quiet."

The lawyers, sweating, suddenly breathing heavily, braced themselves for the worst.

Antoinette pulled one of the folders closer to her. "For the record, I am signing the document labeled Petitioners' One, the temporary restraining order against the government."

She pulled over another file as the lawyers flinched. "For the record, I am signing the document labeled Petitioners' Three, the injunction against arrest or detention of the named individuals."

Gavilan opened his mouth, but nothing came out. Capers studied her closely.

She opened another folder. "For the record, I am signing the document labeled Petitioners' Four, the request for transactional immunity for the named individuals. Such immunity is so granted." She paused while she concentrated on capping her pen.

"We'll deal with the request for files and exhibits, Petitioners' Two, later. We'll go off the record now until the arrival of the government's attorney." She nodded the reporter out of the room.

"Your honor?" Capers sounded stunned.

"Something wrong, Lin?"

Gavilan was instructing Magda, who was already dialing numbers on a cell phone.

"What just happened here, Toni?" Capers asked with obvious curiosity.

"You just crossed the threshold of proof that I demanded."

"How?"

She smiled rather bitterly. "When the attorney general of the United States calls me after midnight his time, to sweet-talk me into not acting on what he describes as, and I'm quoting here, 'a lot of fuss and bother signifying absolutely nothing,' that's all the proof I need."

She sipped a Styrofoam cup of coffee.

"*He's* your proof. The old jackass never deigns to talk to lowly folk like district judges. He leaves stuff like that to his flunky solicitor general." She shook her head. "Let alone do business after the cocktail hour. Looks like you stirred up a hornet's nest this time."

She handed the folders to her clerk for certification. "I'm just covering myself in case there *are* little green men running around out there, being chased by government agents. Just being cautious."

"Thank God," Gavilan whispered.

"Thank me, Mr. Gavilan. That fool of an A.G. got you in the door, but you'll still have to counter the national security arguments I expect to hear."

"We're ready, your honor."

"You're ready," she repeated in a whisper as she took another sip of coffee. "Better get some more of this, looks like it's going to be a long night." She chuckled. "A long, loud night."

She flipped the TV back on.

"Dreamland, Mischief Leader."

"Mischief Leader, Dreamland. Copy."

"Dreamland, Mischief Leader. We've reached the outer leg of alpha pattern with negative results. Can you advise how we should proceed from here, sir?"

"Mischief Leader, Dreamland. We're working on triangulating from here, while we continue the satellite back-trace. Tracking recommends you split your flight into grids one four seven Baker and Zulu, sir."

"Dreamland, Mischief Leader. Copy that. Mischief Leader to Second Division. Break left to two four zero and continue your search in grid one four seven Zulu."

"Second Division Lead. Copy that, Mischief Leader. Second Division, break left in three, two, one. Break."

"First Division, Mischief Leader. Form a diamond and one on me, then come right to three three four degrees. On my mark, in three, two, one. Mark."

Megan sat on the steps of the door to the truck, wiping her face with a damp towel.

"I think that's the longest I've ever talked in my life."

One of the technicians nodded at her. "Sounded like a kid trying to talk his way out of trouble."

"Wasn't I?"

One of the girls came out of the truck. She stepped over Megan, taking a sip from an offered bottle. "Tape's up and running."

"And?"

The girl smiled. "We're up to forty-seven affiliates, sixteen going live with the feed." She handed Megan a small piece of paper. "That came in on the downlink from some guy calls himself Moyer."

Megan glanced at the paper. "My boss. Former boss, I guess." She paused. "Whatever." She read the message out loud. "Welcome back to the land of the living. Your behavior in going underground without notifying us is completely unacceptable and will result in your immediate termination. Unless this story proves itself out. In which case, you get my job."

She laughed as she crumbled the paper, then tossed it away into the night.

"To hell with him."

She took a long slug from the bottle handed her, then checked her watch. "They should be here soon."

"Dreamland. Dreamland. This is Mischief Leader. We have the target."

"Mischief Leader, Dreamland. Say again, sir. You have a contact?"

"Dreamland, Mischief Leader. That is affirmative. We paint the target as mobile satellite transmitter, white in color. Position follows. Grid one four seven Zulu. Section one four Baker."

"Copy that, Leader."

"Dreamland, we show five individuals moving around the target. No other vehicles or individuals in range."

"Mischief Leader, Dreamland. Stand by."

"Mischief Leader, Dreamland. Strike is inbound. ETA nine minutes. They request you paint the target for them."

"Dreamland, Mischief Leader. Copy that. Niner minutes for inbound strike. Mischief three eight two, warm up your targeting lasers."

Greg stood by himself in front of the Justice Center.

Completely alone, unarmed, unwatched. Just one man standing in the soft glow from the landscape lights, apparently caught up in the rough-hewn beauty of the building.

He watched as the local police arrived, setting up roadblocks at either end of the street.

He watched as the sheriff's deputies set up a cordon around the building itself.

He watched as United States marshals arrived to take up security positions just inside the large glass doors.

All three groups questioned him, all three groups checked with Judge Alexander.

All three groups left him alone.

As he'd told Gavilan in a terse conversation two minutes earlier, he wasn't ready to give himself over to the "tender ministrations" of the American justice system quite yet. Not until he was sure.

Not until *they* were safe.

The press had begun to arrive, kept at bay by the roadblocks and the no-nonsense Vegas cops.

Where the cameras turned on their lights, crowds of curious by-standers began to form. Their camcorders, disposable cameras' strobes, all added to the growing unreality of the place.

But Greg held his ground.

Waiting.

Five minutes later, he watched as three limousines were passed through the roadblock. They pulled to a stop at the curb directly in front of him.

Big men, doors with heads on them, got out, looked around, then nodded. Rear doors popped open and four or five people from each car climbed out.

Straightening their jackets as they went, they walked, lemming-like, past Greg; never giving him a second (or first for that matter) glance. They were passed, one at a time, into the building after being thoroughly searched by the sheriffs, then the marshals.

Then they were gone, all vanishing into the depths of the building as their limos pulled away.

All except one.

Greg turned to look at the last limo, as he was sure its passenger was looking at him. He felt a strong, almost overwhelming desire to turn away, rush into the building where unquestioned safety lay. Where, for the first time in more than half a year, he could close his eyes and rest.

But he held his ground.

Compelled by the memories of a dead girl and old man in a luxury penthouse. By visions of a sacrificed/slaughtered patriot and his daughter-in-law, lying butchered in the garage of a middle-class tract house.

By two pairs of the most trusting, however strange, eyes he'd ever looked into.

The rear door of the car opened and closed quickly, leaving an elderly man standing on the sidewalk.

Kilbourne.

Greg opened his cell phone, speed-dialing a number.

"Magyarovar. This is Tapestry," Megan answered.

"We should know something soon."

"Right. We'll keep running the tape until we hear differently."

Greg watched the old man pause, giving Greg his privacy on the phone. "Is everything all right?"

Megan actually laughed. "That's what I'm waiting for you to tell me."

"Right." His voice was hard, like the granite walls behind him. "You hear from them yet?"

"Yeah. Laz, uh, Caravan called saying that they had to stop first for jackets, blankets, and, uh, heating packs. Don't know what he's talking about, it's a warm night and all, but that's what he said."

"It's okay. *I* know. Call me if you hear anything else." Greg folded away the phone, then walked over to the old man.

"Mr. Picaro?"

"Mr. Kilbourne. Or has it changed again?"

The old man forced down a smile at the man's confidence. Real or feigned, it was an impressive sight.

"It would be appreciated if you would meet in the car, sir." Kilbourne was polite, cordial, businesslike. "He guarantees your safety in all respects. He merely wants to talk."

Greg started for the car, glancing at Kilbourne's cane and stiffened leg. "I do that?" he asked casually.

Kilbourne shrugged. "Things happen."

"Things happen." Greg chuckled. "I like that."

"Mischief Leader, this is Strike Leader. We are three minutes inbound your position. You are go to paint the target."

"Strike Leader, this is Mischief Leader. Copy that. Target is laser-lit. Set your pickles for zero zero four point six."

There was a brief pause while the three Apache attack helicopter gunners (flying at almost desert level) set the targeting guidance on their four rocket packs of nineteen air-to-ground missiles each.

"Mischief Leader, this is Strike Leader. Pickles hot and climbing to attack altitude."

"Strike Leader, this is Mischief Leader. God speed."

The limo's back door was opened by Paul as Greg approached it, then he walked away to give the men their privacy as he'd been instructed.

Greg climbed into the backseat without hesitation, settling himself against the center divider, studying the ancient-looking man across from him.

"I've been looking forward to this meeting, Mr. Picaro," the Secretary said in a pleasant tone. "I almost feel as if I know you."

Greg studied the man's face. "I *do* know you. Don't I." It was a flat statement of fact. "Seen your picture on a stamp or something."

The Secretary laughed. "Hardly that, I think."

Greg nodded as he recognized the once famous features beneath the leathered, wrinkled, pale skin.

"Of course," he said with a touch of sarcasm. "Who else would be behind something like this?" He gestured at the courthouse just outside. "Sorry to have spoiled everything."

The Secretary shrugged. "Whatever happens in there, it will have very little bearing on my plans." He offered the young man across from him a glass of wine. "Public pronouncements and judicial decisions notwithstanding, the work of protecting this country will go on."

Greg declined the glass. "Protecting them from who? Joe and Max?" He shook his head. "Try again."

"From what they represent, then. Surely you understand the ramifications of alien life. The chaos it would breed in our society at all levels."

For the first time, Greg noticed that Kilbourne had settled himself in the front seat and was talking on a cell phone.

"What was it Jefferson said?" Greg said as he returned to studying the man in front of him. "A little revolution now and then is a healthy thing?"

"There will be no revolution."

"No?"

The dying man shook his head. "No. There'll be a lot of shouting. Some Senate investigations, TV news specials, that sort of thing.

Ms. Turner will win the Pulitzer Prize and be accused of making it all up at the same time. Probably by the same people." He shrugged. "Then it will all just recede. Fade into cloudy images that everybody will consign their own design to."

He paused, deep in thought, searching for one last lie to add to the fetid pile that was his life. "Our nation's plans will continue with only the barest noticeable tremor on the historical seismograph."

He lowered the divider as Kilbourne gestured to him, then he nodded slightly.

"They may proceed, Mr. Kilbourne," he said after a short silence.

He turned back to Greg. "The administration will take a few whopping bruises for something that was started when the current occupant of the White House was three." He paused. "But then, it *was* exposed on his watch as they say."

He smiled like an understanding grandfather with a puzzled child. "Perhaps there'll even be a big-budget movie on all of this." He chuckled. "And who shall we get to play us, Mr. Hadeon? My apologies. Mr. Picaro."

"You're forgetting about Joe and Max," Greg said solemnly.

The Secretary feigned deep surprise. "Am I? Indeed." He leaned back in his seat. "You didn't take the risks, go through all you've gone through, to put them on display before a gibbering public."

"No?"

The old man shook his head. "No." He closed his eyes for a moment as a ripple of pain played through his decomposing body. "You and I are of a mind on this. To cage them was necessary, once. Today, well, necessity has devolved into a crime against God, any and all gods, and their laws. They had to be allowed their freedom. Their chance to go home. I had to make things right."

Greg shook his head. "So why didn't you just let them go your-self?"

A deep, painful intake of breath. "Because the militocracy is not about to listen to one old, crippled, former self; a man confined to a wheelchair being pushed by a figure in a dark robe with a scythe."

"You are the militocracy."

A brief spasmodic smile from the Secretary in acknowledgment.

"So you decided to use me as a cat's paw," Greg continued after a long pause.

"A tumbler would be more accurate, Mr. Picaro. And, just so the record is straight, you were an afterthought forced on me by your unexpected appearance in Jack Kerry's apartment. Until then, I'd simply hoped to use Ms. Turner, without her knowledge of course, to bring enough pressure on the powers-that-be to allow me to release Joe and Max. You were a bonus."

"More bullshit," Greg mumbled. "Why a tumbler?" he asked in an offhanded way as he considered what the man had said.

The Secretary smiled a secret smile. "There were locks that needed to be opened, Mr. Picaro. Locks that required just the right manipulation of just the right tumblers." He suddenly looked disappointed. "I was sure you'd like the analogy."

"And the rest of it?"

The old man shook his head. "There is no rest of it. Now you know it all."

Greg sighed. "Well, there is one other . . ." He was cut off by the ringing of his cell phone. "Yeah?"

"They're dead!" Megan's voice was breaking up as she shouted into the phone on her end.

Greg froze. "What's going on?"

"They blew it up! They blew it up and killed Georgi and Petra!" She was silent for a moment and explosions could be heard in the background. "Oh God," she whispered. "Oh God! They're coming back! I can hear them! Help us! Help—"

The line went dead.

"Megan? Megan?" He dropped the phone to the seat, then leaned forward toward the Secretary. "What the hell are you up to?"

But the .45 in the old man's steady hand was his only answer.

Greg took a deep breath, but in all other respects seemed calm, collected, resigned.

"Please don't make us kill you here, Victor. May I call you Victor?"

Kilbourne frisked Greg from behind. The thief never took his eyes off the pleasantly smiling old man in front of him.

"I thought you'd guaranteed my safety," he said in an ice-cold voice.

"I lied."

"Of course." Greg could hear Kilbourne moving around in the front seat and estimated that he had moments before a syringe would be plunged into his neck.

"Good-bye, Victor," the Secretary said with a dark glint in his eyes. "You've made my last months most entertaining. Thank you for that."

"I'm glad you like entertainment," Greg said in a flat tone. "Because you're about to get lots of it." He paused as he saw that the old man was watching Kilbourne, behind Greg, presumably about to strike with the sedative or poison.

Something about Greg's stillness caught the Secretary's attention. "One moment, Tom," he said as he studied the thief in front of him. "You have some last words, Victor?"

The desert seemed to be exploding around them. The burning, long-destroyed satellite truck crackled and hissed in sadistic glee as it watched the few survivors crouch behind some rocks and pray for a miracle that couldn't happen.

Half the Gypsy crew was dead, parts of their bodies strewn around the improvised camp. Two of the Gypsies, wounded but conscious, lay behind Megan. Her bodyguard crowded her close to the primordial granite, his finger on the Ingram's trigger, praying that the bastards would fly low enough and slow enough for him to get one clean shot at them.

Then they all stopped breathing as five bright lights sped toward them from the desert night sky. The lights that meant that the next, most probably *last,* volley of missiles was on its way from their invisible attackers.

Megan watched, panicked but transfixed, as her bodyguard stood up and calmly emptied his magazine at onrushing death.

Greg looked the Secretary in the eye, then slowly, carefully played his next-to-last card. "They're not at the satellite truck."

"Who?"

"Joe and Max. They're not there."

The reaction in the dying man was so subtle, so instantly concealed, that it might have only been in Greg's prayers.

"Why would I want them there? I don't want them dead. I told you that."

"You lied. Or told a half-truth, if you prefer." Greg actually managed a half-smile. "You don't *want* them dead; you *need* them dead."

The Secretary leaned painfully forward. "What do you *think* you know?'' His voice was a foul thing, filled with menace, threat, and a hint of doubt.

"Nobody's safe," Greg said steadily. "Certainly not Van Ness, not your plans, not your *vision*"—he spit out the word—"as long as there are any witnesses to history." He shook his head sadly. "Especially Joe and Max."

The Secretary studied him, the expression without affect, the steely gaze. The mettle that he'd thought bred out of the current generation.

"Nice try," he finally said in a voice more steady than he felt.

But Greg heard what he needed in the old man's voice. "Call it off. Now. Or Joe and Max will be on *Letterman* doing Stupid Alien Tricks by the end of the week."

A deadly silence settled between them as both men stared unblinkingly at each other.

"You're bluffing."

Greg's face was stone, his voice iron. "Call it off. Or it'll all have been for nothing."

For almost a full minute, neither man moved, seemed to breathe.

"Abort the mission," the Secretary suddenly called out.

"Mr. Secretary?"

"Do it!" the Secretary almost shouted to his stunned aide. "Do it now!"

Kilbourne dropped his syringe and reached for his cell phone. "It may be too late."

Greg just looked into the Secretary's panicked eyes.

"I've got through to Dreamland, sir," Kilbourne said as he listened to his phone. "They're contacting the strike leader now." A long pause. "Strike Leader reports . . ." He looked relieved. "They made two passes but aborted before the third."

"Survivors?" Greg continued to stare at the old man who seemed to be shrinking before him.

Kilbourne concentrated on the small phone. "Mischief Leader's going in for a check now. Just a minute, wait . . . He reports two possible survivors on the ground."

"I want them medevacked to a civilian hospital immediately," Greg demanded.

The Secretary nodded, and then Kilbourne began to whisper urgently into the phone.

□   □   □

She watched two lights come bouncing up the road toward her. Heard tires scream against the sand-covered road as it jerked to a stop. Barely made out two forms running toward her.

But she was past caring.

There was little pain, little *feeling*, no caring. Just the waiting and regretting.

Megan would've laughed—if she'd been able—at the absurdity of the situation. All she'd ever cared about, the one true love of her life, had been *getting it*. The grades. The jobs. Her distant father's love. And now she *absolutely had it!* The greatest story in the history of the universe whether she really believed in it or not!

And she would die before she could tell it to anyone.

Lazslo bent close to her charred body, wiping the blood from her eyes, balling his jacket into a pillow for her stoved-in head.

"Il ne lui reste rien," the French Gypsy driver said in low tones as he swept the horizon and the sky with the barrel of his MP-5K.

"I know," Lazslo said as he gently wiped the tiny face with the searching eyes, with his bloodstained handkerchief. "But we will wait with her." He bent over, kissing her lightly on the lips.

A noise from behind caught his attention and he looked back toward the truck. "I told you to keep them quiet, under cover," he shouted at Lukacs as he chased after Joe and Max.

"You try it sometime," he yelled back as he followed the two aliens to the attack scene.

Megan sensed but didn't care about the commotion next to her. Her mind was drifting; floating over the missed opportunities, the lost chances, the mistakes, and the unfulfillments that made up her oozing-away life. She wished she could believe in God, in a power beyond our own fragility as we floated alone through the universe.

But there was no God, no divine force or nature to any of it. We were alone and that was that.

A shadow seemed to pass between her and the stars for a moment. She concentrated with what strength she had left to bring the image into focus. To have one final memory of something real before she blinked out of existence.

"Oh God," she moaned weakly as Joe tilted his head to the side to study her. "God, *you're real."* Tears flowed down both cheeks as her voice decayed and drifted off beyond any *human* ears. *"You're real."* She tried to reach up to the vision of the thing she'd never really believed in. But her strength was gone.

Max reached down, took her hand, then touched it to his alien lips, soft, warm, loving. Then Joe did the same.

"Thank you," she whispered as she finally gave herself over to the infiniteness that she now *knew for certain* existed.

The three men crossed themselves and muttered personal prayers. Then, with a look of amazement, Lukacs held out the translator monitor for them all to see.

FREE SHE IS///

After a second report of "at least two survivors on the ground," Greg opened the car door.

"You're leaving?" The Secretary looked confused.

"We're done here."

Panic crossed the old man's face in an instant. "What are you going to do?"

Greg hesitated, then climbed out of the car. On the sidewalk he stopped, then turned back to the open door. "Make things right." A bitter laugh seemed to escape his lips. "Maybe for the first time in my life."

"I can stop you." The old man slid over by the open door. "No matter what happens in that court, I can stop you. Hunt down you, all your friends, anyone who's helping you in this!" He lowered his voice as he became aware of the deputies not twenty meters away. "We'll find all of you, and there'll be . . . *accidents.*" He paused. "You understand me, I think."

"I understand you," Greg replied in an oddly discordant, seemingly sad tone.

"We can still make a deal. You and I. Terms that will work for everybody." He seemed to be calming himself. "Deal now," he said in a finally calm but still-threatening voice, "or we'll find you later." He paused to gather his breath. "And that includes the Hesperians."

"Who?"

"The Hesperians. Joe. Max." Black madness dripped from the man's voice.

"Oh."

"So? Do we deal, do we both come out of this with something?"

"No," Greg said in that same sad voice. "You can probably find us. You might even get away with some of the accidents." He raised his eyebrows in a look of fatalism and disbelief. "But your secret's out now. Whether everybody believes it or not, enough will."

He sighed deeply. "We've both worked for the same lunatics in their hallucinogenic crusades. We both know the way they think." He hesitated, as if he didn't want to go on, but the challenge still in the dying man's rheumy eyes forced him on. "We both know what they'll do to protect themselves."

Another pause. When he spoke again, his voice was filled with pity, sorrow, and regret.

"Majestic is dead, or soon will be, which amounts to the same thing. And you yourself have demonstrated how to deal with sloppy loose ends."

Greg turned to leave, then turned back one last time. "By the way, that's a big desert out there. And there are so many more throughout the world. A lot of sand. Do you really think you'll ever find Joe and Max again? Especially now that they don't want to be found. At least by you." He shook his head. "Some things just won't stay locked up, Mr. Secretary. No matter how much you may want them to."

He walked away, straight toward the doors of the Justice Center.

The Secretary watched him go. His mind a turmoil of truths mixed with lies, of wrong rights and justified wrongs. Of ambitions, personal and national, irrevocably merged together to the point where he wasn't sure any longer where his country ended—where he began.

And he thought of his immortality, of the man he'd chosen, out of expediency rather than love (for love of anything other than country was impossible for the dying man). But the one, nonetheless, who was to carry forward his mantle of *the protector of the nation.* A mantle that now lay on the verge of a chasm of destruction. A thing that would be covered in a mountain of spittle and remembered with revulsion. Unless . . .

The old man aimed, with shaking hands, at the retreating form of the thief who'd demonstrated more honor than any of the so-called public servants the old man had ever known or been.

Then, slowly, with growing strength and commitment, he readjusted his aim, took a deep breath, and pulled the trigger.

"Thank you," Kilbourne mumbled as he collapsed in a bloody heap on the front seat. He died before he could see the second shot explode the shooter's head.

Greg ignored the shots, followed by the race of police to the backseat of the limo. He ignored the surprising cry of dismay from Paul—who had so faithfully served and admired both men that he would be. He ignored the chaos that would lie fresh born from the gaping wound in the Secretary's head.

He was only surprised it had taken so long.

TWENTY

T HE MOON, already low against the distant horizon, seemed reluctant to leave the crystalline sky.

Already, far off to the east, the slightest slivers of lightening blue stood out against the dark canopy. Stars began to fade from sight. A new taste seemed to rise in the damp air as the first of the morning birds could be heard in the tree below the mansion's balcony.

And "greatness" seemed to hang unspoken in the air.

President-Elect Jesse James Van Ness smiled as he took it all in. Breathed in the scents of his coming triumph, saw in the coming dawn . . . his time! Then, reluctantly, he turned his back on the sensations, both real and imagined, and returned to the bedroom.

"It feels good, Moll."

His wife continued taking off her jewelry. "It'll feel even better in a few days." She examined how her face had held up through the all-night party. "Do you think I should go to the spa for a few days before Washington?"

Van Ness shrugged. "Whatever." He began to pull off his tie and tux as the nervous energy from the party began to run out. "I think we should have a few less of these all-nighters, is what I think."

Molly smiled. "We've waited a long time for this. Let's enjoy it while we can."

"I suppose."

Molly stopped brushing her hair. "What's wrong?" she asked as she studied his suddenly somber expression in the mirror.

"Nothing."

The dedicated political wife sighed, then walked over to the bed.

"It's not your fault," she said as she sat down next to him on the bed. "He was dying anyway, you knew that."

"I just wish he'd lived to see it happen. For him to . . ." He shook his head. "So stupid."

His wife looked remarkably unmoved. "Stupid or not, it was the perfect final move. You've got to give the old bastard that." She actually laughed. "Hell! It was probably a helluva lot easier than the way he was gonna go out. And we both know how scared he was of . . ."

Van Ness whirled to his side, violently backhanding the laughing woman across the face.

"I will not have you speaking of him in that way!" His face had become a twisted mask of fury, hatred, and despair. "That man was a hero," he said between clenched teeth. "And I will not have the likes of you disparaging his memory in any way. Do you understand me?"

"I'm sorry," she whispered, truly shocked by her husband for the first time in years.

"That man gave his entire life to this country," Van Ness said as he slowly stood. "No thought ever crossed his mind that didn't touch on the protection of our nation's way or security. Without him, whatever he may have become in the end, I shudder to think where this country would be today."

He started for his dressing room. "Or where I would be for that matter." He stopped in the doorway, turning back to her, the fury replaced by soul pain in his eyes. "So I refuse to allow you to even whisper his name!" He turned back to the door. "Ever."

Molly still lay where she'd fallen on the bed. "You still love him," she mumbled.

Van Ness stiffened, then closed the door behind him.

He stood with his back to the door for a long time, sobbing uncontrollably in the dark room. Allowing the darkness to conceal, even from himself, the one thing he didn't dare acknowledge anywhere but in the dark.

The truth that had begun more than five decades before in the New Mexico desert; that had led through a twisted path to, in nine more days, the most exalted place in the universe that Van Ness could conceive of.

A path that had been lit, periodically at first, then steadily, unwaveringly, by the only person Van Ness had ever felt truly believed in him.

The Secretary might be dead, buried without pomp or prestige in a public cemetery in a vacant corner of Nevada, but through Van Ness, his dream would continue.

With a series of deep breaths, Van Ness gradually gained control of himself, then reached for the light switch.

"No lights, Mr. President-Elect."

Van Ness froze as a soft voice called out to him from somewhere ahead in the dark. "Who is that? I told the Secret Service no one was permitted in here."

A muffled movement from the unseen intruder. "Swell."

Something about that voice, its lack of any human emotion, swept through Van Ness, filling him with certainty about its deadly earnest.

"I can have agents in here in seconds," he said, trying to pierce the dark around him.

"You'll be dead before they're through the door." It was said flatly, without emotion or braggadocio. As a cold, hard fact.

"You can't kill the president." Van Ness said it with the innocent belief of a child.

A short, bitter laugh. "Tell it to Lincoln, McKinley, or Kennedy," the voice replied. "And you're not the president." The slightest of pauses. "Not yet, anyway."

"What—what do you want?"

"I've got a list, actually."

"You'll never get away with it," Van Ness said weakly.

"Why not?" the voice replied calmly. "How hard could it be for a dead Mafia hit man?"

A light was turned on across the room, revealing a man sitting in a rocking chair, a nine-millimeter Glock casually cradled in his lap.

"Picaro?"

Greg nodded at the frightened man. "I'm flattered, Mr. President-Elect." His face seemed set in stone; dark bags under eyes that seemed to have finally seen too much. "Truly flattered. Now sit down."

Van Ness slowly moved to a workout bench to his right. "The Secret Service are everywhere," he said in a hushed voice. "I didn't think it was possible for anyone to . . ." He hesitated, trying to gauge the commitment in that blank face. "How'd you get in here?"

The tired, soul-sore thief shook his head as if the question itself defied belief.

"It's what I do," was all he said.

Oddly that answer seemed to satisfy and calm the man across from him.

"I've heard the tape from the car," Van Ness said after a long silence. "I don't think he'd realized that you'd figured it out." He tried to look relaxed. "At least not all of it."

He started to reach into his pocket, then froze when Greg raised the big gun, pointing it between the president-elect's eyes. "Just a handkerchief," he said softly.

"Slowly."

For a moment, Van Ness considered activating the personal alarm that his handkerchief lay against. But he didn't.

And would never know, beyond doubt, why not.

He wiped his face, then forced a business-as-usual smile. "So which of us starts?"

Greg lowered the gun. "You do." He paused. "And don't even think about trying to lie."

Now Van Ness laughed. "Of course not. Why should I, when the truth is far more confusing?"

"You start telling it and we'll see how confused I get."

Van Ness nodded easily. "Where should I start?"

"The beginning."

For a moment, a cloud of deep concentration swept across the president-elect's face.

"It might be easier," he finally said, "if we start in the middle." He looked up into Greg's eyes. "I promise you won't be disappointed. And it'll save a lot of time."

Greg nodded.

"Fine," the former senator said. He paused to organize his thoughts.

"Get on with it."

A spasmodic smile from the man who had been elected the next president of the United States. "Right."

February 20, 1954
3:25 P.M.
North of Palm Springs, California

You could smell the tension in the room.

An unmarked helicopter flying at low altitude across the desert north of Palm Springs was normally not a cause for sweat soaking through the coveralls of the officers in the Edwards Air Force Base control tower.

The air traffic controllers at Edwards had handled dozens in the last few weeks. Ever since the so-called flying saucer sightings. In fact, there were more every day since the UFO enthusiasts and crackpots had announced they were going to hold some kind of convention just outside the base. But usually one brief warning about "violating secured airspace" and the air tourists would veer off, giving the semisecret air base a wide berth.

If not, well, that's why two older-model jet fighters were kept on constant standby alert.

But the helicopter that the five controllers were tracking was different somehow.

They didn't know why it was different, where it was going, or who was on board, but they knew their orders.

Which were definitely reinforced by the three fierce-looking men in business suits that were carrying Thompson submachine guns. Just to "make sure."

"Majestic Zero Zero One, Muroc Control." The flight controller checked his radar screen, then his written orders, while he listened for the reply.

"Muroc Control, Majestic Zero Zero One. Copy five by."

Glancing over at the closest "special security" man's machine gun, the controller keyed his microphone.

"Zero Zero One, Muroc. Turn left three and maintain two six four. Report when you have the outer marker."

"Copy, Muroc. Zero Zero One turning."

A controller standing nervously by another radar monitor concentrated intently on the screen in front of him. Hell, that was easier than looking at the intimidating men or his colleagues' frightened expressions.

Only two years out of the academy, this specialist in instruments guidance had hoped for a posting in Asia, maybe the Philippines. Anything but this unimproved, backwater, *rusty* backwater, base. His frustration had been compounded by his assignment to a part of the field away from the Dryden Flight Test Center. The only times he'd ever even seen some of the legendary test pilots on the base, like

Yeager and Cooper, had been in the primitive, understocked, base PX.

So, cursing his luck, he worked his assignment of routing cargo planes, chasing off weekend pilots, and working crossword puzzles.

Until today.

A blip suddenly appeared on his screen. He bent down, putting his forehead against the viewing cone as his headset came to life.

"Muroc Control, Majestic Zero Zero One."

"Majestic Zero Zero One, Muroc Control. Read you five by."

"Copy, Muroc. We've just crossed the outer marker."

"Zero Zero One, copy that. We have you now, sir. Come right bearing two seven one true. Descend and maintain zero four zero feet. Maintain course until you acquire the perimeter fencing. At that time, Lima Zulu will be to your eleven o'clock at two miles."

"Copy, Muroc, and thank you, sir."

The young controller straightened after he saw the blip make a slight turn to its right.

"They'll be down in three minutes." He didn't know why he said it, but, somehow, felt it should be said.

The senior controller nodded, then picked up a microphone. "All civilian aviation in vicinity of Rogers Dry Lake. All civilian aviation in vicinity of Rogers Dry Lake." He paused, being careful to read exactly what was written in his orders. "Aviation corridor Delta Lima Foxtrot, one seven five, is now closed to all traffic until further notice."

He repeated the message, then put the microphone down.

The head security man seemed satisfied.

"Job well done, gentlemen. Now if you'll please lie facedown on the floor."

Slowly, reluctantly, they followed their orders.

The young controller fighting a near-overwhelming desire to peek through the tower's large windows as he heard the helicopter approach.

But he didn't.

3:45 P.M.
Outside Edwards Building 18-127

"Dr. Bush, it's been too long."

The thin, aging, former academic shook the big man's hand as firmly as he could. The cancer, and other things, had sapped most of his strength. Age taking almost all the remainder. But he still managed to find a hidden reserve when in the presence of . . .

"Good afternoon, Mr. President. How was your flight over?"

Eisenhower shook his head as he ran his hand over his scalp. "We caught some wind going over the mountains. I'd rather have taken a plane but . . ."

"Precautions, Mr. President," Bush continued in a weak voice. "With the contents of these buildings, we cannot take too many precautions." He was fading and he knew it. "May I introduce my assistant?"

A man in his late forties stepped forward.

"Mr. President, I'd like you to meet Assistant Undersecretary of Defense for Special Projects Michael Robertson Coleman."

"Coleman."

"Mr. President."

Coleman tried to remember everything he'd read about the man in front of him, in the highly classified Majic dossier. *Be tough, be forthright, don't mince words,* the intimate psychological profile of the president had almost screamed.

Dr. Bush hid a cough. "If you'll excuse me, Mr. President. I'll have Secretary Coleman conduct you through, then catch up on the other side."

The president studied the man who had created the Majestic Project seven years earlier, wondering if the rumors about his health were true. "Of course, Doctor. I look forward to seeing you later."

Coleman opened the door to the hangar, waited for the president and his solitary aide to pass, then smiled at Bush and followed them through. "Mr. President, I think you know everyone here."

Eisenhower smiled, barely, as he shook hands with the executive from a news syndicate; the Nobel Prize–winning scientist from the Brookings Institute; and a bishop (rumored to be in line for elevation to cardinal) from one of California's largest archdioceses.

"So," he said as he pulled on the white coveralls, goggles, and helmet that the others already wore, "how long you fellows been out here?"

"Yesterday and today, Mr. President," the news executive said in a near whisper.

"And what do you think so far?"

Silence settled over the small anteroom.

"Bishop?" the president asked, turning his intense stare on the clergyman.

"Well, Mr. President. It's disturbing." He seemed to be deep in thought . . . or turmoil. "Yes. Disturbing is the word."

The president turned away from the man he had previously known to be unflappable. "How much have they seen?"

Coleman looked serious. "Just the outer ring, sir. Preliminary briefings, some of the smaller exhibits. Some photographs from the recovery sites."

"I see." He looked at the inner door. "Through there, then?"

"Yes, Mr. President."

Eisenhower took a deep breath, then nodded. "Let's get on with it, then."

Coleman gestured at a guard by the door, who then put a key in the top of two locks. Coleman put his key in the other. They turned them at the same moment.

This time, Coleman walked through first.

5:20 P.M.

In the most intense silence he'd ever experienced, the president settled himself at the head of the long conference table. No one looked at anyone else. No one spoke, made notes, moved. They just sat, staring at the tabletop, trying to comprehend the most formidable hour and a half in their lives.

Eisenhower accepted the offered lemonade from Coleman.

"Just before the D-day decision," he said after an intentionally long drink, "when it was still raining, I wandered out to this little garden we had at Telegraph Cottage. Tiny little thing. You wouldn't think you could get all that . . ."

He stopped, forcing the comforting memory away. Realizing, for the first time, that he was as affected as the others by what they'd just seen. So he took refuge in the memory for a brief time longer.

"I remember thinking that if the rain didn't stop, if the weather didn't clear . . ." His voice trailed off.

"But a decision had to be made, gentlemen." His expression, as well as his voice, was starting to firm, to be hardened by the enormity of the task ahead. "At the time, I thought it the most important decision I'd ever have to make." He actually forced a laugh. "Little did I know."

He let them join in the weak laughter, then fixed them each with his "commander's gaze."

"I made it then, and I'll make it now. But first, I'd like to hear from each of you gentlemen."

When no one volunteered to go first, as he'd feared, the president tried to think of a way to start things off. His experience had shown him that a discussion in his presence always needed someone, other than him, to get things rolling. He looked around the table.

The bishop? No. The religious implications of it all might leave him tied in knots for weeks to come.

The news executive? Also no. He was, in effect, being asked to subvert the very industry he was representing.

The scientist would only dwell on the technical stuff. Things the president barely understood to begin with.

No, none of them would voluntarily jump-start this conference. What he needed was a good old-fashioned military viewpoint.

"Assistant Undersecretary Coleman."

"Mr. President?"

"Bring in that officer, the one who gave us the facilities construction briefing."

"Sir." Coleman picked up a nearby telephone, issuing some whispered instructions. Two minutes later, an army captain was let into the room.

"Captain."

The man snapped to attention. "Sir!"

Eisenhower smiled, remembering hundreds like him. Men to whom bullshit and obfuscation were as foreign as gills on a lizard.

"We speak the same language, Captain, uh . . ."

"Van Ness, sir! Jesse James Van Ness. Academy class of '44, sir!"

"Well, Captain *Jesse James* Van Ness," the president said with the hint of a smile, "I need some plain talk. And I think an academy grad is just the man for the job."

Van Ness pulled himself to an even tighter attention. "Sir! Yes, sir!"

"You were there at the beginning, right?"

"Sir! Yes, sir!"

"At ease, Captain. Have a seat."

Coleman watched Van Ness find a seat near him at the table. For seven years now, he'd been watching the young man, helping him when he could. The assistant undersecretary saw . . . possibilities in the young man.

Now those possibilities presented themselves as opportunity.

"Mr. President, if I might?"

"Secretary Coleman?"

"Sir, I just wanted to point out that Captain Van Ness is uniquely placed to answer any of your, or the group's, questions. Having worked in all aspects of the Majestic Twelve operation, not just facilities construction." He looked at the younger man. "In fact, I've only recently recommended him for promotion."

It was the first Van Ness had heard of it. He hoped the president hadn't noticed the mixed look of surprise and triumph in his eyes.

"Well, Captain, let's see if we can't earn you those oak leaves."

"Sir?"

"Tell me about Roswell."

Van Ness took a deep breath, reminded himself to speak "plain soldier," then began.

"Mr. President, gentlemen. When I arrived at the site in early July of '47, it was the second day of the recovery effort. The air force people were concentrating on recovering the vehicle's airframe, so my unit was given the job of perimeter reconnaissance. An airborne scout reported possible wreckage at a second site late on the third day. I was the closest to it and got there well in advance of the others."

"What was it like?" the news executive asked timidly.

Van Ness continued matter-of-factly. "I remember the smell in particular. Like spoiled meat." He seemed to relive it for a moment. "Then I saw the disc, well, half a disc actually. The displacement of the wreckage was such that it appeared that the airframe had impacted on the top of the ridge, splitting evenly between the two sides." Another, even briefer pause. "The bodies were on my side of the ridge. One of them, I could see he was dead right away. He was laid open from knee to groin. But the other two, they were kind of sitting next to him. Looking up at the sky as I came up. Then right at me."

The bishop leaned forward. "What made you go up to them?"

Van Ness took a deep breath, snuck a glance at Coleman, who seemed to barely nod. "Well, sir, they were friendly enough. And I could see plain they were hurting. One of them was burned on the head and the other was holding his hand kind of funny. I just figured they were hurt, needed help, and we'd best be making friends with them. At least right then." He looked at the president. "I figured higher authority would decide what to do with them later."

Eisenhower nodded. "Well done." He turned to the others. "You've all been briefed on the wreckage recovery and about the decision to move the survivors. I'd like to move on to the trip to Muroc."

No one disagreed.

"Very well." He turned back to the soldier across from him. "Tell us about the attack."

Van Ness hesitated.

"Mr. President?"

"Coleman."

"Sir, considering the other, uh . . ."

Eisenhower shook his head. "We've trusted them this far. Give them the rest. You can't expect them to give their opinions without all the information."

Coleman seemed to hesitate, then sat back.

"We saw the first ships the second night we were on the road," Van Ness began after a moment. "I mean we talked about what would happen if their buddies tried to recover them and all, but seeing those ships . . ."

"I can imagine," the scientist said as he made notes.

"Well, they finally came down on the third night. Bright lights sweeping over the convoy, scaring the shit—" He stopped, embarrassed.

Eisenhower smiled, gesturing for him to go on.

"Well, we were plenty scared, sir. The engines wouldn't work, radios went down, nothing electrical was working. We formed a circle around the truck carrying the two live ones. The ship landed in a field, just off the road, and they came walking out toward us.

"That first night, all the boys on the ship side of the truck seemed to freeze."

The president's aide nodded grimly. "Natural reaction under the circumstances."

"No, sir," Van Ness disagreed. "These were combat veterans from the Pacific and the ETO. Besides, it wasn't that kind of freezing. More like those creatures were using some kind of stun ray on them."

"Go on, Van Ness," Coleman urged quietly.

"Well, sir, we fired into them and they fell back to their ship. Took their dead and wounded with them too. The next night, same thing happened again. Only this time, we were ready for 'em.

"As soon as the hatch or whatever it was on the side of the ship came open, we let 'em have it! Tore 'em a new asshole before they knew what hit 'em! The two in the truck went crazy and we had to butt-stroke 'em a couple times before they stayed quiet. They've been real cooperative since."

He paused, clearly caught up in the memory. "Afterward, the techs had themselves a helluva lot of new Martian arms and legs to play with."

The bishop looked down, pasty-faced. Eisenhower leaned forward, concentrating more on the man than on what he was saying.

"We hid during the night, only traveled briefly during the day. Even then, we would change our direction randomly, barely staying close to our base course. We also kept on firing at them as soon as they got out of their ship, before they could warm up that stun ray of theirs."

Van Ness suddenly grew quiet. "But we still lost some of the boys. Some kind of radiation poisoning, the doctors called it. Those that were hit by that damned stun ray of theirs more than once."

"Goddamn the bastards," Eisenhower muttered.

"Merciful God," the bishop whispered as he crossed himself.

Van Ness interrupted. "But they *never* got their boys back, Mr. President. I can promise you that! And they never will, not as long as I have something to say about it!"

"Excuse me, Mr. President," the news executive said softly. "Captain Van Ness, did anyone ever try talking to the aliens? To try to find out what they wanted? To negotiate?"

Van Ness glanced at Coleman, who barely nodded. "No, sir. An' I didn't negotiate with the little yellow bastards that were trying to kill me and my boys at Peleliu, Ulithi, and Ngulu, either. Sir." He took a deep breath. "I just did my job, carried out my orders, and *took care of my men.*" The anger that came off the man was like a living thing, standing between the young captain and the news executive.

Eisenhower looked at the pain and fury in the young officer's face. "Finish it, Mr. Coleman."

"Sir. When we got the aliens here to what was then Muroc Field, we stored them under guard, in an underground rocket test silo. Every night, we flew combat air patrols, preventing the alien ships from landing." His voice trailed off as he got caught up in the memory. "We lost some damn good men in those fights. Good boys, aces from the ETO and the Pacific." His voice strengthened as he returned to his briefing mode.

"They may have their damned death rays or whatever the hell you want to call them, but they bleed pretty good too when they take a hit from a fifty. And their ships got busted up pretty good from our quad forties and air-to-air.

"Anyway, we were holding off their strikes okay, but they just kept coming closer and closer, like they were getting directions or something. At first we thought it had something to do with those diamonds we took off them, but the tech boys said no. Then the fifth time we strip-searched those little bastards, we found that they had some kind of tracking device that broke down into multiple parts. We immediately confiscated it. The rescue attacks began to lessen starting that night. We now average just over three a month. And nowhere near as accurate, either."

"I'd like to see that device, Mr. Assistant Undersecretary," the scientist asked intently.

Coleman smiled a bureaucratic smile. "Regretfully, sir, it was deemed unsafe to allow the reassembly of the device. Each piece was carefully studied, photographed, diagrammed, then split up among senior members of the security detail. They wear it on their persons at all times to prevent its reassembly and use."

"I'd still like to examine one of them."

Coleman shrugged. "Captain Van Ness?"

Van Ness nodded, loosened his tie, unbuttoned his collar, and then pulled out the plastic-encased component. He handed it to the scientist, who used his eyeglasses as a magnifier to study it.

"Captain Van Ness?"

"Yes, Mr. President?" Van Ness quickly fixed his shirt.

Eisenhower hesitated, then tried to look supportively at the much younger man. "I know how it feels to lose brothers-in-arms. We've both tasted that kind of loss, felt that pain."

"Yes, sir." Van Ness tried not to move as the president seemed to study him.

"Captain, I'm going to ask you to do maybe the hardest thing you've ever done. Maybe will ever have to do."

"Yes, sir."

Eisenhower took a deep breath, then leaned back in his chair.

"Captain," he said as his aide went to the door to get a message from a WAC. "Captain, I want you to put aside your personal feelings, your very right anger. I want you to think about what I'm about to ask you calmly, without rancor." He paused. "Can you do that for me?"

"I'll try, sir." Van Ness tried to clear his mind as all eyes around the table locked on him.

"Captain Van Ness, you know what this briefing has been all about?"

"I believe so, Mr. President."

Eisenhower hesitated. "Well then, in your opinion, based on seven years of exemplary service to your country, and regular exposure to the—" He turned to Coleman. "What did you call them?"

"EBEs, Mr. President."

"Right. I read that in one of the reports." He took a sip of his drink. "Captain, in your opinion, should the, uh, extraterrestrial biological entities be executed, or should the study program be continued and accelerated?"

Van Ness waited a full minute before answering. "Sir. All I can say is this. We have those two little bastards. Their buddies seem to still want them back. I mean they may be trying less often but I think they're up there, just waiting for us to make a mistake, you know?" The briefest pause possible. "To me, that's a good enough reason to hang on to them. In my book, it's the best shot we got at getting even for what they did to my men."

Eisenhower stared at the unrepentant rage behind the man's eyes. He continued to stare into Van Ness's soul as his aide handed him a note.

"Mr. Coleman, it seems the press has begun to suspect my absence from Smoke Tree Ranch," he said as he read the note.

Coleman looked concerned. "Will you have to leave immediately?"

The president looked at his aide, who looked unhappy. "We'll finish this first," he said as he stood up. "One way or the other." He turned to his aide. "Sherm, come up with some excuse or other."

The aide nodded. "If anyone presses, we'll say you had to go to the doctor unexpectedly."

Eisenhower flinched. "And let them think it's a heart attack? Hell no!" He turned to the bishop. "Apologies."

The president winced as he remembered the pain, embarrassment, and complications involved in keeping his still-classified heart attack of six months before quiet. The world was in crisis then—as it was today—and the Russians must never be given a reason to believe that America was vulnerable, leaderless, weak.

To avoid that, Eisenhower would go to almost any length. It hadn't been lie or cover-up—merely "national security exigencies" or "simple prudence."

Much as his decisions this day would be rationalized.

"If you have to say anything," the president said to his aide, "make it a trip to the dentist."

He turned to Coleman. "I want to see them before we go any further."

Coleman stood, walked over, then led the way out.

Eisenhower paused in the doorway, turning back to Van Ness. "Captain Van Ness?"

The young officer jumped to attention. "Sir!"

"You have the most sincere appreciation of your president and of your unknowing countrymen. You've done your country a great service at a terrible price, son. And I'd like to recognize that." He paused as he headed out. "I would consider it a personal compliment if the survivors of your security team, that are still with the project, would join me at a little barbecue I'm throwing tomorrow night."

"Mr. President, are you sure that . . ." His aide was cut off by a withering look.

"They deserve the recognition, Sherman. Even if we can't come out and say why." He walked through the door, a smiling Coleman closing it behind them.

As they walked across the base to the specially secured "habitat," the three men were silent.

"How much would this new facility in Nevada cost us?" the president asked as they were cleared through the first of three doors.

"Just over three hundred million in the first five years, Mr. President."

"Astronomical," the president's aide mumbled, then looked embarrassed as both men looked at him in shock. "Sorry," he said sheepishly.

"I can give you a detailed breakdown of the proposed spending program, sir."

Eisenhower shook his head. "Later, Coleman. Tomorrow night, after the barbecue. You'll be my guest at Smoke Tree."

"Thank you, Mr. President." Coleman could barely contain his satisfaction at the unexpected turn of events. "Should I have Dr. Bush bring anything special to . . ."

"Let the man rest," the president said as they were passed on to a long staircase that seemed to go straight down into the airfield's depths. "Besides, I think it's probably time to put my own man at the head of this Chinese fire drill." He paused on the long steps to catch his breath. "Bush is Truman's man. I need someone in there whose loyalty is to me."

How far should I push? Coleman concentrated intensely. *How far?*

"I can recommend several top people, Mr. President."

Eisenhower shook his head at the seemingly endless stairs. "I can't abide game players, Coleman. If you get the job, always give it to me straight, right?"

This time Coleman allowed the smile. "Yes, sir."

"You want the job?"

"Yes, sir."

"Then put a damned elevator in the new facility, goddammit!"

At the bottom of the stairs, they were cleared into a viewing room that was a smaller version of one that would be built in the Nevada desert in the years to come.

"Mr. President, this is Captain Lewis McCutcheon, day supervisor of our two subjects."

Eisenhower shook the man's hand. "They giving you much trouble, Captain McCutcheon?"

McCutcheon had been prepared for the presidential arrival. His lines had been carefully rehearsed, then committed to memory.

"It'd be easier if we could talk to them, Mr. President. But they're generally pretty easy to get along with. They're actually kinda playful most of the time."

Coleman nodded, then McCutcheon pulled the curtain back from the window. "Mr. President, may I present Joe and Max Gray."

Eisenhower took a step forward, almost touching the glass as he looked into the room just beyond.

He stared through the thick glass for fifteen minutes, never speaking, only his eyes moving as he followed the antics of the seemingly harmless creatures playing in the thin layer of sand that covered the floor.

"Mr. Coleman?" he finally said in a muffled voice.

"Sir?"

He never took his eyes off the two creatures as they rolled in the sand in front of him. "Have the others sign security oaths, briefed, then returned to wherever they came from with my gratitude."

"Yes, sir."

As Coleman went to the telephone, the president's aide took his place beside the obviously fascinated chief executive.

"But, Mr. President, what about the decision? What do we do with . . ." He didn't have to gesture to make his point.

"I've made my decision, Sherm." He looked over at McCutcheon. "Can I go in there?"

"Absolutely, sir," Coleman said as he came back up to the president. "Absolutely."

Twice in the last hour, sounds from the bedroom caused the tension-filled president-elect to stop. Frozen into silence by Greg's upraised gun. Then, long minutes of undiscovery later, the same gun would be used to gesture continuance of the story.

He had told it all simply, a recitation of crystalline memories that could have easily come from last week. Rather than over fifty years ago. He forced no spin on the story, took no positions as to the relative rightness of his role in it all. Just told it all, to the nonreacting face across from him.

"We all went to the barbecue at the president's ranch the next night. Were even given special citations of merit by Ike. They even saw that the story got written up, in vague terms of course, in all our hometown papers.

"Then, three months later, we broke ground on Dreamland, what the media calls Area 51. A year later Eisenhower had another heart attack, this one too big and too public to cover up. He started to delegate more and more things, to be less hands-on—at least with Majic—than he'd been before. Secretary Coleman was named head of Majestic Twelve, with almost unlimited authority, and I was brought along as his aide-de-camp." He stopped. "That's all there is."

But the nonexpressive eyes and the accusing silence across from him demanded more.

"Uh, in 1968, I left the army," Van Ness continued reluctantly. "All of us in the three-digit circle always had the option of changing our names. Some even agreed to be given test drugs that had been developed from stuff the aliens had. Some kind of a deep hypnotic that allowed the users to replace parts of their memory with entirely fictitious ones. That scared me, *and* I had other plans, so I passed."

"Unlike McCutcheon," Greg said quietly.

Van Ness physically looked away from the thought of his murdered friend. "He knew that his morality would one day betray us. Always said that there was something basically, *morally* wrong with what we did." He paused, sighing deeply. "He said he had nightmares where he would see the arms and legs of the other aliens, the dead ones, floating in front of him. *Accusing* him, he said."

Greg flinched. "So he decided to take the hypnotic."

Van Ness hesitated. "Well, it was decided for him."

Greg stared down at the floor for what seemed interminable minutes. "Finish it."

"Well, uh, with the Secretary's contacts, opportunities in politics were, uh, made available. Which brings us to here."

Greg leaned forward. "You left some things out."

Van Ness studied him for a long moment. "You *do* know all of it, don't you?"

Greg ignored him. "The times have changed, open-budgeted black ops aren't in fashion anymore. More and more people want to know what happened in New Mexico, in Roswell, all those years ago. Freedom of Information Act requests, congressional inquiries, even the Freedom Ridge Society lawsuits are starting to be taken seriously." He paused, as if considering his own argument. "Something had to be done."

Van Ness nervously glanced at his watch. "The sun'll be up soon. If it isn't already. You'd better—"

"So," Greg cut him off, "all of this was concocted. The perfect double-headed plan. Admit, reluctantly of course, what everyone already suspected. Leak information to Megan Turner, enough for the current administration to have to either lie about it . . . in which case they get caught by more leaked information. Or they tell the truth, and try to explain why they've been perpetuating this lie for the last four years. I'm impressed."

Van Ness sighed. "Mike Coleman was sincere about winning the release of the EBEs. He, *we*, both felt that it was the only right thing to—"

Greg jumped to his feet, roughly shoving the barrel of his gun against the president-elect's left eye.

"No more lies," he growled in a hoarse whisper. "No more, right?" His eyes narrowed with an otherworldly rage. "Just nod for the truth or die for a lie. Just that simple, you understand?"

Van Ness, sweat pouring from him, slowly nodded.

"It was a double-headed plan, right?"

A quick nod.

"First, undermine the credibility of the incumbent administration, right?"

Nod.

"Second, destroy anyone who could possibly link you to Majestic Twelve. Anyone who might threaten your candidacy. Anyone. Kerry. McCutcheon. Kilbourne." A brief pause. "Especially Joe and Max."

A hesitation brought more pressure from the blue-steel automatic pressed against the president-elect's eye.

Then a reluctant nod.

"Sure," Greg said reasonably as he eased the pressure. "Even if I hadn't broken them out, the administration probably would've ordered them killed to, literally, bury the evidence."

His breathing slowed, he seemed to calm. "Then what? You slowly uncover the plot in the first year or so of your administration? Expose the murders, the cover-up, then lay them at the door of the previous administration, I suppose."

A nod.

"What about Majestic? What happens to the project?"

Van Ness took a deep breath, tried to think of a convincing lie. Then, suddenly, he felt . . . calm. A calm from understanding that, although the man before him was completely capable of murder, he would only do it if he, Van Ness, gave him a reason.

"Joe and Max have been providing less and less of real use in the last few years," he said in a near whisper. "Majic is all about the technology now. And privatization deals have been arranged."

"Of course." Greg lowered his gun, returning to his seat.

"You have no idea, Mr. Picaro, the advances to our society that are owed to the Hesperian technology."

Greg looked up at that. "The Secretary used that word."

"Hesperians?" Van Ness smiled. "It comes from the name Hesperos Astor. Or the Eastern Star. The technical astronomical term for Venus."

Greg nodded. "Swell."

Van Ness continued on. "From light-years in advances for microchip technologies to high-impact plastics and disease inoculants. They even had a process for creating perfect synthetic diamonds. So perfect that they are completely indistinguishable from natural-occurring stones."

A smile began playing at the corners of his mouth. "We each got a set on our retirement." A slight laugh. "We called them parts of the Giant Rock Collection, after the convention of UFO enthusiasts in '54 near Muroc."

He paused, remembering the shining stones. "Although they never quite got the shape right. They always came out looking like marbles." The smile disappeared. "I assure you we took full advantage of our time with Joe and Max."

"Took advantage is right," Greg mumbled.

All at once, Van Ness looked angry. "And what would you have done? Tell me, Mr. Picaro, tell me how you would've acted humanely to the cute little ETs."

He stood up, actually taking a semithreatening step toward the armed man. "We were less than two years from the Second World War and we all believed another war, this one nuclear and with the Russians, was inevitable. So tell me, with your young, pure, idealistic insight, what you would've done. When you stood there face-to-face with beings from another world with clearly superior technology. Beings who were slaughtering men you'd barely survived the last war with, all within days of their arrival!

"My God, man! You don't think it ended with our finding their homing device, do you?" Breathing heavily, red-faced, the man's passion seemed *mostly* genuine. "They've never stopped looking for Joe and Max. Never will. It's almost as if they have an organic *need* to find them. Without the homers, it's been hard, and we've thrown them some red herrings, but they're still there. Dividing the entire planet up into grids and regularly searching specific areas."

For the first time, the president-elect seemed completely sure of himself.

"But we understand them now, know when and where they'll appear and are prepared to meet and repel them at each encounter." He casually looked up at the ceiling as if to contemplate his foe somewhere in the stars above.

"Their technology *is* superior to ours. But their ships conduct heat as they pass through the atmosphere, give off radar signatures—if you know what to look for, and they are *far* from invisible at the lower altitudes. We usually have twenty to forty minutes lead time when they come." He returned a steely gaze to the thief in front of him. "And high explosives *will* destroy them. As they've learned rather painfully over the years." He shrugged. "As long as they're looking in the wrong places, we're content to warn them off. If they ever got close to Dreamland, well . . ."

His shrug was Black Death.

The president-elect laughed banefully. "I wasn't prepared to give them back Joe and Max half a century ago, and I won't do it now." Another laugh, this time sarcastically. "No matter how many 'random' UFO sightings shows like Ms. Turner's promote."

Greg shook his head. "Unbelievable," he mumbled as if he was the most exhausted man in the universe.

"Oh no," Van Ness said easily. "Quite believable. *You* should understand that better than most." He paused to catch his breath. When he spoke again, the older man was, not calmed, but committed. "But you never answered my question, Mr. Picaro. What would you have done? Hypothetically I give you the complete and total responsibility. What would you have done?"

Silence from the depressed, angry man across from him.

"You would protect your country, sir," Van Ness said simply. "As we did. You would make irrevocable decisions in hours on matters that should've been discussed for years. You would make the aliens' killings of your friends look like random murders. You would shoot first, lie, conceal, obscure, or"—he hesitated—"murder. You would do whatever you had to do."

He collapsed back down into his seat, wiping his face with his handkerchief.

Greg took a deep breath as he tried to deny the hidden truths in the president-elect's pile of lies.

"It's been fifty years," he said quietly. "And it wasn't Hesperians that I saw kill Jack Kerry or the girl with him. Or try to kill Megan Turner or me."

Van Ness nodded sadly. "One last truth, Mr. Picaro." He paused to compose his thoughts. "It took us the better part of twenty years to begin any meaningful communication with the Hesperians. One of the first things we discovered was that they were a communal people. So closely attenuated to the group ethic that they would go to almost any length to avoid the death of any member of the group. Joe and Max told us that they *felt*—in physical and visceral senses— the deaths of their comrades who'd tried to rescue them. That those sensations *alone* almost killed them.

"The best we can tell, their arrival here was accidental, a fluke engine malfunction resulting in the Roswell crash. But our instinctive act of detaining them, the too-rushed decisions I referred to earlier, have resulted in well . . ." His voice trailed off. "The Secretary called it a 'technical state of war.' Both sides actively probing the other's defenses. Both sides studying, learning, inhaling everything and anything they can about their enemy. But neither side willing to risk the stakes of going completely to an active footing."

"The stakes?"

Van Ness nodded. "For us, two and a half billion people. For the Hesperians"—he laughed—"Joe and Max. For them, an even greater, more personal loss than the world's population would be to us."

He took several deep breaths, then straightened the wilting, sweat-soaked tuxedo shirt and pants he still wore from the party the night before.

Greg just shook his head. "So this was all about compassion?" he asked bitterly. "The greater good and the public's welfare!"

"It was *about* necessity." The president-elect looked into the angry eyes, the also somehow searching eyes, then sighed. "Now," he said in a suddenly all-business tone, "you said something about a list."

Greg studied the man, reluctantly put away his gun, then took a typed sheet of paper from his pocket. He handed it across to the president-elect. "They're nonnegotiable," he said firmly.

Van Ness oddly chuckled as he pulled out a pair of reading glasses.

"Nonsense, Mr. Picaro," he said as he began to read. "The one thing I learned from Secretary Coleman, the one thing that I can truly say he was completely right about is . . ." He glanced over the top of the paper at Greg.

". . . everything's negotiable."

TWENTY-ONE

S O, MY FELLOW CITIZENS, my friends, I stand before you at
this watershed moment in history, humbled by your trust.
Christened by your call. Imbued with a sense of the mighty majesty
of the American people as they proclaim their readiness to march
forward into our ever-widening universe!''

The old Mafia boss chuckled as he reached out, turning off the
small TV on the patio table. "Old song, new singer," he said as he
poured his houseguests coffee.

They'd been sitting there, on the back patio of the man's palatial
ranch, watching the pomp of the inauguration unfold. Each completely absorbed, not by the pageantry, but by their own (very personal) thoughts.

To Deo, the ceremony was mildly interesting, but paled beside the
private auto collection the semiretired Mafia legend had allowed
him access to. He would be there now, but some unspoken thing
seemed to demand his presence for the final act.

Lazslo searched the crowd of millions for the four familiar faces
that he knew were there somewhere. Thinking less about the sym-
bolism of the event than the missed opportunity of a crowd of over a
million for one skilled pickpocket.

Foss was angry! Visibly so. He clenched and unclenched his fist,
ground his teeth, and wished every ill known to man upon Van Ness
as he spoke of "liberty," "democracy," and "personal freedoms."
All the while praying that there was a Heaven. Only for the Hell that
it then implied. And the hope that in the cosmic sense of things, at

the very least, Van Ness would receive what the former junkie fervently believed he deserved.

Grandmother Peterkezs, having a simple and sustaining belief in the existence of Heaven and Hell (as well as the eventual fate of the new president), simply smiled, knitted, while occasionally glancing out at the desert that lay just beyond the small greenscape of the backyard.

"So," the old Mafia boss said, turning to Foss. "Have you thought about your future?"

Foss shook his head. "Having too much trouble dealing with the past to get around to that yet."

"There's an old Sicilian saying," the former Mafia kingpin smiled. "Loosely translated it means: the past can only cut your throat if you give it the knife. You understand?"

"I think so."

The nattily dressed older man nodded. "Good. You see, I got more past than any two of you put together. Stuff I did, I can't believe I did it. Can't believe I was that guy I was." He leaned close to Foss. "But I can't do shit about all that now. Just try to do better in the future."

Lazslo interrupted him. "Speaking of future . . ."

The semiretired Mafia boss smiled and gestured for the Gypsy to join him as he stood up. "We'll talk while we walk . . . partner."

Lazslo beamed, then fell into step alongside him.

Foss reached over, turning the TV back on.

Van Ness looked out at him seriously. As if he was talking directly to the man whom his plans had almost killed.

"Perhaps we may never know what really happened in the desert of Roswell, New Mexico, in 1947. Perhaps we shall never know the full truth about the heinous and despicable crimes of this past year, events that seem somehow tied to those strange doings in the New Mexico desert.

"But I pledge the spirit, the energy, all the resources of this administration to uncovering the truth. To discovering if life does exist on distant worlds. And I pledge one more thing as well."

He looked dramatically into the camera.

"We will punish the guilty and, if possible, contact, and embrace as friends, any life-force not of this world."

Thunderous ovation.

Except on a desert patio outside Las Vegas.

"Bastard," Foss muttered.

"More like delusional," Greg said as he strolled up to the table.

Deo put down the car collection catalog that he'd been leafing through. "You up for real this time?"

Greg nodded. "More or less." He took the offered cup of coffee from Foss. "How long I been out?"

"Four or five days," the driver said casually. "More or less."

Greg downed half the cup in one drink. "What's been going on?" He leaned over Foss's shoulder, looking at the TV.

"Pornography," Foss said bitterly as the inaugural address continued.

"Everyone get off all right?"

Foss nodded. "Yesterday. Crew cleared out the day before, paid in full and pledging undying loyalty and friendship."

Deo laughed. "In Polish, Hungarian, French, *and* English."

Greg took another drink of the hot, strong liquid. "What about . . ." He nodded toward the desert.

"Like kids on Christmas morning," Deo said as he stood up. "After that place they were in, four hundred acres of guarded, private, wild desert is paradise."

"Megan? The others?" Greg's voice was suddenly choked, strained, uneven.

Grandmother Peterkezs looked up at the thief, put down her knitting, then stood up. "Was grand Gypsy celebration. Our people take care of our people back in their homes. But we prepare bodies here. Had very grand celebration of lifes. Last three days. More even."

Greg took a deep breath. "Did we ever find out who Megan's people . . ." He never finished the sentence, emotion briefly taking over the usually controlled exterior.

The old Gypsy woman locked eyes with him. "I stood for her myself," she said in a comforting tone. "Was proper, good. Of her faith. Not Gypsy, but good." The old woman smiled. "After, with some her friends, with others from the Romany, we dance for her soul. For her life." She leaned up, kissing the semishattered man on both cheeks.

One of the few to know just how deeply, how personally, Greg had taken the death of Megan and her Gypsy assistants—the final lie had been about possible survivors of the attack—she carefully studied the man. In the days after the chaos of Megan's broadcast, the old woman had worried over the young thief. Saw in his eyes and spirit a deep personal acceptance of the horror and bloodshed. The loss of life. Of friends.

But she also saw that the man would never admit to any of it to anyone. It was who he was, his strength.

His curse.

The government had, sacrilegiously the old Gypsy woman believed, held the bodies for over two months before releasing them for burial.

Greg's late night/early morning visit to Van Ness had finally solved that painful problem.

Now Grandmother Peterkezs looked up into the iron eyes that hid so much. "No guilt. No fault on you. Fate is as will be. The Lord God placed Megan on this path, just as he placed you on yours." She pinched his cheek. "Even you cannot *steal* another's fate from them. It was her time."

It was said flatly, a statement of fact, not comfort.

"Now you," she said as she pulled his hand up to her eyes, studying the palm closely. "You time still very far away. And you fate still tied, in impossible knot, to the Majic Eyes."

"So this was all inevitable?" he said weakly. "I won't accept that."

The old woman shrugged. "No *thing* is inevitable. Only God that creates man to choose for self." She laughed. "So many not-smart choices man make, God also have to create men to make thing right. He give you your life. You make you choices, you path lead here to save these, these . . . magic ones."

"I wish I could believe that."

She simply shrugged. "Palm no lie."

Greg laughed weakly. "And have you tried reading their palms?"

The old woman shook her head as if the sky had changed to plaid and only she'd noticed. "Big headache. Life line, fate line, line of romance, lines of past, present, of future, all places shouldn't be. Also many lines I never see anytime, anyplace!"

Greg laughed, bent down, then kissed her on the cheek. "If anybody can figure it out, it's you." He turned, starting to walk toward the desert.

"Sure," Grandmother Peterkezs said with confidence. "Why you think I still here?"

Foss and Deo followed him toward the sand.

As they left the lawn, they could see Lukacs sitting on a boulder about thirty meters into the desert.

"Did you ever find out what it was all about?" Foss asked as Greg waved to the young Gypsy.

Greg nodded, his jaw tight, teeth virtually clenched. "Politics, mostly." He stopped, standing silently as he looked out across the desert, then climbed up on the boulder with Lukacs.

Lukacs looked Greg over carefully. "Welcome back to the land of the living," he said in an entirely new tone of voice. It was more adult, more experienced.

More bitter.

Greg grimaced, patted him on the back, then nodded toward the desert. "How're the kiddies?"

In answer, the Gypsy thief picked up a small air horn, pointed it out at the desert that reached the horizon without a fence or wall in sight, then pressed the activator for three, short, bone-shaking blasts.

It took several minutes for Greg to notice any changes in the warming sand. Then, suddenly, he spotted two familiar sand berms rushing toward the boulder.

Joe and Max erupted from the desert, showering the four men with sand and pebbles.

Lukacs handed one of the translators to Greg.

JOE IS///
PICARO BACK WELCOME///
MAX IS///
MISS PICARO PERSON LOT A///

Greg smiled at them. "I missed you guys too. And I brought you something." He reached into his shirt pocket, pulling out a plastic-encased component, identical to the one he'd taken from Jack Kerry's safe when it had all begun.

He tossed it to Joe, and the air was instantly filled with a loud chattering, screeching, high-pitched noise.

"That's their happy sound," Lukacs said confidently.

MAX IS///
ZERO COMPONENT PART IS///
REST YOU HAVE///

"No. Not yet. But we're still looking."

The Hesperians looked at him, an expression of gratitude seeming to come into their large, childlike eyes.

BOTH IS///

THANKFUL IS BOTH///

PICARO THIS KNOW///

YOU///

WE///

FRIENDS///

FOREVER///

Before Greg could respond, before his eyes could fill with tears, both aliens dived beneath the sand, taking the second element of their missing life beacon with them.

"Where'd you get it?" Lukacs asked as they watched the sand berms head off toward the horizon.

"Van Ness. He was wearing it."

"He know where the others are?" Foss asked with genuine curiosity. " 'Cause I ain't finding shit on the Net."

Greg watched the berms crisscross, race each other, make designs in the sand. He watched both aliens leap into the air, like whales breaching, then slide effortlessly back beneath the warm grains.

"He says he doesn't. Just this, and one other. He says he'll use his 'best efforts' to find the rest."

"So we're on our own, after we get the other one he mentioned."

Greg nodded. "That's about it."

"So," Deo asked as he could see a burden being lifted from his friend's shoulders, as he watched the aliens at play. "Where is this other component?"

For the first time in months, so far as any of the other three men could remember, Greg smiled broadly and easily. "In a specially designed safe that's locked away in an impregnable vault, protected by an even more sophisticated, more state-of-the-art security system than the one we beat to get them," he said distractedly as he gestured at the playing aliens.

"How did I know that?" Foss said glumly.

"Them's the breaks," Greg said in the same strange tone as he started back to the ranch house.

"And where is this unhittable place?"

Greg put his arm around his old friend. "In a bank surrounded by thirty million dollars in used bills."

The ex-junkie suddenly looked up with sparkling eyes.

"Well," the old computer hacker said after a brief, impressed pause, "I think we should help the little fellas out." He grinned broadly. "I mean, it's the right thing to do, right?"

"My thoughts exactly, old man," the young thief answered happily. "Right after I take care of some personal business."

"Unhittable, huh?"

Greg half nodded. "Unhittable. Safest bank in America, they say. But you know something . . ."

Foss started laughing even before the remaining words came out of the other man's mouth. "Nobody's safe," he chuckled.

"Damn straight, old man."

Greg glanced out at the aliens, who seemed almost to be surfing on the shimmering heat waves that were already dancing off the desert sands.

"Nobody."

Van Ness had been president for just under an hour when he was escorted into the private study of the Speaker's Rotunda office. Along with his wife and an aide (Paul, formerly the Secretary's and Kilbourne's aide), the president sat down in a row of chairs that had been set up for that purpose.

Across from them sat the lawyers (Gavilan and Capers), along with Roman and Magda.

Behind the large, ornate, ceremonial desk sat Judge Alexander. A stern expression, as she thought befitted the occasion, displayed against her otherwise attractive features.

When the Secret Service had been cleared from the room, she nodded for her court reporter to begin. "Back on the record in the matter of Joe Gray and Max Gray. Present are Mr. Linwood Capers and Mr. John Gavilan of the Clark County Public Defender's Office. Along with Ms. Jane Smith and"—she looked at Roman—"would you state and spell your name for the record, sir?"

"Roman Peterkezs." He spelled it for the reporter. "Present as an observer for the petitioners." His look was solemn, wary, with a natural distrust for all things official.

Antoinette nodded. "Also present, representing the government, is President Jesse Van Ness; the First Lady, Molly Van Ness; and . . ."

"John Smith," the aide known as Paul said quickly.

Antoinette shook her head. "There does seem to be a lot of Smiths in this case." She looked directly at Van Ness. "Mr. President, I recognize your authority as the nation's chief executive, but are you sure you wouldn't prefer to have a U.S. Attorney or perhaps your attorney general designate present?"

He never hesitated with his answer or professional smile. "Quite sure, your honor. After all"—he brought the smile to bear on the other side—"this isn't an adversarial proceeding."

The lawyers looked away in disgust; but Roman studied the man, seeing the black soul behind the smiling eyes.

"Very well," Antoinette said softly. She lifted a packet of papers that had been given her earlier by Gavilan. "I have before me an out-of-chambers agreement that has been reached by counsel for the petitioners and the government. Are both sides in agreement on the implementation of this agreement?"

"Yes, your honor," both sides said almost simultaneously.

"For the record," she continued, "the court is in agreement with both the form and the implementation of the agreement." She paused again, thinking (for not the first time either) about the un-charted waters she was about to dive into.

She picked up a large parchment document. "In final execution of the out-of-chambers agreement I am handing the president a document titled 'Act of Full Amnesty.'" She handed him the paper. "Mr. President, would you read it into the record, then sign, date, and affix the presidential seal to it?"

Van Ness read in a monotone.

"Act of Full Amnesty. I, Jesse James Van Ness, in my position as President of the United States of America, in accordance with the pardon and amnesty powers granted me by Article Two, Section Two of the Constitution of the United States, do hereby grant a complete and full amnesty, reprieve, or pardon for any and all crimes that may have been committed by individuals (listed in a separate sealed appendix) in the course of their attempts to liberate two other individuals (Joe Gray and Max Gray) from improper fed-eral custody. I do hereby affix my signature and seal as guarantee of such amnesty, reprieve, or pardon."

He signed then dated the document; had Paul affix the presiden-tial seal, then return it to the judge.

Judge Alexander examined it, then handed another parchment to Van Ness. "Mr. President, would you also read then sign, date, and seal the second document I have just handed you?"

"Executive Order, number 2001-0001." He glanced down the

two-paragraph document, his hands slightly shaking as he began to
read. When he'd finished, he paused to pull himself together.

It seemed as though the contents of this document had acted to
knock all the supports out of the new president's life. It was either a
deeply emotionally charged moment or the performance of a lifetime.

Roman wasn't sure which.

"Order to all departments, branches, and bureaus of the Federal
Government of the United States of America," Van Ness read.
"One: Whereas two individuals of extraterrestrial origin, known as
Joe Gray and Max Gray, have been detained illegally and in violation
of their constitutional rights under Article Three, Section Two, Para-
graph Two; and the Sixth, Eighth, Ninth, and Thirteenth Amend-
ments; and . . .

"Two: Whereas organs of the Federal Government continue to
engage in illegal actions to reinstate the above-named detention
conditions; I do hereby order all representatives or agents of said
government to stop, refrain, and cease said activities in recognition
of the inalienable rights of these individuals."

As he signed the order, he chuckled bitterly. "*Inalienable.* Inalienable, by God."

The signed, dated, and sealed document was returned to Antoinette.

"Good," she said firmly. "Now for my part of the deal." She put
two boxes of documents on the desk in front of her. "I hereby place
under strict court seal all transcripts from these proceedings. Further, all documents, exhibits, or evidence labeled Court's 1 through
Court's 341 will be made part of the public record. However,
Court's 342 through 497 will likewise be placed under seal. Anno-
tated list of document headings to be amended to this record.

"Finally I do hereby instruct all parties to this matter to refrain,
under all circumstances, from making any statements to the press or
other media as to the contents, general subject matter, text, or tone
of these proceedings." She paused. "Okay. Anything else?"

Silence from both sides answered her.

"Then I do declare these proceedings at an end, pending recall
for adjudication of violations of any of the court's orders or of the
documents signed in the court's presence." She brought down her
gavel on the mahogany desk.

The room emptied out in less than two minutes, leaving President Van Ness, his wife, and Paul alone.

"The bastards!" Molly almost screamed. "How dare they blackmail us!"

Van Ness just sat down behind the desk, lifting the receiver on the phone. "Easy, old girl. We won on all the big things." He began to dial a number, then looked up at the aide. "The line *is* clear, Paul?"

"Yes, Mr. President."

Satisfied, Van Ness continued to dial, then entered a touch-tone code after the ringing stopped.

"Mr. President?"

"Yes, Paul," he said as he waited for the connection to be made.

"I'm sorry we lost Joe and Max and the program, sir. We . . ."

"Go on, son."

"Sir, we did everything we could, but, well, still we should've . . ."

He seemed to want to say more, but the president waived it away. "Small potatoes, Paul. Small potatoes." He turned his attention to the receiver. "Hello, General. This is the president." He listened, then smiled. "Thank you very much. I appreciate that."

More listening. "Tempest in a teapot, General. Don't waste another minute thinking about all that noise. But you see, it has made me think about activating the Imperial Plan." A pause. "Of course. Of course. I'd be glad to."

He pulled a card from his inside jacket pocket, then began to read. "One, nine, five, zero. Sam, Alpha, Niagara. Alpha, Gamma, Union, Sam, Tom, Ice, Niagara."

More listening. "Very good, General. You still have your two witnesses on the line . . . Good." He cleared his voice. "By my authority as Commander in Chief of the Armed Forces of the United States of America, I do hereby authorize you to activate Imperial." A brief pause. "As it happens, I *do* have an initial order."

He checked again that only his wife and aide were in the room. When he continued, it was in a tone of both zealotry and cold calculation.

"Find the fuckers!"

TWENTY-TWO

THERE WAS A TIME (there had to be, didn't there?) when the street had a purpose. Somebody, sometime, must have drawn a line on a city plan and declared "the reason for this street is . . ."

But none of the human debris that existed on Gravesend Avenue ever heard the rest of the sentence.

Because, as its name implied, it was where people came to die.

Well, at the very least, they came, they died.

Even a small boy—he looked younger than his seven years—understood *that* truth.

He stood in the narrow aisle of the convenience store, seemingly enraptured by the cereal box offers in front of him. But the bright colors, spectacular offers, and pirate treasures advertised there held little interest for him.

The man behind the counter was ringing up an order; the shelf in front of the boy couldn't be seen in the ceiling mirror's reflection behind him; and the timing of the closed-circuit camera was a known thing. All familiar to the boy, but reconfirmed in an instant.

He acted!

The tiny hand cradling a bent-out paper clip flashed forward, the little fingers easily sensing the almost unfelt tensions of the small tumblers. The display case door slid open and he instantly returned to studying the cereal boxes.

After rechecking the counterman, the mirror, the camera, he

acted again and the prize was his—buried deep in the lining of his thin jacket.

He paid for his few groceries, smiled with unabashed innocence (even took a free gum ball from the counterman), then calmly left the store.

Heading down Gravesend.

He weaved his way around the pervs (*Watch their hands, Victor! Always watch their hands!*); never looked down the alleys (*They don' see you lookin' at 'em, they let you be!*); and always kept the nearest escape routes in sight.

The small sack of groceries tucked inside his ragged jacket, change wrapped in a tissue so it wouldn't make any sound as he ran, he dashed across the street and into a decaying red brick walk-up.

Them stairs, Victor. Stay off them stairs when you can. They gets you on them stairs!

He ran through the ground floor of the building, out the back, easily jumping up on the rickety fire escape. The gate leading to the second-floor fire escape (and unfettered access up the side of the building) was padlocked, but Victor somehow understood such things. A child's facility that had kept them fed on more than one occasion.

Moments later, he was standing outside the fifth-floor fire escape, peering in the window to see if it was all right to go in.

His mother lay on the bed, her dress and slip pushed up under her chin; her bare feet raised, pushing in a jagged rhythm against the pressed-wood footboard.

Victor ignored the man on top of her (with his pants open but not pulled completely down), shrugged, then sat down on the fire escape to wait. He set the groceries aside, turning to his *prize*—the black-faced combination lock that he'd lifted from the convenience store.

For twenty minutes in the growing gloom, the little boy lost himself in twisting the dial. Listening to the clicks. Peering into the mechanism, feeling the mysteries inside the carbide casing.

As the shadows lengthened, as night and the street's greater dangers began to creep over the building, the little boy intensified his concentration on the lock. Trying desperately to ignore the sky filling with the stars that he found so threatening. The same stars his mother blamed "for 'bout every damn thing happen to us." That shone like so many eyes staring down at him. Watching his every move with far more menace than any convenience store camera he'd ever run across.

A slamming door called him inside.

The woman wrapped a lightweight floral robe around herself, then took the groceries, counted the change, and fixed the meager meal they shared in silence.

"What you got there?"

"Yale Series 114A, combination padlock, Mama."

"What you gonna do with it?"

"I'm figurin' it out, Mama."

"We gonna make some money out that thing you do with them locks one day. Mark me on that." Then she disappeared into the bedroom for her "wake-up" before the evening's work.

Time passed. An hour, two maybe, the little boy couldn't be sure. But it was time, past time for his mother to be on the street.

He went to wake her.

She lay half on, half off the bed. Wearing her best half-slip, her best dress hanging on the side of the bureau.

Her syringe hanging from her limp arm.

"Mama?"

He knew she was dead, had seen dead before. But he put his ear against her cold chest to listen for a heartbeat anyway.

He'd seen it in a movie once.

For the better part of an hour he sat on a trunk, studying her, thinking as intently as he ever had. Not about his mother though. Dead was dead on Gravesend Avenue. Everyone knew that.

No.

He thought about "the home."

The place they took the lost ones, the weak ones, the crazy ones, who didn't have nobody to stand for them. The place they would take him as soon as they found out he was alone.

He didn't fear being alone, wasn't exactly sure what fear was. Didn't feel it any more than he'd felt any other particular emotion in his short life. And there was no remorse or grieving. His mother was a junkie, as was his father (whichever of the parade he was; a white college man, Mama sometimes said); and junkies *always* died.

But he did know "the home." And he knew he couldn't survive there.

It took just ten minutes for him to go through the two-room apartment to gather the few things he would take with him. His locks. A clean shirt and untorn jeans his mother'd stolen earlier in the week. His one dog-eared pamphlet/book written by his namesake idol. The cash the last trick had given his mother.

Then he was out the window and down the fire escape.

Suddenly, on the third-floor landing, he stopped.

He looked up at the open window, then turned, slowly climbing back up.

She was heavier than he'd expected, her limbs stiff with the early stages of rigor. But somehow the small boy struggled her corpse fully onto the bed, smoothing down her slip, pulling the covers over her exposed breasts.

Pulling the needle from her stiffened arm; carefully putting a Band-Aid over the raw puncture.

A brief kiss on the forehead (he'd seen that in the movies too) and he was gone.

In a few days, a small boy would be found in the train station of an upscale part of another city. Seemingly abandoned, a pathetic but courageous little tyke who'd asked a policeman if he could "wait around the station until my mommy and daddy come get me."

His picture would be in all the papers.

Eleven families, good people whose hearts were broken by the youngster's plight, would come forward.

One would eventually give him a home and a semblance of a life.

And he wouldn't return to Gravesend Avenue for almost thirty years.

The man stood where the boy had stood, on the rickety fire escape overlooking the lost world of his infancy.

The building was long deserted, now only home to vermin (animal and human) or the lost. Much as it had been in his time. And the room beyond the fire escape looked unfamiliar, its graffiti-splashed walls shouting back defiance to his silent accusations.

Below him, Gravesend Avenue ran like a dark snake through the heart of the once great city. Even on the fifth floor, he could smell the fear, the anger, the disappointment of its dying populace. Sense their desperation.

As he breathed it in, allowed the smells, the sounds, to bring up this buried memory or that suppressed revelation, he began to understand.

He'd thought that somehow the odious street had been born into him. Had occupied the place where his soul should have been. Had robbed him of his humanity.

He almost laughed at the number of things he remembered blaming Gravesend for. Failures (both personal and otherwise), life choices (uniformly bad he believed), his attitude of complete disregard for all the conventionalities of a society he so despised.

So wanted to be part of.

But as he looked across and down the street of his nightmares; as he looked up at the building where, months before, he'd blamed the presence of the godforsaken street for the beginning of the waking nightmare he'd just emerged from, he was forced to smile.

Gravesend Avenue *had* been born in him. Not, however, as a tumor or disease that lay wrack and ruin to his life. No, that had just been the easiest excuse for a confused little boy who didn't know any better. Who no one saw fit to take the time or commit the effort and energy to help. To explain the confusions.

Gravesend Avenue had been born in him. It had given him the gift of strength. The power of rage. That rarest of all abilities . . . an inborn, native skill at survival.

Without any of which, he would never have gotten away from this earthbound black hole. The fire that had stoked the cauldron of his life.

The man looked up into the glittering night sky. At the stars that, in the little boy's world, had seemed so distant, so foreboding.

That now seemed close, intimate, familiar.

The dream still came to him. Unbidden, some nights the small, perfect arm clutching the doll invaded his sleep, demanding his attention. But now there was something else besides. A quiet thing. Not a voice, exactly, but a . . . sense.

Now he would reach out, hold, caress this sense. And cry. Begging not for denial, for it to go away and never return, but rather he begged for forgiveness, for the compassion that he'd never known.

For understanding.

Somehow he thought he was beginning to receive it. From himself as well as the sense/memory/dream.

So he would look up into the glittering night sky. At the stars that, in the grown man's world, seemed to accuse, demand, judge. Had seemed so mocking and foreboding for so long; and for the first time in his life, this or any of his many broken lives, he thought about the future.

They were waiting for him below, he knew. The Hesperians, Foss, Lukacs. Waiting for him to tell them their next move. The next gambit in their seemingly never-ending game of lethal hide-and-seek. Because despite court orders, gentleman's agreements, or the protection of Mafia kingpins, he knew Van Ness would never, *could* never, stop.

It wasn't in the man's nature.

Any more than giving up was in Greg's.

ACKNOWLEDGMENTS

Nobody's Safe would not have been possible without the generous assistance, support, and belief of many people, both now and in the past. Too many to thank individually. So I'll take this opportunity to thank a special few; and through them, the rest.

Among the many are: Congressmen John Siberling and Steven Schiff; Lance Oliver, Robert Lazar, Mary Manning, U.S. District Judge Philip Pro, Jonathan Turley, Kim Pagliaro, Glenn Campbell (not the singer), and Pat Travis; as well as the archives of the *Las Vegas Sun, Maariv,* the *Jerusalem Post,* the *Los Angeles Times,* MUFON, the *New York Times, Encarta,* and Yale University.

Also: Professors Ariel Cohen and Benjamin Beit-Hallahmi; Gadi Doron of the Tel Aviv Police Department, Michael Kobi, Thomas R. McDonough, the late Carl Sagan, David W. Swift, Raymond E. Fowler, the Masterlock Company, Yale Locks, William Hooper, Teri Diamond, Bill DeLonge, Gerry Dashkin, and for teaching me more about the dark side of society than I ever cared to know—Howard Steinberg.

Thanks are also owed to: the Gemological Institute of America, Communication Control Services (CCS), the American Rom Society, particularly Mr. Sacha Pienez, "Flatman" Corinth, Robert Brawley, Louis Gay, and particularly the late Jeremy "Coke Bottles" Goodman and his family.

Less technically, and more personally, this novel would not have been possible if not for the kindness, support, friendship, and unwavering belief of a select few.

Particularly all of "Team Steinberg"—Jack Kratsas, Rolf Egelandsdal, and Pat Glynn—without whom I'd be stuck in place forever; Pat Nohrden, David Emry (with Peggy and Nancy of course), Gary Smith, and Jerrilyn Betts, who came through like champs; Bernie Kurman, my most trusted face to the world; and the Aguila family, who've always been there for me.

Also: my mother—Gloria Steinberg—who has put up with all the nonsense and who now deserves to reap the treasures; the comically malevolent Antosha Kameniensky (who has kept me alive despite my best efforts to the contrary); and my constant musical companion on this journey, Bob Seger.

A very special and very personal thanks to Jack Hoeft, Arlene Friedman, *believer* Brandon Saltz, and all the other champions and stone pros of Bantam Doubleday Dell, past and present. Particularly: Steve Rubin, Irwyn Applebaum, Erik Engstrom, Michael Palgon, Nita Taublib, and Kate Miciak.

To Shawn Coyne—editor and friend—thank you. Your "nudges" continue to improve the work, sharpen the message, to keep me out of my own way, so that the story can shine through. Two joyously down, a great many to go!

A surgeon I know once told me that what lay beneath the skin was far more beautiful, far more interesting, than what lay on the surface. So, too, with *Nobody's Safe.*

For the incisive/insightful questions and answers, for the patience, the calmness, the E-mailed suggestions/solutions, sympathetically taking the muddled, too-long phone calls and inspiring clarity of message, for being there for me despite my bullshit . . . my complete soulful thanks and appreciation to the *PINDER LANE ALL STARS!!!*

Robert Thixton, Dick Duane, Jean Free, Nancy Coffey, and Roger Hayes, all of that tireless, selfless, remarkable staff are in a large way responsible for what's under the skin of *Nobody's Safe,* the guts of the thing. It's a better book, and I'm a better man, for having been with them.

Success!
Richard Steinberg
Somewhere in America
1998

F
Ste

Steinberg, R
Nobody's Safe

DATE DUE		
JUN 2 2003		
OCT 2 9 2003		WITHDRAWN
SEP 0 6 2004		
MAR 0 6 2012		
AUG 0 3 2016		

12-02